PURE YOGA

In its Historical Context and Today

YOGA

History • Philosophy • Practice

- **Yoga and Indian Philosophy** — Karel Werner
  [978-81-208-1609-1]
- **Pure Yoga in the Historical Context and Today** — Karel Werner
  [978-81-208-4108-6]

PURE YOGA

DR. KAREL WERNER

In its Historical Context and Today

PURE YOGA : *In its Historical Context and Today*/DR. KAREL WERNER

First Edition : Delhi, 2021

ISBN: 978 81 950 553 7 1

Published by
Motilal Banarsidass Publications
93, Shyam Lal Marg, Darya Ganj,
New Delhi-110002 (India)
mlbd@mlbd.com / www.mlbd.com

MLBD Cataloging-in-Publication Data
PURE YOGA
DR. KAREL WERNER
(YOGA : HISTORY, PHILOSOPHY-PRACTICE)
ISBN : 978 81 950 553 7 1
Abbreviations, Preface, Notes,
Bibliography, Index

Printed by Repro Books Ltd.

Table of Contents

List of Abbreviations

AB - Aitareya Brāhmaṇa

AU - Aitareya Upaniṣad

AV - Atharva Veda

BCE - before common era

BhG - Bhagavad Gītā

BU - Bṛhadāraṇyaka Upaniṣad

cca - *circa*

cf. - compare

CE - common era

ChU - Chāndogya Upaniṣad

DN - Dīgha Nikāya

IU - Īṣā Upaniṣad

J - Jātaka

KathU - Kaṭha Upaniṣad

KauU - Kauśītakī Upaniṣad

KenU - Kena Upaniṣad

MaiU - Maitrayānīya (Maitrī) Upaniṣad

ManU - Māṇḍūkya Upaniṣad

Mbh - Mahābhārata

Mdh - Mokṣadharma

MN - Majjhima Nikāya

MunU - Muṇḍaka Upaniṣad

P. - Pāli

PU - Praśṇa Upaniṣad

RV - Ṛg Veda

Ry - Rāmāyaṇa

ŚB - Śatapatha Brāhmaṇa

ŚU - Śvetāṣvatara Upaniṣad

Skt. - Sanskrit

SN - Saṁyutta Nikāya

SV - Sāma Veda

TU - Taittirīya Upaniṣad

Ud - Udāna

Vin - Vinaya Piṭaka

YS - Yoga Sūtras of Patañjali

YV - Yajur Veda

Yvas - Yogavāsiṣṭha

PREFACE

Why another book on Yoga? The simple answer is that nobody has so far written a book on pure Yoga. By pure Yoga I mean Yoga as a spiritual practice which is not a part of some definite philosophical system and is not affiliated to a religious doctrine which has to be accepted on faith. The only assumption to be made about pure Yoga as a practical discipline is its preliminary implications and its goal. Its goal is individual liberation from the necessity of being born into a changing world in which one cannot achieve lasting fulfilment of one's aspirations before one passes from it. The preliminary implications are that an individual's life continues beyond the death of the body and that the individual is reborn in this world or in some other dimension of existence and continues to be reborn in an endless sequence of deaths and births in which one seeks but never finds fulfilment, until one makes a firm decision to aim for liberation and eventually achieves it.

This is the basic philosophical outlook of Yoga. It cannot be verified by everyday human experience, but it has a high degree of probability in comparison with all other possible views which are often held firmly, even though they cannot be proved, being mostly based on inherited or adopted religious faith. Similarly, the tenets of so-called scientific materialism cannot be proved, yet are usually held by scientists with full conviction. Thus some astrophysicists believe that sentient life 'emerged' at some point during the formation of galactic systems in the evolving universe when it produced sun-like stars with orbiting planets. Some biologists maintain, without being able to prove it, that individual life depends entirely on the nervous system and the brain and does not continue beyond the death of the body. I regard such firm convictions of scientists as the equivalent of religious faith. Those pitfalls are avoided by some scientists who are agnostics, but their stance that we can never know the answers to questions about the ultimate nature of existence is too farfetched. Yoga promises to provide answers in the form of personal experience and although someone who has found the final answer may not be able to provide proof of it in the way required by science, the possibility that one day proofs may be available should not be ruled out.

The problem is that throughout the history of Yoga its answers have frequently been prematurely anticipated by philosophical speculations and elaborate religious teachings, not to mention fraudulent claims by unscrupulous self-designated yogis to know the truth and promise to pass it to others in exchange for payment. The aim of this work is to trace the origin and history of Yoga as a spiritual practice, point out at each stage of its development the way in which its aim was obscured rather than illuminated by these entanglements, and to try to assess whether in different times there were genuine yogis.

In the oldest period of Indian prehistory we are limited to archaeological discoveries, yet the occurrence of pictorial finds, of a few statues and of some telling ruins makes it possible to adumbrate a plausible picture of the religious situation of the time and of yogic elements within or alongside it. Subsequent periods produced writings which are, however, mostly of a religious nature, with some early philosophical attempts. But even so, from these sources, mainly the Vedas and the Upaniṣads, we learn that unaffiliated yogic trends existed and were developing not within but alongside or completely outside the religious establishment which, however, eventually started appropriating them for its own purpose. Philosophical speculation joined the trend and Yoga has never become fully dissociated from these accretions.

Yet indirect evidence makes it clear that something approaching pure Yoga was already being practised among homeless wanderers in the times of the Vedas and it can even be surmised that there was a link to the prehistoric period. In the time of the early Upaniṣads there is also evidence of Yoga practice in settled communities of disciples assembled around teachers in forest *āśrams.* From them emerged eventually a comprehensive text dealing with several methods of Yoga practice which is known as Patañjali's *Yoga Sūtra* (YS). Each one of these methods probably originated in a different *āśram,* but the assembled text is the work of a single compiler. The great merit of the *Yoga Sūtra* is the fact that it is basically unaffiliated to any particular religion or philosophical system and that there are in it only minor religious and philosophical elements. The most important part of the *Yoga Sūtra* is its fifth chapter dealing with 'eightfold Yoga', succinctly defined in one single stanza (II.29) and elaborated in the rest of the chapter.

At the same time as various teachers in the forest *āśrams* were instructing their disciples in their particular methods of Yoga, but some two hundred years before the finalisation of the *Yoga Sūtra* by a compiler into the textbook-style collection known today, the Buddha formulated his 'noble eightfold path' as a way to liberation. It is a Yoga path in all but name and it undoubtedly influenced the formulation of the eightfold Yoga in Patañjali's *Yoga Sūtra.* The notion of 'pure Yoga' as understood in this book is derived from these two eightfold paths and elucidations in their respective sources. This notion is used as a yardstick or criterion when describing and evaluating the historical developments of Yoga throughout the centuries and in different contexts. In the last two chapters of the book an attempt is made to outline the way in which pure Yoga could be practised in the conditions of modern life.

The book has been written on the basis of original research in sources and of research results of experts but with the intention of making it readable for members of the general public interested in the theory and practice of Yoga. Quotations of original Sanskrit texts with translations and references to other works relevant for discussed topics as well as some personal explanations and the author's assessments and opinions have been put into endnotes. It is advisable to ignore them during the first reading of the book in order to obtain an overall picture of the subject of Yoga in the author's understanding. On the second reading the notes should be read in the appropriate order as their numbers occur in the text.

* * *

Readers of this book would greatly benefit from knowledge of the author's earlier book *Yoga and Indian Philosophy* which deals with Yoga in a wider conceptual context. Its fourth reprint has already been published and is available on the market.

London
2018

1. Introduction

What is Yoga?

In popular parlance Yoga is often understood as referring to the practice of 'postural Yoga', usually described as beneficial for physical health and fitness. To use the word that way is strictly speaking misleading, the correct term for it is Haṭha Yoga which will be dealt with in Chapter VII, on 'The Rise of Specialised Schools'. Nevertheless, many people are aware, even if they are not themselves practitioners, that Yoga is a spiritual and ascetic discipline geared to discovering the meaning and goal of life and, in the last instance, to realising that goal by personal experience.

To some degree that understanding penetrated into the widely respected publication, *The Concise Oxford Dictionary*, although its definitions of Yoga have to be regarded with some caution. A rather imprecise definition of Yoga appears in its 11th edition in electronic form (OUP 2006) as "a Hindu spiritual and ascetic discipline, a part of which, including breath control, simple meditation, and the adoption of specific bodily postures, is widely practised in the West for health and relaxation". It is not correct to refer to Yoga as a 'Hindu' discipline, since it considerably predates the formation of the complicated religious system known as Hinduism. Yoga started acquiring its systematic form under this term cca 400 BCE in the time of the Upaniṣads when the then current religious system was dominated by

Brāhmanic ritualism and is therefore referred to as Brāhmanism. But Yoga as a discipline was not its product.

The sources of Yoga are composed mainly in Sanskrit, an ancient member of the extensive Indo-European family of languages which share many verbal similarities, some of which are recognisable even in the modern forms of Indo-European languages (Werner 1987). Thus the term Yoga is akin to the English word 'yoke' and Latin *iugum*. It is derived from the Sanskrit verbal root *yuj* (present tense *yunakti*) which corresponds to two English verbs: 'to join' and 'to unite'. The meanings of all the three expressions ('yoke', 'join' and 'unite') reverberate in the term Yoga. It designates a discipline which 'yokes' the mind or the whole personality of the practitioner to a precise procedure whose final aim is to join or be united with the ultimate reality or the final truth. So a brief definition of Yoga can be tentatively formulated as follows:

> Yoga is a system of training the mind and the whole personality, by way of specialised techniques, with the aim of eventually achieving a direct encounter with, or knowledge of, the ultimate reality or truth.

It is unnecessary to consider or even mention the multifarious uses of the term in different contexts in India over the centuries (as does White 2012, 2-4) in a publication such as this whose purpose is, in the final instance, to penetrate to the essence of Yoga and to unwrap or extract from the historical sources a pure form of its practice, the aim of which is the practitioner's personal salvation.

Yoga, religion, mysticism and metaphysics

The above brief definition suggests that Yoga is a spiritual discipline in its own right and is independent of particular religious beliefs and philosophical assumptions. When it is thus understood, it contrasts with spiritual practices of a higher order in different religious and spiritual traditions, often referred to as mysticism. This was not always clearly understood. Thus the 5th edition of the *Concise Oxford Dictionary* in hardback (OUP 1964) still regards Yoga as a "Hindu system of philosophic meditation & asceticism designed to effect the reunion of the devotee's soul with the universal spirit". This description has obvious religious and philosophical connotations. It presupposes the existence of individual souls and of a spiritual source from which at some point these souls emerged or by which they were created and to which they aim to return. To be united or reunited with the universal spirit or ultimate reality (variously defined) is the goal of practically all religions based on belief in the existence of a God Creator. It is also the goal of deeper trends in some philosophical schools of thought with strong metaphysical leanings towards monism, such as Greek neo-Platonism or Indian Vedāntism. It may even apply to some spiritual traditions which do not quite fit the label of religion or philosophy, for example Chinese Daoism. It could further apply to modern varieties of spiritual teachings such as Theosophy and various 'New Age' trends on the one hand and the still strong contemporary theistic religions (Judaism, Christianity and Islam) on the other. Each of these systems has specific ideas about the nature of the final goal or salvation and about the spiritual practice through which it is to be achieved.

In the neo-Platonism of Plotinus of Alexandria (203-270 CE) the final goal was the unification of the practitioner with 'that one' (*to hén*), a kind of original and ultimate 'singularity' underlying and, at the same time, transcending phenomenal reality, which can supposedly be apprehended in this life in ecstatic (supra-sensory and supra-rational) visions. Plotinus disclosed that he had experienced such a vision three times during his life, but hoped to realise it for good after death. His concept of the ultimate oneness resembles the Vedāntic teachings of non-duality (*advaita*) which emerged in the early Upaniṣads (cca 600 BCE) and were later elaborated into various systems of Vedāntic philosophy. Plotinus may have become acquainted with them and been inspired by them when he travelled to the East.

The basic tenet of Vedāntic systems states that individual beings emerge as emanations from one divine source called *brahman* to which they eventually return, merging with it as do rivers with the sea or, since *brahman* is conceived in some Vedāntic systems also in personal terms as the god Brahma, they dwell, when they reach salvation, forever in his presence, while preserving a semblance of their individuality. In Chinese philosophy or spiritual traditions it is Daoism which concerns itself with the ultimate reality. It posits an absolute dynamic principle called *dao*, the 'way'. Its dynamism manifests itself, in the course of a polarised process oscillating between its two poles called *yang* and *yin*, by producing phenomenal reality with all its individual objects and life forms (plants and living beings). Individuals on the human level can find fulfilment if they exist in harmony with the eternal rhythm of *dao*. But Daoism also envisages a possibility of mastering the eternal rhythm of *dao* with the result that one can achieve personal immortality in the body. Daoist philosophy and beliefs are expressed on different levels, from a popular religious one bordering on primitive magic, to lofty ones expressed in metaphysical concepts, symbolical imagery and poetical creations.

There are many other 'semi-mystical' and 'semi-religious' and philosophical approaches to the quest for the ultimate. Thus Theosophy regards all religions as being in essence one, although differently expressed, and asserts that there is a steady evolutionary process of individuals and mankind as a whole, which will culminate in a state of universal salvation, with a hint of eternal cyclic repetition. Under the 'New Age' label there are hiding diverse trends, from neo-paganism and resurrected witchcraft to occult teachings, such as the so-called 'Fourth Way' of George Gurdjieff (cca 1872–1949) or the highly verbalised 'pathless land' to be achieved through 'pure awareness' which was preached by Jiddu Krishnamurti (1895-1986).

Although according to the definition of Yoga given above, it is, in its pure form, free from religious or philosophical beliefs and assumptions and is geared to direct knowing, some authors attach the name of Yoga to spiritual trends in all possible traditions and employ for them designations such as 'Hindu Yoga', 'Jain Yoga', 'Christian Yoga', also 'Zen Yoga', 'Yoga of Sufism' and even 'Yoga of J. Krishnamurti', in the belief that all these trends aim, in essence, for the same final goal. However, those types of spiritual endeavour within religious and other doctrinal traditions and New Age type movements which do not fit the strict methodical criteria of Yoga practice as such should be more correctly referred to as 'mysticism'. It has to be admitted, though, that certain practices of yogis and mystics bear a degree of mutual similarity or in some aspects overlap with each other. That is why Yoga may appear to some to be a specific variety of mysticism. That view seems to transpire from the quoted hardback *Concise Oxford Dictionary*'s definition of a mystic as "One who seeks by contemplation & self-surrender to obtain union with or absorption into the Deity, or who believes in spiritual apprehension of truths beyond the understanding", and from its definition in its later electronic version as "a person who seeks by contemplation and self-surrender to attain unity with the Deity or the absolute, and so reach truths beyond human understanding". But it certainly does not transpire from the electronic dictionary's definition of mysticism, which gives two alternatives, the first referring to mysticism as "the beliefs or state of mind characteristic of mystics", while the second describes it as a "vague or ill-defined religious or spiritual belief, especially as associated with a belief in the occult".

Neither of these definitions can possibly include true Yoga. In any case, broadening the usage of the term Yoga to include various spiritual trends in other traditions is inappropriate, because Yoga is an expression with a precise meaning as defined above.

So what exactly distinguishes Yoga from, say, Taoist mysticism, the Zen Buddhist approach or the way of a Christian mystic? The answer is: mainly its methodical approach, which is characterised by conceptual clarity, a high degree of systematisation and a variety of developed technical procedures, and particularly by its already stated feature, namely that it can stand alone without a link to a specific religious belief or philosophical world view. Besides, it does not indulge in anticipating the final knowledge by speculation or intuitive apprehension, let alone by poetic imagery, but insists that it must be apprehended by direct experience.

As already indicated, mysticism is normally steeped in a doctrinal tradition and this is very often a religious tradition with an elaborate system of theology. The mystic then strives for the ultimate goal under the name of the personal God of his particular religion. It may be, for example, Christ or Allah, Kṛṣṇa or Śiva or even Ādi Buddha, a personification of the ultimate reality in Mahāyāna Buddhism, even though the designation 'god' is not a fitting label for him. In some cases the mystic may eventually transcend the particular personalised notion of the ultimate reality current in his tradition, as did Master Eckhart (Eckhart von Hochheim, cca 1260 – cca 1328) in medieval Europe who went beyond the notion of God and the Trinity to that of Godhead and finally even beyond Godhead. Or a mystic may sense that behind the image of God in his as well as other traditions there is an underlying unity, as did Ramakrishna (1836-86) in India. He can then continue in his devotion to the deity of his own tradition while being aware of the shared higher reality of which the different forms of deities of diverse traditions are supposed to be outward symbols. But more often than not the mystic remains at least to some extent in the sway of the imagery of his particular tradition, and if there are no indications that he can see beyond it as could Master Eckhart or Ramakrishna, it may be because his achievement has stopped short of the final break-through.

Yoga at its best, however, is free from any particular religious or metaphysical affiliation not only at the end of the journey, but right from the start. Yogis of the free type do not pray or perform rituals directed to a personal God. When they refer to the ultimate reality, the goal of their efforts, they use a philosophically neutral term without religious connotations.

There are three such terms which have emerged in the historical process of the development of Yoga terminology: *nirvāṇa* (blowing out, namely of the flame of passions), *kaivalya* (autonomy, 'aloneness') and *sat-cit-ānanda* (being-knowing-bliss). A completely neutral term used by religious and philosophical traditions in India is *mokṣa* (liberation, in Pāli Buddhism usually *vimutti*).[1]

Nevertheless, even the yogi may sometimes end with the admission that there is in the final experience of the ultimate an indication of an infinite personality factor which accounts for the insistence of religions and most mystics on referring to the ultimate reality in terms of God. And so even the so-called Classical Yoga of Patañjali's *Yoga Sūtra* admits of the possibility of the existence of an absolute personality in transcendence, either from time immemorial or from the time when the first ever yogi reached perfection and passed away. But unlike in religions, he is referred to in the YS as *īśvara* (the Lord), not as God. The usefulness of turning to him for possible assistance on the part of those who feel the need to do so is admitted also in the pure Yoga chapter of the YS dealing with the eightfold path (*aṣṭāṅga yoga*).

The problem of God and *īśvara* is a complicated and to some extent obscure and controversial topic stemming from the overlapping of mystical and yogic practices, outlooks and conceptions of the ultimate goal. It will be further discussed in the appropriate chapter, but we can suggest here that a mystic may start his prayers and meditative endeavours with some definite form of religious faith in God, but when he has tasted the fruits of his devotion to him he may widen his perception and come back with an understanding which puts philosophical terms into his mouth. These then may go far beyond his original religious beliefs so that he may come to be regarded within his religious tradition as a heretic and even become subjected to persecution. Such a fate was in store for Master Eckhart, who was summoned by the Pope to justify himself, but escaped by a timely natural death on his way to Avignon, where Popes were residing at the time. But the avenging hand of the Catholic Church then fell heavily on his followers. Another mystic who went beyond the concepts approved of by the theological doctrines of the Roman church was St John of the Cross (1542-1591) who suffered temporary imprisonment as a result.

By contrast an aspiring yogi may start with a philosophical belief in a metaphysical principle such as the impersonal *brahman* or even without any commitment save to gaining liberation (*mokṣa*) from the round of rebirths and, without having any preconceptions about its nature, may be able in the end to appreciate the religious believer's predilection for viewing the ultimate as an infinite person, which is how God is sometimes referred to even by orthodox theologians. But it is important to bear in mind that in the religious and philosophical teachings of India God bears virtually no resemblance to the God of theologians or ordinary believers of any organised monotheistic religion, such as Judaism and Islam and their sects, as well as of the triune Christianity and other Christian denominations.

The Systematisation of Yoga

In its methodical approach to the goal, usually referred to as liberation, whose hallmark is the ultimate knowledge through direct experience of the nature of existence as such, Yoga shows some affinity with Western scientific procedures. It would seem that the Indian mind developed scientific skills, remarkably, in the context of Vedic worship, the dominant feature of which was the recitation of certain verses of Vedic hymns, called *mantras*, and sometimes of selected whole hymns. The Vedic hymns were regarded as sacred and as endowed with magic power when correctly recited. This view was an important dogma developed within Brāhmanism, a ritualistic religious system which was establishing itself as a dominant force in the tribal Āryan society several centuries after the codification of the Ṛg Veda accomplished by cca 1500 BCE. The Ṛg Veda was believed to have come down to ancient seers (*ṛṣis*) over a period of time as divine revelation through internal hearing of its verses. It was therefore called *śruti* (that which was heard) and it became the most important sacred text of Brāhmanism. Consequently the predominant concern of the officiating Brahmins (priests) using the Vedic texts during sacrificial rites was accuracy in their unaltered preservation for repeated use and absolute precision in their pronunciation during recitation. It was not just the Ṛg Veda as a whole or the individual Vedic hymns which were seen as sacred, but every word, syllable and even letter, whether a consonant or a vowel, was regarded as sacred and had to be preserved and clearly as well as fully pronounced. That led to the development of a method of careful analysis which was applied to the structure of the texts and sentences and to the way in which the individual sounds of consonants and vowels were produced.

This greatly facilitated the ability to implant the Vedic collections of hymns into memory and preserve them unaltered for the use of subsequent generations. It eventually resulted in the early creation of a perfect system of phonetics and of an unparalleled scientific grammar of Sanskrit which was in due course codified by Pāṇini (probably in the 4th century BCE), an achievement hardly surpassed even by modern European philology.

The spirit of scientific investigation and analysis thus developed was applied in subsequent centuries also to the mystical experiences and insights into the nature of reality gained by the ancient Vedic seers, wandering ascetics (*śramaṇas*) and Upaniṣadic sages. This resulted in the creation of methodical procedures which enabled accomplished spiritual masters from the ranks of wandering ascetics and sages settled in forest hermitages of subsequent times to guide other aspirants on the spiritual path so that they could develop coherently the same insights and reach their culmination in the form of a direct apprehension of the ultimate reality as a result of systematic effort, instead of by haphazard individual search.

The first recorded account of an accomplished master who had reached the goal by his individual search and then provided guidance to his disciples on the basis of his own experience was that of the Buddha (cca 543-463 BCE), preserved in the Pāli Canon of Theravāda Buddhism. The Buddha's teaching method, geared to making it possible for his disciples to reach the highest goal, was individual, taking into account the personal capacity of each pupil. Having been born as an aristocrat, the Buddha did not undergo the Brāhmanic training in the Vedic lore with its tendency to systematisation, but would still have been aware of the methodical skill applied by Brahmins when reciting *mantras* during courtly rituals. Many parts of his recorded teachings show similar methodical skill in their presentation. The case in point is his 'noble eightfold path' (*ariya aṭṭhaṅgika magga*, see below, Chapter III) which later on undoubtedly influenced the formulation of the eightfold Yoga path (*aṣṭāṅga yoga*) contained in the already mentioned collection of texts known as Patañjali's *Yoga Sūtra.* The YS outlines several distinct Yoga techniques and contains also a treatment of Yoga's elementary philosophical basis. The collection as a whole, including its philosophical part, came to be looked upon as one system of Yoga practice and philosophy and obtained the designation Classical Yoga. However, what is truly classical in it is its comprehensive account of just the eightfold technique (YS II.28-55 & III.1-55 & IV.1) which is actually free from philosophical speculation and any particular religious affiliation. It truly is, like the Buddhist eightfold path, pure Yoga. As a technique for practice it came to be constituted through a very long process — from visionary experiences and mystical insights of ancient seers, who produced the Vedic lore, via meditative absorptions of wandering ascetics (*śramaṇas*) and of renunciants settled in forest hermitages and also from the Buddha's descriptions of his own spiritual struggles which eventually brought him enlightenment. The Buddha's eightfold path is now a comprehensive system accessible to virtually everybody with an average intelligence and interest to try it out. It has survived in purity for some two and a half thousand years till the present day, despite having often been set into sectarian contexts as well as used and misused by a variety of religious cults and even by movements bordering on magic which were often geared to struggles for political power and acquisition of wealth rather than for gaining ultimate knowledge and salvation. Its status in the modern world will be discussed in the last chapter.

Yoga and modernism

As already hinted, India has developed a 'classical' form of Yoga, represented by Patañjali's slender collection of texts, which in itself is free from affiliation to any religious sect or doctrine or metaphysical school of thought, although, curiously enough, it is designated in Hinduism as one of its six 'orthodox' systems (*darśaṇas*) of philosophy under the simple term Yoga and treated as philosophy also by academic researchers. However, few yogis truly succeed in following the methods of Patañjali's Yoga in its pure form while remaining free from any religious or doctrinal involvements. Many Western Yoga teachers and *gurus* from India who are active in Western countries present Yoga in the contexts of various types of Hindu mysticism and religious sectarian frameworks. This is the case particularly with respect to Bhakti Yoga. Often they mix it also with the popularised metaphysics of Śaṅkara's monistic system known as Advaita Vedānta. In India the neutral Yoga system of Patañjali has often been associated also with the metaphysical system of the Sāṅkhya school of thought (another one of the six Hindu *darśaṇas*) owing to the commentaries interpreting its difficult aphorisms in that way. Quite a number of Western scholars and various other exponents or interpreters of Indian philosophical thought accept this view and regard the Sāṅkhya dualism as the background philosophy of Patañjali's *Yoga Sūtra.* They often describe the two systems together under the heading 'Sāṅkhya-Yoga', which blurs their respective individual teachings and fails to do justice to the essential differences in their basic positions and outlooks (a typical example is Larson 2012, 76-78).

When we survey the contemporary yogic scene, we cannot fail to notice the fact that Yoga procedures are being appreciated and utilised for spiritual uplift in all possible religious and philosophical contexts, not least also by some committed Christians. This in itself proves that in essence Yoga is truly independent of all of them. It does not at all subscribe to any religious belief or metaphysical theory about the ultimate reality, but simply offers the methodical means for trying to develop a direct experience of it.

Because Yoga is thus doctrinally neutral or uncommitted and does not require faith, not even in the existence of some ultimate reality, it can be of assistance even to the modern atheist. Many people nowadays who have no religious allegiance or faith have a somewhat vague or superficial view of life and the world, often underpinned by an attitudinal materialist outlook which they do not care to define clearly for themselves. This outlook has been moulded to a large degree by the impact of applied science or technology on people's lives which have been made, in comparison with the pre-scientific age, safer, healthier and far more comfortable. Nevertheless many people, sooner or later, experience on some occasions a certain dissatisfaction, even boredom, amidst their material comforts. They develop spontaneously a feeling that there should or even must be some higher meaning to life. Science can enrich their lives with new discoveries and provide them with further temporary excitements, but it can never give a meaning to life or solve the riddle of existence. Even when science pushes itself to its limits in its investigations into the subatomic microcosm and the astrophysical macrocosm, it is still confronted by a mystery. Some scientists readily recognise that in the last instance they face an unknown dimension of reality perhaps accessible only to the vision of mystics. [2]

Few scientists, however, can or will want to become mystics, one reason being that most of them probably lack the depth of religious faith and commitment which is a prerequisite for embarking on a mystical path in any religious tradition, and many have no religious belief whatsoever. But the practice of pure Yoga, which requires no kind of religious faith at the outset, is available even to them if they manage to disassociate it in their minds from the religious and other accretions of the centuries which is unfortunately the image of Yoga they often encounter first, to say nothing about distortions in popular literature and commercial tendencies in Yoga centres run by Indian *gurus* both in India and in the West.

Anybody who has an inquiring mind should be interested in the possibility of unveiling the mystery of life's meaning. Scientists of course do have inquiring minds. So a scientist willing to experiment on a systematic basis with his own mind can make use of the neutral methodology of Yoga, become a regular practitioner and experience in due course a certain widening of his vision and a deeper understanding of the nature of life and of the direction in which the true goal of life should be sought and might eventually be found. Besides, there are certain worthwhile side benefits of Yoga practice in terms of improved health and mental balance, now widely recognised even in medical circles. Scientific training and the discipline learned during research work would be enhancing factors in a scientist's practice of Yoga so that some results could be expected in a not too distant future which in turn would be an encouragement to persevere. What is needed on the part of scientists is to overcome their reluctance and scepticism with respect to personal involvement in procedures whose results cannot be objectively demonstrated under controlled conditions for others to see.

As to the proverbial man in the street, he seldom has a truly inquiring mind. He has benefited materially from the progress of science, does not care much, if at all, for religion and has absorbed much of the materialistically orientated outlook of the majority of scientists. Yet in spite of that even he occasionally feels dissatisfied and unfulfilled. Yoga is here even for him. He can adopt some of its moderate techniques which aim at modest initial achievements whose benefits he can readily appreciate. These may be just a slimmer figure by practising only the physical variety of Yoga (Haṭha Yoga), or the reduced chance of a heart attack, and a better overall feeling of mental and physical well-being which even modest periods of Yoga meditation can provide, or it may be the restoration of a measure of mental balance amidst the hectic conditions of living. Yoga is there for him to benefit from. Many have been convinced of its effectiveness once they have tried it. This and the wider issues of Yoga as adapted to modern conditions will be discussed in the final chapter.

The basic philosophical outlook of Yoga

Yet, despite the fact that religious faith, some ideology or a commitment to a metaphysical doctrine are not necessary and may even act as hindrances for effective Yoga practice, a certain basic philosophical outlook is in many cases an accompanying feature of Yoga practice. For many people it undoubtedly serves as motivation for taking it up and persevering. This philosophical outlook may be rather simple or it may be more or less elaborate. Even if the motive is purely one of physical health or even just bodily appearance, it still represents a philosophical outlook in which a slimmer and healthier body gained at the cost of regular effort and a portion of restraint in food intake has a higher value than a body bearing signs of indulgence and idleness. A measure of mental balance brought about by relaxation, which is a part of physical Yoga practice and which helps practitioners cope with mental stress caused by their modern lifestyle, may arouse curiosity about what benefits can be gained by more advanced mental procedures of Yoga. Taking up occasional mild meditation sessions may be the next step.

However, embarking on a serious Yoga practice requires more than that. It involves obeying certain rules, holding regular meditation sessions and maintaining a portion of watchful mindfulness during the day. All this may eventually even change the practitioner's whole lifestyle, so that it undoubtedly requires much deeper motivation than do moderate physical exercises and mild meditation sessions. This motivation comes from the realisation that the short span of life spent in ignorance about its meaning and goal does not make sense even if one is 'lucky enough' to enjoy relatively agreeable conditions, perhaps enhanced by moderate Yoga practice. But it is impossible to ignore the fact that no one is entirely safe from diseases and possible other misfortunes or tragedies. More than that, the inevitability of dying casts a kind of shadow over every life, even though it is usually kept at the back of one's mind or driven into the subconscious. When for any reason one becomes acutely aware of these raw facts of life, it is the moment when one goes beyond the purely practical involvement in Yoga and tentatively turns to its philosophical background.

Yoga, besides being by definition an aspiration to realise the final truth about existence and its meaning or goal, aims in the last instance, as all sources maintain, at the aspiring individual's liberation (*mokṣa*). But liberation from what? The answer which all Indian sources on Yoga provide, whether in a fully spelled out or implied form is: from the repetitive nature of life in ignorance which continues after death in a never ending sequence of further lives during endless cycles of the manifestation and dissolution of the universe – unless at some point in time the liberating knowledge of the final or ultimate truth is realised.

The wandering ascetics in ancient India who gave up all involvement in ordinary life in society and reduced their individual needs to a bare minimum in search of the final goal and liberation were fully aware that they might not reach it before dying. Yet they carried on with their efforts with confidence that they would continue in their quest and endeavours in their subsequent lives. The same goes for the fully committed yogis or practitioners of Yoga throughout centuries till the present day.

In India the view of the life of an individual as proceeding in a virtually beginningless and endless sequence of births and deaths until, or unless, he reaches liberation is in some form or another a part of the doctrines of all religious sects (some of which ascribe a limited role in the process to God) and of all schools of indigenous philosophy. One exception is the defunct *lokāyata*, a materialistic doctrine whose origin is ascribed to a mythical founder by the name of Cārvāka; it is known only from polemical sources opposed to his teaching. Of course, with the introduction of the European educational system into 19th century India, enabling her people access to Western philosophical ideas, modern Western materialism found footing also in some sections of the Indian population and also in some philosophical departments of Indian universities. However, this trend produced also a reaction against this imported materialistic world view and even strengthened the efforts in some circles to preserve the ancient Indian spiritual traditions, sometimes reformulated for modern times to make them accessible worldwide. Yoga visibly benefited from these efforts.

Hymns of the Ṛg Veda which are at least three and a half thousand years old make it clear that belief in the continuity of life after death was then universally held. This clearly transpires from the prayers and supplications in a number of Ṛg Vedic hymns asking in many cases for life in heaven. However, in some hymns they go further and ask for immortality. The implication is that if it were believed that life in heaven was everlasting, there would be no need to ask for immortality. There is even direct evidence for the teaching of or belief in successive lives, although an entirely clear statement to that effect can be found, to my knowledge, in only one hymn (RV 4,54,2). Other hymns indicate that there are various destinations for departed individuals according to the eternal law and the nature of their actions. As well as heaven, the destination may be the abode of departed ancestors, a place where good deeds are rewarded, or return to earth, and even embodiment in plants. Evil-doers go to hell (although not for eternity). The reason for somewhat haphazard references to this important topic in Vedic hymns is the very nature of hymnic poetry. It is not in the nature of Vedic hymns to present systematic information on any particular theme. Nevertheless the belief in transmigration would have been a part of the outlook of more thoughtful people and the outcome of personal insights of Āryan seers and mystics into the nature of life since very ancient times, perhaps even in their original home in Eastern Europe.[3]

It may have been a common outlook of all Indo-European people before they split up and migrated in all directions to colonise the whole of Europe, the Near East, Middle Asia, Īrān and India. This can be deduced from surviving evidence in those areas. For example, some Greek and Roman philosophers and mystery cults taught reincarnation or sequential rebirth under the term 'metempsychosis'. It was taught as their central doctrine by Druids in ancient Britain, from where it spread also into Gaul, as testified by Julius Cesar (*De bello Gallico*, Book VI). Some indications of it can be found in remnants of pre-Christian Slavonic and Germanic mythology and in folklore. It is quite feasible to assume that it was the central teaching of priests or shamans in Indo-European antiquity in the presumed Indo-European homeland in Southern Russia before the dispersal of its growing population, resulting in the formation of distinct Indo-European nations (Werner, 1987).

To recapitulate: The ancient insights of the sages in Vedic times about successive lives were preserved in the subsequent period of literary creativity, in the so-called Brāhmaṇas ('priestly books') in which they are referred to as 'repeated death' (*punarmṛtyu*, ŚB 10.4.3.10). The view of repeated births and deaths was newly formulated and clearly explained in terms of successive incarnations in several passages in the early Upaniṣads. But the most comprehensive exposition of the teaching of transmigration or rebirth can be found soon after in a number of the discourses of the Buddha. In all these systems it is believed or taken for granted that once the Yoga path has been embarked upon by an individual, the journey can be continued, life after life, until the final goal of liberation is reached.

A necessary corollary to the doctrine of reincarnation or rebirth is the idea of justice, often understood in terms of rewards for good actions and retribution for evil ones. Evidence for it can already be found in the Vedas and Brāhmaṇas, clear statements to that effect appear in the Upaniṣads and the issue is comprehensively dealt with again in the discourses of the Buddha. The natural feeling that human actions have consequences not only for those at whom they are directed, but also for their doers according to the moral character of their actions, found expression in monotheistic religions in the belief that God (regarded as the Creator who is omniscient and omnipotent and metaphorically viewed as the heavenly Father) rewards the doers for their good actions and punishes them for evil ones by analogy to a human father in relation to his children. When in the modern secular age religious belief declined, the notion of moral retribution lost its divine sanction and was only imperfectly replaced by a system of human laws enforced by police and administered by judiciary. Their efficiency depends on detection, which is not a very effective deterrent.

In Indian religious and philosophical traditions the concept of law is not derived from an omnipotent and omniscient God, but is anchored in the Vedic notion of *ṛta*, the universal law or cosmic order, which emerges from the primeval creative force (*tapas*) together with 'truth' (*satya*) or reality, i.e. with everything that is (*sat*).[4] This universal law governs not only the external processes of nature, being in this respect comparable to the concept of the laws of nature of modern science derived from observation and experimentation, but governs with equal efficiency also the processes of what we can call inner nature. These processes are of mental character and consequently come under the heading of ethics. They therefore include man's volitional activities (decision making) which lead to external actions, classified as good, evil or neutral, and resulting in corresponding consequences for the doer. The force and efficacy of the universal law in the context of ethical behaviour cannot be escaped, but its consequences can be modified by purposeful action. This is fully parallelled by the force and efficacy of the laws of external nature which cannot be changed, but whose consequences can be modified by conscious manipulation.

The Vedic texts were composed in an archaic version of Sanskrit, but sacred texts of the post-Vedic time were written in a different version of Sanskrit which was not the direct successor of the Vedic one but became, since Pāṇini, the classical norm. In classical Sanskrit the word *ṛta* has a less prominent meaning than in the Vedas. The notion of universal law came to be expressed mostly by the word *dharma* which, however, has multifarious meanings too, so an adjective is usually added to form a notion of *sanātana dharma*, the everlasting law, which acquired a truly comprehensive meaning. It also applies to the central teaching of Hinduism about the continuous cyclic returns of the manifestation (*sṛṣṭi*) of the universe out of its divine source (or out of the dimension of the unmanifest), its duration for a time (*sthiti*) and its dissolution (*laya*) back into its hidden source, only to re-emerge again and again in the continuous creative process in ever-recurring cycles. The living beings who are subjected, under the all-pervading cosmic law, to transmigration in successive lives preserve their individuality in the latent state even during the period of dissolution of the universe to emerge in a new rebirth in the next period of manifestation. Their character, which was shaped by their deeds, accompanies them and so do the consequences of their volitional actions which have not yet reached their fruition. All that is proceeding in accordance with the universal law which is known in its application in the sphere of ethics as the law of *karma*. Expressed in simple terms it means that as one has sown so one will reap from life to life.

Without continuation of life after death the idea of final liberation would be meaningless and any effort beyond securing a reasonably comfortable life would be wasted. If by dying one would cease to exist altogether, everybody would be, in a way, 'liberated' from existence regardless of the type of life he had led. Suicide would be the best solution to a life full of hopeless hardships or frustrations and euthanasia would be fully justified. Selfless service, sacrifice and work for the good of others could be looked upon as folly (which, unfortunately, is not an unknown occurrence).

Not a few people hold similar views and many behave accordingly without giving much thought to ethical issues. This state of affairs, a result of professed or virtual materialistic outlook of many people in the modern world, is more or less the result of the philosophical inadequacy of the Christian religious tradition dominated by rigid dogmatic thinking based on rather primitive ideas developed in times when divine revelation was believed to be the only source of knowledge about the world, its origin, its nature and its future. It dominated European thinking throughout the medieval time into the first two or three centuries of the modern age. Almighty God was believed to have created the world and mankind only a few thousand years before, decreeing the laws of nature and formulating commands for human behaviour with subsequent rewards and punishments in eternity. With scientific discoveries about the enormous age of the universe and its peculiar nature governed by laws which can be expressed in mathematical equations, and about the long evolution of life on earth and mankind's progress from primitive stages to *homo sapiens*, inevitable conflicts with religious authorities, wielding political power and insisting on their dogmatic beliefs, eventually resulted in the parting of the ways between religion and science. Many scientists have become agnostics or even downright atheists. Some of them have overstepped the boundaries within which their science could formulate valid conclusions, for example by ruling out the possibility of an afterlife. Some biologists even regard the impossibility of afterlife as proved because of lack of laboratory evidence for it. But if one adheres strictly to logic, evidence *ex silentio* is not admissible.

The popularisation of science thus greatly contributed to the spread of a materialistic outlook, as already mentioned, and the resulting loss of faith in God and life after death had an undesirable side effect in that for many people moral values lost their force. Even philosophy contributed to this trend. Nietzsche's proclamation about god being dead (in several of his books) led to a cynical slogan: 'If god is dead, anything goes' The voices of some scientists admitting the possibility of an unknown dimension of reality accessible perhaps only to the vision of mystics are less influential.

Unlike the three monotheistic (Abrahamic) traditions (Judaism, Christianity and Islam), Indian religious and philosophical traditions are not in conflict with modern scientific thinking and the laws of nature as understood by science can be regarded as a mere extension of the ancient Indian notion of a universal law. Moral laws are, according to the Indian religious and philosophical traditions, anchored in this universal law as firmly as the physical laws of nature and do not depend for their efficacy on the agency of a personal god to back them with rewards and punishments. Unfortunately, with the transplanting of Western scientific knowledge and modern technological miracles which benefit the economy and population at large, the unwelcome materialist trend just described has rooted itself also in India. Nevertheless, since Indian religions are not, in essence, dogmatic and allow symbolical and philosophical interpretations of their cosmological mythology, their pantheon of deities and a plethora of other unseen beings, there need not be in India a parting of the ways between religion and science. Scientists and other educated people in India need not follow in the footsteps of Western materialism and can reconcile scientific discoveries with valuable insights of their spiritual traditions. After all, the interpretation of mythical and religious beliefs and practices on different levels of understanding, including the rational one, started already in Vedic times and has continued throughout the centuries till the present day.[5]

Yoga, its practices and its theoretical and philosophical foundations, have also been subjected to elaboration and interpretation on different levels. Some involve a search for an accomplished *guru* and then require unquestioning obedience to him. But there is a simpler approach. As has been pointed out before, the initial practice of Yoga does not require firm faith in any of its theoretical and philosophical tenets, only an open mind and a spirit of enquiry with a willingness to test the effectiveness of the practical methods on offer. Some positive results, be it only in terms of indefinite or vague feelings of satisfaction or pleasant reaction, may result in a certain degree of confidence that it may work and in time provide concrete results in the form of deep states of meditation. These then will inspire in the Yoga practitioner confidence in the insights of the sages of old about the continuity of life in successive existences during the periods of the manifestations and dissolutions of the universe and also in the balancing power of the cosmic law in the field of moral actions as well as in the possibility of the final salvation. Therefore the practitioner of Yoga will consistently uphold moral and spiritual values in life while working, however slowly, for his own final face to face encounter with truth.

II. The Prehistory of Yoga

Before the Buddha and Patañjali

Our understanding of Yoga as a doctrinally neutral and systematically presented spiritual discipline is based mainly on expositions of the spiritual path to liberation, the socalled 'noble truth of the path leading to the elimination of suffering' (*dukkha nirodha gāminīpaṭipadā ariya sacca*), expounded several times in the discourses of the Buddha and in thesuccinct text of the eightfold Yoga path (*aṣṭāṅga yoga*) in Patañjali's *Yoga Sūtra*. Thus the Buddha and Patañjali are two beacons signifying the beginning of the history of pure Yoga, unburdened by ideology or religious teachings. What went before can be called Yoga's prehistory, because it is known only from indirect sources, such as archaeological excavations, the religious poetry of the Vedas or Upaniṣadic musings, often burdened by mythological imagery and metaphysical speculations. In evaluating the evidence for the existence of Yoga or Yoga-like practices in pre-Buddhist times one has to use the Buddha's and Patañjali's systems as the criteria in order to extricate possible Yoga elements from the religious set-up of older times in which they are usually clothed. For the earliest indications of Yoga-like procedures one has to make some assumptions or tentative interpretations on the basis of archaeological materials.

The earliest indication of Yoga

One feature of Yoga training described as essential by

the Buddha and mentioned in Patañjali's text is a cross-legged posture (*āsana*) for meditation whose varieties are readily recognisable and have been practised in India for millennia, even long before the arrival of Āryans in the beginning of the second millennium BCE. One or other of the varieties of the cross-legged postures are now used for Yoga practice and meditation throughout the world. A proof of the early knowledge of several types of sitting positions and their practical use in prehistoric India was supplied by archaeological excavations at Harappa, Mohenjo-daro and other sites in North West India (now mostly in Pakistan) around the river Indus and its tributaries where a highly sophisticated pre-Vedic urban civilisation flourished between the years 2900-1900 BCE. One or two varieties of these sitting positions are depicted on a number of excavated steatite seals. Steatite seals were found in profusion in the prehistoric sites just mentioned, depicting human figures, animals, trees and whole scenes, some of them quite dramatic, and others clearly of mythological or religious character. Most of them bear inscriptions which have yet to be deciphered.[6]

Three types of pictures of a human figure which are significant in the context of Yoga have been found on several seals. They depict the figure sitting in a position which can be identified from much later (post-Vedic) Sanskrit texts on Yoga as *siddhāsana* (wisdom posture) or *bhadrāsana* (auspicious posture); other terms are in use for this position in some texts. It is a position which is not cross-legged, because the knees are more apart so that the soles of the feet are touching each other – in fact on at least two seals it appears that the soles of the depicted figure are not even touching, but that there is a small gap between them. It is possible to identify three types of human figures on the clay seals or copper tablets. All of them are male:

(1) The first type of picture shows a human figure sitting on a pedestal or stool. He has three faces and is adorned with horns and a tall headdress or a crown. He may have a

scarf around his shoulders and what appear to be bangles on his arms and legs. His member of procreation (*liṅga*) appears erect and his hands are resting on his knees. On either side of him are animals, on his right an elephant and a tiger and on his left a rhino and a buffalo. Above the tiger there is a standing human figure and there is another one above the rhino. Under the stool there are two antelopes. Horns being in antiquity usually associated with divinity, it is surmised that what we see here is an icon representing a god or perhaps even the God Creator which may be suggested by his erect member (Marshall, 1831, I, Pl XII/ 17). This figure was already identified by Marshall as a possible prototype of the god OEiva (and is often referred to as 'Proto-Śiva').

(2) The second type of picture is of a solitary human figure either with or without horns. On one or two of the seals he seems to wear bangles on his arms and is possibly looking upwards; he could be reciting prayers or ritual texts or magic formulae (*mantras*). Another seal shows a figure without bangles conveying the impression of being absorbed in meditation. The figures on these seals are sitting on a stool in the same position as the figure under (1). (Mackay, 1938, II, Pl LXXXVII/222 & 235; Fairservis, 1971, 276, seal 16; Newberry. 1985, seal M-D 222.)

(3) On the third type of picture is a human figure in the same sitting position as the others on a stool, but it is flanked by two kneeling human figures sitting on their heels, recognisably in *vajrāsana* (diamond posture). They are raising their hands in salutation. Behind each of them is a cobra raising its head poised like a canopy over them (Marshall, 1931, III, Pl CXVI/29, Pl CXVIII/Vs210; Fairservis, 1971, 276, seal 18).

There can be hardly any doubt that all these pictures have religious or spiritual significance and point to scenes and activities which are subsequently commonplace among early Āryan inhabitants of India. It would appear that the spiritual culture of the Harappan civilisation managed to survive the calamity of decline and collapse of its urban centres and in a way remained alive in the smaller fortified settlements which the Harappan tribes or communities were able to establish in the countryside. These were eventually conquered by Āryans and their inhabitants were partly subdued and partly assimilated, but in the process the surviving features of Harappan culture exercised a powerful influence on āryan society on all its levels.

Links to the *Śramaṇa* movement, Jainism, Buddhism and Hinduism

The first icon described above was already identified by Marshall as a possible prototype of the god Śiva, who came to be worshipped some two and a half thousand years later by Hindus, and is so worshipped till the present day. One of his many names is Paśupati (the lord of creatures) which is well foreshadowed by the picture on the seal on which the horned figure is surrounded by various living beings, including men. He is a god with many attributes, some of them even mutually contradictory, for example his protracted periods of asceticism on the one hand and long periods of sexual indulgence with many sexual exploits on the other. In the cosmic context Śiva is viewed as the lord of procreation and is as such worshipped under the symbol of *linga,* whose varieties are installed in many oeivaistic temples, often in combination with the female symbol of *yoni.* This tallies well with the ithyphallic nature of the figure. Stone phalluses were also found in Harappan sites (Marshall, 1831, III, Pl CXXX; Pl CXL), as were emblems of *yoni* (Marshall, 1831, I, Pl XIII/11 & 12; Pl XIV/6) as well as their combination, so their installation in Hindu temples suggests a clear link to Harappa. Ṛgvedic hymns express enmity to worshippers 'whose god is phallus' (*śiśnadevāḥ*). They were killed whenever the Āryans conquered their forts. [7]

Śiva's sexual feats do not seem to hinder him adversely in the practice of austerities and meditation during equally protracted periods. Indeed, for long periods in his life he does not do anything else and so as *the* great ascetic and meditator he bears the title Yogapati (the lord of Yoga). Śivaistic yogis regard him as their Divine Guru. It is because of this obvious connection with later Hinduism that the Harappan figure on the seals is still often referred to in academic literature as the proto-Śiva.

But on the same seal of the first type there is also a recognisable link to the early Buddhist iconography (Dikshit, 1939, 34 and 35). As reported in the discourses of the Buddha in which he reminisces about his struggles for liberation (MN I, 26, 163-173 & MN I, 36, 246-250), when he renounced life in luxury as a prince, he joined the hosts of wandering ascetics. First he found, one after the other, two teachers, Āḷāra Kālāma and Uddaka Rāmaputta, and stayed with each for a time. Each, in turn, taught him a specific metaphysical doctrine and a method of meditation leading to a corresponding blissful state of absorption. Each regarded his particular absorption as liberation which would be his final lot after death. The future Buddha mastered both the doctrines and the states of absorption in equal perfection as his teachers, but felt that neither of their meditative achievements guaranteed final liberation. So he left them and took up the practice of severe austerities followed at the time by many wanderers. They included reducing the intake of food to the bare minimum. According to the prevailing belief among wandering ascetics of the time (which in some ascetic circles persists till the present day) this was the way to lessen and eventually completely eradicate the natural clinging to life and thereby to achieve release from the necessity to be reborn in successive lives in *samsāra* ('global flow' of existences), thus reaching the final liberation in *nibbāna.* His determination and enormous zeal impressed five other ascetics who joined him in the hope that he would soon be liberated and then be able to guide them in their struggle for the same goal. But the future Buddha almost died from exhaustion and starvation without experiencing any signs of approaching liberation. He therefore resumed the normal intake of food given by people to ascetics as alms, to regain his strength and clarity of mind so that he could continue his search. The five ascetics regarded this as indulgence and abandonment of his effort to reach liberation and left him. But the future Buddha turned back to meditation, deepening it with internal concentration and eventually managed to break through to enlightenment (*bodhi*). He then pondered who would be able to grasp his message of the middle way between indulgence and severe austerities and apply his newly found methods of meditation, and first thought of his two teachers mentioned above, but found that they had died in the meantime and were now stuck in their respective blissful abodes, corresponding to their meditative achievements, for the rest of the present world period, to be reborn again in the next world period. Next the Buddha thought of the five ascetics who had previously deserted him. Finding that they were staying in the Deer Park (*migadāya*) near Benares, he went there and delivered his first discourse to them.

This park, reportedly a gift by the ruler of Benares (J I.145ff), was in constant use by ascetics alongside numerous deer for whom it was a safe haven. It is mentioned that the five ascetics offered the Buddha a stool and a vessel with water for washing his feet, so he sat on a stool while delivering his first discourse to them. When two or three hundred years after the Buddha's demise the initial reluctance to depict him in human form was abandoned, numerous icons of him started appearing. Some, showing him sitting cross-legged on a stool and preaching, have two antelopes under his seat and other figures following the example of the 'Proto-Śiva'. (One can be seen in Cave I at Ajanta, see Munsterberg 1970, 69.)

Other icons which show a human type figure sitting in meditation have been a familiar phenomenon in post-Harappan India for centuries. This icon is still the embodiment of Yoga in its aspect of meditative endeavour, although a less strenuous position than the one depicted on the seals (with soles pressing against or pointing to each other) is usually adopted. It is either the cross-legged lotus position (*padmāsana*) or the more comfortable one with shins parallel (*sukhāsana*). The first textual description of a suitable position for the practice of meditation, which could be the full lotus or half-lotus (*ardhapadmāsana*) can be found in two discourses of the Buddha (DN 22 & MN 10) in connection with the method of meditation known as 'mindfulness of breathing' (*anāpāna sati*).{8}

Further descriptions of varieties of sitting postures are given in the commentaries to Patañjali's *Yoga Sūtra* and in medieval and later textbooks. {9}

The third type of icon originating from Harappan seals, showing the central human figure sitting in *siddhāsana*, can be interpreted as a spiritual teacher with his revering disciples sitting at his feet, as already suggested. It is a scene which could perfectly illustrate a situation in an *āśram* centuries later and even in modern times. The motif of protecting cobras reappears in early Buddhism in the form of the King of *nāgas* (cobra-like beings living at the bottom of lakes and rivers) by the name of Mucalinda who, according to a legendary narration, protected the Buddha from a rainstorm when he was sitting under a tree in the third week after his enlightenment, by holding his extended hood over his head (Vin, I. 3; Ud II. 1). The added detail to this image in Buddhist icons is that Mucalinda coiled himself seven times round the Buddha's body to keep him warm. The sculptural icon depicting this scene has become very popular in all countries to which Buddhism spread, but instead of coiling himself round the Buddha's body, Mucalinda is sitting on his coils. The Harappan seal with a sitting human figure with cobras in front of him also reminds us of the still surviving popular phenomenon in India of a fakir playing a pipe to a cobra rearing in front of him.

The described images along with a variety of other scenes and motifs on numerous other Harappan seals as well as further relevant archaeological finds suggest the existence, in the Harappan civilisation, of a highly developed and stratified spiritual culture set probably within a religious system professed by the educated upper classes of the population. It was obviously parallelled by a popular worship prevailing among the lower classes, probably centred around the cult of a Mother Goddess (which also reappeared later in Hinduism), suggested by numerous rather crude clay statuettes. There is also evidence of cults of tree spirits (Marshall, 1831, I, Pl XII/18) and some animals (Marshall, 1831, I & III containing pictures of numerous seals on several plates). But was there also in Harappan time an independent spiritual trend outside the possibly organised religious establishment and popular cults? We cannot be certain. However, what is remarkable about all the described traits and images on seals is their continuity. They were obviously strongly enough ingrained in people's minds to survive the decline of the Harappan urban civilisation and the upheavals caused by the incoming Āryan tribes with their own Vedic culture, and to reemerge centuries later in the āryan religious and philosophical systems as well as in popular cults. By then the Āryan tribes and clans had consolidated themselves into a pattern of settled communities, rural and urban, socially stratified into castes. Groups of tribes coalesced in the course of struggles for territory among themselves and with the indigenous post-Harappan population into state formations most of which became kingdoms. A few Āryan tribes and clans managed to preserve their earlier tribal identity and developed into aristocratic republics with differing constitutions

Religion and spirituality in the Harappan culture

On the basis of what has been described, we have sufficient grounds for assuming that an important feature of the ancient Indus civilisation was a living religion which included a sophisticated element of worship of a powerful God who was obviously the lord of creatures and possibly perceived as their Creator. His procreative prowess may be indicated by his ithyphallic state, which could also be interpreted as a symbol of the divine creative force in the universe. At the same time one has to take into account his posture, which precludes outward activity and suggests a meditative state of mind of cosmic proportions assumed after the creation. This would make him a prototype of a human renunciant who gave up active life in the world and became engaged in an internal struggle for spiritual progress, in other words of a yogi or a monk practising meditation. The ithyphallic feature of this 'proto-Śiva' immersed in meditation could also be viewed as foreshadowing later Tantric elements in the Vedic and Brāhmanic times, and in Buddhist and Hindu Tantrism; supporting evidence for some kind of Tantric trend in Harappan culture may be seen in additional finds of separate stone *liṅgas* and of emblems of its female counterparts (*yoni*) as referred to above.

The existence of a community of monks in Harappan culture is suggested by a large building which was excavated in Mohenjo-daro and may have been a monastery (Marshall, 1931, III, Pl VII & VIII, Pl XXI/b). It has in its central courtyard a large rectangular communal tank (very much like tanks in later Hindu temples) with two staircases at each end. On one side is a range of small rooms like cells for individual monks, each with a small private tank underneath reached by a small staircase. At one end there are a few bigger rooms on a slightly higher level than the courtyard, probably for gatherings. If it was a cloister or monastery, it certainly provided the resident monks with opportunity for communal events as well as seclusion for private meditation.

Evidence for monks is suggested by a statue which looks exactly like a Buddhist monk today, providing another example of a feature which survived into later centuries (Marshall, 1931, III, Pl C/1-3). He wears a simple garment which leaves his right shoulder bare and is sitting in a cross-legged position. His legs are covered by his garment so that the exact posture cannot be established, but his knees are not widely apart as are those of the figures of yogis on the seals sitting on stools, so it cannot be *siddhāsana,* but it could be *padmāsana, ardhapadmāsana* or *sukhāsana.* He seems to be carrying some object under the garment (perhaps a begging bowl?).

One impressive statuette of a man in a ceremonial garment suggests a priest (Marshall, 1931, III, Pl XCVIII). His garment leaves his right shoulder bare in the same manner as the statue of the monk above, but he could not have been a monk, because of the rich decoration on his garment and his careful hairstyle with a head ornament on a hairband whose ends fall down his neck. He has a beard, but his upper lip is shaved. His garment has a trefoil decoration (in the form of three rounded lobes like a clover leaf). The trefoils show traces of red pigment so one can assume that the garment may have displayed other colours as could the hairband. All this would hardly point to an ordinary priest, it rather suggests someone of a higher status, some kind of religious dignitary. There must also have been temples in the cities, but none has been excavated so far. There is in the central part of Mohenjo-daro a mound, usually referred to as 'citadel', which is surmounted by a later construction of a Buddhist stūpa (Marshall, 1931, III, Pl XV/a). It is generally assumed that underneath the stūpa must be a temple from Harappan time, but it cannot be excavated for religious reasons because it would destroy the stūpa.

From the point of view of searching for evidence or indications of Yoga as an independent spiritual discipline the most interesting and even telling image is the human figure without horns sitting in *siddhāsana* which could be interpreted, as suggested above, as portraying a spiritual teacher, an advanced yogi, perhaps just instructing his two disciples sitting at his feet and displaying a reverential gesture. Absence of any religious imagery in this scene makes a sharp contrast with the symbolism of the 'Proto-Śiva' which eloquently conveys his religious and metaphysical status that would probably be confirmed by the inscription above him, if it could be read. The seal with the image of the yogi on the stool with the two revering figures flanking him has no inscription and he appears to be completely naked in the manner of some of the later renunciant *śramanas.* This feature was also adopted in post-Vedic time by Jina Mahāvīra, the founder of Jainism, and is still adhered to by his followers of the *digambara* tradition.

The cobras in this scene may be a marginal feature which is in keeping with popular ideas about animals being affected by the atmosphere surrounding a spiritually advanced person, but there might be a more profound explanation in view of the Mucalinda story in the Buddhist Canon.

We can conclude (leaving aside popular cults) that there is a possibility or even a high degree of probability that there existed side by side in Harappan culture two tendencies in the practice of advanced spiritual disciplines. One would have been rooted in or be a part of the religious establishment run by a priesthood, probably officiating in temples. Spiritual endeavours involving meditation and concentration of the mind and consequently requiring permanent or at least temporary seclusion could have been practised in monasteries which would have allowed freedom from the strictures of organised religion and community life and could even have led to the adoption of a solitary itinerant life or living as a hermit in a cave or a makeshift hut. In some cases an advanced practitioner of a spiritual discipline, which we can with reason call Yoga, would have with him one or two or a group of disciples.

Transition to the Vedas

The Harappan civilisation was already in decline when Āryan tribes started moving into Northern India from Īrān in consecutive waves from around 1900 BCE. It was the last leg of their long migration from their original homeland in Southern Russia which they had shared with other Indo-European groups of tribes (some of whom also migrated — to Anatolia, and southern and Western Europe). Prior to the arrival of the first wave of Āryans to India the main Harappan cities appear to have suffered for some time from overpopulation, apparently as a result of the influx of refugees from flooded rural areas. Floods were eventually encroaching on cities as well, which led to raising the floors of houses and building further upper stories.

In time there was also a breakdown in the system which supplied the cities with agricultural produce and the inhabitants had to move away. There is no evidence of wholesale conquest of the cities by Āryans, only signs of sporadic fires and of minor skirmishes which left behind a small number of skeletons.

The incoming Āryan tribes and clans do not seem to have shown much interest in the largely deserted cities and were settling down outside the flooded areas in the countryside, much of which was wooded, in North Western India in the area of the five rivers (called by them Pañcasindhu, hence later Pañjāb which comprises the Indus and its tributaries). Later most Āryans moved beyond Pañcasindhu, everywhere establishing their agricultural settlements. [10] In the process they had to fight with Harappan communities living by then in small fortified enclosures and fiercely defending their cultivated fields and herds of cattle. When deforesting wooded areas to establish more agricultural land, the Āryans came into contact also with primitive aboriginal tribes. Those whose villages were destroyed in the process of deforestation were subdued and incorporated into Āryan society as serfs. However, at that stage the Āryan tribes and clans were not yet integrated and competed with each other for land, occasionally even fighting among themselves. Sometimes some Āryan tribes entered into alliance with upperclass Harappans who were near to them racially or by the colour of their skin. Nevertheless consolidation and relative integration of the Āryan society was achieved within two or three hundred years, even though political unification was not reached until much later.

The Āryans brought with them from their original home to India a sophisticated religious and spiritual culture as well as a tripartite social organisation which was at the time already intrinsic to all Indo-European nations. Each Āryan tribe or clan had a seer (*ṛsi*) or a few seers who safeguarded their religious and spiritual tradition in the form of hymnic poetry to which the gifted ones among them were adding their inspired visions. They and their disciples also performed religious rituals for their tribes and were members of the elite social class. Next was the class of warriors who were important during the long migration and occupation of new territories on the way and finally when conquering the new home in India. In settled conditions they developed into an aristocracy. The remaining members of the tribe formed the menial class which included herders of cattle and workers in the fields as well as various craftsmen. With the subjugation of the original inhabitants of India — Harappans of the lower classes and the conquered jungle tribes — who were made into serfs, a fourth social class was formed.

The Āryans were extremely race- and colour-conscious and so there was a deeper social barrier between them and the serfs, who were mostly of darker skin. This backfired on them and resulted in the deepening of the barriers even between the three upper classes. As a result the class system eventually turned into the specifically Indian rigid caste system. The Harappan population itself was racially mixed; at least four racial types were suggested on the basis of the analysis of preserved skulls, among them was also a contingent of Alpine or Indo- European type (Hrozý, 1941, 228; Dikshit, 1939, 36). These and some other groups of the original inhabitants who were racially or by colour of their skin akin to the Āryans managed to be incorporated into the Āryan upper classes.

The system of four castes (Skt. *varna*, meaning originally 'colour') may have been established already by 1,000 BCE, because the Ṛgvedic hymn 10,90 on the cosmic person, called *Puruṣa Sūkta*, mentions the names of the four castes. Soon thereafter the Āryan tribes were more or less integrated, forming a homogeneous Vedic culture, as already mentioned. Their religious and spiritual heritage was preserved in hymnic form and each tribe had originally its own version of it (with some overlaps). Prior to codification it was safeguarded by seers within each tribe and could be supplemented with new hymns. Any member of the elite social class who managed to compose a hymn and get it accepted for recitation at public ceremonies earned the designation 'seer' (*ṛsi*). It would seem that some of the latest hymns were felt to be of inferior value compared with those inherited from previous generations and that was the reason for sifting out and coordinating the best valued hymns of all the tribal communities. They were arranged into ten books which comprise altogether 1028 hymns of varying length, but on average a hymn has about ten stanzas. Six of the books are named after famous ancient families which produced one or more outstanding seers who had composed hymns handed down orally within the family for generations until they were included in the codified collection.

At the same time, as the process of integration of the tribes continued, each of the four social classes within different tribes came to be integrated 'across the board', as it were, and they were then regarded as forming four castes within the wider Āryan social setup. Members of the spiritual elite, now no longer regarded as seers, retained the officiating function in public ritual gatherings, virtually becoming priests (*brāhmanas*) and forming the caste of Brahmins. The warriors whose task had been to secure by combat the existence of the Āryan society as a whole (when on the move), formed in settled conditions the caste of warriors (*kshatriyas*). They became virtually aristocrats within the newly formed state formations. Common folks formed the caste of *vaioeyas* and serfs the caste of *śūdras.* The whole process during which the system of social classes, which allowed limited mobility between them, hardened into a rigid caste system separated by almost unbridgeable barriers, was gradual and rather complicated. Its genesis has never been fully or satisfactorily explained, but it is obvious that the main protagonists of the rigid caste system were the Brahmins, who regarded themselves as forming the top layer of society. They may have managed to smuggle the *Puruṣa Sūkta* mentioned above into the *Rg Veda* at a late stage, perhaps even after its codification, to give the caste system a divine sanction.

The full name of the selected and carefully redacted collection of hymns is *Rg Veda Samhitā* (collection of knowledge in verses). It comprises the spiritual and religious knowledge of the Āryan tribes accumulated over many centuries. The seers who had produced the hymns were probably always regarded as divinely inspired and that is how this first and subsequent Vedic collections compiled on its basis came to be looked upon. The *Rg Veda* and subsequent Vedic collections were safeguarded by specialised groups of Brahmins who had implanted parts of the collections into their memory and were responsible for passing them unchanged to subsequent generations. When a specialised group of memorising Brahmins assembled, they could recite the whole collection. Knowledge of the sacred scriptures was what gave the Brahmin caste its high status.

The hymnic creativity, of course, did not stop after the codification of the *Rg Veda,* despite the fact that no new hymns could be added to the *Rg Veda Samhitā.* Some of the new hymns were probably ephemeral and were soon forgotten, others caught on and were sung on public occasions, but no special effort was made to preserve them, and most of them were lost in the course of time. However, when within a few centuries writing became current, some of the favourite post-Vedic hymnic poems (called *stotras,* hymns of praise) were written down and thus preserved. In fact, this kind of poetry never ceased to be produced and among the authors of preserved *stotras* are some illustrious names, e.g. Śankara, although their authorship cannot usually be established with certainty. Nowadays they are referred to as devotional songs. They are very popular and have become an art form presented also by professional performers in concert halls and even utilised in films.

The spiritual message of some of the Ṛgvedic hymns inspired by mystical experiences of ancient seers was probably originally meant for individual contemplation, but the vehicle of their partial dissemination was public recitation, usually accompanied by rituals. The hymns which became most popular with the public were those which contained supplications for long life, prosperity, offspring and heaven after death, usually combined with praising individual gods and their heroic deeds. Ritual accompanied by recitation was becoming ever more important for the bulk of the population and the Brahmins eventually made use for liturgical purposes of only selected portions of Rgvedic hymns for recitation, which accompanied the ever more elaborate rituals in public gatherings. In the course of time the rituals became standardised, which required set texts of a precise length. This led within about two hundred years after the codification of Rgvedic hymns into *Rg Veda Samhitā* to the adaptation of some of its hymns and to the compilation of a special collection of certain stanzas of selected hymns for ritual purposes, called *Sāma Veda Samhitā* (collection of knowledge in songs). It has altogether 1549 stanzas of which only 76 are not taken from the *Rg Veda Samhitā.* These came probably from hymns which, for some reason, were not included into the redacted Rgvedic collection, but were popular enough to be regularly used. Their full version has not been preserved.

A component of public religious practice was the sacrifice of domesticated animals and agricultural produce to the gods which was to secure their favour and rewards, such as long life, offspring and well-being. The sacrificial rites were also becoming very complicated. They were expanded by Brahmins as a means of dominating the lives of the population and increasing their own importance in the developing state formations. A third collection of texts of ritual character was created in this connection by Brahmins. It came to be called *Yajur Veda Samhitā* (collection of sacrificial knowledge). The three Vedas were compiled in the North Western part of India where the process of merging the Āryan tribes and the transformation of their social setup into urban civilisation were taking place.

A fourth Vedic collection, called *Atharva Veda Samhitā,* named after an ancient family of seers, was codified between 600-500 BCE. It is quite different from the above three Vedas in that it contains spiritual lore of a rather esoteric nature. It originated with a smaller contingent of Āryan communities which were organised in kinds of combatant fraternities bound together by religious vows (Skt. *vrata*) and so they came to be referred to as Vrātyas. They were the advance party of invaders into North Western India from Īrān and probably secured domination of the new country for the Āryans by force, subduing parts of the indigenous settled population, but they did not at first create fixed settlements, remaining itinerant and living off the subdued local inhabitants. When the bulk of Āryan tribes started arriving from Īrān over the Hindukush into Pañcasindhu and settling down with their families and herds of cattle, the Vrātyas moved further East to the area around the river basins of the Gangā and the Yamunā (later known as Magadha, today's

Bihār and West Bengal). At the peak of the Vedic culture, the growth of the Āryan population in Pañcasindhu led to the migration of its surplus population in the footsteps of the Vrātyas to include the upper Gangā and Yamunā, later proceeding as far as the eastern seacoast. The whole area of the Vedic culture then expanded around seven mighty rivers and the expression Saptasindhu probably referred to it (cf. RV 4.28.1; 8.25.27). The arrival of large contingents of Āryan communities from the Pañjāb into the Vrātya territory created pressure on Vrātya fraternities who were eventually incorporated into the Vedic social setup. Their spiritual elite was given the status of Brahmins and their ancient sacred lore was redacted and codified, as mentioned above, to become *Atharva Veda Samhitā*, the fourth Veda. It is in some parts more explicitly spiritual than the *Rg Veda Samhitā* and exercised great influence on the Upaniṣads, which started appearing just at that time. The *Atharva Veda* is particularly conspicuous for its frequent use of the term *brahman* for the essence or highest level of reality and is therefore also referred to as *Brahma Veda.* Some small groups of Vrātyas remained itinerant and became famous by practising magic rituals which they had been offering to the settled population in Pañcasindhu even before its surplus population started moving east. They were thus in competition with Brahmins when the Vedic rituals appeared ineffective, for example in times of poor harvest because of drought.

Yoga and the Vedas

There is no proof that Yoga was known to the Vedic Āryans in any systematic form. The originators of the Vedas known as *ṛṣis.* (seers) can be regarded as accomplished mystics. Some Vedic hymns contain their profoundest insights into the mysteries of human existence. They also suggest their acquaintance with higher forms of life in transcendent dimensions of reality and some of them claimed to have experienced the essence of reality as such. As this knowledge was being passed from generation to generation in a kind of teacher-pupil relationship, a way or path for the development and transmission of these highest insights would have been gradually developed or 'found'; the attitude to new knowledge in the Vedas appears to suggest that matters related to spirituality and even to religious procedures, such as ritual, are not developed by the human mind, but are found through vision. That is the case also with the conceiving of a new divinely inspired hymn or a practical task of transmitting insights from a teacher to his disciples. The teacher finds the way, becoming a pathfinder (*gātuvid*, cf. RV 1.105.15). It would probably have to be structured so that it could be passed on to learners by stages; in other words it would have been methodical. It could be called a Yoga path, but in the absence of any details in the Vedic hymns about its shape and character it is better to refer to it as a mystic path.[11]

Tapas - the inner flame

One element of the later system of Yoga transmitted in Patañjali's *Yoga Sūtra*, however, does stem from the Vedic experience: the practice of *tapas*. As is explained in note 4, it designates in the Vedas an impersonal creative force enhancing the cosmic manifestation. In post-hymnic creation myths recorded in the Brāhmanas (priestly books, cca 900-700 BCE) and some mythical portions of the oldest Upaniṣads (cca 700-600 BCE) *tapas* became a personal technique which the demiurge god adopted (*tapo 'tapyata*) in preparation for his task of fashioning the universe (e.g. Brhadāranyaka Upaniṣad 3.2.1).

In the middle Upaniṣads (cca 600-400 BCE) the word came to designate the flame of inner exertion needed to achieve final knowledge: 'Through inner effort seek to know *brahman*' (*tapasā brahma vijijñāsasva*, Taittirīya Upaniṣad 3,2,1). Later Upaniṣads (from 400 BCE onwards), which already deal expressly with Yoga, frequently employ the term *tapas*. Patañjali includes it in the second step of his eightfold

Yoga path as the third of the five observances (*niyamas*) which is usually translated as 'austerity'. Its purpose is to free the mind from dependence on sensory pleasures and all manner of bodily satisfactions. But the connection with the meaning 'heat' should even here be borne in mind; it is well known that an experience of inner bodily warmth if not heat accompanies efforts to discipline the body and occurs also during quiet meditational sittings. Generating extreme bodily heat is also the objective of specialised Yoga exercises known from Tibetan sources as *tummo.*

The wandering sages

The seers of old (*ṛṣiṣ*) who had found the mystic path, had achieved their spiritual accomplishment and composed most of the Vedic hymns, chose to live within their Indo-Āryan tribal communities in order to lead them on the path of order (*ṛta*) by instituting a religious tradition based on recurring rituals which was instrumental for establishing a well functioning society. But there was also in this system the seed of degeneration, not for the original path-finding seers, but for their successors. Living within the society involved them in family life and other worldly concerns. This was reflected also in their hymnic poetry. That was no doubt one contributing factor for the codification of the *Rg Veda Samhitā,* intended to prevent the spiritual heritage from being watered down. Successors of the seers became members of the caste of Brahmins (priests), as already explained.

However there were also probably from very early Vedic times wandering outsiders called *munis,* who were conspicuous by their long hair; they had a reputation of accomplished sages, but they did not choose to spread their message within the Āryan tribal communities.

Their way of life was described as 'following the path of the wind' and they implied that their real nature was not open to scrutiny by people.[12]

The *muni* was a noble figure with the features of a spiritual teacher and that is how this expression was mostly used subsequently as in the case of the Buddha, whose frequent designation is Śakyamuni, the sage from the Śakya clan. Less illustrious wanderers were called *śeramanas* (from the verbal root *śram*, to exert oneself), mentioned a few times in different contexts above. A *śramana* was an equally old phenomenon as a *muni*, existing in parallel with, but outside of, the developing Vedic religion and predating the post-Vedic system of Brāhmanism. The most conspicuous feature of wandering *śramanas* was asceticism, so the word is usually translated as 'ascetic'. The procedures adopted by some ascetics were sometimes of a quite severe nature, involving even self-torture in the belief that it would speed up the dissolution of 'bad *karma*' and bring them nearer to liberation.

One might be inclined to regard as yogis those wandering sages who accepted disciples and also the sages who settled in hermitages. They must have had a way of transmitting their accomplishment to their close disciples, but there is no evidence of any kind of systematic method. The transmission was probably a matter of adopting the same lifestyle as their master and living in constant proximity to him.

The Vrātya contribution

Those Vrātyas who resisted incorporation into the Brāhmanic setup continued their itinerant life and carried on with some of their specific religious and spiritual practices. An important part of the communal religious practice of the Vrātyas had been singing (accompanied by music and dance) and the recitation of *mantras* and litanies performed in a solemn and precisely regulated way, which led to the preoccupation with the breath and eventually to the development of *prānāyāma.* This influenced Brāhmanic practices, including rituals, and also obviously led to the inclusion of *prānāyāma* into Patañjali's *aṣṭāṇga yoga.*

Among Vrātyas who retained their itinerant way of life there were solitary wanderers called *ekavrātyas.* They practised austerities, breathing exercises and mystical contemplation. They feature prominently in the *Atharva Veda Samhitā.* Others formed wandering groups among whom there were conspicuous teams of three members headed by a master (known as *māgadha* after Magadha, the geographical centre of the Vrātya tradition in the east) with a young pupil (called *brahmacārī*, i.e. 'one who fares according to *brahman*'), and a young female attendant (called *pumoecalī*). They were the successors of those who used to stray into the Western part of Northern India, the heartland of the Vedic civilisation before it started spreading East, offering their services to the settled population, as already described. At the request of patrons they engaged in magic and performed special rituals such as fertility rites in the fields, which included ritual copulation (*maithuna*) — a clear antecedent of the later 'lefthand' practices in Tantric Yoga.{13}

'Divine Faring'

When advanced masters accepted disciples in order to pass on to them instructions in methods of spiritual practice, as described earlier, the necessity would have arisen to formulate a set of rules for the disciples to live by. This set of rules received the designation *brahmacarya* which can be translated as 'divine faring' and interpreted also as 'moving according to or towards *brahman*', i.e. towards union with the source and goal of all existence. This interpretation is derived from those Upaniṣads which identified the goal of spiritual practice and, indeed, the goal of existence *par excellence* with *brahman*, which they proclaimed to be the divine source and inmost core of the world and, indeed, of the whole of reality. That includes individual beings whose inner core, *ātman*, was felt to be identical with *brahman.*

In some Upaniṣadic passages *brahman* is conceived in personalised form as the god Brahma or the god Brahma is regarded as the first emanation from *brahman*. The term *brahmacarya* would then be interpreted as 'moving towards Brahma'. We can be satisfied with the definition of *brahmacarya* as 'the way of living according to the set of rules to be observed by disciples of a master'. In other words the term denotes the state of discipleship, of being under training for the attainment of the highest goal of human existence. The derivative term *brahmacārī* then denotes one who is under such training, usually as a pupil of an experienced or perhaps even accomplished master.

Stemming from the Vrātya tradition, both these terms came to be used in the above meanings in the *Atharva Veda Samhitā*. Then their meaning became broadened and they were adopted throughout the Vedic culture for all youngsters during their period of studentship or apprenticeship. The Indo-Āryan youngsters underwent such a period for twelve years before they achieved adulthood and, being then capable of earning a living, became householders.

During those years the youngsters were usually living with their teachers as members of their household and were, naturally enough, bound by the rule of chastity. Thus the term *brahmacarya* became synonymous with chastity and with this meaning it was adopted also as the fourth of the five 'abstinences' (*niyamas*) in Patañjali's system of eightfold Yoga. The original Vrātya meaning of the term (faring towards *brahman*) has been preserved in the Tantric tradition, even the left-handed one which includes ritual *maithuna*, but does require chastity outside the ritual practice.

The teacher-pupil relationship

The life-style of a Brāhmanic apprentice living in the household of his Brahmin teacher was one of strict obedience to, reverence for, and personal service extended towards his teacher. This applied also to the relation between a spiritual teacher (*guru*) and his disciple (*śiṣya*). This stricter form of the *guru-śiṣya* relationship was later incorporated into and is, in fact, still reflected in those Yoga schools and *āśrams* which have been based on the Brāhmanic tradition or have closer links to Hindu religious systems. On the other hand, this relationship was much freer in most Yoga schools of the independent forest tradition. That has a precedent already in the hymn on the 'long-haired one' (*keśin*, RV 10,136) in which the accomplished long-haired wanderer who helps others on the path is described as a 'sweet and most uplifting friend' (RV 10.136.6) rather than a stern *guru*. A similar freer relationship between the teacher and his pupils was adopted also in early Buddhism as will be explained later, but Mahāyāna and Tibetan Buddhist sects were influenced by the Hindu tradition of the strict *guru-śiṣya* relationship.

Brāhmanism and yogic trends

In the post-hymnic period the established Vedic religion turned, as already mentioned, towards an increasing involvement in ritualism which eventually became rather excessive, to the detriment of spiritual and mystical trends in the Vedic tradition. The Brahmins concentrated in their writings, called *brāhmanas*, on the cosmic symbolism of the sacrificial rites, their mythological justification and social application, and so there is hardly any textual evidence about spiritual and mystical or Yoga-like practices from this time.

Yet there is no doubt that these activities did not disappear. The Vedic *ṛṣi* line may have virtually dried up, but *munis, śramanas* and Vrātyas undoubtedly continued roaming the land and their spiritual practices must have been undergoing some kind of articulation and systematisation while being passed on from teacher to pupil. There is no doubt that not only the Vrātyas, but also the *śramanas* and even *munis* were outside the mainstream of the orthodox Vedic-Brāhmanic line. They may have found some of their inspiration also in the surviving remnants of

Harappan spirituality and this may have given their endeavours that particular twist which resulted in the emergence of purely yogic spirituality rather than a somewhat modified ancient Vedic mysticism.

This does not mean, however, that the Brāhmanic circles committed to the Vedic tradition did not contribute anything at all to the formation of Yoga. Some Brahmins did retain interest in a personal spiritual approach to the riddle of existence and when they retired from active service as priests in the community to spend the rest of their lives in forest hermitages, they devoted their time to contemplation and some of them to some extent rekindled in themselves the vanishing mystical flame (*tapas*) of the ancient Vedic seerhood. They may also have come into contact with itinerant sages and ascetics from the unorthodox circles. Some of them later also settled down in the woods and became hermits, possibly even in the neighbourhood of hermitages of retired Brahmins.

Accustomed from their active life to formulate their thoughts for others, the Brāhmanic hermits now started producing from their solitary meditations new sets of scriptures which came to be called *āranyakas* (forest books). Those which were recognised as inspired were attached to the Vedic collections and undoubtedly contributed to the revival of mystical trends even among the actively serving Brahmins. From them the interest in these trends spread into aristocratic circles and influenced more articulate members of the public for whom Brahmins continued performing traditional rituals. In the course of time it became commonplace even in public to discuss matters of life and death, of human destiny and the goal of life. Inevitably the discussions also generated speculation about insights gained from meditative absorptions. Some discussions were recorded and combined with traditional knowledge and from all this emerged a new type of text known as the Upaniṣads which continued to be produced for centuries up to modern time. The thirteen oldest Upaniṣads are highly valued because in them Brāhmanic spirituality reached a new peak. Formally 108 Upaniṣads were recognised as inspired, were attached to the Vedic collections and are designated as the 'end of the Veda' (*Vedānta*).

Forest Yoga schools

Meanwhile we have to assume that early during the historically little known period of the *brāhmanas, āranyakas* and older Upaniṣads (cca 900-600 BCE), a new phenomenon of forest centres of spiritual quest and practice appeared on the scene. They were probably started by those renunciants who preferred a settled way of life as hermits to a wandering life-style. When some of them had gained the reputation of accomplished sages, a circle of disciples would have gathered around them and in time such circles developed into *āśram* type hermitages or schools with a clearly non-Vedic and non-Brahminic background.

Direct evidence about them is comparatively late and comes from the discourses of the Buddha in the Pāli Canon, where there is mention of two schools headed by the two teachers of the Buddha before his enlightenment, as described in the Introduction and summarised in the next chapter. There can be hardly any doubt that many more such *āśrams* or forest schools existed. One can speculate that some of these schools may even have been of Harappan origin, but one has also to remember the Indo-Āryan origin of the Vrātya tradition with its Indo-European past and the above-mentioned Vedic influence of Brāhmanic hermits. The situation is not very clear, but that Yoga as a specific path was taking shape under diverse influences can also be inferred from its subsequent methodical versatility and variety.

III From Forest Schools to Buddhist Yoga

As described in the chapter on The Prehistory of Yoga, evidence about the forest Yoga schools was supplied by the discourses of the Buddha in which he gave some autobiographical reminiscences which it is opportune to summarise partly here. When he became a renunciant, he first spent some time with various teachers in the hope of gaining enlightenment under their guidance. He related the names of two of them who appear to have earned his esteem (Āḷāra Kālāma and Uddaka Rāmaputta). They were obviously very advanced on their spiritual pathsand both of them behaved in a way which made an impression of accomplished masters. Eachwas living in his forest hermitage surrounded by a host of disciples to whom they presented their teachings about the state of final liberation and a meditation technique for reaching it. Those techniques would have been systematic and efficient as the future Buddha mastered them quickly. They can therefore be regarded as virtual Yoga systems and the *āśrams* where they were taught and practised as forest Yoga schools even in the absence of this designation. However, the resulting blissful states of mind which both the teachers of Gotama Sakyamuni regarded as the final liberation which would be theirs after death, did not satisfy the future Buddha. He felt that when he emerged from these blissful states he was still tied to this world and did not feel sure that they would be permanent after deatḥ evertheless, they were recognised by him as genuine higher spiritual states of mind and when he reached final liberation and became the Buddha, he incorporated them into his system of higher states of meditation under the term of *arūpa jhānas* (which may be rendered as 'abstract absorptions'). They were uplifting and profound, but in a way only 'recreational' and therefore suitable for respite from the strenuous efforts needed on the path to genuine liberation, but if unduly indulged in could become a hindrance obscuring the vision of the final truth.

Having been disappointed in his two Yoga teachers, the future Buddha for a time practised severe austerities as a *śramana* and tackled *prānāyāma*, although the way his attempts to master it as described in the discourses seem rather incompetent compared with the methodical descriptions in later yogic literature. But that may be because of ignorance on the part of the redactors of the discourses who finalised them after the Buddha's death. Neither of these practices produced for the future Buddha the desired final effect, but — to say the least — we need not doubt that his experience and proficiency in them contributed significantly to his final success. *Prānāyāma*, even if correctly applied, would not in itself bring the practitioner to the point of liberation. But, as mentioned above, it found its place later as the fourth part of Patañjali's eightfold Yoga path. In the Buddha's scheme *prānāyāma* as an elaborate system known from later sources has no place, but the process of breathing is one of the recommended objects of meditation termed 'mindfulness of breathing' (*anāpānasati*).

Meditative absorption

The technique of absorption which the future Buddha learned from his two teachers has a long and complicated history. The Sanskrit equivalent of its Pāli version (*jhāna*) which the Buddha used for it, is *dhyāna* and it is derived from the root *dhī* used in the Ṛgvedic texts to denote the mystical vision of the ancient seers (Gonda, 1963). But this link of *dhyāna* to the original meaning of the Vedic *dhī* appears to have been obscured in the Brāhmanic tradition, which preserved only a dim understanding of what the expression means. Even the early Upaniṣads, which must have been contemporary to some of the forest schools in which *dhyāna* was practised, have only sporadic passages about it. One of them, however, is of considerable interest (Chāndogya Upaniṣad 7.6.1).

In this passage *dhyāna* is regarded as a natural state of existence superior to the usual activity of mind called here mentation (*citta*) which creates only conflicts and upheavals. Essentially, heaven, space and earth, the waters and mountains, gods and even men exist in *dhyāna*, but only a distinguished person, a master (*prabhu*, which can be interpreted as 'one in his original state of being'), experiences it that way, that is as if in contemplation.[14]

This virtually says that for a mature mind everything is in deep harmony, because such a mind perceives everything in its true essence. This kind of living in constant meditation transforms one's vision of the world. A more extensive and elaborate account of a mind which experiences everything in its true essence and how it is achieved is given in a rather extensive discourse of the Buddha (MN 1,1). There may be a link in it to the source on which the Upaniṣadic passage was based. When the Buddhist scriptures with descriptions of the Buddhist *dhyāna/jhāna* meditative techniques reached China, they gave rise there to the Ch'an school of Buddhism which then reached Japan to become Zen and under that name it became popular in the West in modern time.

The Zen Buddhist description of the accomplished state of mind is called 'no mind' since it views reality as it presents itself without being mentally appropriated. A kind of constant meditative frame of mind, as against limited sessions dedicated to meditation, was also advocated by J. Krishnamurti and described by him as 'choiceless awareness'. But a caution is needed here (see later).

It would appear that this notion of a constant meditative frame of mind was derived from the Vedic *dhī* and was a line of development which preserved for the notion of *dhyāna* the implication that it ultimately represents the final liberation including final knowledge or enlightenment, just like the *dhī* of the ancient *rshiṣ*. This appears implied also in Zen accounts of its notion of the final or highest *satori* — Zen *satori* appears to have initial and advanced stages preceding supposedly the final one which brings liberation. But it is not possible to extricate a clear picture from Zen sources, since they contain spontaneous utterances which defy interpretation and can be easily imitated by anybody.

As already described, the Buddha learned states of deep absorption (*jhāna*) from his two forest teachers and after his enlightenment incorporated them into his system of eight *jhānas*. He actually, according to his description, experienced the first *jhāna* spontaneously as a boy and used that reminiscence as a starting point in his struggle for enlightenment under the Bodhi tree. He then passed through three increasingly deeper and purer *jhānas* and achieved enlightenment from the fourth one. He described them in the Satipatthāna Sutta under 'right concentration' (*sammā samādhi*); they received the designation *rūpa jhānas* (concrete absorptions). The jhānic absorptions which were taught by his two forest teachers are not among them, as he knew that they secured for his teachers only temporary respite in their samsāric wanderings. Nevertheless he recommended their development to his monks, as they produced calmness (*samatha*). He added two more varieties and the resulting four absorptions became known as *arūpa jhānas* (abstract absorptions). The higher status of *rūpa jhānas* is demonstrated also by the Buddha's passing from this world. He is said to have gone first through the four *rūpa jhānas* and then through the four *arūpa jhānas* and to the state of suspension of perception and feeling (*nirodha samāpatti*). Then he emerged from the state of suspension and proceeded through all eight *jhānas* in reverse order. Finally he proceeded from the first *rūpa jhāna*, through the second, the third and into the fourth *rūpa jhāna* and from it passed away. This description related in the *Mahāparinibbāna Sutta* (DN 16) was reportedly provided by Anuruddha Thera, an *arahat* who was present and could follow the Buddha's mind by going himself through the same sequence of *jhānas*.

Maybe the Ch'an/Zen understanding of the *jhāna/dhyāna* technique was derived from sources originating in the forest schools without knowledge of the discourses of the Buddha, some of which focus specifically on the system of *jhānas* (SN III,13; IV.6; V.9). On the other hand, a few centuries after the Buddha, Patañjali's eightfold Yoga path (*aṣṭānga yoga*) incorporated *dhyāna* as its seventh 'limb', the last and most important stepping-stone to the final achievement of *samādhi*, which agrees well with the Buddha's scheme.

Yoga and the early Upaniṣads

The early Upaniṣads (particularly BU and ChU) deal with the important questions of the origin and nature of the world, man's place within it and the meaning and goal of life. Many passages present these topics in mythological imagery, but they also struggle for the creation of a conceptual language, perhaps in follow-up to similar tendencies in some parts of the *Rg Veda Samhitā* (cf. hymn 10,129). Some passages are truly philosophical or mystical texts and approach the ultimate reality through metaphysical speculation as well as through contemplative vision. They postulate a common core or essence of reality underlying all that is and refer to it as *brahman*, as has been repeatedly explained. At the same time they purport to develop direct knowledge of that ultimate reality through direct inner vision which in their understanding amounts to liberation. Then they conclude that *brahman* as underlying essence of reality is also man's inner core and they refer to it as *ātman.* This expression designated 'breath' in the *Rg Veda Samhitā* (and has been preserved with the same meaning in modern German as *der Atem*), but subsequently changed its meaning to designate the 'self'. The Upaniṣads thereby claim that the experience of ultimate reality reveals the essential unity of the individual and the universal (*ātman=brahman*). To know this by direct vision, not just conceptually or verbally, would mean being liberated. But there is not yet any trace in the oldest Upaniṣads of a methodical approach to the task of developing the final direct knowledge and passing it on. The pupils of Upaniṣadic masters could hope to start developing it by living with or near them and emulating their lifestyle. They would memorize their discourses and ponder on their meaning, live lives of strict discipline, perform mindfully the traditional rituals and contemplate their symbolical significance.

It is most likely that the Upaniṣadic masters would eventually have developed a truly methodical mystical path, but at this stage contacts with the forest schools were becoming more frequent and some knowledge of their developing Yoga methods percolated through into the Upaniṣadic movement where they were gradually taken up and developed 'limb by limb'.

The term *Yoga* is mentioned for the first time in the Taittirīya Upaniṣad (TU 2,4,1), which is still pre-Buddhist. The first chapter deals with fairly orthodox Brāhmanic teachings, such as phonetics, prayer, scriptural allegories, symbolism of sacred syllables and the parallelism of micro- and macrocosm etc., in the form of instructions of a teacher to his pupil. The second chapter, *Brahmānanda vallī,* on the Brahmic bliss (TU II,1-9) represents one of the peaks of Upaniṣadic teachings, albeit expressed in a style peculiar to Brahmins, with repetitions and symbolical comparisons. It gives first (II,1,1) a brief outline of the evolution of the *ātman* in descending sequence through the five elements (ether, air, fire, water, earth); from earth spring herbs which become food to living beings. At the end of the food chain appears the person (*puruśa*) as the highest evolutionary product of *ātman* on the phenomenal level. Extended explanations of the stages of the evolution of the *ātman* follow in the form of descriptions of how the structure of the human personality comes about. Food enables life (II,2,1), whose chief mark is breath (*prāna*), life includes mentality or intellect (*manas*) and from it arises cognitive consciousness, which can be linked by Yoga to the cosmic mind called Mahat, the Great (II.3.1-4,1). This enables consciousness to know bliss (II.5.1). But then unbridled speculation continues (II.6.1-7.1): there is a 'non-existing *brahman* (*asad brahma*) and *brahman* who exists (*asti brahma*). When *brahma* or Brahma finds himself at the beginning alone, he desires (*so'kāmayata*) to become many and then as *brahman* he (or it) enters as essence into everything. To penetrate to this essence produces bliss. The Upaniṣad plays here on the ambiguity of *brahma*/Brahma as an impersonal essence and as God the creator. A whole section (II.8.1) is devoted to descriptions of progressively higher bliss and it ends with the recapitulation of the 'levels of self', thus reiterating the ātmic origin of the whole personality, although on the lowest level there is a slight difference because of its corporeality. The last section (II.9.1) seems to suggest that, after all, the mind may return from this verbal exercise without reaching any achievement (*aprāpya*). Is this an admission of doubt as to whether the Upaniṣadic quest is not on the wrong track? Nevertheless, the goal still remains, namely to get to know the bliss of *brahman*, thereby becoming free from fear and doubt.

It is difficult to make clear sense of this Upaniṣad and it is hardly feasible to translate it into a straightforward conceptual idiom. But it is possible to extricate from it a systematised and compressed scheme of the structure of the human personality as understood at the time:

The personality complex and its cosmic connection

For the sake of convenience the extrication and presentation of the layers of this personality complex will be done in reverse order:

(1) Bodily self — *annarasamaya ātmā* — literally the 'self made of the essence of food' (II.1.1); also — *annamaya ātmā* — literally the 'self made of food' (II.8.1). This difference in terminology appears between two recapitulations of the personality layers in the TU. The first one is more to the point. The bodily self is what one experiences when one says, for example: "I wash myself".

(2) Vital self — *prāṇamaya ātmā* — the 'self made of the vital force or vitality'. One experiences it as just being alive. This level is the domain of feelings which can be pleasant, unpleasant or neutral.

(3) Mental self — *manomaya ātmā* — the 'mind-made self' is the level of thinking and other conscious mental activity. On this level one has just conceptual understanding of teachings when studying, for example the Vedas, or even poetry. There is no intuitive grasp of the deeper meaning of symbols and metaphors on this level.

(4) Cognitive self — *vijñānamaya ātmā* — the 'self made of consciousness'. On this level one has immediate grasp of the meaning of sensory perceptions and ideas; it is sometimes deepened by spontaneous intuition and may be further enhanced by insight gained through effort in which Yoga plays its part.

(5) Blissful self — *ānandamaya ātmā* — the 'self made of bliss' is the level of the indescribably blissful experience which comes when one penetrates deep into one's inner essence and feels at one with the cosmic essence (*ātman* =

brahman). However, this blissful feeling should not be regarded as a guarantee of the absolute truth of the underlying monistic philosophy of the TU.

It is hardly possible to comprehend fully the frame of mind within which the obscure text of this Upaniṣad was formulated. But it does make a valid point about the complexity of the human personality. In Indian understanding man was never conceived as a simple duality of soul and body, namely two completely different entities temporarily combined into one unit, as happened in medieval Europe in the teachings of Thomas of Aquinas (1226-1274), which were adopted by the Roman Catholic Church. From then on the dualism of body and soul became the common view in the West and was given philosophical backing by René Descartes (1596-1650). The above systematised presentation of the personality complex provides us with a possibility to understand in conceptual terms, which were not at the disposal of the compilers of this Upaniṣad, their experienced reality of human personality as a harmoniously functioning structure of hierarchically graded constituents. It may not therefore be purely speculative, but it may have been partially also a result of a kind of introspective viewing, however vague. Neither is this Upaniṣadic text the first evidence of man trying to gain an internal picture of himself. Sporadic attempts are scattered throughout the hymns of the Rg Veda and Atharva Veda and can be pieced together to show how early Vedic man tried to unravel the complex nature of the human personality.[15]

But despite this early stage in the development of the personality scheme in the TU, it has theoretical or philosophical importance in that it, in its own peculiar way, brings out the multi-layered nature of the human personality. It is worthwhile to contemplate this scheme in the light of self-knowledge — how one experiences oneself in one's daily life and where one can expect to raise one's consciousness to if one progresses in spiritual efforts. In everyday life man functions fully on just the first three levels. He experiences the functioning of his bodily organism (1), is aware of being alive (2), and is engaged in almost ceaseless conscious and half-conscious mental activity, such as directed or purposeful thought processes, haphazard thinking, drifting thoughts or daydreaming (3).

The level (4) is on the verge of the spiritual. It starts quite inconspicuously, with a position which involves normal perception accompanied by conceptual understanding, but it is underpinned by intelligence. That may result in a sudden penetration of meanings previously hidden. Besides, there is on this level an element of effort which includes a tendency for deepening and clarifying one's knowledge. The result is a kind of awareness: one knows what one knows and one knows what one does not know, and one knows that one knows. There is also an indication of a possibility of occasional flashes of intuition which may occur unexpectedly, triggered by seemingly insignificant events, and of insights gained by effort on a spiritual path. As to level (5), it is, in human experience, the highest approximation to, although not yet the full realisation of, the ultimate reality, in Upaniṣadic parlance of course, *brahman.*

Yoga is mentioned in connection with level (4), the cognitive or cognising self. With effort there comes the realisation of oneself as a striving person (*purusha*) who needs as his guiding principle faith (*śraddhā*), has to fulfil the preconditions of righteousness (*ṛta*) and truth (*satya*) and has to penetrate to the very essence of Yoga. The top achievement of this process will be an encounter with *Mahat,* ('the great one', i.e. the cosmic mind, the first emanation of *brahman*). *Mahat* is, in this scheme, the basis of all cognition on all levels, but individual awareness is graded. At the highest stage it becomes the experience of the universal consciousness which is the threshold to the final attainment of the blissful experience of the inner self, *ātman,* and its cosmic basis, *brahman*. This is, of course, a speculative anticipation of what can hardly be regarded as the compilers' actual achievement, as is obvious from the terms used. This historical survey of the speculative passages of the Upaniṣads has in the last instance the purpose of disassociating Yoga practice from all philosophical assumptions. {16}

The TU is written in cryptic language and uses many metaphors. It has always presented difficulties to interpreters. It likens faith to the head of the striving person, righteousness to his right side, truth to his left side and Yoga to his inner self, while *Mahat* is his foundation (*puccha pratishthā*). It may be that the originators of TU themselves struggled with the problem of expressing the efforts and procedures of the spiritual quest of the time. The oldest Upaniṣads display the tendency, as was stressed in earlier pages, to search for the ultimate knowledge through metaphysical speculation which should become eventually, by a kind of leap, a direct realisation of man's inmost self (*ātman*) as identical with *brahman*, the ultimate essence of reality. Yoga in its purer form — as a practical discipline to struggle for the direct experience of absolute truth — was pursued outside the Brāhmanic elite by renunciant wanderers (*śramanas*). The discussed parts of the TU appear to be the earliest indication of the meeting of these two different trends in the attempt to arrive on a path towards the final realisation of the ultimate goal. This meeting may have started when some earlier outstanding Upaniṣadic thinkers, like Yājñavalkya of the Brhadāranyaka Upaniṣad (BU), following the Brāhmanic scheme of four stages, left home to become hermits and eventually wanderers. {17}

The percolation of yogic procedures into Upaniṣadic circles was very slow. The TU did not yet manage to describe them in understandable terms, nevertheless it listed certain important conditions for a successful spiritual practice, already mentioned above, which were no doubt required by the teachers from their pupils outside the Upaniṣadic circles and remained indispensable in the later systems of Yoga. First was *śraddhā,* understood as faith, trust or confidence in the existence of the ultimate reality and the possibility of reaching it.

A further unavoidable condition for a successful practice of Yoga is adherence to certain fundamental principles or values on which all manifestation of reality in the world rests. These values are expressed in the Vedas as cosmic factors: *ṛta,* the eternal law, and *satya,* truth, literally 'that which is' (*sat-ya*) or simply: reality. In the human context they mean righteousness and truthfulness and they are preconditions for spiritual progress both in Buddhism as *śīla* (Pāli *sīla,* morality) represented by the third, fourth and fifth parts of the eightfold path (right speech, right conduct and right livelihood) and in Patañjali's eightfold Yoga path as five *yamas* and five *niyamas* (abstentions and observances). They will be dealt with in due course. Without these ethical preliminaries spiritual progress through meditation is not feasible.

The TU (1.9.1) also provides the term *svādhyāya* (self-development or self-education) which Patañjali incorporated as his fourth *niyama.* It proves that both in Brāhmanic religious instructions and in Yoga training the role of a teacher is not absolutely paramount. Selfinstruction can replace it, and even under the guidance of a teacher self-education remains important.

The Buddha's approach

TU probably originated close to the start of the Buddha's mission. As already mentioned, when the future Buddha renounced his position as a prince and joined the ranks of *śramanas,* he probably sampled a number of forest Yoga schools besides the two whose teachers he named. He would have learned not only the techniques of *jhāna/dhyāna,* but also other current Yoga procedures which he may not have regarded as important to describe. But due to some coincidences it is quite possible that he may have been in contact with the same circles with which the compilers of TU were also acquainted and from which they drew some of TU's materials.

Like most Upaniṣadic compilers and the two named teachers of the future Buddha, most if not all teachers of the other forest schools would have expounded metaphysical doctrines about the ultimate reality. We know nothing of their doctrines, but the Buddha's teachers taught the theory and practice of *dhyāna* and maintained that their respective achievements represented the experience of the ultimate reality; they built their metaphysical doctrines on them, but the future Buddha found them wanting and rejected them. That was probably the point at which he realised that premature speculation on the nature of the goal could lead to overestimation of the spiritual experience reached; it might have been profound, but not yet ultimate. This could hamper or preclude further progress. Consequently when the renunciant prince eventually did become enlightened and resumed his mission as the Buddha of our era of history, he was careful to avoid the mistakes of his two earlier teachers. He related in his discourses that he became absolutely sure of the genuine nature of his enlightenment and final liberation, besides other criteria{18}, by retracing the footsteps of the Buddhas of past periods of world history and becoming aware of their methods of teaching. When he himself started teaching, he therefore concentrated on basic facts, motivations for taking up the path to liberation and the actual practice.

The four noble truths

The Buddha, if we take the preserved records of his message as trustworthy, was in a unique position from which he could confirm on the basis of his own enlightened knowledge the fact of the continuation of life in a beginningless and endless round of rebirths (*samsāra*) and could describe the way in which life within it should be correctly evaluated and coped with in four succinct statements, traditionally referred to as 'the four noble truths'. They can be described as follows:

(1) Life in limited saṁsāric forms of existence is transitory, repetitive, unsatisfactory and does not by itself lead to any final outcome or lasting solution.

(2) Beings are caught in this round of unsatisfactory existences because of their attachment, longing or craving (*tanhā*, literally 'thirst') for limited and temporary satisfactions and fulfilments and their thoughtless clinging to them as if they were lasting.

(3) This thirst can be abandoned, given up and uprooted and consequently liberation from the necessity of endless rebirths can be won.

(4) There is a method to achieve this goal, namely by following 'the eightfold path to liberation'.

This path is the first systematic and comprehensive system of spiritual practice ever recorded and although the Buddhist sources do not use the expression Yoga for it, it is for all practical purposes the first known integral system of Yoga practice in a pure form, without religious or metaphysical accretions.

The Buddhist Yoga path

Referred to throughout the Buddhist Pāli Canon as the Noble Eightfold Path (*ariyaatthaṇgika magga*), the Buddhist Yoga comprises the following parts:

1) Right viewing (*sammā ditthi*). It can be summarised as a way of looking at experienced reality — all things, all events and all individual life forms, including human beings —from a vantage point which is devoid of self-centredness. One

allows the perceived reality to reveal itself fully without commenting on it, forming a judgment about it or relating it to oneself.

2) Right resolve (*sammā sankappa*). It can be explained as deciding whether to act or not to act in a particular situation on the basis of objective knowledge gained by right viewing with motivation in which there is no bias or self-interest.

3) Right speech (*sammā vāca*) is defined in negative terms as abstaining from lying, tale-bearing, harsh language and vain talk, thereby implementing right thinking and right resolve.

4) Right acting (*sammā kammanta*). This requirement demands avoidance of killing, injuring, stealing, sexual misconduct and taking intoxicants, again in fact implementing right thinking and right resolve.

5) Right livelihood (*sammā-ājīva*). This requirement allows taking up only professions for making one's living in which one can observe the moral principles defined by right resolve, right speech and right acting.

6) Right effort (*sammā vāyāma*) is defined as conscious endeavour, in other words the resolute application of one's will, to implement the previous five demands by removing from one's mind all tendencies adverse to them and strengthening those which support them.

7) Right mindfulness (*sammā sati*) is an attitude of watchful observation which requires constant awareness of what enters one's mind in terms of thoughts, feelings, desires or urges so that one is not prompted by them to act without first assessing them. If action is required, it will then be done as a result of conscious decision. If no action is the right course, the pure awareness clears the mind of any residual promptings. The opposite of mindfulness is thoughtlessness, negligence, daydreaming and mental laziness.

8) Right contemplation (*sammā samādhi*) is the culmination of the path which involves the process of purifying one's mind by developing, through meditation, successive stages of deepening absorptions (*jhānas*) so that the mind becomes calm and eventually capable of the ultimate inner apprehension of the truth.

These eight parts of the path are not supposed to be treated as progressive steps, but should be regarded as simultaneous requirements. Initially applied in mild doses, they should be gradually perfected. Parts (1) and (2) represent in initial stages the yogic philosophical outlook which was described earlier. When perfected they turn into wisdom (*paññā*). Parts (3), (4) and (5) represent the moral requirements (*sīla*), in preliminary stages of practice as rules to be imposed on oneself and scrupulously observed, later as a natural way of behaving which stems from a growing understanding and finally from right wisdom. Parts (6), (7) and (8) represent the Yoga training proper which leads to progressively purer contemplative states of mind (jhānic stages of *samādhi*) and culminate in knowledge and liberation.

Of the numerous meditation techniques which have been used in Buddhism the best known is perhaps the observation of one's breathing. It is referred to in several discourses of the Buddha as a method to which he himself often resorted. It is obvious that it was then already widely known and taught probably in the forest schools which he had frequented. The Pāli texts call it *anāpānasati* (mindfulness of in and out breathing).[19]

When the path is perfected, one will have developed right wisdom (*sammā paññā*) and experienced right liberation (*sammā vimutti*). One is then free from the necessity to undergo any further rebirths or re-incarnations in the phenomenal world of *samsāra*. One has reached the incomparable bond-free *nibbāna* (Skt. *nirvāna*), an achievement equal to the status of the Buddha when he achieved enlightenment.[20] The literal meaning of the word is 'blowing out' and the metaphorical interpretation suggests the blowing out of the flame of passions or of desire (*kāma*), the driving force of samsāric life. All descriptions of *nibbāna* avoid evoking any positive ideas about the liberated state because of the inadequacy of verbal communications which consist of concepts derived from sensory perception and are conceived by the mind. Another reason is that once a definite idea of the ultimate is formed it could hinder the actual achievement. The Buddha must have been familiar with the then current *brahman-ātman* doctrine of the early Upaniṣads, but he avoided using those terms in order to spare his followers the temptation of preoccupation with metaphysical descriptions of the goal (e.g. whether it is divine and is the original source of life, whether it is personal, i.e. God, or an impersonal principle or force etc.). Instead he urged them to strive so that they realise the goal and thus acquire direct knowledge of the final truth.

This is why it can be affirmed that the Buddha's expositions of the path made it actually possible to understand that Yoga in its essence — pure Yoga — is and should be understood as a doctrinally neutral spiritual discipline u committed to any religious faith or school of thought. That is also why Yoga can be taken up even by religious unbelievers and philosophically uncommitted truth-seekers (which includes scientists as well as ordinary people who have an open mind).

The personality issue

The Buddha must also have been familiar with the early Upaniṣadic attempt to understand the nature of the human personality which was in many parts speculative and in fact a diversion from Yoga practice, because it did not in any way enhance it. Whether the Buddha turned his attention to this problem because of the inadequacy of the Upaniṣadic scheme or because he knew all along that knowledge of a realistic scheme would be a help in the practice of his Yoga path, he produced a teaching about constituents of the human personality which is an empirical analysis of man's experience of himself. It results in a kind of self-knowledge on the level of everyday living and that is where effective Yoga effort starts, not in speculations about the cosmic anchorage of man's inner core. The Buddha's empirical analysis confirms and makes more obvious the complexity of human personality without resorting to any kind of speculation and without claiming that it is a result of some higher vision. The analysis reveals the human personality as being composed of five groups or 'bundles' (*khandhas*) of distinct constituents:

1) The group of corporeality (*rūpa khandha*); *rūpa* means literally 'shape' which does not suggest hard materiality, but in everyday language one speaks about 'material body'. Science of course describes matter as composed of molecules, atoms and, in the last resort, of subatomic particles which can be understood from another angle as vibrations of force; the materiality of the body is a result of our sense perception. In ancient understanding matter is composed of the four elemental forces of nature which are readily recognisable by perception, although there is a touch of symbolism in their names. They are earth or solidity, water or fluidity, fire or temperature and air or vibrations. In Buddhist understanding this makes clear that man's experience of himself as an individual material body is produced by a conglomerate of forces which are universal and not his possession.

2) The group of feelings (*vedanā khandha*) of pleasant, unpleasant or indifferent nature which are constantly changing; no one is ever without them until one develops some meditational skills.

3) The group of perceptions (*saññā khandha*) — visual, audial or aural, olfactory, gustatory, tactile and mental (i.e. ideas, thoughts, images, memories). They are dependent on sensory organs, but the mind perceives them internally. It also has the capacity to recover them as memories, but it can moreover produce internally new perceptions, for example when a composer creates a melody in his mind which he can put into notation even before it has been heard by ears.

4) The group of 'confections' (*saṅkhāra khandha*) — volitional formations or active mental factors such as instincts, urges, inclinations, desires, greed, intentions, wishes, decisions or their opposites such as laziness, indecision, aversion, hate.

5) The group of consciousness (*viññāna khandha*) is a continuous process of being aware of perceptions and mental contents interrupted only by oblivion in deep sleep. It is quite obvious that the Buddha's analysis of the human personality is not a theoretical or visionary scheme, but a tool meant for Yoga with a practical purpose — to reduce and eventually overcome the yogi's attachment to his phenomenal form of existence in the world. It leaves open the question about what is the coordinating factor or force which makes the five constantly changing *khandhas* into a self-conscious person convinced of his existence as a unique individual despite the fact that the internal configuration of *khandhas* is fluid which accounts for the changes in the individual's character during his lifetime and from life to life. Patañjali's *Yoga Sūtra* also concentrated chiefly on practice, but it did not produce a scheme of personality, although there is an awareness of a self-conscious personality complex in the background.

The earlier described Upaniṣadic personality scheme, which surfaces in various modifications in some Hindu systems of thought, came again into prominence in the

Advaita Vedānta philosophical doctrine of Śankara (788-820) with additional explanatory factors. It is based partly on empirical analysis and partly on speculation and it is also somewhat visionary.

In agreement with Śankara's metaphysical non-dualism, the innermost kernel of reality and therefore of the world is *brahman* which is, in the context of life, *ātman,* the universal self. But this universal self is obscured in individual living beings by ignorance so that it becomes a separate individual *jīvātman,* 'lived' self, which is the kernel of each individual's personality. This kernel is enveloped on different levels by 'sheaths' and 'bodies'. Starting with the lowest level, the scheme looks as follows:

I) *Sthūla śarīra* (gross body) which is identical to *annamayakośa* (sheath made of food). This body is experienced in the individual's waking state (*jāgarita sthāna*).

II) *Sūkshma śarīra* (subtle body) also called *linga śarīra* (character body) is composed of progressively subtler sheaths:

1) *prānamaya kośa* (sheath made of vital force) produces awareness of being alive;

2) *manomaya kośa* (mind-made sheath) produces awareness of mental processes such as ideation and conceptualisation;

3) *vijñānamaya kośa* (sheath made of consciousness) practically equals awareness and produces understanding and intelligence. It is also called *buddhi.*

The subtle body is experienced in the individual's dream state (*svapna sthāna*).

III) *Kārana śarīra* (causal or volitional body) corresponds to the *ānandamaya kośa* (sheath made of bliss) which envelops *jīvātman.* Deprived of its grosser sheaths when one dies, *jīvātman* transmigrates as the bearer of the accumulated *karma,* i.e. the unripened consequences of the individual's volitional activities. In dreamless deep sleep (*sushupti sthāna*) the individual's volitional activities are at rest which is blissful, but it is experienced by the individual only as an aftertaste of bliss on waking up.

There is still the 'fourth state' (*turīya sthāna*) which equals *samādhi* and is achieved when the goal of Yoga efforts is realized by the yogi's awakening to *ātman,* the universal self (Werner, 1977a, 60-70).

Further elaboration of the personality structure appeared in the advanced Hatha Yoga system and is the hallmark of Tantric theory and practice. Both the Hatha Yoga system and Tantrism posit the existence in the subtle body of spiritual centres known as *cakras* (see chapter VII).

IV. Parallel Searches

The Jaina path

Like Buddhism, Jainism originated from forest movements of wanderers outside the Vedic tradition and has some similarities and overlaps with Buddhism. Its saviour-teachers are called *tīrthankaras* (ford-makers) or *jinas* (victors, hence Jainism). The last Jina, Vardhamana Jñātriputra (Pāli: Nātaputta), also called Mahāvīra (great hero), was the Buddha's older contemporary (cca. 549-477 BCE).{21}

Unlike Buddhism, Jainism formulated definite views about the nature of the world and the living beings within it. Cosmos (*lokāloka*) consists of 'non-world' (*aloka*) — which has to be understood as infinite and empty space (*nabha*) — and the world (*loka*) which has the shape of the cosmic person (*loka-purusha*). The cosmic person comprises numerous compartments or levels of existence. The purest one is in his forehead, the abode of perfect individual beings. This level of existence is outside time. Lower down is the world of 'global flow' or *samsāra* existing in time. Its upper parts (*rūdhva-loka*) are divided into many graded heavens (*svarga*). The human world is in the narrow part (*madhya-loka*), i.e. the waist of the cosmic person, and lower down is the underworld (*adho-loka*), consisting of abodes of a variety of beings, including demons. In his feet are numerous compartments of hell (*naraka*). A description of all the regions within the cosmic person would fill a book.

An individual living being (*jīva*) is an indestructible substance (*dravya*) which can be understood as corresponding to the Western notion of 'soul' (the notion surviving from medieval scholastic theology derived by Thomas Aquinas on the basis of Aristotle's notion of substance). The philosophically more accurate rendering of *jīva* would be 'mental monad', because it can inhabit, or incarnate into, all categories of beings, including plants and microscopic organisms. In its original state in the highest abode a *jīva* is a perfect mental and sexless monad, omniscient, and with infinite consciousness. It experiences total freedom and boundless bliss. When a *jīva* takes an interest in particular happenings in regions lower down and if it starts reacting to them, the perceptions of these samsāric events become what the *jīva* experiences as influx (*āśrava*) into his consciousness which gets thereby narrowed, the *jīva* loses his omniscience and turns into a *samsārī*, a transmigrating wanderer. He then roams up and down through regions of the cosmic man according to the ethical quality of his actions, in other words he becomes subject to karmic laws. This may bring him down even into the lowest form of incarnation as a *nigoda*, an infinitesimally small being with subdued consciousness based only on the sense of touch. But even on this level a longing for betterment may initiate upward progress for the *nigoda*. At some point a *samsārī jīva* may decide, usually while incarnate as a human, to embark on the path to liberation and he can eventually regain the original state of purity. Jainist ethics endorses the existence of a measure of free will or capacity to make decisions on all levels of being. Some spiritually advanced *jīvas* may feel drawn to or be destined for a teaching career, and when they become ripe for it, they reach liberation in their last incarnation as victors (*jinas*) over the influx of samsāric happenings. For the rest of their lives as teachers they obtain the status of *thīrthankaras*, 'ford-makers', who help other struggling wanderers to cross over the stream of samsāric incarnations onto the 'other shore' of liberation more quickly than they could do on their own. When a ford-maker departs from his material body to resume existence in the forehead of the cosmic person, the highest abode of timeless freedom and boundless bliss, he leaves behind his formulated doctrine which continues to be a help to seekers of liberation as long as it is preserved.

To be able to recognise the Jina's teaching as the right view (*samyag drshṭi*) and adopt it presupposes a certain level of intelligence developed during many lives as a result of one's effort to acquire knowledge about the world and life. The adoption of the right view is not instantaneous. Even after it starts dawning in one, many false views (*mithyādrshṭi*) still clutter one's mind. The Jaina way to liberation therefore developed a method of progressive elimination of false views and of developing restraint (*virati*), discipline (*samyata*) and other qualities (*gunasthānas*) in fourteen stages. The scheme is somewhat formalistic. It proceeds from the worldly stage of completely false views (*mithyādrshṭi-guṇasthāna*) to the stage in which one gets a taste of the right view (*sāsvādana-samyagdrshti-guṇasthāna*) until one reaches the twelfth stage of the scheme, which is free from passion and clinging (*kshīnakaoeāya-vītarāga-gunasthāna*). At this stage one has already burnt all past *karma* and if one chooses to die by starvation, one is born in a heavenly world and then only once more on earth before quickly reaching liberation. If one still lingers for a time on earth, one is in the thirteenth stage, 'liberation with yoke' (*sayogi-kevalī-gunasthāna*). After death one reaches the fourteenth stage, 'liberation without yoke' (*ayogi-kevalī-gunasthāna*) which is permanent.

But it seems that right from the start Jainism has been predominantly focussed in its striving for liberation on the eradication of past karmic bonds and on avoiding the creation of new karmic bonds through any kind of involved action. The heaviest karmic bonds are created in Jainist understanding by killing living beings or inflicting injury on them, not only on purpose, but also inadvertently. Therefore non-killing and non-injury (*ahimsā*) is the strongest commandment both for renunciants or monks striving for direct liberation and equally for lay followers who may be intent only on favourable rebirth. Non-injury is thus even stronger in Jainism than in Buddhism and it was instrumental in its inclusion among *yamas* in Patañjali's synthesis.

In its practical approach to the task of self-perfection Jainism has been open to influences from all Yoga movements, without involving itself in their religious doctrines, if they were accompanied by any. It adopted comparatively late the method of *dhyāna*, but it seems that it was understood more as contemplation of Jina's teachings than meditation leading to absorptions. At a still later stage Jainism even adopted wholesale Patañjali's eightfold Yoga scheme. The result may have been that such specifically Jaina techniques as may have existed earlier became obliterated.

The brahmanisation of Yoga

We saw that the Brāhmanic authors or redactors of the early Upaniṣads were not acquainted with Yoga as a spiritual method, but they gradually came to know about it.

Eventually they began tentatively to experiment with its technical procedures and combine them with their visionary and mystic ways as well as with their philosophical speculation. A further stage was reached when the Upaniṣadic schools became actively involved in adopting yogic procedures and started contributing to their formulation. They linked them, to begin with, to their metaphysical teaching on *brahman* and *ātman* and then the more traditional schools among them began introducing into them their religious ideas and beliefs. This was happening parallel with the formation of the Buddhist and Jainist movements, during the period of the middle Upaniṣads.

The three schools most representative of this

development are also important steppingstones to Patañjali's system, despite their religious leanings. We learn about them from the Śvetāśvatara Upaniṣad, Kaṭha Upaniṣad and Maitrayānīya (Maitrī) Upaniṣad. Their basic religious position is monotheistic.

Yoga and the theistic trends

Although the early Upaniṣads favoured the impersonal conception of the ultimate reality expressed by their equation *ātman=brahman,* theistic tendencies were never completely absent from the scene and eventually made a break-through into them. The first one which was thus influenced is probably the ŚU. At first its compiler asks those who proclaim the doctrine of *brahman* as the core of reality: from where comes birth, by what do we live, and on what basis do we experience pleasure and pain. Natural processes cannot account for it and neither can our innermost self (*ātman*). Yet those who took up the technique of yogic absorption (*dhyānayogānugatā*) had a glimpse of a divine power vested in the Self. This power stems from God who alone supervises all causes (ŚU I, 1-3).

This passage is not entirely clear. There is ambiguity as to whether *ātman* refers to the self as the core of individual personality (later known as *jīvātman*) or perhaps to the innermost Self which is regarded as the same in all and therefore identical with *brahman,* the core of all reality, as taught by the early Upaniṣads. However, what comes across right at the beginning of this passage is an indication of an overseeing God, a clearly theistic feature. Later the text seems clearer and *ātman,* self, does refer to an individual who experiences the empirical world (being an enjoyer, *bhoktṛ bhāvāt*). The highest reality is the supreme *brahman* which is the firm, imperishable support and contains a triad. Liberation from rebirth is reached by knowing this (ŚU I, 6-7). Here we have the usual Upaniṣadic trend based on philosophical speculation which is supposed to intensify into direct vision and liberating knowledge. The triad within *brahman* is: (1) the Lord (*īśa,* literally 'the powerful one'), called also the 'Turner' (of the wheel of rebirths) or 'Impeller' (*preritṛ*) or God (*deva*), who supports everything (i.e. the manifested reality); (2) the conscious individual self (*ātman*) who, although unborn, is the bound enjoyer of the manifested reality; (3) the manifested reality (*bhogya,* that which is enjoyed). By directly getting to know the triad, one realises *brahman* and one's own self which deep down is in fact the infinite Self (ŚU I, 8-9, cf. I, 12). In this roundabout way ŚU arrives at the previously mentioned equation *ātman=brahman.*[22]

The achievement of final direct vision may have been in practice supported by techniques of Yoga, probably derived from the example of *śramaṇas* or hermitage dwellers. The aspirant should choose a clean and sheltered place and sit holding the three parts of the body erect (meaning undoubtedly the spine, neck and head). He should withdraw attention from the senses and the mind's activity and turn it inside (into the heart, says the text). He should also control his movements and breathing which is done through the nostrils (ŚU II, 8-10).

A further theistic feature 'smuggled' into Yoga procedures in the Upaniṣads appears when God is named Hara (later an epithet of Śiva) and a progressive meditation technique involving him is recommended through absorption (*abhidhyāna*), unification (*yojana*) and becoming his 'thatness' (*tattva bhāvana*) which leads to the cessation of all illusion (ŚU I, 10). As Hara comes from the verbal root *hṛ, harati* (to take away), the name may allude to the cessation of illusion when one merges with him.

The next name given to God in ŚU (III *passim*) is Rudra, known to us already from RV (10,136, see note 12). Derived from the verbal root *rud, rudati or rodati* (to roar), it is originally the name of the Vedic god of storms, and therefore his character is associated with the destructive power of nature. Consequently he is very much feared and it was probably for this reason that he was given the epithet *oeiva*, the auspicious or gracious one, with the intention of appeasing him (ŚU III, 11), although this epithet did not become one of his names until it happened in the epics and *purāṇas*.

As the *keśin* hymn suggests about Rudra and the Purāṇic myth about Śiva, Rudra/Śiva became the saviour of gods and other beings by drinking the deadly poison that emerged as a byproduct when gods and demons collaborated on churning the world ocean in order to obtain the drink of immortality. The destructive powers of storms gave Rudra/Śiva also the task of destroying the world at the end of the world period. But ŚU describes him mainly as the sovereign Lord and protector of all the worlds which he emanated from himself and will in due course re-absorb (ŚU III, 2).

ŚU's celebration of the god Rudra/Śiva as the highest among the gods made him virtually equal to *brahman*. This position of his may have originated from the early circles of the *keśins*, the long-haired ascetics, described earlier. Rudra was their mythical preceptor with a possible link to the Harappan so-called proto-Śiva. ŚU also represents a step towards Śiva's elevation to the status of Yogapati (the Lord of Yoga) in Hinduism. Apart from descriptions of elements of Yoga practice which echo procedures similar to those in Buddhism and anticipate some steps in Patañjali's eightfold Yoga path, there is also in the ŚU an anticipation of advanced Tantric practices, some of which are dealt with also in medieval Yoga textbooks, such as *Haṭha Yoga Pradīpikā*. The yogi is promised a 'body made of the fire of Yoga' (*yogāgnimaya śarīra*), which is beyond sickness, old age and death (ŚU II, 12).

The theistic trend is expressed also by the tendency to understand the goal of Yoga — the ultimate reality — as the person *par excellence* (*puruṣa*). There is a shorter section about him already in the ŚU (III, 11-21), but a more interesting account of the theme is contained in the Kaṭha Upaniṣad (KathU I. 1. 1-29 & I. 2. 1-25). The stages of progress towards experiencing oneself as this supreme person are outlined in the famous allegorical story of Naciketas. His father was having a sacrificial ritual performed by Brahmins, presumably offering them cows to gain rewards such as prosperity, long life and the like. Naciketas disliked ritual and asked his father, possibly in irony, "To whom will you give me?" The annoyed father replied: "To Death." Although he did not mean it seriously, Naciketas resolved to obey so that his father's word would be respected, knowing anyway that death is followed by rebirth. He goes to the house of Death who, however, is not present. Naciketas was not expected because it was not his appointed time to die. When Death returns after three nights, he is guilty of failing in hospitality and grants Naciketas three wishes. First Naciketas asks to be recognised and graciously accepted by his father when he is released by Death. Second he asks about the proper fire sacrifice which secures heaven and how from heaven one secures immortality. He gets an explanation about that and the meaning of fire sacrifice, including detailed instructions for building the altar for it. This sacrifice will from then on bear his name. The third question is rather profound. Naciketas asks about the status of one who has departed beyond death and birth; there are doubts whether he then is or is not. This echoes the question often put to the Buddha in an extended form — whether the one who reached *nibbāna* is, is not, is as well as is not, or neither is nor is not. The Buddha never answered these questions, maintaining 'noble silence'. Death is also reluctant to answer Naciketas' question and replies that even gods have doubts about it. He offers Naciketas the fulfilment of all possible desires instead. But Naciketas knows that all such fulfilments would be impermanent and presses Death for the answer. Death eventually concedes and uses a comparison of the driver, chariot and reins to illustrate the way in which the aspirant should control the senses and the mind.

When in the process of spiritual endeavour the senses (*indriyas*) and the mind (*manas*) are tamed and transcended, one succeeds in awakening the inner intelligence (*buddhi*) and beyond *buddhi* one discovers the 'great self' (*Ātma Mahan* — which corresponds to the *Mahat*, the great cosmic mind of the TU 2.4.1). Through it one discovers the unmanifest (*avyakta*) which stands here for *brahman* (and corresponds to *prakṛti* or 'nature' of the Sāṅkhya system). The unmanifest is the source and the goal of everything and therefore also a trap for unenlightened beings who find in it a temporary respite at the end of the world period only to emerge back into the world at the dawn of a new manifestation. Only a yogi can pass through it to the highest achievement (*para gati*) of the supreme personhood. 'There is nothing beyond the supreme person' (*purusan na paran. kincit*, KathU I. 3. 1-11).

The path of the yogi is still described in this Upanisad as a method which the authors learned from outside their circles, but they managed to include a clear description of the essential procedure, virtually a definition of Yoga: 'When the fivefold sense perception together with the mind stand still and the inner intelligence (*buddhi*) does not waver, that, they say, is the supreme way, that is Yoga. That, they consider, is Yoga; when through sustained stopping of the senses one becomes undistracted, then Yoga prospers' (Ka II. 3. 12-18). This already points to Patañjali's succinct definition (YS I, 2).

The sixfold Yoga (*ṣaḍaṅga yoga*)

Of the three Upaniṣads with theistic trends named above, the MaiU contains the most important evidence of efforts to produce a systematic description of the Yoga technique. It presents, in fact, the closest approximation to Patañjali's Yoga path, although it deals with Yoga practice in only a few short passages. The bulk of MaiU is steeped in metaphysical speculation about the nature of the ultimate reality and in religious imagery, involving a whole spectrum of Vedic and Brāhmanic deities. But its name, reminiscent of the future Buddha Maitreya (Pāli Metteya), and some of its contents show that its practical approach was originally derived from practices pursued in the same circles of *śramaṇas* as was the path of Buddhism, or in their proximity, and that it was influenced by Buddhism when its textual form was being fixed. This is obvious from many formulations despite the overall Brāhmanic character of the MaiU. One example is its highlighting of suffering in the bodily existence because of its impermanence and another is its dwelling on the repulsiveness of the body's parts. It enumerates them in some detail in a similar way to comparable passages in the Buddha's discourses in the Pāli Canon, which uses them as a subject of meditation in order to develop detachment from the body. Another example of highlighting suffering is its use of formulations closely following Buddhist ones when it defines suffering as 'separation from what is desired, association with what is undesired, disease, old age and death' (MaiU I, 3).

In its involvement with Vedic and Brāhmanic deities MaiU brings together, probably for the first time, three of them — Brahma, Rudra and Viṣṇu — and makes them into a triad, while still regarding them as manifestations of the ultimate reality variously referred to as the highest (*param*), deeply hidden, without beginning and end, the 'Self of all' (*viśvātmā*) and the tranquil Self (*śāntātmā*) (MaiU V, 1-2). Thereby it anticipates the Hindu Trinity in which Rudra acquired the new name Śiva, originally just his epithet. Philosophically the three gods continue to be understood as emanations from *brahman* or from the cosmic *puruṣa*, with individually distinct functions in the drama of the world process. Brahma is the 'creator' or fashioner, Viṣṇu the preserver and Śiva the destroyer in the process of the periodic formation and dissolution of the universe. In the context of religious sectarianism, each one of the three gods came to be regarded by their followers as the highest ruler and simultaneously the transcendental, timeless and ultimate divine force. Brahma had his heyday as the sectarian as well as the absolute top god a few centuries before and after the common era as is evident from Buddhist sources, but his sect has not been much in evidence since then. In sharp contrast Viṣṇuism and Śivaism have remained strong sectarian movements within Hinduism till the present day.

In its philosophically orientated sections the MaiU puts forth several interpretations of the ultimate reality, the individual and their relationship. One of them proclaims the greatness of the Self (*ātmano mahināmam*), which is transcendental and thus free from involvement in the world process, and recognises beside it an 'elemental self' (*bhūtātman*), which is blinded by delusion and affected by fruits of action in the course of rebirth. But there is a way of achieving union (*sāyujyam*) of the two by acquiring knowledge of the Veda and pursuing one's duties according to the successive stages of life which in the last stage, when the aspirant becomes a wanderer, culminate in asceticism (*tapas*). All along he can enhance his chances by meditating (*cintayā*). Having been freed from previous attachments through meditation, he can reach *brahman* and find himself in union with *ātman*, the Self (MaiU IV, 1-4). In short, MaiU accepts the metaphysics of *brahman* as the ultimate reality and its essential unity with *ātman*, the self of individuals who can realise this unity by direct knowledge or vision. In that MaiU follows in the footsteps of older Upaniṣads (BU, ChU), despite its many passages which are sidetracks; among them are passages which have the character of philosophical deliberation pointing in the dualistic direction. They became the basis from which the Sāṅkhya system of philosophy developed much later. Some descriptions of meditational procedures and achievements tally with Buddhist and even later Mahāyāna understanding and one can also find in this Upaniṣad some traces of Tantric attitudes.

In instructions geared to spiritual practice the MaiU manages to go further than the older Upaniṣads, which assert the achievement of the ultimate by direct knowledge or vision if one is attached to and guided by an accomplished teacher. The MaiU supplies the aspirant with a reasonably clear basic set of instructions for practice which would lead him even without the personal guidance of a teacher to eventual achievement of the ultimate oneness. This set "is said to be the sixfold Yoga" (*ṣaḍaṅgā ity ucyate yoga,* VI. 18). The formulation of this phrase suggests that knowledge of this practical technique was acquired from outside the circle of the Brāhmanic compilers of the MaiU, presumably from a master of a hermitage or his pupils or from homeless wanderers who sometimes gave advice to their supporters if they asked pertinent questions, as we know from the discourses in the Pāli Canon.

The form of this sixfold Yoga path suggests that it predates the formulation of the eightfold path of the Buddha or that those who were responsible for the sixfold scheme would not have been in contact with Buddhist monks among whom the 'noble eightfold path' would have been well known. The MaiU just enumerates the six *aṅgas* in one sentence without any explanation of the detailed procedures which would have been conveyed orally to aspirants in forest schools by their teacher. Some of the practical procedures are mentioned in other contexts in the Upaniṣad. But the actual meaning of each part and the description of the procedure which it entails cannot be clearly established from the text of this Upaniṣad. It will be attempted in some detail when dealing with Patañjali's scheme. But the following enumeration of the six 'limbs' with a literal or approximate translation and tentative interpretation of each 'limb' will show its similarity to Patañjali's eightfold path.

Sixfold Yoga:

1) *prāṇāyāma,* breathing exercise; the control of the breathing process;

2) *pratyāhāra,* drawing back; withdrawing [one's attention from sensory perception];

3) *dhyāna,* reflection; meditation; absorption;

4) *dhāraṇā,* holding; bearing; retention; concentration upon [a chosen object of meditation];

5) *tarka,* inquiry; conjecture; speculation; reasoning; intuitive apprehension;

6) *samādhi,* joining together; union; concentration; [final realisation of truth].

The similarity of the sixfold Yoga in MaiU and Patañjali's eightfold Yoga is obvious, but one should not assume that one developed from the other. It is more likely to have been a parallel development. Patañjali's system soon became universally known and after a period of obscurity, during which it would have been followed in small circles, was 'rediscovered' in modern time and spread round the world. The sixfold Yoga continued to be followed in some quarters, sometimes with minor modifications or additions, for example in *Gorakṣa Saṁhitā* by Gorakṣanātha (referred to again later). A sixfold Yoga scheme was used also in medieval time in a school of Kaśmīrī Śaivism and one modified scheme is described in Garuda Purāṇa (CCXXVII, 18) with the addition of recitation (*japa*). If we disregard the religious and metaphysical context within which the sixfold Yoga is set in the MaiU, the differences between the two Yoga schemes are not significant. There are just some omissions in one system and additions in the other system when they are confronted. Conspicuous is the absence, in the sixfold scheme, of the two ethical limbs of *yama* (restrictions; abstinences) and *niyama* (observances), and of *āsana* (posture). But there is no doubt that there were some rules of conduct current among wandering *śramaṇas* and hermitage dwellers anyway. As to the posture it would have been a matter of course for everybody to assume a cross-legged position when engaging in a scheme involving meditation so that its inclusion in the MaiU's sixfold scheme would have been seen as superfluous. Sitting cross-legged has been so natural in India that advanced yogis have been known to assume this posture when they felt death approaching. The reasons for inclusion of the limbs omitted by MaiU into Patañjali YS will be considered in the next chapter.

Conspicuous in MaiU is also the placing of *dhāraṇā* after *dhyāna,* but the meaning of the two concepts is close and overlapping so that their respective definitions may easily have been different with different teachers or schools of practice. If *dhyāna* is understood as meaning just meditation, as it often is, its meaning approaches more the idea of reflection on a chosen object with some ongoing conceptual activity, whereas *dhāraṇā*'s basic meaning of 'holding' (from the verbal root *dhṛ, dharati*) suggests a steady holding of the chosen object in attention to the exclusion of any movement of thought, thereby becoming virtually sustained concentration. Rather unusual is the inclusion of *tarka* as one fully fledged step in the sixfold Yoga, so it requires a search for similar usage elsewhere. In the Pāli Canon *takka* usually means 'reasoning' and may be translated also as 'logic'. In the context of meditational endeavour it appears with a prefix as *vittaka* (Skt. *vitarka*), a concomitant of the first concrete absorption (*rūpa jhāna*). It is an absorption with a line of sustained thought. Patañjali's system was clearly influenced by early Buddhism in several instances and one of them is his inclusion of *vitarka* within the multiple conception of *samādhi* as *saitarka samāpatti,* a form of *samprajñāta samādhi.* This suggests that MaiU, although post-Buddhist, did not adopt *tarka* from Buddhist circles, but inherited its deeper meaning from some older sources. Its depth is corroborated by its position just after *dhāraṇā,* thus being virtually the threshold to *samādhi.* The subsequent usage of *tarka* in the logical system of Nyāya in the sense of 'reasoning' or even 'confutation' suggests a direct discriminatory element within its meaning, making the discernment and rejection of something instantly obvious. In the context of Yoga aiming at union and leaving behind multiplicity as irrelevant if not illusory, we may settle for *tarka* to mean 'intuitive apprehension'.

V. Patañjali's *Yoga Sūtra*

It is apparent from the preceding chapters that Yoga as a spiritual discipline was practised in one way or another from very early times, first by individuals and in small specialised circles, but eventually interest in and practice of it became widespread. There were individuals who resorted to living as hermits or homeless wanderers in order to be free from worldly ties so that they could direct their effort to Yoga's goal of liberation from rebirths in *saṁsāra* without interruption. There were forest hermitages, virtually schools of Yoga, in which beginners were being instructed by advanced teachers in the theory and practice of the Yoga discipline. And there were itinerant teachers accompanied by disciples who were conveying their message also to the wider circles of the population living in homes who were not completely satisfied with the teachings and practices of Brāhmanism, the established religion. They became impressed by the earnestness of the wanderers and their message and started supporting them with the basic necessities of life. For some householders one or other of the groups of wanderers headed by a master completely replaced the established religion. Thus came into being communities of lay followers of a particular teacher and his pupils who came to be regarded as monks. A few of these groups known only by their name eventually petered out, such as Ājīvikas, but there must have been quite a number of groups whose names have not been preserved. Only two of them won large numbers of lay followers and survived till the present day, under the names of Buddhism and Jainism. As religions they developed rituals and eventually built temples, even though their main message was to teach a practical Yoga path to liberation.

All these movements greatly influenced the established priesthood of Brāhmanism and led to the gradual brāhmanisation of Yoga as described earlier. Obviously, the appeal of Yoga in the post-Upaniṣadic and post-Buddhist times was enormous and continued producing further elaborations of Yoga methods. But what is important is that the Buddhist formulation of the eightfold path can be viewed as a neutral method of training the mind for suprasensory vision which transcends also the rational capacity of the mind. The final aim is liberation from the necessity of continual rebirth and the achievement of a state beyond any conceptual grasp so that it cannot be described, save by metaphors. What is also apparent is that in the process of the appropriation of Yoga procedures by the Brāhmanic elite and their development into the sixfold Yoga it was often understood within the framework of a religious belief or a philosophical world view. In other words, the practice of Yoga was often used by religious believers and metaphysical thinkers seeking confirmation of their articles of faith or doctrinal postulates by way of a higher experience. They embarked on the practice of Yoga with preconceived beliefs or philosophical ideas and thereby were conditioning their minds by autosuggestion. If, while meditating, they achieved a kind of yogic absorption of the type of *savitarka* (in which focussed mentation is still possible), their minds retained preconceived beliefs or ideas so that on emerging into the everyday state of consciousness they would feel reassured — the believers about the existence of God as taught by their religious denomination, and philosophical speculators about the validity of their particular notion of the absolute or the ultimate reality. With the latter it is usually a variety of monism, i.e. a philosophy of oneness, later known as advaitism. The progress of both types — those holding preconceived religious beliefs and those cherishing preconceived philosophical tenets — towards the final vision of the unknown would thereby be blocked. An example of the first type is described by the Buddha in the Brahmajāla sutta (DN I.2.6; PTS p. 18). An ascetic, virtually a yogi, reached by his efforts an absorption in which he remembered that before he was born on earth, he had dwelled in the heavenly world and lived there in bliss for a very long time, during which other persons were also born there. After a time some of them passed away. One mighty being was already in the heavenly world when the yogi himself was born there and so he believed him to be Brahma, the god creator. Born thereafter on earth and having reached the recollection of that one past life, the ascetic would now worship Brahma and concentrate in his yogic effort on returning to him, hoping to stay in his presence forever. To the second type of yogi — with a preconceived metaphysical view of the ultimate state of liberation — belonged the Buddha's two named teachers as described earlier.

Another danger when practising meditation comes from partial spiritual experiences which are often accompanied by sensations of uplift and even moments of ecstatic exaltation. One can find these states of mind so satisfying that one may become addicted to them. One then practises with the aim of experiencing them repeatedly, in other words, one indulges in them. It is virtually a misuse of Yoga and a diversion. The ecstatic sensation of such experiences, however, tends to wear off. In order to revive or heighten their intensity one may resort to combining them with eroticism in pseudo-Tantric practices or with taking drugs obtained from various herbṣ

Some of these developments can be studied in later sectarian Upaniṣads, in the epics and in other types of literature. Evidence for these developments is scanty and often indirect, which suggests that the more devious trends were short-lived and not prominent among Yoga practitioners. It was at a time when a systematic technique of Yoga practice was probably being gradually and tentatively formed and articulated by a number of individuals and various groups. There must also have been a strong awareness of the importance of a strict moral and mental discipline born from observing the failures of those who did not get rid of preconceived frames of mind and those who strayed into following the devious trends. The widespread proliferation of Yoga in a general population involved in a worldly life must have led to considerable confusion about spiritual practices and methods of Yoga and the goal. This probably prompted a reaction on the part of some advanced yogis or even some groups, for example of some teachers of their specific versions of Yoga philosophy and practice in their forest Yoga schools, to make their teaching accessible to outsiders who approached them as inquisitive visitors. Such oral expositions may or may not have been written down by visitors in the form of notes, but versions of them must have been floating around for some time before a need for them to be fixed in writing in a systematic arrangement came to be felt. In this atmosphere the *Yoga Sūtra* came to be shaped.

Authorship and dating of the *Yoga Sūtra* text

The synthesis of all sound Yoga trends and methods and their codification into a system of instructions suitable to be put down in writing certainly was not a simple process and, as suggested above, could hardly have been the work of one individual. When the need for bringing some kind of order into the Yoga scene was strongly felt, various expositions would have been collected, compared in discussions and perhaps to some extent harmonised. Finally, at a certain point someone or some group would have arranged the collected texts into one single volume which became known as Patañjali's *Yoga Sūtra*. It acquired a high reputation and was centuries later afforded the title of Classical Yoga.

To recapitulate, the state and character of the text of the YS points to the conclusion that several different texts composed in different times within a period of five or six hundred years were put together to produce the final shape of the work as we know it. The descriptions of the Yoga practice in different sections or chapters of the YS partly overlap and partly run parallel to each other but are produced from different standpoints, possibly stemming from a number of forest schools with different teachers heading them (cf. Hauer 1958, 222ff). Whether one of them bore the name of Patañjali is impossible to say. Maybe Patañjali was not the author of any of the components, but was the final redactor of the collection. There are different opinions about this and also the dating of the individual components and the final redaction of the text.

There is an author by the name of Patañjali (2nd century BCE) who is well known especially by his commentary to the Sanskrit grammar written by Pāṇini (5th century BCE). The view that the grammarian Patañjali was also the writer or at least the redactor of the whole *Yoga Sūtra* prevailed for a long time and some academic scholars in the past accepted it. The prevailing opinion now is that the author, compiler or redactor was someone else, perhaps bearing the same name as the grammarian. Or the name may have been chosen by the redactor to connect the work with the famous grammarian in order to give it greater respectability.[23]

As yet there is no general agreement about the date of the various parts of the work and of its final redaction. In view of the influence of early Buddhism, especially in the part of the work outlining the eightfold Yoga, it can be assumed that this part may have been formulated some time between 400 to 300 BCE. It has been suggested that the other parts were taking shape also between 400 BCE to 300 or even 400 CE (cf. Hauer, 1958, 239). The final redaction of the collection would have taken place towards the end of this period. The language of some sections of the work is closer to what is called Buddhist Hybrid Sanskrit rather than to classical Sanskrit, which suggests the influence of initial texts of Mahāyāna Buddhism. From the fact that there is no reference to the YS in Buddhist polemical works it has even been suggested that Buddhists of the time regarded the YS as a Buddhist work (White 2014, 230).

The composition of the text

The traditional division of the YS and the captions of the chapters in the preserved manuscripts are as follows:

(1) I.1-51 Samādhi Pāda — Chapter on accomplishment

(2) II.1-55 Sādhanā Pāda — Chapter on Practice (*kriyā* and *aṣṭāṅgha yogas*)

(3) III.1-55 Vibhūti Pāda — Chapter on powers (*siddhis*)

(4) IV.1-34 Kaivalya Pāda — Chapter on transcendental autonomy

This division into four chapters, each with a heading, is not logical. It does not adequately reflect the contents of the work's topics so that many scholars have tried to rearrange them, increase the number of chapters, change some captions and provide new ones.

This process has been going on since early in the last century and is still continuing, lately especially in the translations and interpretations of the YS by Indian Yoga teachers and *gurus*, some of whom are active in Western countries. Their views and interpretations have to be regarded with extreme caution. An early, well thought out scheme of chapters which is flexible enough to allow its use in practice according to individual preferences is the one provided by J. W. Hauer, a leading indologist of the last century (1958, 223-258). He divided the YS into five parts or chapters and gave them special names according to the main topic of each one. His analysis of the parts has a bearing also on their dating. This is his division:

(1) I.1-22 The Chapter on Cessation (*nirodha*).

(2) I.23-51 The Devotional Path (*Īśvarapraṇidhāna*).

(3) II.1-27 The Active Path (*kriyā yoga*).

(4) II.28-55 & III.1-55 & IV.1 The Eightfold Path (*aṣṭānga yoga*).

(5) IV.2-34 Manifestations of the Mind (*nirmāṇacitta*).[24]

This is a much more logical division of the *Yoga Sūtra* text into thematic chapters than the traditional division. Looking at the long traditional first chapter, Hauer argued credibly (1958, 225) that the term *vā* in the verse I, 23, meaning 'or', indicates the start of another Yoga path, namely the devotional one, and so he split the traditional (1) I.1-51 Samādhi Pāda at verse I,23 and created his (2) I.23-51 Devotional Path (*īśvarapraṇidhāna)*. But there is another *vā* in the aphorism I.34 which by the same token suggests a further alternative path and the start of another independent chapter which no longer contains any reference to the devotional approach and ends with explanations of the stages of *samādhi.* Therefore it seems to me appropriate to split Hauer's chapter 2 and create a new chapter I,34-51 'Towards the final achievement (*samādhi*)'. The resulting new division of the YS used in subsequent pages is the following:

(1) I.1-22 The Chapter on Cessation (*nirodha*).

(2) I.23-33 The Devotional Path (*īśvarapraṇidhāna*).

(3) I.34-51 Towards the final achievement (*samādhi*)

(4) II.1-27 The Active Path (*kriyā yoga*).

(5) II.28-55 & III,1-55 & IV,1 The Eightfold Path (*aṣṭāṇga yoga*).

(6) IV.2-34 Manifestations of the Mind (*nirmāṇacitta*).

The four chapters (2), (3), (4) and (5) deal with techniques of Yoga practice which were probably taught in different forest schools or circles of renunciant wanderers headed by different teachers for a considerable time. They would hardly have been practised one after the other as if in a methodical sequence. The assembling of different texts into one collection and dividing it into chapters appears to have been done without careful consideration and full understanding of their contents. The final redactor of the text does not appear to have been a practising yogi; the incongruous division into chapters testifies to that. The traditional division splits the description and explanation of the *aṣṭāṅga yoga* into two chapters, but they belong logically together. The traditional chapter (2) is describing in the last two aphorisms *dhāraṇā* (II.54-55) and chapter (3) continues with that description in its first aphorism (III,1) and in the next aphorism (III.2) it is *dhyāna* which starts being described. So putting together aphorisms II.28-55 and III.1-55 to get a continuous chapter (5) on *aṣṭāṅga yoga* is fully justified.

The last chapter (6) attempts to formulate a philosophical basis, in fact a rudimentary ontology and epistemology of Yoga by speculative elaboration of a few small hints contained in the practical chapters. It may have been composed by the redactor of the collected text of the YS and therefore not by a practising yogi. He may have been a philosophical thinker with some knowledge of other budding systems of Indian philosophy which were later codified as 'orthodox' *darśaṇa*s, among them Sāṅkhya and Yoga.

In Hauer's view the first chapter was written by the compiler of the YS as an introduction to the other four chapters, of which more below. As already explained, I use some of Hauer's division of the YS into chapters as it is quite logical. I also approve of his inclusion of aphorism IV,1 in his chapter (4) — which is chapter (5) in my division — as its last aphorism. This makes sense because it points to alternative ways of acquiring supernatural or magic powers (*siddhis*) which have nothing to do with Yoga in its pure variety. These powers have always been regarded as highly desirable, particularly in the circles of wanderers who failed to make progress in Yoga practice itself. That is why aphorism IV.1 describes alternative methods for attaining them. The display of *siddhis* would have impressed the population, who would consequently supply the wanderers with their material needs more readily. This aphorism on *siddhis* may have been an interpolation inserted later by a scribe copying the manuscript who might have had a fascination for magic powers, as has been suggested by several scholars.

According to Hauer (1958, 235ff.) the chapter which deals with *aṣṭāṅga yoga*, the eightfold Yoga path (II.28-55 & III.1-55+IV.1 in my division), is to be regarded as older than the other chapters of the YS, but that is difficult to substantiate. All four chapters on practice were somehow gradually receiving their formulation in the period between the fourth and second century BCE. That was the time when the Buddha's message of liberation by following his 'noble eightfold path' was widespread. A practitioner or teacher of Yoga with a group of disciples somewhere in a forest hermitage or 'Yoga school' may have decided to formulate the description of his Yoga path on the lines of the Buddhist one as eightfold Yoga (*aṣṭāṅga yoga*), but to remain independent of the Buddhist movement of monks and lay followers. The goal of this eightfold Yoga is to be achieved by spiritual practice (*anuṣṭhāna*, YS II,28) which means by one's own effort aiming for transcendence, as in Buddhism. In one respect, however, the eightfold Yoga differs from the Buddhist eightfold path, namely by including among observances (*niyama*) respect for or veneration of the Lord (*Īśvara praṇidhāna*). But the Buddha was himself often referred to as the Lord and respect and even veneration was indeed shown to him by his monks and lay followers during his lifetime as well as after his passing to *parinirvāṇa*, but it was not and is not a requirement. In both systems veneration of the Lord, whether Brahma, another god or the Buddha is felt to be of great help in the struggle on the path to liberation, but it is of psychological character, namely by creating the right frame of mind.

The notion of the Lord is not explained in the short aphorisms on him in the *aṣṭāṅga yoga* chapter and he is not given a name. (It is defined in the *īśvara praṇidhāna* chapter, see below.) As explained earlier the Lord of Brāhmanism at the time of the formation of the YS was Brahma — not the creator, but the 'ordainer' (demiurge) of the universe — who would be the first being to appear at the beginning of a great world period and preside over it till its end. There would have been in the notion of Brahma the resonance of the Upaniṣadic *brahman*, but there is no indication of metaphysical speculations in the *aṣṭāṅga yoga* chapter. It deals with practice which is geared primarily to eliminating obstacles on the way to liberation. So it deserves to be viewed, like the Buddha's eightfold path, as *pure Yoga.*

The text of the *aṣṭāṅga yoga* chapter of the YS as it stands would have provided a sufficient set of instructions for practice to be further elaborated orally. This oral elaboration would not have been available to lay followers of Yoga, who would have been interested mainly in Yoga's philosophical background. So the thinkers among them provided their own elaborations which were attached to the YS as commentaries and in time came to be regarded as an indispensable part of it. These commentarial elaborations are disregarded in this work, as was already pointed out, because most of them were written centuries later and are of a highly speculative nature. In contrast the Buddhist Canon was written down in the first century BCE, having been preserved up till then by a more or less reliable oral tradition. This might have been the case also with this earliest part of Patañjali's Yoga, which would then have been a single independent text memorised perhaps even in several forest

Yoga schools, obviously not in the full narrative form as were the discourses of the Buddha, but in short mnemonic aphorisms. That would account also for the not quite systematic shape of the presentation of the topics throughout the YS, except for the enumeration of the eight limbs of the path (II,29) which, as a systematised scheme, was an improvement on the eightfold scheme of the Buddha's path. This makes it almost certain that the enumeration of the eight 'limbs' in the YS was post-Buddhist. While the date when the Buddhist Pāli Canon was recorded is known, we do not know the exact time when the whole YS was fixed in writing, following its redaction.

For some wanderers or yogis in hermitages the notion of devotion to the Lord had a greater significance than it had for the followers of the *aṣṭāṅga* text, and that provided them with an alternative method of practice focussed on the Lord. This would have resulted in a set of instructions which would have become another independent text, later added to the YS as chapter (2) on Devotion to the Lord (*īśvarapraṇidhāna*) when its final redaction was taking shape. Right at the outset the *īśvarapraṇidhāna* chapter provides us with a definition of the Lord as a rather special kind of person (*puruṣa viśeṣa īśvara*) who is free from afflictions and karmic bonds and all-knowing, unbounded by time and having been the teacher of the previous yogis (*pūrveṣām api guruḥ*, I.24-26). This non-Brāhmanic definition of the Lord in the *īśvarapraṇidhāna* chapter may have been formulated in direct opposition to the description of Kṛṣṇa as the supreme God and creator of the world and the object of the path of devotion (*bhakti mārga*) expounded in the Bhagavad Gītā which was being formulated around the same time as the Ys. Bhakti Yoga is not a systematic path and is based on faith in and devotion to Kṛṣṇa. It will be dealt with later.

Another school of Yoga greatly emphasised in their practice asceticism (*tapas*) and repetition or recitation of sacred texts (*svādhyāya*) supplemented by devotion to the

Lord, who may have been for them one of the traditional Vedic-Brāhmanic gods individually chosen (as *iṣṭ a devatā*). These procedures (*tapas* and *svādhyāya*) are also included among observances (*niyama*) in the *aṣṭāṅga* text, but again they had a much greater significance for the practice in this particular Yoga school so as to warrant the creation of a separate text, in my scheme chapter (4), which was later added to the YS, when it was being assembled under the heading 'Active Yoga' (*kriyā yoga*). The heading is taken from the Bhāgavata Purāṇa which refers to the eightfold Yoga but does not mention the name of Patañjali. The renunciants practising this variety of Yoga were obviously pronounced theistic traditionalists and had close links to Brāhmanic circles partly described earlier (in the section 'The brahmanisation of Yoga').

The last, sixth, chapter of the YS in my division, 'Manifestations of the Mind' (*nirmāṇacitta*), presupposes the existence of the philosophical texts of early Mahāyāna Buddhism and therefore could not have been composed earlier than the third to fourth century CE (cf. Hauer, 1958, 233). It summarises, albeit in an unsystematic and aphoristic way, the philosophical basis of Patañjali's Yoga — its understanding of the nature of existence both in its cosmic and individual contexts. That means, to use terms from the general pool of Indian philosophy, existence as *saṁsāra* or the 'global flow' of world periods on the one hand and the individual sequence of rebirths into *saṁsāra* on the other, with a chance of liberation from it by the individuals' own efforts. Expounding the philosophical basis of Yoga would not have been the prime concern of teachers in forest Yoga schools since it was, anyway, in some form a preliminary philosophical outlook or motivation for renouncing life in society and becoming a wanderer, hermit or disciple of a Yoga master, as described earlier in the relevant section of the Introduction.

The early centuries of the CE witnessed the growth of Buddhist philosophical doctrines such as Madhyamaka and Yogācāra/Vijñānavāda, and the development and initial formulations of the later five 'orthodox' systems of Hindu philosophy — Sāṅkhya, Vaiśeṣika, Nyāya, Pūrva Mīmāṁsā, and Uttara Mīmāṁsā (Vedānta) — into which the YS was, not quite appropriately, included as the sixth under the simple term Yoga. This inclusion was felt to be necessary in the later form of an advanced, conceptually explicit and to some extent systematic formulation of Yoga metaphysics, epistemology and psychology, comparable in its sophistication to the five rival systems. It served three purposes. One was to make it clear that Yoga, although its practical part was influenced by early Buddhism, did not share in Mahāyāna speculative doctrines. The second purpose was to make it clear that Yoga, although it shared some philosophical concepts with the early budding sāṅkhya thought such as *puruṣa* and *prakṛti*, never shared in the *sāṅkhya* thought in the speculative elaboration of its metaphysics into a complete dualistic philosophical Sāṅkhya system rivalling the other Hindu systems, particularly the monistic Vedāntism. The final purpose for including Yoga among the orthodox Hindu systems was to provide for Yoga followers a basic, rather modest but conceptually clear philosophical framework as a safeguard against the lure of those other grand systems describing in conceptual terms the final knowledge prior to experiencing it. This point got lost over the centuries to commentators on the YS whose voluminous elucidations were and still are regarded as indispensable for understanding the terse style of the YS's aphorisms. But the commentators' understanding of Sāṅkhya and Yoga as virtually one system, Sāṅkhya being its theoretical and Yoga its practical part, is totally misguided. It has nevertheless been accepted by many Western scholars so that the two systems are often lumped together in Western histories of Indian philosophy under the heading 'Sāṅkhya-Yoga', as already pointed out in the section on 'Yoga and modernism'.

When reading, studying and attempting to interpret the YS, we have to be aware and constantly remind ourselves that none of its parts forms a continuous text. All of them consist of short, highly condensed aphorisms which could not have been intended for continuous reading. They appear to be mnemonic aids. The question is: who would have conceived the idea of fixing them in writing and for what purpose? We do not know whether they were notes which the teachers would have scribbled for themselves to use when expounding their teaching to a group of disciples, which is rather unlikely, or whether they, more likely, originated with pupils wanting to record the gist of their lessons so that they could ponder over or memorise them and perhaps repeatedly recite them. However, it is highly unlikely that wandering teachers and disciples would have made any written records. Making notes was possible only in hermitages. We know that the Buddha's disciples (monks) used to make an effort to memorise his discourses *verbatim* and not as short mnemonic tools. The memorised discourses were passed to subsequent generations of monks by frequent recitation. The collection of the discourses — together with additional texts: rules of discipline and *abhidhamma*, the analyses of the doctrine — were eventually written down some 500 years after the Buddha's death. The origins of the final portions of the Vedic scriptures — the Āraṇyakas ('forest books') and the early Upaniṣads are also known. The former were actual speeches or conversations which took place in forest hermitages inhabited by retired Brahmins (*vānaprasthas*) when visited by people still living in households (as *gṛhasthas*) and the latter took place in diverse community settings, even in market places and at the courts of kings.

They would have been written down while still in living memory, relatively soon after they were heard. Nothing similar would have happened with respect to what at some point of time surfaced as collections of aphorisms on different types of Yoga which may have been preserved for a while by memorisation through frequent recitation before written preservation would have been seen as necessary.

Be that as it may, interpreting the YS aphorisms is not an easy task. When rivalry arose between religious sects and schools of thought and polemical works started to be produced just when individual aphoristic Yoga texts were being assembled into Patañjali's *Yoga Sūtra*, some of its adherents joined the fray by producing voluminous interpretative commentaries to the YS as a whole. This process never stopped and continues to this day, but only the commentators up to the sixteenth century earned the designation 'classical' in the eyes of modern scholars. Outstanding among the commentators is the first one, named Vyāsa. Some scholars suggested that he was contemporary or even identical with Patañjali using another name, which does not seem very likely. Subsequent classical commentators are Śaṅkara (eighth century), Vācaspati Miṣra (ninth century), Bhoja (eleventh century) and Vijñāna Bhikṣu (sixteenth century). All the commentaries disagree with each other on various points and are rather speculative. Their authors do not create the impression of having been practitioners of any of the varieties of Yoga described in the Ys. We can disregard commentaries and interpretations by modern Indian and self-styled Western *gurus* who are usually practitioners but are almost without exception adherents of some Hindu sectarian movement or philosophical school of thought or are making use of the YS to promote their own varieties of elaborate forms of Yoga.

At the beginning of the last century new kinds of commentaries started to be produced, namely by Western scholars as a result of academic research, in due course followed by Indian and other Asian scholars as Western style universities proliferated all over the world; this is an ongoing process. [25] It appears that all scholars use the commentaries as aids in understanding the aphorisms of the Ys. But Vyāsa's commentary already interprets the YS in the light of Sāṇkhya philosophy and subsequent commentators were influenced by him. Vyāsa is therefore the originator of the misguided trend which occurs also in modern histories o Indian philosophy when dealing with the 'six orthodox Hindu systems of philosophy', namely to treat *de facto* only five, describing Yoga and Sāṇkhya together under the heading Sāṇkhya-Yoga, as already mentioned. Pure Yoga is thus lost from most modern works on Yoga.

I.1-22 The Chapter on Cessation (*nirodha*){26}

The first part of the YS, 'The Chapter on Cessation', starts with the shortest and best known definition of Yoga as 'the elimination (or cessation) of the activity (or fluctuations) of the mind' (*yogaoe citta vṛtti nirodhaḥ*). Individual minds are the product of nature (*prakṛti*), the original substance of phenomenal reality, which produces a mind for every originally free person (*puruṣa*) who possesses in his free state just awareness (*citi* cf. IV.22). The awareness or *citi* of the free person presumably includes an uninvolved knowledge of the processes of nature in *saṁsāra* which *puruṣa*, the free person, knows about, because he is omniscient. However, if the free *puruṣa* takes an interest in nature's creative drive, he thereby identifies himself with the mind created for him by *prakṛti* and becomes an acting person in the world. The text of this chapter refers to the individual person, whether involved in nature's activities or free from them, also as a perceiver (*draṣṭṛ*). A person or perceiver living an ordinary life in the world becomes completely shaped by or takes the shape of the mind's fluctuations (*vṛtti sā-rūpyam*). When free from fluctuations, he is characterised as dwelling in his own nature (*svarūpe 'vasthānam*).

As an acting person in the world the perceiver has some negative experiences which produce suffering and some benign ones which delude him into desiring them. This and the actions he takes to satisfy his desires and avoid suffering fill his mind with passion and leave subliminal traces in his mind which carry him after death into his next life. Nevertheless, he somehow retains a faint memory of his essential freedom from involvement with nature's forces, a state far superior to his present entanglement, and he may decide to strive for disentanglement. He then has to achieve the stilling (*nirodha*) of all the mind's activities as well as the eradication of subliminal traces left by his past passions. He can achieve it with continuous effort by sustained practice of dispassionateness. When he is able to view himself as a person no longer thirsting for attributes of nature, he may recover his original free status.

This chapter presents a sort of psychology of the human mind in its entanglement and in its striving for liberation. In describing some empirical states of consciousness, it produces a kind of basic theory of knowledge (noetics), followed by hints on practice.

Hauer (1958, 225) was of the view that this chapter was written and added by the redactor of the YS as an introduction to the collection of the aphoristic treatises on different types of Yoga practice — Hauer's chapters (2), (3), (4) and my chapters (2), (3), (4) and (5) — which originated independently from each other before they were assembled. That appears to be a credible theory which would date the *nirodha* chapter in the fourth century CE, especially because Buddhist terms, such as *vitarka, vicāra* and *smṛti*, are much in evidence in it. The compiler of this chapter certainly knew well the other chapters and its aphorisms are less cryptic and almost make the impression of being a directly written text.

I.23-33 The Devotional Path (*īśvarapraṇidhāna*)[{27}]

The YS recognises the existence of God throughout, but not as a creator. He is the Lord (*īśvara*) by virtue of his being an absolute all-knowing person (*puruṣa*) forever untouched by afflictions of the karmic process. He was the teacher of the ancient seers and his primeval manifestation in sound is *om,* called *praṇava* ('murmur', 'humming') and understood as composed of three sounds — *a-u-m.* The way to encounter him is by the 'murmuring meditation' (*japa*) of the syllable '*om*'. Many other meditational devices can also be used to reach inner unity (*ekatattva,* I.32), peace of mind and sorrowlessness. Among them is the meditative development of the four mental states, known in early Buddhism as *brahma vihāras,* divine abodes. They are: love, compassion, shared joy and equanimity (*maitrīkaruṇā-muditā-upekṣā*). Further methods are: breath control and meditation on dream and deep-sleep experiences. All these methods will lead the devotee through deeper and deeper dhyānic stages to the final *samādhi.*

It is quite obvious that success on the devotional path of the YS is not a gift of the Lord, but requires a great deal of effort. It is believed, however, that the devotee's progress is greatly enhanced by having faith in and surrendering to the Lord.

I.34-51 Towards the final achievement (*samādhi*)[{28}]

This section may have originated with an accomplished master yogi heading a group of wanderers or a forest Yoga school and using several methods of Yoga practice which are enumerated and briefly characterised. Some may have been used singly, others alternately or one after the other according to need. Their successful mastery would result in aloofness from the external world and pure mental absorption without a remnant or trace of phenomenality. This is expressed by the word *samādhi* which implies liberation from having to be born again. It is here an equivalent of the Buddhist *nirvāṇa.* As mentioned above, the compiler added it as a further alternative after the section describing the devotional path.

The first method mentioned reminds one of the system of *prāṇāyāma.* The text describes the procedure as 'expulsion' and 'retention' of breathing, so it does not suggest an elaborate system. The next method is described as steady observation of the arising of mental phenomena. An alternative is to retain in attention those mental phenomena which are luminous and to free the mind of worry and passion (*rāga*). One can also contemplate insights derived from dreams. Or one can meditate on any chosen object. Each of these methods may lead to mastery (*vaśīkāra*), whereupon the mind becomes transparent and unaffected by the process of perceiving and by what is perceived. The result is 'unified contemplation' (*samāpatti*) which may still be accompanied by subtle reflection, i.e. conceptualisation. But when this is eliminated and even past memories stop emerging, the consciousness reaches undifferentiated ultimateness revealing the lucidity of the inner self (*adhyātma prasāda*). It should result in wisdom which is superior to knowledge based on scriptures or logical conclusions. Everything, including subtle mental formations, is stilled. There remains just the seedless direct apprehension of unification [with truth] (*abīja samādhi*).

II.1-27 The Active Path (*kriyā yoga*){29}

The brief outline of *kriyā yoga* in the YS appears to have come from the śramaṇic circles close to the earlier forest schools of Yoga of a certain type reminiscent of ŚU in which, as we saw, Yoga was for the first time fully brahmanised. They greatly stressed renunciation and austerity (*tapas*), interpreted self-study (*svādhyāya*) as the study of sacred scriptures, and valued personal surrender to the Lord (*īśvarapraṇidhāna*) as the most important part of their path because it helped combat the main obstacle to the removal of ignorance (*avidyā*), namely the egoity (*asmitā*) and other associated afflictions (*kleśas*) such as passion (*rāga*) and hate (*dvesa*). The active path consists of the three practices: austerity, self-education and self-surrender. In order to abolish ignorance and achieve freedom the active path must be accompanied also by the practice of meditative absorptions (*dhyānas*) and, besides, one must develop discriminative vision (*viveka-khyāti*) as to what is eternal and what is impermanent, what is pure and what is impure and what leads to bliss and what leads to suffering.

The final result of having successfully trodden the path is described as *kaivalya* (autonomy, 'aloneness', non-involvement in the passing phenomena of the world process). What the section on Active Yoga does not contain are any direct methodical instructions about the technicalities of its practice. Therefore most commentators regard it as a general summary or as a preliminary introduction to the eightfold Yoga path, but that does not do justice to it. Its wording makes a definite impression that quite specific practices are underlying it. The section as it was handed down may have originally been a basic text of a particular school with its own form of a practical path and methodical techniques which would have been taught orally and by day-to-day discipline in the context of communal living under a master.

II.28-55 & III.1-55 & IV.1 The Eightfold Path (*aṣṭānga yoga*){30}

The individual 'limbs' of the eightfold scheme of the path are enumerated in just one single aphorism (II. 29). Their supplementation with details and further explanations and elucidations with practical hints follow throughout the chapter. Before enumerating the eight limbs the text promises that by practising them impurities are eliminated and discriminative understanding (*viveka*) starts developing. After enumerating the eight limbs the text deals with moral requirements without which Yoga practice cannot be successful. They must be practised by everybody, regardless of status by birth, place, time or circumstance. They are, first, the five commands which represent a truly great commitment and are known also as the Great Vow. They aim to eliminate violence, dishonesty, stealing, indulgence in sexuality and attachment to possessions. All these negative activities and inclinations are rooted in greed, ill-will and delusion (*lobha-krodha-moha*). Besides guarding oneself against them, one should cultivate states of mind which are the direct opposites of the negative ones.

Second come five observances. They demand purity of body and mind and require the practitioner to rest content at all times with his actual situation, whatever it is. This can be achieved in the course of ascetic practices (*tapas*). But intellect, the conceptual and verbal capability, is also important on the spiritual path and should not be neglected. It is expressed in the text by the word *svādhyāya*, meaning basically 'recitation' or 'rehearsing'. Traditionally it is interpreted as 'recitation of the Veda or any sacred texts' done semi-silently, but with full attention to the meaning of the words and sentences. It is also interpreted as 'self-study' or 'self-education'. By scrutinising conceptually one's experiences during ascetic practices and meditation one sharpens one's intellect and is able to correct one's practice, should a deviation occur. The striking example of intellect being used to correct one's practice on the spiritual path is the future Buddha's scrutiny of his practice of *tapas* when he became emaciated and weak and nearly died of exhaustion. He then came to the conclusion that severe asceticism is as bad as indulgence in sensory satisfactions and as a result formulated his 'middle way'.

Subsequently the text also admits that if one is capable of feeling devotion to the Lord (*īśvarapraṇidhāna*), whose real nature does not include the function of the creator, as already described, it may increase one's power of concentration. It often also involves a kind of worship or ritual which may be performed in front of a house shrine with a statue of a chosen representation of the Lord. The *īśvara* as such does not have a physical representation, so one of the great numbers of gods, in which the Vedas and subsequent texts abound — although philosophically there is behind them an underlying unity — can become the yogi's chosen deity (*iṣṭa devatā*) for the purpose. As the texts of Buddhism refer frequently to its founder as the Lord Buddha, there is no reason why a practitioner of the eightfold Yoga path could not choose his statue or even the statue of one of the Mahāyāna transcendent Buddhas or Bodhisattvas as his chosen representation for his devotional ritual.

The next requirement for practice is the adoption of a suitable position, which is traditionally one of the cross-legged varieties. After assuming it, one proceeds to the next requirement which is controlling one's life force (*prāṇa*) through breathing. This is done first by observing the passing in and out of air during the breathing process and holding it briefly between its phases. To help concentration one can count the breaths. One follows the whole process of breathing in the body with its effect on the movement of the chest and abdomen. With time the breathing becomes increasingly subtle and eventually — in the long run — results in the suspension of breathing altogether. But there is no indication in the YS of a later elaborate system of *prāṇāyāma.* Controlling one's life force through breathing can be done also in the form of the Buddhist technique of 'mindfulness of breathing'. It involves just observing the process of breathing in and out without influencing it, only noting the length of its phases and the possible spontaneous gaps between them. Any lengthening of the gaps between the phases or suspension of the breathing process is to be left to the inner mechanism of the organism. Observing the process of breathing in this way is in itself an efficient meditation object and so it can serve for the purpose of the next limb of withdrawal of one's attention from perceiving sensory objects and further on for proceeding to deeper and deeper absorption (*dhyāna*). This step can be developed, besides by mindfulness of breathing, by using a variety of meditation objects. With experience one can then succeed in withdrawing one's attention from sensory perception altogether and acquire the capacity of 'holding' (*dhāraṇā*) the chosen meditation object without any distraction. This 'holding' is not a static state but an increasingly subtle process during which the meditation object slowly fades, which is a sign that deep absorption (*dhyāna*) has been reached revealing the emptiness of one's own being (*svarūpa-śūnyam*). This is already like completion (*samādhi*), but not yet fully implemented. The yogi is now able to see the whole complex of mental dimensions which have to be gone through to eliminate previously accumulated impressions (*saṁskāras*) which are normally latent. Only when this is achieved is the mind imbued with stillness and completion is achieved. This is total mastery which enables the developing of wisdom. The text asserts that there are many 'side-effects' which may appear while the three highest stages are being developed. They amount to extraordinary capabilities (*siddhis*) and knowledges for the yogi with respect to the external world. He acquires power over his bodily organism, remembers his own and can see other beings' previous incarnations, can read their minds and can scrutinise the world as a whole as well as in detail.

A word of warning is given with respect to these supernormal powers. They are, of course, viewed as valuable attainments, but they may hinder completion (*samādhi*) and seduce one to go astray if wisdom is not accompanying their application at all times. The text enumerates a number of feats which one can perform using the powers. But the chief concern is disassociation from materiality which, paradoxically, leads not only to the ability to control elements of the world, but also to a kind of spontaneous flowering of one's body, resulting in beauty, grace, strength and diamond-like durability. One of the capabilities achieved at this stage is to perceive at will all dimensions of existence, including the extremely blissful heavenly realms, from which there could still arise a danger of succumbing to the lure of the unimaginable celestial bliss. That would lead to renewed suffering (when the period of enjoying the celestial bliss would sooner or later come to an end), but knowledge born of discrimination maintained from moment to moment enables the dismantling of and going beyond all seductive objects and influences. Discrimination, mastery, supremacy and simultaneous non-attachment even to the highest attainments will make all the harmful seeds from the past vanish. Thus the individual person (*puruṣa*) will reach his original purity and the result will be his 'autonomy' (*kaivalya*) meaning total liberation from rebirth and any active involvement in saṃsāric processes.

The extraordinary powers described so extensively in the text may be inborn in some individuals, but may also be derived from certain plants or may be won through recitation of formulas (*mantras*). They may emerge even unwanted as a byproduct of ascetic practice (*tapas*) or may be spontaneously generated on reaching completion (*samādhi*, IV.1).

To correlate the two eightfold paths it is necessary first to present a summary scheme of the *aṣṭāṅga yoga* with brief descriptions of the individual steps similar to the one of the Buddha's eightfold path presented earlier. As in the case of the Buddhist eightfold path, the individual steps of the eightfold Yoga should not be regarded as entirely successive. After initial perusal and contemplative preoccupation with them, all the steps should be practised right from the start alternately and simultaneously, at first in a mild way and gradually with fuller application. Not even fully committed yogis expect to reach perfection in them, with the final realisation to follow, within one lifetime. As mentioned earlier they expect to recover a level of proficiency in them in subsequent lives and carry on with the effort to make further progress.

The summary of the eightfold Yoga scheme goes as follows:

1) *Yama* (restriction; self-control) comprises five commands: [1] *ahiṁsā* (non-violence),

[2] *satya* (truthfulness), [3] *asteya* (non-stealing, not taking what has not been given),

[4] *brahmacarya* (pure living — chastity and eventually celibacy) and [5] *aparigraha* (non-grasping, non-acquisitiveness).

2) *Niyama* (obligation) consists of five observances: [1] *śauca* (purity of mind and body),

[2] *saṅtoṣa* (contentment with one's situation), [3] *tapas* (inner creative flame; austerity; asceticism), [4] *svādhyāya* (self-development, self-education; in traditional Hindu understanding: recitation, memorisation and study of sacred texts) and [5] *īśvarapraṇidhāna* (respect for or devotion to the Lord).

3) *Āsana* (posture) is usually understood as assuming a steady and comfortable position for meditation.

4) *Prāṇāyāma* (control of the life force through breathing) was later developed into an elaborate system of breathing exercises, but in Patañjali's time it meant just observing the process of breathing in and out and holding it briefly between its phases.

5) *Pratyāhāra* (withdrawal) means withdrawing attention from the sensory perception of the multiple external objects and the mind's unguarded preoccupations, such as daydreaming and haphazard thinking, thus preparing the mind for conscious inner perception during the period of sustained meditation.

6) *Dhāraṇā* (holding) means striving consciously to keep in focus a chosen object of meditation.

7) *Dhyāna* (absorption) means developing a deep state of mind resulting from meditation, and experiencing it for a considerable time.

8) *Samādhi* (concentration; completion, joining, union) is a term which is used in Yoga for several progressively deeper or more advanced states of mind leading to contemplative vision or 'cognitive unification' and to direct apprehension of or unification with absolute truth which is variously described.

The first step of the scheme deals with ethics or moral requirements without whose observation an effective spiritual practice cannot be successful and is virtually impossible. It is accepted both by Buddhism and in the YS that some technicalities of the practice can be mastered even without commitment to strictly ethical principles with the result that certain powers could be developed and misused for unethical purposes. That would mean going astray and it would eventually have dire karmic consequences. In the case of mild practice by lay people aiming at some uplifting experience even slight transgressions would have a disturbing influence on their meditational efforts. Step two is straightforward. All observances can be practised by laymen, even *tapas* in the form of giving up some satisfactions. The fact that the *aṣṭāṅga yoga* text allows for communion with one's chosen deity (*iṣṭa devatā*, II.44) might have been a concession to modest practitioners living as householders who might have been turning to their chosen god with petitions. This is the case also in Buddhism where turning with petitions to Vedic-Brāhmanic gods (whose existence the Buddha did not dispute) has been in evidence among lay Buddhist followers for centuries. Even nowadays many Buddhist temples in Theravāda countries have in their courtyards shrines for that purpose. Some Buddhists in Western countries adopt for their ritual worship Mahāyāna Buddhas or Bodhisattvas, often in their Tibetan form.

The cross-legged position may not be easy for many people, but sitting upright on a chair with or without a straight backrest is satisfactory enough. Controlling the life force by breathing is not described in any detail in the YS and it is advisable to avoid later *prāṇāyāma* techniques introduced and often insisted on by contemporary *gurus* in their books and even in their *āśrams* in the West. The 'mindfulness of breathing' procedure is advisable because it is also effective for and supportive of further steps on the path. It can be practised even casually whenever one has nothing else to do, for example while travelling on public transport.

Step five if perfected would reveal one's inner 'emptiness', but what actually happens to begin with is the discovery of the mind's 'fluctuations' (*vṛtti*). Ideas and images continuously emerge, develop for a while and pass. The procedure is to notice an emerging idea or image at its first appearance and focus on it, which leads to its almost immediate disappearance, and to a brief gap before another one surfaces. The aim is then to focus on that gap and put into it one's chosen meditation object. This then may develop into step six when one can hold the meditation object for a time. When one develops the ability to hold it almost indefinitely, one dismisses it to allow a deeper state of the mind to develop, thereby passing into absorption. This is step seven which has several levels marked by subtle mentation and emotions before equanimity is achieved. That is already a transition to step eight with all its levels to be successively mastered, which is a long-term task.

The correlation of the two eightfold paths looks as follows:

Patañjali's *aṣṭaṅga yoga*:

1) *Yama* (restrictions):

[1] *ahiṁsā* (non-violence)

[2] *satya* (truthfulness)

[3] *asteya* (non-stealing)

[4] *brahmacarya* (pure living)

[5] *aparigraha* (non-grasping).

2) *Niyama* (obligations):

[1] *śauca* (purity)

[2] *santoṣa* (contentment)

[3] *tapas* (austerity, exertion)

[4] *svādhyāya* (self-development)

[5] *īśvarapraṇidhāna* (respect for the Lord)

3) *Āsana* (posture)

4) *Prāṇāyāma* (control of the life force through breathing)

5) *Pratyāhāra* (withdrawal)

6) *Dhāraṇā* (holding)

7) *Dhyāna* (absorption)

8) *Samādhi* (completion)

Buddha's *aṭṭhangika magga*:

1) *Sammā diṭṭhi* (right viewing)

2) *Sammā sankappa* (right resolve)

3) *Sammā vāca* (right speech)

4) *Sammā kammanta* (right acting)

5) *Sammā ājīva* (right livelihood)

6) *Sammā vāyāma* (right effort)

7) *Sammā sati* (right mindfulness)

8) *Sammā samādhi* (right contemplation)

Starting with ethics, we can see that the Buddha's sequence follows a different logic and is less explicit. What

Patañjali enumerated systematically and in more detail, the Buddha explained at length in different discourses. But the essential similarity or almost sameness of the two schemes comes across clearly from the comparison. In some respects they are complementary.

1) [1] Non-violence corresponds to 4) Right acting and 5) Right livelihood. It excludes harming other creatures and their killing. Therefore making one's living in occupations which involve killing is ruled out. It further implies vegetarianism, because buying meat increases demand. (Buddhist monks are supposedly allowed meat if it is put into their bowl when begging for food from door to door, but it is a disputed point.)

1) [2] Truthfulness corresponds to 3) right speech. Both require silence in case telling the truth would harm someone, which would come under non-violence and right acting. In the Buddhist context right speech also excludes vain chatter and repeating what somebody said to somebody else, i.e. 'tale-bearing' which could cause dissent.

1) [3] Non-stealing corresponds to 4) right acting and it is self-explanatory. In Buddhism it is explained as 'not taking what is not given' which excludes also picking up abandoned objects and even fruit fallen from trees.

1) [4] Pure living corresponds to 4) Right acting. It demands celibacy from monks and excludes self-satisfying.

1) [5] Non-grasping means to be content with mere basics for surviving, but without endangering one's health. It would come under 5) Right livelihood. It is explained in a similar way in the Buddha's discourses which enumerated what monks may possess; it is summarised in the Vinaya rules.

2) [1] Purity refers to bodily cleanliness and pure mind free from worldly ideas and daydreaming. It is similarly referred to in the Buddha's discourses and may be regarded as coming under 4) right acting.

2) [2] Contentment is virtually synonymous with 'non-grasping'.

2) [3] *Tapas* is a loaded concept which is variously translated; as austerity it is akin to nongrasping and contentment, but excludes inflicting hardship or pain on oneself as is practised by some ascetic movements; as exertion it expresses the necessity of wilful drive on the path. It corresponds to 6) right effort.

2) [4] Self-development can be understood as being intent on one's progress on the path and it would also be a part of 6) right effort.

2) [5] 'Respect for the Lord' is something of an embarrassment for Yoga interpreters, should it refer to God. It is variously explained away, for example as meaning 'primarily psychological and pedagogical needs rather than providing a purely ontological category' (Whicher, 1998, 83-85). Another explanation is that it refers to Matsyendra, the supposed first teacher of Yoga; respect would surely be owed to him. In Buddhist texts respect is shown to 'the Lord Buddha' which would go under 4) Right acting.

3) Posture to be assumed for practice of the subsequent five limbs of the path would be one of the cross-legged sort. The one called comfortable or 'happy' position (*sukhāsana*), may include sitting on a stool or chair. The Buddha described them all in his discourses and added also meditation while walking.

4) Control of the life force through breathing as an elaborate technique in later Hindu systems does not go back to Patañjali's YS, which describes only breathing through the nostrils (without mentioning their alternation) and retention of breathing. The Buddha found even retention unhelpful and recommended only observing breath as it is passing in and out through both nostrils (*anāpāna sati*) without interfering with it. He praised it as an efficient technique of meditation (see note 8).

5-7) Withdrawal, holding and absorption represent progressive stages of deepening in the process of meditation. They correspond more or less to the Buddhist 6) right effort.

8) Completion is the final realisation. In Buddhism 8) Right contemplation comprises all stages of progressively deepening meditation as far as the threshold of the final realisation, all of them described at length in the discourses, together with the subsequent liberation and right wisdom.

The Buddhist 7) Right mindfulness (*sammā sati*) does not have an independent equivalent in the PataÒjali scheme. It is mentioned just once in the YS (I,20), together with other qualities necessary for emancipation, which are faith, heroic energy, mindfulness, contemplation and wisdom. The technique of applying mindfulness (Skt. *smṛti*) on the path was probably the subject of oral instructions by the teacher. At the time when the *Yoga Sūtra* was being assembled, the compilers of its *aṣṭaṅga yoga* chapter either did not regard it necessary to include a description of the technique of applying mindfulness or it was no longer known in detail. The commentaries to the *Yoga Sūtra* are useless in this respect. Their authors wrote them in later centuries and, besides, were not practitioners so that they did not understand the techniques, substituting speculation for knowledge. In the Buddhist Pāli Canon, on the other hand, the technique is described in detail in two almost identical discourses on the 'Foundations of Mindfulness' (Satipaṭṭhāna Sutta, MN, 10 & DN 22).

In the absence of a proper description of what was meant by cultivating mindfulness in the circles from which the *aṣṭāṅga yoga* chapter of *Yoga Sūtra* emerged, it is important to go over the account of *sati* in Satipaṭṭhāna Sutta in some detail. It was delivered by the Buddha only to his monks and never repeated in his time to his lay followers. Only when an advanced lay follower was sick and near death, would he have been instructed in the basics of the practice of the four foundations of mindfulness.

At the beginning of the discourse the Buddha says: "This is the sole way, monks, for the purification of beings, for the overcoming of sorrow and lamentation, for the destroying of pain and grief, for reaching the right path, for the realisation of *nibbāna,* namely the four foundations of mindfulness. " They are then explained by the Buddha not as concepts, but by describing a monk practising them: "Here, monks, a monk dwells contemplating the body in the body..." (*idha bhikkhave bhikkhu kāye kāyānupassī viharati*). Similarly he contemplates feelings (*vedanā*), the mind (*citta*) and the contents of the mind (*dhammā*). The discourse then proceeds with details which can be summarised as follows:

1. Contemplation of the body proceeds by turning one's attention to several bodily parts or processes successively or intermittently:

(1) Contemplation of breathing involves following the phases of breathing in and out, their length and *knowing* that one does so, while becoming aware of the whole process of breathing. One also, on occasion, observes the breathing process in others and alternately in oneself and in others. This is an intermittent practice separate from the regular meditation sessions in which one may have chosen mindfulness of breathing as one's meditation object.

(2) Contemplation of bodily positions and movements. One should always *know* when one is walking, standing, sitting or lying down.

(3) Whatever one does one should be doing it always with full understanding (*sampajānakārī*) as to the purpose of it. This means that a monk or full-time 'pure' yogi would not even lift his arm if there is not a clear reason for it such as, for example, holding back a branch obstructing the footpath on which he is walking. If there is no reason to do anything, he would turn to one or other of the described contemplations.

(4) Contemplation of the body in all its external and internal parts by looking at those one can see and visualising those one cannot see. The text enumerates them extensively: hair of the head and of the body, skin, nails, teeth, flesh, sinews, bones, marrow, kidneys, heart, liver, diaphragm, spleen, lungs, intestines, stomach, bowels, faeces, bile phlegm, pus, blood, sweat, fat, tears, saliva, mucus, urine. The aim is to develop detachment from the body by realising that its beauty is only skin-deep. This contemplation enables the yogi to free himself from the sexual urge and to lead a life of celibacy.

(5) Contemplation of the body as consisting of four 'elements' (*dhātu*), traditionally named as earth, water, fire and air, usually interpreted as solidity (solid parts such as bones etc.), fluidity (blood etc.), vibration (breathing etc.) and bodily heat. It basically brings home the recognition that one is not identical with the body, because it is composed of impersonal elements. In the modern context the traditional four elements may be replaced in contemplation by atoms and subatomic particles with empty space between them.

(6) Visualising a dead body in successive stages of decay which would be possible to see in India in former times (and possibly even today) on charnel grounds. One should then imagine one's own body in those stages of decay. With a bit of imagination one can do this without actually viewing corpses and can easily imagine one's body decaying or simply consumed by fire during cremation. The desired result should again be to stop identifying oneself with one's body, another way of developing detachment from it.

2. Contemplation of feelings which may be pleasant, unpleasant or neither (neutral). One should always know one's feelings. Whenever a particular feeling arises, one should be fully aware of it and observe it for its duration without actively dwelling on it or interfering with it, until it passes under one's watchful observation.

3. Contemplation of the mind involves knowing the states of one's mind, both negative and positive, as they occur or are developed — such as attraction, desire, repulsion, anger, confusion or distraction and also sympathy, joy or concentration. Whenever a state of mind arises, one tries just to observe it until it passes.

4. Contemplation of the contents of the mind is described in the text under specifically Buddhist schemata — under five hindrances, five constituents of the personality (*khandhas*), five sense organs and their objects (eye and shapes, ear and sounds etc.), seven qualities necessary for eventually reaching enlightenment (so-called 'factors of enlightenment') and the four noble truths. This very advanced contemplation would be possible only after a high degree of progress has been reached on the path.

The Buddha's discourse on mindfulness promises that following its instructions fulltime meticulously and intensely may result in attaining *nibbāna* in seven years or in seven months or weeks or even in seven days. This would nowadays mean living as a solitary monk in a cave or in a forest (*arañña*). There is a territory on Sri Lanka for that purpose protected by the government where a number of monks are reportedly living as 'forest dwellers' (*araññavāsa*s, often shortened to *arañña*s) for whom necessities — food and, when needed, medicine and garments — are left on agreed places to be collected. Living in monasteries is hardly conducive to quick liberation, especially as monks usually perform other functions, for example teaching, advising lay communities or pursuing scholarly research etc., and hoping to progress further in future lives. Even in the Buddha's time some monks chose as their main task, instead of full-time meditational effort with round the clock mindfulness, to preserve his teaching in their memory. A number of monks would form a group, each one of them would memorize a specific number of the Buddha's discourses and they could then together recite between themselves the whole 'basket' of discourses (Sutta Piṭaka). The same happened for the rules (Vinaya Piṭaka) and possibly also for the gradually composed analytical basket (Abhidhamma Piṭaka) so that the whole Canon could be passed down the generations until it was written down, dictated by a group of monks to a scribe, in the first century BCE.

To recapitulate, it is obvious at first glance that Patañjali's scheme truly is systematic.

It is the result of a long process which originated in forest schools where Yoga was taught by a master to his disciples. The instructions they received gradually developed into a system, albeit in aphoristic style, which describes progressive steps from the beginning to completion and could be easily handed down from generation to generation and eventually committed to writing. It is significant that the scheme starts with 'limbs' (*aṅgas*) of ethical character. The Buddha's scheme, on the other hand, was the result of his discourses being delivered mostly in the open to an audience which would assemble round him, drawn by his reputation as a prince turned wanderer who was rumoured to have reached enlightenment. His listeners would have had different levels of understanding and different expectations and aims in life. But the Buddha was ready to listen and talk also to individuals and groups. His ultimate aim was, of course, to point out to his listeners the way to liberation, but when he saw those among them who were not ripe for it, because they were too involved in worldly affairs such as family life, social tasks or a professional career, he instructed them in ways how best to conduct their affairs and fulfil their tasks and duties for their own benefit without harming anybody. These instructions would be of ethical character. Those among his listeners in whom he saw an ability for deeper understanding, although they may have lacked an aim in life, he invited to join him as his wandering disciples forming, as was usual in his time, a community of monks (*saṅgha*). To them he taught the direct path to liberation.

What is noteworthy in the *aṣṭāṅga yoga* text is that it does not employ the terminology current later in the Sāṅkhya system of thought which was being formulated around the same time. The *aṣṭāṅga* text uses mostly the term *sattva* for nature as the basis of the phenomenal reality which conjures up the world and the empirical personality, including its mind. If the person as such (*puruṣa*) fails to discriminate himself from the active *sattva*, he is bound by it and identifies himself with the empirical personality through the mind produced for him by *sattva*. When he applies discrimination, both he and *sattva* become purified and emancipation (*kaivalya*) follows. The liberated person's separation from sattvic activities means that no mind is again created for him and his worldly personality vanishes. The Sāṅkhya system uses for the 'original substance' or essence of reality the term *prakṛti*, usually translated as 'nature'. It is described there as a dynamic force made of three constituents (*guṇas*) of which *sattva* (here with a new meaning of 'lucidity') is one, the other two being *rajas* (excitation) and *tamas* (stolidity). When involved with *puruṣa*, the term *prakṛti* can be translated as 'phenomenal world'. In the *Yoga Sūtra* the term *prakṛti* is used only three times, in the later chapters of slightly philosophical character: twice in the *nirmāṇacitta* chapter (IV,2-3) and once in the *nirodha* chapter (I,19). These differences between the YS and Sāṅkhya confirm that the two systems were formed independently of each other, as has been mentioned a few times before.

IV.2-34 Manifestations of the Mind (*nirmāṇacitta*) {31}

This chapter of the YS outlines the philosophical outlook of Classical Yoga, not another specific method of practice. Its basic conception of existence includes the teaching on rebirth governed by karmic laws and the possibility of liberation into the ultimate state of perfect freedom, just like in early Buddhism. But unlike in Buddhism, this last chapter of the YS teaches that behind each transmigrating being there is an originally pure spirit termed 'person' (*purusa*), so that there is a multiplicity of them. Each *puruṣa* somehow persists in a transcendent, totally separate dimension beyond time and space, and remains in his essence unaffected by the process of transmigration through sequences of births and deaths, although on that level he loses his awareness of his true status. Originally this chapter may have been an independent text which was added to the collection of chapters outlining Yoga practice by someone after the separate Yoga texts were assembled into one volume, but before the final redaction of the complete YS was finalised. This would make it the latest chapter of all, dated perhaps around 400 CE, if not later.

The pure person's loss of awareness of his true status so that he identifies himself with the process of transmigration seems to be a kind of delusion and somehow appears to be the work of the original substance of nature (*prakṛti*), a dynamic force which conjures up phenomenal reality by its abundant creativity. This original substance of nature produces, first, the Cosmic Mind (*Citta*) from which emanates the matrix of individuality called I-am-ness (*asmitā*). Through this principle of individuality the one Cosmic Mind generates individual minds (*cittas*) for *puruṣas.* Whenever one of the *puruṣas* somehow loses awareness of his original purity so that it becomes obscured in him, he becomes identified with a single mind generated specially for him by the Cosmic Mind. This individual *citta* is never pure, because it is subject to unending fluctuations (*cittavṛttayas*). Because many *puruṣas* obviously must have suffered at some point in time the loss of their original purity, there is now a multiplicity of transmigrating individual persons on the phenomenal level (in *saṁsāra*). The chapter never explains why and how the originally pure individual persons (*puruṣas*) became contaminated by the abundant dynamic force of nature. The text only employs a metaphor that it happens in the way a farmer divides a stream to allow its water to flow through many channels onto his fields to irrigate them. The dividing of the stream is an act of volition (*varaṇa-bhedas*, IV,3), but whose? Metaphors always offer only a partial explanation. So it remains unclear where this decision took place. Perhaps in the awareness (*citi*) of the first *puruṣa* who was lured to partake in the abundant creativity of *prakṛti* and became identified with an individual *citta* provided for him by the Cosmic Mind via the matrix of individuality (*asmitā*)? Other *puruṣas* would then follow the example of the first one and thus *saṁsāra* (the 'global flow' of phenomenal of existence) would have got going. This problem was discussed (but never really solved) in subsequent centuries in commentaries which became influenced in the process, as already stated, by the 'orthodox' Sāṅkya system. (The final result then led, by the imposition of the Sāṅkya system's metaphysics on Yoga, to the creation of the hybrid Sāṅkya-Yoga Darśaṇa.)

a.) Once identified with individual minds, the essentially pure *puruṣas* experience themselves as individuals in a world of objects which obtained reality (*tattva*) as phenomena by the process of the (unexplained) transformation of oneness into manifoldness. This would have happened simultaneously with at least one *puruṣa* obtaining his mind just created by the Cosmic Mind. Within the context of the world the objects are real, independently of whether they are perceived by any individual mind or not. (This statement perhaps represents a refutation of idealistic monism which was at the time already in the making, to develop in later centuries into the classical system of Advaita Vedānta.) The individual mind-possessing *puruṣas* involve themselves in the world by acting on the objects and among themselves; through their actions they create in themselves specific characteristic tendencies (*vāsanā*) which turn into latent impressions (*saṁskāra*) and drive them to yet further actions. This perpetuates karmic processes which lead to transmigration. The text suggests how it is that different actions — bad, good and neutral — have corresponding effects (*vipāka*) even when the doer is thereafter reborn in a different life separated from his previous actions by time and space. It is the latent impressions within the individual mind which bridge over the separateness, like memory (*smṛti*) does within one life, when what was done during one's youth brings effects in old age. Curiously, the latent impressions are said to be beginningless (*anāditva*) because of the perpetuity of the urge to exist (*āśiṣo nityatvāt*). Here is a hint that the whole process of saṁsāric existence may not have had a beginning, which is an insoluble issue. It is expressed quite clearly by the Buddha: 'Unknown is the beginning, monks, of faring on.' The earliest point in wandering of transmigrating beings hindered by ignorance and yoked by craving is not evident (*saṁsāro pubbākoṭi na paññāyati* - SN II, 179 = II,XV,3,2).

The text of this final chapter of the YS also contains some practical points. It makes clear that liberation from transmigration is possible and gives a few hints about how to achieve it. One can practise meditation and if a deep absorption (*dhyāna*) is developed, the individual mind loses its natural (sattvic or prakṛtic) basis and becomes no-mind (vanishes) and that particular *puruṣa* becomes free and possesses only pure awareness (*citi*) of his true nature. A few slightly unclear aphorisms (IV.23-26) nevertheless seem to suggest that the individual empirical mind somehow collaborates with the transmigrating *puruṣa* for his as well as its own release. It is actually the mind which is capable of developing discrimination and can realise the distinction between essence (*ātma*) and existence (or becoming, *bhāva*), whereupon it ceases its activities. If it persists with its discrimination without lapse, liberation (*kaivalya*) of the *puruṣa* may follow. The mind, no longer needed, dissolves. If a lapse occurs, mental activity starts again, triggered by the not yet uprooted latent formations (*saṁskāras*). The *puruṣa*, acting through his mind then has to undergo a thorough process of cleansing his mind from these impurities by practising one of the methods described in previous chapters and by concentrating on developing knowledge. If the mind then experiences, through meditation and while maintaining discrimination, the highest states of mind without getting stuck in them, the *puruṣa* experiences the total unified, boundless knowledge of the whole of empirical reality or the contemplative vision of the totality of truth (*dharma-megha-samādhi*). This amounts to the cessation of the flow of instances of phenomenal happenings or the activities of nature, i.e. of the original substance of phenomenality (*sattva, prakṛti*). Nature's dynamic forces (*guṇas*) then return to their original state. Consequently, the mind of this particular *puruṣa,* having become superfluous, dissolves, and he is restored to pure awareness (*citi*) of his true status and reaches emancipation (*kaivalya*) from the prakṛtic enticements, presumably for good.

A question remains as to the status of liberated individuals who still linger in the world before they physically die. One aphorism (IV.7) refers to yogis (in this context undoubtedly meaning accomplished ones) whose actions are ethically neutral and therefore not producing karmic effects. Besides, the context of chapters 2-5 is one of presumably accomplished teachers instructing their pupils. So one has to assume that there is a certain momentum of the phenomenal personality which continues to function on earth even after its *puruṣa* realises *kaivalya,* at least in some cases, perhaps when a decision is taken to teach the Yoga path. This parallels early Buddhism whose extensive scriptures record that the Buddha lived and taught for 45 years after his liberation from the round of rebirths. Some of his accomplished disciples (*arahants*) also taught, others awaited quietly the natural demise of the body.

The above suggestion that the individual empirical mind somehow collaborates with the free person (*puruṣa*) for his as well as for its own release (i.e. dissolution) is supported by the fact that it is the mind which has to make the decision to embark on the Yoga path, presumably out of its free will. Every practitioner of Yoga experiences the hard fact that he has to make a firm and conscious decision to start the practice and keep renewing his determination on a daily basis, until it has become for him a matter of course.

The usual aphoristic nature of even this concluding chapter, which does not proceed systematically and repeats similar topics in different parts, again suggests that it was most likely based on notes taken by a listener, perhaps supplemented from memory later on.

It would be futile to wish to create a metaphysical system from this basic set of philosophical ideas. It can be regarded as a kind of invitation to turn to practice and see the final truth directly (cf. Werner, 1977a. 130-140).

VI. The Popularisation of Yoga

Yoga and specialised Upaniṣads

The classical Yoga of Patañjali's YS, particularly its 'pure Yoga' of the *aṣṭāṅga* yoga chapter may be seen as a crystallisation of yogic teachings and practices pursued by individuals as well as by various groupings of a most diverse nature. When it established its reputation it became a corrective for trends in danger of going astray and a focal point or a beacon for future Yoga endeavours. But it did not stop further exploration and diversification of methods of Yoga practice and uses of Yoga as a springboard for promoting metaphysical, theological and popular religious interests. All these trends pushed ahead and are reflected in subsequent writings with specialised themes and many of them take as their model the early Upaniṣads. They even include this designation in their name, but they no longer belong to the bulk of Vedic scriptures which is a status afforded to only the thirteen oldest Upaniṣads (Bṛhadāraṇyaka, Chāndogya, Taittirīya, Aitareya, Kauṣītaki, Kena, Kaṭha, Īśā, Muṇḍaka, Praśna, Māṇḍūkya, Śvetāśevatara, Maitrī — also called Maitrāyaṇīya — and Mahānārāyaṇa). These Upaniṣads constitute the end of the Vedas and are therefore summarily designated as Vedānta.

Subsequent texts with specialised topics called Upaniṣads are numerous. Their composition has been a continuous process for centuries, both in Sanskrit and in vernaculars, and it may still be going on. Only a limited number of them has been collected and published in different anthologies. A traditional Indian anthology, which also includes the oldest thirteen, comprises 108 Upaniṣads considered by most Hindu sects to be 'canonical'. The oldest known anthology of 108 Upaniṣads is the so-called Muktikā Canon which dates from around the middle of the 17th century (Deussen, 1920, 31-35; cf. Tripathi, 2010).

A representative selection of easily accessible specialised Upaniṣads has been made by Deussen (1897, XXV-XXVII) and grouped under specific headings expressing their nature:

(1) Pure Vedānta Upaniṣads comprise three early (Mundaka, Praoena and Māṇḍūkya) and six later ones (Garbha, Prāṇāgnihotra, Piṇḍa, Ātma, Sarva-upaniṣat-sāra, Gāruḍa).

(2) Yoga Upaniṣads, eleven in number, are all of later date (Brahmavidyā, Kṣurikā, Śūlikā, Nādābindu, Brahmabindu, Amṛtabindu, Dhyānabindu, Tejobindu, Yogaśikhā, Yogatattva, Haṅsa).

(3) Saṅnyāsa Upaniṣads, of later date, are seven in number (Brahma, Saṅnyāsa, Āruṇeya, Kaṇṭhaśruti, Paramahaṅsa, Jābāla, Āśrama).

The subsequent two groups comprise mostly medieval sectarian Upaniṣads:

(4) Śiva Upaniṣads are five in number (Atharvaśira, Atharvaśikhā, Nīlarudra, Kālāgnirudra, Kaivalya).

(5) Viṣṇu Upaniṣads are seven in number (Mahā, Nārāyaṇa, Ātmabodha, Nṛsiṅhapūrvatāpanīya, Nṛsihotaratāpanīya, Rāmapūrvatāpanīya, Rāmottaratāpanīya).

These Upaniṣads refer to Yoga and meditative practices in various ways and to some extent anticipate later developments in Indian thought and in Yoga practice to be described in some detail in subsequent chapters. They also contain philosophical speculations and diverse religious trends.

Pure Vedānta Upaniṣads point to the later classical system of Advaita Vedānta of Śaṅkara by anticipating his monistic teaching about the sole reality of *brahman* and the illusory nature of the world as expressed in the Muṇḍaka and Māṇḍūkya Upaniṣads in combination with speculations on the nature of consciousness in the dream state and in deep sleep in the Praoena Upaniṣad. The Ātma-Upaniṣad redefines the notion of self (*ātman*) by introducing three layers of it: (1) The external self when one experiences oneself as a bodily organism; (2) the internal self when one is aware of one's actions and mental functions and gets an understanding of oneself as a person (*puruṣa*), in effect a functioning mental structure; (3) the highest self which is realised through mental withdrawal, meditation and Yoga. One is then the pure and absolute Ātman, who yet at the same time remains a person, totally free from karmic effects. Other Upaniṣads of this group deal with marginal topics.

Yoga Upaniṣads combine Yoga procedures with many features current in Hindu sectarian movements. They frequently make use of the sacred syllable *om* as a meditation object, by both loud and silent repetition, and also by inner visualisation. Although it is now written and usually pronounced as a single syllable '*om*', the ancient form was always understood to be composed of three letters *a-u-m* as mentioned earlier. In Sanskrit script (*devanāgarī*) the final letter '*m*' is written as a dot (*bindu*) above the preceding vowel (in this case the diphthong 'au' is written by one letter in Sanskrit script). The dot above it symbolically represents the spaceless and timeless *brahman* as described, for example, in the Brahmabindu Upaniṣad. A good example of non-systematic references to Yoga practice among the late Upaniṣads is Amṛtabindu. It quotes all the limbs of the *ṣaḍaṅga yoga* and anticipates Haṭha Yoga, particularly in the detailed descriptions of the correct sitting positions and of complicated *prāṇāyāma* exercises and other specific methods, including some elements of Tantra. Another Upaniṣad, Yogaśikhā, obviously presupposes the knowledge of the system of inner channels (*nadīs*) in the subtle body by mentioning *suṣumnā*, the central channel along the spine. The Yogatattva Upaniṣad describes the variety of relationships through which one proceeds in the course of re-incarnations: one's present mother may become one's wife or daughter in future successive lives, one's father may be reborn as one's son, and so on. The *om* meditation is then used to associate with its triple nature other tripartite elements of the Hindu religion such as the three Vedas and the three gods of the Hindu Trinity, or of philosophy like the three *guṇas* of *prakṛti* in the Sāṇkya system. Yoga is proclaimed to be the medium to the highest *ātman* through *pratyāhāra* and *prāṇāyāma*, which interestingly consists of just breathing in and breathing out with the in-between 'windless' gap through which unification with the highest may be won, as also through the *bindu* between the eyebrows.

The Saṅnyāsa group of Upaniṣads gives quite a profound insight into the thinking and practice of the homeless wanderers, the ancient phenomenon which may predate even the forming of the Vedas. It truly glorifies homelessness as the basis for Yoga at a time when the majority of the population followed established religious practices in the hope of heavenly rewards. But even this group of Upaniṣads is, in the last analysis, geared towards the Vedāntic philosophy of oneness expressed by the old Upaniṣadic dictum *brahman=ātman*. This is most clearly reiterated in the Brahma Upaniṣad. The Saṅnyāsa Upaniṣad, after which the whole group is named, begins with the description of complicated procedures which a householder should perform before leaving home for good. He should light a sacrificial fire and bring offerings for the ancestors, distribute his wealth to his children and depart with only basic possessions, to live on alms food. He then practises mental withdrawal, concentration and breath control to the point when the breath leaves through the skull to bring him to the 'highest place' (*parama-vastha*). The Āruṇeya Upaniṣad advocates total renunciation by enumerating at length all that one has to give up physically and mentally in order to become totally free from past actions (*karma*) and to reach liberation. It includes renouncing family ties, social status, conceptual learning, liturgy, hope for rebirth in higher dimensions of existence and 'everything else'. There are echoes of Buddhist thinking in this Upaniṣad which finishes by referring to *nirvāṇa.* The Kaṇṭhaśruti, Jābāla and Āśrama Upaniṣads advocate going through the traditional four stages of life as student, householder and forest-dweller before entering the fourth stage as a wanderer. Then one is a true *saṇnyāsī.* The Paramahaṁsa Upaniṣad uses the symbol of the 'swan' to refer to the free wanderer. When he achieves liberation, he is the 'supreme swan'. Otherwise it reiterates what the other Upaniṣads proclaim in various ways.

The two sectarian groups — the Śiva and Viṣṇu Upaniṣads — are of minor interest for the study of Yoga because of their theistic character, resulting in the elevation of either Śiva or Viṣṇu, respectively, to the position of the highest personal god as well as the transcendental principle and creative force in the universe and the goal of yogic endeavours. The practice of sectarian yogis is therefore impaired by their respective religious beliefs. This is not to say that they may not achieve high spiritual experiences, but in the last resort they would have to rise beyond their allegiances if they should proceed to the threshold of liberation. There is also in the sectarian Upaniṣads, particularly in those with Viṣṇu as the Lord, a trend to *bhakti yoga* which was brought to explicit formulations in the epics and will be dealt with below.

One has also to bear in mind that the above division of the Upaniṣads into the described groups is more or less tentative and approximate. Traces of all the trends can be found in all of them.

Yoga in the epics

The proliferation of Yoga into all classes of Indian society is best reflected in the epic literature. The Upaniṣads used to be produced in upper echelons of society and until comparatively recently their circulation was limited, but epic poetry was openly recited in public places and memorised by the common people. In both Indian national epics, the *Mahābhārata* (Mbh) and the *Rāmāyaṇa,* which started in ancient times in the form of heroic ballads and over the centuries grew enormously in size, Yoga, the qualities gained through Yoga practice and the possibility of penetrating even to the threshold of liberation without becoming a wanderer, began to be described and propagated in passages inserted at about the same time as the first steps were being taken to codify Classical Yoga (cca 300 BCE). These passages concerned with Yoga were being constantly reworked and enlarged and eventually grew into lengthy narrative episodes which were inserted into the epics, most probably between 300 BCE and 300 CE. Four such major episodes were incorporated into the Mbh (Deussen, 1906), the best known among them being the *Bhagavad Gītā* (BhG).

Yoga in the *Bhagavad Gītā*

The BhG, which is inserted into book 6 of the Mbh, is basically a religious text of a theistic nature with a Viṣṇuistic background. In the wider context of Hinduism Viṣṇu is the second member of the Hindu Trinity as the preserver (the first member, Brahma, being the creator and the third, Śiva, the destroyer), but in the sectarian context Viṣṇu and Śiva are each elevated to the position of the supreme God within their respective sects. One of the main features of Viṣṇuism is the teaching on periodic incarnations (*avatāras*) of the God Viṣṇu in order to restore righteousness (*dharma*) on earth and assist beings on their way to salvation. Viṣṇu's eighth incarnation is Kṛṣṇa. The BhG is composed in the form of questions by prince Arjuna and answers by Kṛṣṇa, who reveals himself in the process as not just a subordinate incarnation of Viṣṇu, but as the supreme God in his own right. As such he proclaims himself to be unborn and imperishable and reveals that by his intrinsic power he can enter incarnate existence. He does so from time to time — whenever conditions in the world deteriorate to the point of lawlessness — to protect the good and destroy the evil-doers. By this statement the BhG appropriated for itself the well-established Hindu teaching of periodic divine incarnations (which has a precursor even in the Vedas). Kṛṣṇa then makes a further important statement to the effect that whoever gets to know him in this his true nature as the supreme deity as well as the incarnating saviour will after bodily death be liberated from rebirth in the world and will come straight to him, presumably forever, or into a timeless state (IV. 6-9). Kṛṣṇa claims further (VIII. 16) that, for example, worshippers of Brahma follow him, reincarnating throughout the sequence of recurring world creations and world destructions (known in Hindu mythology as Brahma's days and Brahma's nights). It is only Kṛṣṇa, as the supreme God, who guarantees his worshippers freedom from the sequence of rebirths. He even maintains that it is not *brahman* which is the ultimate principle of existence, but he himself, *brahman* being based on him and therefore secondary to him or derivative from him.

I think that we do not have to take these statements too literally, for statements in other parts of the BhG contradict them. What we can conclude from them is that in this way the BhG places Kṛṣṇa on a par with the ultimate reality like the *brahman* and *ātman* of the early Upaniṣads, the *nirvāṇa* of Buddhism and the *kaivalya* of Jainism. The BhG's teachings are highly syncretic and virtually all-inclusive; they allow for diverse metaphysical teachings and yogic as well as religious practices of the time, including Vedic rituals, to exist side by side.

This is because the BhG grew over a long period into its final shape as inserted into the Mbh so that there are older and younger layers. Numerous interpolations in various parts from various times abound in it.

The BhG in its tolerance of all possible approaches aiming at salvation describes also the basics of the path of *direct* knowledge — i.e. knowledge which is not mediated by concepts and which came to be termed Jñāna Yoga (III, 3). Its emergence in the BhG and further development will be dealt with later, as will be another innovation of the BhG, the method of 'selfless action' called Karma Yoga.

The insertion of the BhG and other philosophical and mystical episodes into the Mhb may have been a device to utilise the great popularity of the epic to secure wider publicity for the spiritual teachings those episodes convey. In the case of the BhG it obviously worked and elevated it almost to the level of sacred scriptures rivalling the Vedas and the Upaniṣads.

The BhG gives only a passing reference to the method of meditational absorption (*dhyāna*), saying that through it some can see themselves as the Self (XIII, 24).

One relatively short section of the BhG (VI,10-32) contains a description of the Yoga practice which follows procedures known from the YS, but does not use the YS's technical terms. The yogi should practise in a solitary place, be comfortably seated, restrain his senses and focus his gaze on the tip of his nose. His main task is to bring his mind under control. That requires him to be tranquil and unperturbed by emotional upheavals brought about by sexual activity; then he "abides in the vow of chastity" (*brahmacārivrate sthitaḥ*). When he has fully succeeded in controlling his mind, he attains the peace of the supreme *nirvāṇa* which is coterminous with the bliss of contemplating *ātman* and *brahman*. This is a conception of Yoga based on renunciation whose goal of liberation is impersonal (*brahman*, *ātman, nirvāṇa, kaivalya*). Ultimately, however, it is Kṛṣṇa himself in his transcendence and simultaneous immanence in everybody and everything who is the true final goal. So by identifying the ultimate goal with Kṛṣṇa with whom one can have a personal relation, the BhG points even in its popular summary of the YS's path to its own prevailing theme, namely to the way involving love of and to God, i.e. Bhakti Yoga (foreshadowed in the Upaniṣads, particularly ŚU, 6. 21-23 and KathU, 2.20).[32]

Despite its syncretism and tolerance of all possible methods and procedures, the BhG is thoroughly theistic and relies on devout faith. Although it contains many inspiring and profound ideas, it is at root misleading so far as an independent search for truth is concerned.

Yoga in the *Mokṣadharma* (Mdh)

Much less known than the BhG, the *Mokṣadharma* (the doctrine of salvation) is another spiritual text inserted into the Mbh, book 12. It is dedicated in most parts to syncretistic philosophical and theological speculations and polemics, interspersed with repeated recommendations of renunciation and austerity (*tapas*). In some parts the text seems to be accepting, to a degree, the usefulness of correctly performed Vedic rituals and it recommends adherence to the four stages in life (pupil, householder, hermit and wanderer), as described by a Brahmin father giving instructions to his son. But the son sees further and points out to his father that death can snatch one away at any stage before one has reached the stage of renunciation so it will be followed by rebirth and repeated dying in the world again. Typical of youthful zeal, which was already in evidence early in the time of the Upaniṣads, the son insists that the time to renounce is before one gets tied up in family life.

In its speculative parts the text posits a spiritual principle (*mānasa*), which is unmanifest (*avyakta*) and unending, and is called *ātman*. From it stem all beings. The text also follows, in a somewhat piecemeal way, the Sāṅkhya philosophy. It describes the process of the world's manifestation from the Great (Mahān), which is followed by the principle of egoity (Ahaṅkāra), accounting for the existence of individual beings. Then emerges space/ether (*ākāśa*) followed by the four great elements (fire, air or wind, water and earth which work as forces of heat, movement, fluidity and compactness); they make up the visible world, including the 'materiality' of beings (their bodies), as well as their mentality. Somehow there is within the unmanifest Great the self-existing (*svayambhū*) divine being or entity which creates a heavenly lotus from which springs the god Brahm, who acts as the divine Ahaṅkāra so that other Vedic deities appear. The text also presents basics of primitive psychology. It operates with the notion of individual life (*jīva*) which, in pure form, reflects *ātman*, but it gets involved with forces of nature (*guṇas* of *prakṛti*, which stick to *jīva*). When experiencing the world, *jīva* is called the 'knower of the field' (*kṣetrajña*). Freed from association with *prakṛti*, it becomes *paramātman*. We have here a thoroughly syncretic teaching with hardly any originality. It does not represent in itself any special contribution to Yoga as practice.

But the theme of renunciation and austerity (*tapas*) keeps recurring and these practices are praised as bringing appropriate reward even for those who live in homes and have not fully renounced. A practising householder should conscientiously care for his family, limit his intake of food, reduce or give up eating meat and visit his wife only at fixed times (not driven by uncontrolled passion) or abstain from intercourse altogether after begetting offspring. If he then gives some serious consideration to the web of this world which is decaying in all its aspects, it will make him turn away from it. A reasonable man's main concern must therefore be to search for the means to save himself (or one's Self) from it. In essence the world is full of suffering which has its source in craving or thirst (*tṛṣṇā*), but also in pleasure, since the two inevitably alternate. The main domicile of man's awareness of himself is the body and as a result of ignorance he makes the effort to avoid pain and accumulate pleasures while living in the body. This proves to be the character-building force which determines his life during the sequence of incarnations and even in the hereafter, in the subtle dimensions. But the ultimate result of involvement in worldly experiences of whatever kind is always suffering and repeated death. The world of *samsāra* is suffused with birth, death, old age and pains, illness and mental deficiency. The safest remedy for avoiding these ills lies in avoidance of ownership, freedom from family ties, giving up all ambitions and striving for salvation.

A substantial amount of the Mdh's terminology is reminiscent of Buddhist formulations, to which the preceding paragraph bears witness. Their truth is repeatedly hammered in and illustrated by many narrative passages — stories put into the mouths of famous personalities such as king Janaka, known from old Upaniṣads, and stories in which gods and animals mingle.

Some verses deal extensively with ethical principles, among them truthfulness, generosity, fidelity, modesty, chastity and compassion. One should maintain purity of body, speech and thought and avoid craving, anger, selfishness and harming any living being. Many verses give very detailed advice on decent behaviour in all possible circumstances and repeatedly stress purity of body and mind.

When it comes to the practical procedures to be adopted after renunciation for the sake of liberation, they are dealt with rather briefly. It has to be assumed that they were supplemented by oral instructions and personal guidance by a teacher. There can be little doubt that various Yoga procedures were practised, particularly meditation or the way of deep absorption (Dhyāna Yoga). The recommendation is to adopt a sitting position in which one is straight 'as a wooden stick' and endeavour to calm and concentrate the mind so that it achieves total one-pointedness, while the functioning of the sensory organs is fully suspended. When this has been accomplished, one has reached the first phase of *dhyāna*, although the mind may produce flashes like lightning in clouds any time. This first phase is of short duration, because the mind (*manas*) starts wandering again 'like the wind in space'. Even thoughts, worries and doubts may reappear in it. But the yogi should each time bring the mind back into a state of calmness. Eventually he will, through sustained practice of Yoga meditation, reach total pacification and experience the bliss stemmin from it. In this state he will eventually enter trouble-free *nirvāṇa*, which is an achievement he must earn, it cannot be bestowed on him as a gift of god.

The text also describes the practice of Brāhminic renouncers who constantly murmur Vedic prayers. It regards this practice as detrimental, especially if it is associated with Vedic sacrifices. But if prior to assuming the murmuring meditation (*japa*) at least preliminary attempts have been made on the path of *dhyāna*, then the reward is in a favourable birth on the path of gods (*devayāna*), i.e. a sojourn in higher heavenly dimensions. In a lengthy chapter, however, the text insists that if the murmuring is done as a consistent and ceaseless practice for its own sake without any thought of reward or any aim whatsoever, it may go on indefinitely, perhaps as a kind of eternal wandering — hardly a realistic proposition in the real world.

There are several passages which refer to knowledge (*jñāna*) as the bestower of all possible benefits. Through knowledge everything can be achieved, including salvation, so knowledge can be seen as the highest goal. But there are no practical hints as to what one could regard as the path of knowledge in the sense of Jñāna Yoga. However, there is a hint at a comprehensive approach to achieving perfection:

it cannot be reached without knowledge, wisdom, ardour (*tapas*), restraint of the senses, concentration of the mind up to onepointedness, total renunciation and Yoga. In this way one who has renounced his caste may attain the highest goal and so may even a woman who has been striving to fulfill her duties.

Yoga in the *Anugītā*

This insertion into the Mbh, book 14, is a somewhat more systematic text than the Mdh. It deals extensively with topics of philosophical and theological interest, particularly the process of the world manifestation as did the Mdh but at greater length, with more clarity and better understanding of the Sāṅkhya doctrine. It dwells on questions of transmigration, the nature of the *jīva*, the way to liberation and the theory of Yoga, but not in sufficient practical detail, indulging mainly in extolling the final result.

The process of transmigration is described as very painful. The body, while it is being abandoned by *jīva*, suffers pain as does the new body created in the womb from the past deeds of the incarnating individual. In between the *jīva* is enveloped in his previous deeds (*karma*), his consciousness is obscured and he is tossed about as if by a (karmic) wind. He may temporarily recover his consciousness for a certain time in a place of suffering (hell, *naraka*) or in a higher abode (heaven, *svarga*) according to his merits, only to be sucked again into the process of reincarnation. But liberation can be achieved by following appropriate principles, including ethical ones, among which the highest is non-injury (*ahiṁsā*) of living beings. What is most needed on the way to liberation is self-restraint, austerity, the practice of concentration and meditation and following the 'science of Yoga'. It enables the determined yogi to achieve a state in which he dwells within his own self (*ātman*), unaffected by external circumstances and experiences, being fully liberated. This state is a great mystery even to gods. The liberated one is a person (*puruṣa*) beyond activity who possesses full self-knowledge.

Yoga in the *Sanatsujāta-parvan*

The shortest insertion into the Mbh, book 5, is named after the mythological figure of Sanatsujāta, the 'eternal youngster', the form of *brahman* visible to gods, usually referred to as Brahma, who figures also as the first person of the Hindu Trinity in mainstream Hinduism. He is best known by his pronouncement "Death does not exist" which can be understood as anticipating the Advaitic doctrine of the illusory nature of the world of *saṁsāra.* This illusion comes about by deception which is caused by craving, but can be suppressed by meditation and dispersed by knowledge. Knowledge can be developed if one is tireless in striving and free from acquisitiveness and also by becoming learned, yet as if not being learned (knowing as if not knowing). Truthfulness, uprightness, chasteness, restraint, purity and higher knowledge are also needed to prevent delusion. Higher knowledge is not acquired by being versed in the Vedas. But those who are versed in the Vedas may reach immortality through austerity (*tapas*). The text never tires of enumerating negative states of mind to be avoided and positive ones to be developed. Great praise is voiced towards one's teacher, who is viewed as indispensable. This no doubt indicates, from the total absence in the whole text of any methodical hints on how to practise Yoga, that instructions to that effect were passed on orally.

Yoga and the Rāma tradition

The second of the Indian epics, the *Rāmāyaṇa,* is much more compact than the Mbh and did not lend itself to diverse elaborations and insertions. Rāma, just as Kṛṣṇa of the BhG, is regarded as an incarnation of Viṣṇu and so his devotees, seeing the success of the BhG within the MBh, produced treatises on philosophical, theological and yogic themes and attached them to the Rāmāyaṇa as Rāma Upaniṣads in which *japa* on the name Rāma is prominent. (It also became generally popular as a name for god, probably under the influence of the *Rāmāyaṇa* in the version produced by Tulsi Das, a renowned poet of the 16th century; Mahatma Gandhi — Mahātmā Gāndhī — died with the words 'Rām, Rām...' on his lips.)

The greatest achievement of this movement, however, is the so-called *yoga vāsiṣṭha.* Its basic text is *Yoga Vāsiṣṭha Mahārāmāyaṇa* ascribed to Vālmīki (possibly 8th century), but it was elaborated into a few subsequent versions. It takes the form of a conversation between the legendary sage Vasiṣṭha and Rāma. Originally a part of the sectarian Viṣṇuistic tradition, the movement came also to recognise the roles of Brahma and Śiva, although Rāma is seen as superior to them. Perhaps following the example of Kṛṣṇa of the BhG, the movement also opened itself to viewing the ultimate reality under the aspect of a supra-personal principle under the name of Rāma who is thus regarded both as the ultimate reality, the source of the universe and also the highest god within the manifested universe. But for the supra-personal principle expressions from other traditions are also used liberally, including the Vedāntic *brahman* and the Buddhist *śūnyatā* (emptiness). The movement can be regarded as an example of the influence which spiritual experience, possibly gained through Yoga practice or deep thought, can have in transforming an originally narrow sectarian belief into a universalistic outlook, albeit still committed to religious and philosophical beliefs. The elaborate system of practice which Yogavāsiṣṭha employs can be classified as a combination of Jñāna and Dhyāna Yoga with a Karma Yoga basis and it is stressed that it can be followed amidst active life. It is quite a comprehensive system of practice, but far from the notion of pure Yoga.

Yogavāsiṣṭha's conceptual and faith-based anticipation of the goal may preclude the breakthrough to final truth. It is committed to the advaitic (non-dualist) view, according to which the external world is of illusory nature. The Yoga path to realisation is envisaged as proceeding in seven stages (*bhūmikas*):

(1) *nivṛtti* — abstaining, inactivity, suspension — is interpreted as developing dispassion (*virāga*) by meditation, abstaining from shallow pleasures, guarding oneself against getting involved mentally in external tasks and searching for the way to cross the ocean of *saṁsāra*;

(2) *vicāraṇa* — reflection; musing; also: reluctance, hesitation, doubt — suggests that one reflects over the scriptures but, perhaps doubting that they bring results, turns to Yoga and practises *dhāraṇā* and *dhyāna* which would suggest taking up the Yoga of Patañjali, but the text is not specific enough to confirm this; it may be some kind of meditation practice current at the time;

(3) *asaṁsaṅga* — non-association, non-attachment — means being free from worldly pursuits and involvement with worldly people, yet associating with like-minded renunciants in forest hermitages; the stage seems to culminate in realising that 'I am not the doer, it is God'; the deeds are within the domain of nature (*prakṛti*).

The first three stages of this Yoga proceed in the realm of waking in which this world appears real and the yogi lives in it with dignity. When he dies, he experiences pleasure for a long time before the next rebirth in which he resumes his Yoga practice and continues through further stages:

(4) *svapna loka* — the world of dream vision — is the 'immeasurable' stage of non-dual vision; the yogi sees the world as if in a dream; no specific procedure is revealed about how to glide into this state, but it is predetermined by the commitment of the Vāsiṣṭha Yoga to advaitic philosophy;

(5) *advaita suṣupta* — non-dual deep sleep — appears to be a state akin to deep sleep without any dreams which still allows some feeling ('one awakens to inner joy');

everybody has occasionally, on waking after a good night's sleep, the impression that there was in it nothing to recollect in terms of dream images or events but a feeling lingers of having experienced total rest and satisfaction or even happiness, although of a short duration; again the text is not explicit about how this stage could be fully achieved through some kind of awareness. From here there is just a little step, if a step it can be called, to the next stage:

(6) *jīvan mukti* — being liberated while still living in this world, in *nirvāṇa,* but as if not in nirvāṇa; although being in a body, one is free 'like a piece of sky in a jar' beyond duality as well as non-duality;

(7) *videha mukti* — 'bodyless' liberation is beyond the horizon of the universe; it is called by many names, but can be imagined as the core of everything, the Self (*ātman*)[33] (cf. Key Chapple, 2012).

When the Bhakti movement swept the country, the eclectic Rāma tradition accommodated it by formulating its own path of Bhakti Yoga expounded in the treatise called *Adhyātmarāmāyaṇa* (15th century CE or later) in which Rāma is equated with *ātman* and his wife Sītā is viewed as *cit-śaktī,* his creative power — another instance of the anticipation of the final outcome precluding an unbiased final vision.

VII. The Rise of Specialised Schools

Jñāna Yoga, the path of knowledge

Strictly speaking there is no separate school of Yoga which would have developed from a methodical pursuit of knowledge, creating its own specific Yoga technique in the process. The notion of knowledge is, quite simply, inherent in Yoga endeavours. Each school of Yoga aims at obtaining final and absolute knowledge of the ultimate reality, whether through coming face to face with it or by unification with it. But once Yoga emerged as a methodical path and different emphases started a process of differentiation, the preference in some circles for pursuing analytical knowledge alongside usual Yoga practice eventually led to the development of specific *jñāna* techniques.

The *jñāna* trend stemmed originally from the early Upanisadic direct mystical experience of the ultimate reality and one's essential unity with it (*brahman=ātman*). To get to know *brahman* directly meant to be liberated from the round of rebirths. The early Upanisads appear in parts speculative and employ also symbolic imagery, yet their insistence that one can get to know *brahman* directly suggests a leap beyond conceptual knowledge, but they do not provide methodical hints on how it is achieved. The conception of knowledge as a special kind of apprehension of truth or the absolute or God beyond concepts is comparable to the Greek concept of *gnosis* which is philologically identical to *jñāna,* being derived from the same root of the word with the meaning of 'knowing' in the assumed Indo-European parent language: **ǵṅō* which softens in Sanskrit into *jñā*.

A kind of account of Jñāna Yoga can be found for the first time in the BhG, as has already been pointed out, and it no doubt derives from or is a kind of echo of the quest of the early Upaniṣads. This direct knowledge has, in the BhG, the power to eradicate instantly all accumulated demerit produced by past evil actions, so it is superior to the orthodox practice of ritual sacrifice of one's possessions to God, in which even the acquired knowledge is offered to the Lord as if in a sacrifice (BhG IV, 33 & 36-37). Even if one is the worst villain, the power of direct knowledge transports one across the ocean of *saṁsāra*.[34]

As is the case in the early Upaniṣads, there is no clear methodical device described by the BhG on how to acquire this direct knowledge. It seems that it occurs by a sudden breakthrough, possibly following intense thinking and unshakable belief in the truth of *brahman* as the ultimate reality. Not everybody is capable of this belief, but there are alternatives in other approaches.

The elaboration of the Jñāna Yoga trend continued in the late Vedāntic Upanisads and received its systematic form within the metaphysical school of Advaita Vedānta, whose teachings are summarised in the *Brahma Sūtras* of Bādarāyaṇa (cca 2nd century CE) and expounded by Gaudapāda in his *Kārikā* (before 750 CE) which is attached to the ManU. But the greatest protagonist of Advaitic metaphysics was the famous Śaṅkara (788-820 CE), a great philosopher, mystical poet and *saṅnyāsī* who advocated the sole existence of *brahman* as ultimate reality beside which the world has only illusory being. Salvation can be won by seeing through the illusion, just as by carefully looking one realises that what appeared to be a snake is in fact a piece of rope. This may seem easy, but in practice one has to train oneself thoroughly to achieve the right vision. The preliminaries for achieving it were summarised by Sadānanda (15th century) in his compendium *Vedānta-sāra* which laid down the following requirements:

(1) *Viveka* — discrimination — between what is real and what is unreal. This is virtually the end result, because the underlying philosophy asserts the unreality of the external world which a beginner experiences as real, while the sole reality of *brahman* is beyond his ken. But one can train oneself in a preliminary way by discriminating between false perceptions and correct perceptions even within the seemingly real world of matter, just as in the rope/snake example.

(2) *Vairāgya* — dispassionateness — towards all phenomena. In practical life one should focus progressively first on easier targets to become indifferent to them, for example on holding passionate opinions or being passionately fond of certain foods, before one can hope to tackle sexual passion.

(3) *Ṣaṭsampatti* — six attainments — namely *śama* (tranquillity), *dama* (self-control), *uparati* (giving up), *titiksā* (patience), *śraddhā* (faith) and *samādhāna* (concentration). Faith within the Vedāntic tradition would mean believing in the non-dualistic nature of reality, but one could bypass it by believing just in the efficacy of the path of knowledge without anticipating what will be revealed when the final knowledge is won. This, of course, would be a stance of pure Yoga which when adopted would 'liberate' the practitioner even from the strictures of Advaita Vedānta.

(4) *Mumuksutva* — longing for liberation — is quite an important requirement. It may happen that when one makes a decision to strive for liberation from rebirth, it may remain more or less on a conceptual level. There may be an indefinite feeling of uncertainty about the state of liberation, about *nirvāṇa* as being perhaps non-existence. As a result

the practice is half-hearted. So one should examine one's feelings by introspection or mindfulness and see if one's initial resolution can be turned into real longing.

However, when this happens, one should then practise without anticipation or any thought of liberation. This, again, would be pure Yoga.

The training in Jñāna Yoga proceeds through three stages: (1) *śravaṇa* (hearing), i.e. study and learning; (2) *manana* (mentation), involving analysis of what has been learned and the application thereof to one's experience; and (3) *nididhyāsana* (constant meditation), i.e. the development of a permanent meditative state of mind. The experience of the final state of liberation is described as *sat-cit-ānanda* ('existence-consciousness-bliss' which can be paraphrased as 'being in conscious bliss').

The tradition of Advaitic Jñāna Yoga has been carried through to the present day within monastic fraternities founded by Śaṅkara, several of which still exist. His philosophy has found a wide following, its popularised form being the prevailing Hindu world view ('God dwells deep down in the heart of everybody'). Popularised Jñāna Yoga has been made widely known by Ramakrishna's pupil Vivekananda (1863-1902), who brought it to the West.[35]

The Buddhist path of wisdom

The equivalent of Jñāna Yoga in Buddhism is the meditational technique on *śūnyatā* (emptiness) employed by both the major Mahāyāna schools, Mādhyamaka (the middle way) founded by Nāgārjuna (2nd century CE) and Vijñāvāda (consciousness doctrine) known also as Yogācara (way of Yoga) started by Asaṅga and Vasubandhu (4th century CE). However, it became combined with the *bodhisattva* doctrine so that the Yoga path in Mahāyāna Buddhism turned into a rather grandiose undertaking involving a vow to bring about the deliverance of all beings 'down to the last blade of grass'. The motivation for it is the same as the Buddha had for undertaking his mission, namely boundless compassion for the suffering of beings

However, it can be effective only if it is guided by perfect wisdom (*prajñāpāramitā*) for whose development *śūnyatā* meditation is essential. It is a development which goes beyond the conception of Pure Yoga which is an individual path.{36}

Karma Yoga

As has been pointed out above, Karma Yoga would appear to have been an innovation specific to the BhG. When extolling Karma Yoga, the BhG omits from the spiritual path to salvation the traditional requirement of renunciation of a worldly way of living and advocates full participation in active life. That includes fulfilment of one's duties to family, ancestors, caste, clan and king or state, all performed in a spirit of selfless or disinterested action without expecting any reward. This method is a total contrast in comparison with Jñāna Yoga. Jñāna Yoga requires renunciation of action altogether, whereas Karma Yoga as the way of action requires only renunciation of 'fruits of action'. Both methods are regarded as leading to salvation, but of the two, the way of action is proclaimed to be the better one (BhG V, 2). Descriptions and hints on how to practise Karma Yoga are scattered throughout the whole of the BhG. The gist is that actions should be performed in the line of one's duty while being mentally completely detached. That is how one reaches the highest goal (BhG III,19).

If one's duty (*kāryaṇ karma* — 'acts which are to be done') involves combat in an armed conflict, any hesitation has to be overcome. From the point of view of the Hindu caste system, warriors (*kṣatriyas*) must fulfill their duty, which is to fight and 'disinterestedly' kill their opponents, even if there are relatives and friends among them. That will secure them union with the supreme God Kṛṣṇa. The enormous epic of the Mahābhārata (the great combat of the Bharatas) culminates at the moment before the great fight begins between the assembled armies of two closely related clans — the Bharatas and their opponents the Pāndavas — over a territorial dispute. The BhG is inserted into the epic at this point. The forces of the Bharatas are headed by Arjuna, who is supposed to give the signal for the battle to commence. Kṛṣṇa, in one of his earthly incarnations, is acting as Arjuna's charioteer. But Arjuna trembles and becomes despondent at the sight of all his many relatives and friends facing him on the other side of the battlefield. Rather than slaying them, he would prefer to let himself be slain without raising his arms and he proclaims that he will not fight.

At this moment his charioteer assumes his role as the supreme God Kṛṣṇa and answers him 'with a mocking smile' (*prahasan,* II,10) in the form of a philosophical thesis to the effect that no one ever kills or is killed. That goes for Kṛṣṇa, Arjuna, all those kings and warriors on the battlefield and anyone else. The owner of the body (*dehin*), presumably *ātman* or *jīvātman,* simply passes to another body when the present body is slain (II, 12-13). So without worrying about the oncoming slaughter Arjuna should honour his duty (*svadharma*), for there is nothing higher for a warrior than fighting out of duty (*dharmyād,* II,31). He should pass on all his deeds with all their consequences to Kṛṣṇa, give up all desires and thoughts of owning anything, compose himself and fight (III, 30). In the context of the spiritual interpretation of the BhG, the duty to fight and kill is a disputed point and there are various allegorical interpretations of the battle as taking place in the human mind between conflicting urges, tendencies and aspirations.[37]

Karma Yoga can of course be disassociated from the semi-historical context of the epic and even from the religious context of any personal allegiance to a god, whether in the guise of Kṛṣṇa or Viṣṇu. It can become an independent Yoga technique. This happened to a degree when Karma Yoga was utilised in the system of Yogavāsiṣṭha, as shown above. There are indications that the attempt to establish Karma Yoga as an independent Yoga technique happened tentatively also in modern times and will be further described later.

Bhakti Yoga

As has already been pointed out, Bhakti Yoga is not a systematic path and does not contain any clear methodical Yoga procedures. The chapter of the BhG entitled 'Bhakti Yoga' is rather all-embracing and somewhat vague, only the promise of total liberation being firmly stated. The chapter recommends that the devotee fix his mind on Kṛṣṇa, revere him and have faith in him (XII, 2), restrain his senses and delight in the welfare of all beings (XII, 4). It advises him, in the manner of Karma Yoga, to 'throw down' all his actions (which includes their consequences) on Kṛṣṇa, be devoted to him and adhering to the discipline of Yoga, meditate on him (XII, 6). Kṛṣṇa will then be his deliverer (*samuddhartṛ*) from the sea of the rounds of deaths (*mṛtyusaṃ sírasāragāt,* XII, 7).

But even Kṛṣṇa in this chapter acknowledges that some people are unable to fix their minds totally on him and he recommends to them to adopt any other of the methods of practice ever mentioned by him; they all will also be dear to him. Yet those who have not this impediment, who revere the nectar of righteousness as expressed by him, have faith in him and are utterly devoted to him are the dearest ones to him (XII, 20). In fact, in some other parts of the BhG the aspect of the sole supremacy of Kṛṣṇa over any other personal or impersonal concepts or designations of the ultimate is expressed even more strongly. He is above Brahma, who in the Hindu system presides over periods of world creation and world destruction with people tied to the round of deaths and rebirths. But those who succeed in coming to Kṛṣṇa are forever free from rebirth (VIII,16). He is even above the impersonal principle of *brahman*, the absolute reality, guarantees order and bestows absolute beatitude (XIV, 27). All the BhG requires of the devotee for the sake of his salvation is unshakable faith in Kṛṣṇa and utter devotion or love (*bhakti*) for him. By this devotion he gets to know Kṛṣṇa most intimately, namely by entering him (XVIII, 55). This is more than getting to know him by the meditational 'breakthrough', it suggests total mystical union or penetration.[38]

The Bhakti movement became a widespread phenomenon on the Hindu religious scene. The Bhāgavata Purāṇa expounds it as a way of life and illustrates it in many narratives.

When describing it as a yogic path, it even ascribes to it a knowledge-producing capacity (Matchett, 1993). It even tried to give it a systematic form (Feuerstein, 1975, 20). The concept of *bhakti* as such is not easily defined and it appears to have a wide range of meanings in different traditions (cf. Werner, 1993). As far as our aim of pinpointing what could be seen as 'pure Yoga' is concerned, it does not offer any help.

Tantric Yoga

With the appearance of Tantric Yoga we are entering a new territory in the 'discipline of spiritual practice'. As already hinted, my conception of 'pure Yoga' which I shall try to define in the next chapter is based on two ancient sources: (1) the Buddha's Noble Eightfold Path (*ariya-aṭṭhaṅgika magga*), the source for which is the Suttapiṭaka ('basket of discourses'), the second part of the Buddhist Pāli Canon (partly preserved also in Sanskrit), and (2) the eightfold Yoga path (*aṣṭāṅga yoga*) contained in the collection of texts known as the *Yoga Sūtra*, whose authorship is ascribed to Patañjali. Neither of these sources contains any instructions, descriptions of or even hints at what goes under the designation of Tantric Yoga. Therefore the following outline of Tantric views and practices has in the context of this work only historical value and is not utilised for the purpose of defining 'pure Yoga'.

Tantrism developed from trends in Indian religious and philosophical speculation about the origin, nature and meaning of reality. The main recurring themes in this thought process have been whether reality as we experience it in its manifested form as cosmos ever had a beginning, whether there is a 'beyond', an 'ultimate reality' which we do not normally experience and, if it does exist, whether we can ever get to know it. Tantric Yoga emerged in the course of the search for the way to answer these questions in circles which regarded the hitherto search methods as inadequate or failing.

From the outset it was surised that the ultimate reality would be free from diversity so that it could be understood as 'oneness', as already expressed in the Vedas in the words of the Creation hymn (RV 10,129, see note 4). This would mean that the ultimate reality would be above opposites, while the manifested reality abounds in them, often in the form of polarities. The Creation hymn describes the first polarity at the point of the emergence of manifested reality by the words 'below was self-assertion, above was thrust' which is clearly an early hint with sexual connotation. Subsequently the female/male polarity appeared in ritual symbolism of the Brāhmaṇas and Upaniṣads and further scriptures. The actual symbolical representations of sexual polarity in the form of *liṅga/yoni* statuary in Hindu temples are well known. In contrast to the actual position of women in the Hindu caste system and Indian society in general, the religious and philosophical significance of the 'eternal feminine' is much higher. From about the 4th century CE religious thought, feelings and practices in India became increasingly influenced by the philosophy of Śaktism or the role of the feminine principle in the cosmic scheme expressed in its spiritual discipline (*sādhanā*) aiming at a final solution of the riddle of existence. It led to the exclusive symbolical representations of this philosophical and eschatological topic by the effigy (*mūrti*) combining the male and female principles. In the Hindu tradition the male principle is represented by a god as the ruler of the world, usually Śiva, and the female principle in the form of his female consort, his cosmic power (*śakti*), originally Umā, but usually Pārvatī, in close sexual embrace (*mithuna mūrti*). In Tantric Buddhism or Vajrayāna (the diamond vehicle) in India the male principle came to be represented mainly by the cosmic Buddha and the female principle by Prajñāparamitā, his transcendental wisdom in feminine form, sculpted or painted in close embrace.

Although elements of Tantric beliefs and practices existed long before Buddhism, the earliest sources describing elaborate techniques of Tantric Yoga are Buddhist. Many, however, have been lost in India and are known only from Tibetan translations. Tibet adopted Indian Vajrayāna and Tantric Buddhism wholesale and elaborated it further. The twin effigy of male and female 'deities' is referred to in Tibet as *yab yum* and most rituals and practices associated with it are Tantric.

There is a certain connection between the ancient Vrātya movement and Buddhism and it may well be that some of the Vrātya sexual practices mentioned in an earlier chapter survived and went on developing. After the inception of Mahāyāna and the proliferation of sectarianism they may have penetrated into the Buddhist movement. This would have been helped by the simultaneous growth of Hindu Śaktism. Another influence on both the Buddhist and Hindu Tantric tradition was exercised also by the primitive practices of a sexual nature in the lower classes, perhaps inherited from the pre-Āryan cult of phallus-worshippers referred to as such in the Ṛg Veda; some influence may have come from cultures of jungle tribes as they were being absorbed into the all-embracing Hindu system, while some other Tantric features point back to Harappan times.

The proclaimed objective of Tantric practice is the same as the practice of any other yogic school, namely the experience of the ultimate reality. As the ultimate reality viewed as oneness is above the world's manifoldness and opposites and these are best epitomized in sexual polarity, Tantric methods seek the experience of transcendental unity by attempting to integrate the two poles of the feminine and masculine within the individual. This is in the first place a spiritual process in the practitioner's mind, but the importance of involving the body in the process is, in a way, anticipated in the claim that an accomplished yogi can choose to conquer death and become virtually immortal, which would involve total transformation of his material body. There is an echo of this view in early Buddhism expressed in the claim that the Buddha could have chosen to extend the span of his life to last till the end of the current world period (*Mahāparinibbāna Sutta*, DN 16), which would hardly happen in his aged and aching body. The *sutta* actually says at one point that the Buddha suppressed his illness caused by poisoning, thus extending his life for a short time. He then died at the age of 80, at a time of his choice.

Tantric Yoga developed parallel practices of integrating polarity and reaching transcendental unity in the so-called 'right-hand' (*dakṣinācāra*) and 'left-hand' (*vāmācāra*) varieties, both supposedly leading to the possibility of achieving virtual immortality. The righthand variety is described as using purely mental means. Its method of meditation involves visualisation of the image of a yogi and a yoginī in sexual embrace. The practitioner eventually identifies himself internally with the supposed experience of the blissful unification which the image symbolises whereupon the image is dissolved. The practitioner is then left with an experience of transcendental unity which remains with him while he carries on living in the world.

Tibetan Tantric practice would start with viewing and concentrating on one of the numerous *yab yum* effigies before passing over to mental visualisation by gradual 'interiorisation'. This practice is based on the assumption — accepted also by some trends in modern psychology — that each individual contains both female and male characteristics with one of them prevailing, which determines the gender of an individual's outward appearance.

The left-hand variety requires meditation in motionless sexual congress (*maithuna*) of the male yogi with a female partner or yoginī with full penetration but without culmination, i.e. without the discharge of semen which is supposedly absorbed. The meditation then proceeds mentally in a similar way as the right-hand practice.

Some sources maintain that the final goal can be achieved in the course of strict practice of Tantric Yoga even within one lifetime, but only under the guidance of an enlightened *guru*, although it is admitted that few may succeed. Both varieties of Tantric Yoga would be accessible only to aspirants who are already quite experienced in other types of Yoga, in the techniques of concentration and meditation. But there is, of course, no reason for individuals not to try to meditate, using Tantric visualisation without a *guru*, not expecting early results. That goes equally for couples who feel inclined to meditate in *maithuna* positions.

Traditionally the training in Tantric Yoga takes place in groups. It may be a continuous process in a monastery belonging to a Tantric lineage of Tibetan Buddhism or in retreats which a monastery may regularly organise even for its lay followers. It is described in some sources as proceeding in four stages which can be summarised as follows:

(1) Kriyā Yoga - During this stage the monk or aspirant regularly takes part in a public Tantric ritual, i.e. in an open *pūjā* whose proceedings he gradually memorises. It involves *japa* meditation on special *mantras* known as *dhāraṇīs* and

precisely defined ritual actions which symbolise the path to enlightenment. In the rest of his time dedicated to spiritual endeavour he spends long periods studying relevant texts. He keeps increasing the periods dedicated to his solitary meditations and adheres to strict observance of ethical precepts and virtues. He may decide to perform the open *pūjā* for outside bodies such as Buddhist societies or groups or for interested individuals or for himself in private. No day of his should pass without performing or being present at the performance of a *pūjā*.

(2) Caryā Yoga - It starts for the aspirant with his ceremonial initiation (*abhiśeka*) into the lineage after the performance of the esoteric variety of the ritual *pūjā* in the monastery by its abbot or in a retreat by an experienced member of the lineage. The initiate now has to learn the esoteric *pūjā* and perform it daily for himself in a meditative frame of mind instead of the open *pūjā*.

(3) Mahā Yoga - This is the technique which leads to the 'interiorisation' of the ritual *pujā*. It would have been preceded by preparatory training in 'visualisation' during daily meditational sessions. When mastered, no actual *pūjā* need be performed by the initiate any longer, except when he is entrusted with performing one in the monastic sessions, in retreats or in public gatherings, always of course selecting the correct one for the occasion.

(4) Anuttarā Yoga -. This is the last stage of the Tantric Yoga practice which is supposed to lead to the final integration of the male and female constituents of the initiate's personality. He now has to decide whether he will practise the 'right-hand' (*dakṣinācāra*) or 'left-hand' (*vāmācāra*) variety of the Tantric path. He has undergone sufficient training in visualisation during earlier meditational sessions involving the previous stage, during which he learnt to visualise the esoteric *pūjā*. If he now decides to practise the right-hand variety of Tantric Yoga, he will choose a

mithuna mūrti, an effigy of a male figure, usually sitting in the lotus position, in close embrace with a female consort which implies penetration. The sexual union of the two figures represents full integration of opposites, pointing to the timeless and spaceless beyond.

In Hindu tradition the male figure is a deity representing God as the ruler of the world and his female consort is his cosmic power (*śakti*). Hindu effigies of this kind most often portray Śiva as the supreme deity, but they are relatively rare and bear Buddhist influence so that often an uncertainty may arise as to the affiliation. Even rarer are effigies of Viṣṇu with his *śakti* (a remarkable specimen represents his form as Vaikunthi). Other effigies, looking very similar, have names such as Padmasambhava or Jambhala, pointing to the Tantric period in Indian Buddhism. Much more numerous are the Tibetan *yab yum* effigies, usually very elaborate with names pointing to particular lineages. One rarely finds a plain effigy with no obvious affiliation, which is therefore more suitable for visualisation by uncommitted practitioners.

The initiate now visualises his chosen effigy in daily extended meditation sessions and places it within himself until it becomes fully interiorised. He is then supposed to achieve total unification with it and at this point the interiorised image of the effigy dissolves, the male and female elements of the initiate's personality merge and he becomes an integrated personality.

It is not entirely clear whether this achievement is meant to be the final liberation (*mokṣa*) equivalent to the Buddhist *nirvāṇa*, Jain *kaivalya* and Vedāntic *sat-cit-ānanda*, but if not, it certainly would be on the threshold of it. The task is formidable so that speedy achievement might be realistic only in the case of full-time commitment in a monastery or as a hermit. There is a tradition in Tibetan Buddhism of isolated retreats in mountain caves or in sealed off cells with only a small opening for handing in food. A lay follower would aim at reaching at least a situation in which his stage of progress would be deeply ingrained in his subconscious so that he could expect to resume his practice in his next life from the point he had reached in the present one.

The initiate who chooses the left-hand practice of Anuttara Yoga will have found, or has been for some time in some way associated with, a female practitioner who would, ideally, be experienced in Yoga and from now on their daily meditation sessions will proceed in the position of the ritual union or *maithuna.* Any further procedure is not clear for lack of sources or because of their cryptic language. The practitioners have to rely on the instructions of a *guru* or, if the practice is undertaken independently, it would be a matter of experimentation. What is certain is that if during a meditation session the initiate experiences discharge of semen, the session has to be regarded as unsuccessful and should be discontinued for the day. The same applies if the yoginī experiences an orgasm. We can only assume that the independently practising couple would use a plain effigy. If they were so inclined they could look upon the effigy as representing a cosmic Buddha and Prajñāpāramitā, his transcendental wisdom. They would by then be capable of placing it inside themselves (to interiorise it) to the point of identifying themselves with it, thereby completing the process of total integration of the male and female element within the personality of each one of them and raising their unified consciousness on to a higher plane.

The above survey outlines only one of the Tantric spiritual paths (*sādhanā*). The enormous literature about the sub ject describes a large number of its varieties, often difficult if not impossible to study because of the cryptic or enigmatic and even deliberately misleading language. Therefore a controversy exists among followers as well as scholars about the nature of those sources which introduce obscene features and practices into their scheme, while asserting that their path is genuine and even superior to all other paths. There is no doubt that the introduction of sexuality into religious and spiritual practices led some individuals and groups astray, with resulting corruption in the past centuries up to the present time.[39]

When a Tantric disciple qualifies for a higher stage he usually continues the lower practice as well in periods of relaxation, although he does not have to. He may sometimes officiate at the esoteric *pūjā* on the lower stages for fellow practitioners in retreats or the public *pūjā* in open gatherings. The *pūjā*s make great use of *mudrās*, i.e symbolical hand gestures, and are usually performed in front of an altar which displays an effigy, for example of a Buddha, or a picture of one (Tibetan *thangkas* often serve for this purpose) and objects which have symbolical significance. On rare occasions, usually only in communities following a Tibetan Buddhist tradition, the *pūjā*s are performed inside *maṇḍalas* ('circles'), which are complicated diagrams made from sands of different colours, or assembled from statues of esoteric 'deities', symbolically representing the universe as well as the human mind. In Hindu tradition simpler diagrams, called *yantra*, are also in use.[40]

The Yogas described below have, at least historically, close links to Tantrism and many varieties of Tantra Yoga make use of them. But they can also be practised as independent disciplines without being burdened by sexual associations.

Haṭha Yoga

It is not known whether a system of physical Yoga training existed in the early days of forest Yoga schools or even at the time when the system of Classical Yoga of Patañjali was being formed. The requirement of *āsana* in *aṣṭāṅga yoga* may not have gone beyond a limited number of steady sitting postures for the practice of breathing exercises and meditation.

The likelihood is that Haṭha Yoga developed in connection with Tantric Yoga with its aim of final liberation within one lifetime and that its primary purpose was securing perfect bodily and mental health and long life. The earnestly pursued Tantric path required long years of study and preparation, and the time for the Anuttarā Yoga practice would have come very late in an aspirant's life. Haṭha Yoga was to provide the way to preserve the initiate's bodily and mental potencies to a very advanced age or even, it is maintained in some sources, to transform his body so as to make it virtually everlasting.

The main and oldest preserved textbook of *haṭhayoga* is the *Haṭhapradīpikā* by Svātmārāma (cca 15th century CE). Modern editions of the work usually bear the title *Haṭhayogapradīpikā* and that is how modern writers on Yoga usually refer to it (e.g. Feuerstein, 1990, 136; White, 2012, 392), but as editors of Svātmārāma's *Haṭhapradīpikā* mention in their Preface (1970, p.3), *Haṭhayogapradīpikā* 'is not the title given to this work in any of the manuscripts consulted by us'. Besides, Svātmārāma himself refers to his work as *Haṭhapradīpikā* (I.3).

Basically, Svātmārāma concentrates on the practice of *haṭhayoga,* although he frequently branches off to explain its effects on higher levels, particularly on the subtle body; he took over the details about the subtle body from *Gorakṣa Saṁhitā* (see below). Svātmārāma mentions in his *Haṭhapradīpikā* eighty-four *āsanas,* but describes less than three dozen, some of them in great detail. "After becoming well-versed in (a set of) *āsanas* the yogi, with (his senses under) control and eating moderate agreeable food, should practise *prāṇāyāma* (breathing techniques) as advised by the guru" (Svātmārāma II.1. p. 35). This would lead to physical purification of the subtle body and its ducts (*nāḍis*) through which flows *prāṇa* (the life force). This would make the yogi fit for advanced meditation and have an effect, in the long run, on the mysterious 'serpent power' (*kuṇḍalinī*), lying coiled at the base of the spine in the subtle body. The purification of the body by *haṭhayoga* is a preparation for an eightfold spiritual path, which he calls *rāja*, 'royal' (cf. White 2012, 357). This is what Svātmārāma states right at the beginning of his work (I.2. p.2); he deals with Rāja Yoga more extensively in the fourth chapter, but his Rāja Yoga is not identical with the *aṣṭāṅga yoga* of Patañjali whom he does not even mention. For example, his Rāja Yoga does not contain *yamas* and *niyamas* in its eightfold scheme. Svātmārāma regards these ethical limbs as prerequisites but gives great prominence to *ahiṁsā* and regards a precisely regulated diet as highly important. There are several passages in the *Haṭhapradīpikā* dealing with the basics of meditation — a suitable place, posture, focus of the eyes etc. — intermingled with hints about the effects of *prāṇāyāma* on the subtle body and its ducts (*nādis*) and on the spiritual centres (*cakras*) as they are being awakened in advanced practice by the rising *kuṇḍalinī*. Several times the text stresses that for successful progress guidance by an accomplished *guru* is essential.

The term Rāja Yoga caught on in modern times even for Patañjali's eightfold scheme in the wake of Vivekananda's writings, but it is used mostly in popular books, while scholarly works prefer the designation Classical Yoga. Svātmārāma obviously based his *Haṭhapradīpikā* on previous works, mainly on the *Gorakṣa Saṁhitā* and *Gorakṣaśataka*, both by the presumed founder of the system, Gorakṣanātha (perhaps 14th century CE, although dates as early as the 11th or 10th century are also suggested). The *Gorakṣa Saṁhitā*, known also as the *Gorakṣa Paddhatti*, describes a sixfold Yoga path, presents a detailed anatomy of the subtle body which was taken over from it by Svātmārāma, gives advice on arousing the *kuṇḍalinī* and recommends *japa* on the sacred syllable *om*. The *Gorakṣaśataka* is aimed at those who renounce worldly life and are aiming straight for liberation. The recommended method is mind control through *prāṇāyāma* while sitting in the lotus position (*padmāsana*) or its easier variety known as *sukhāsana*, although this text calls it *vajrāsana* (which in later sources is used for the position in which one sits on one's heels). This is followed by a description of two techniques for arousing the *kuṇḍalinī* (Mallinson, 2012).

Svātmārāma mentions that Gorakṣanātha's *guru* was Matsyendranātha, which would be important for dating him, but all references to Matsyendra in diverse sources are of a mythological character. The addition of *nātha* to some names suggests but does not necessarily guarantee a link to esoteric and controversial as well as obscure practices 'against the current' (*ujāna sādhanā*) of a movement sometimes called the Nāth Cult or 'nāthism'. It is not of help for establishing pure Yoga practice and therefore I do not deal with it (cf. Eliade, 1969, 270; Dasgupta, Sashibhushan, 1969, 191-255). Matsyendra's name comes from a mythological incident in which he assumed the form of a fish and in this guise secretly listened to Śiva explaining to his consort Durgā a secret doctrine about how to gain immortality, part of which was *haṭhayoga* (Eliade, 1969, 270). Matsyendra is regarded as the first human teacher of *haṭhayoga*, but there is no text extant under his name.

Of later works two are worth mentioning. The *Śiva Samhitā* is by an unknown author who was obviously an adherent of the non-dual philosophy of Advaita Vedānta and is variously dated between the 15th and 17th centuries. He deals with *āsanas*, *prāṇāyāma* and *mudrās*, with the anatomy of the subtle body and with some other esoteric practices, yet suggests that even householders and women can make substantial progress on this esoteric path. However, by implication eventual renunciation is an unavoidable condition of the final achievement. The *Gheranda Samhitā* (late 17th century) is written in the form of a dialogue between the Yogi Gheranda, of whom nothing is known, and a disciple of his named Canda Kāpāli. It describes a number of methods of purification, thirty-two *āsanas* and twenty-five *mudrās*. [41]

Kuṇḍalinī Yoga

Once it had been constituted as a system, Haṭha Yoga assumed a life of its own and became another path to the final goal using the subtle body as the vehicle. This esoteric path is sometimes called Kuṇḍalinī Yoga. It would appear that this is an independent path parallel to Tantra Yoga, although there may be some overlaps. The 'physiology' of the subtle body contains a system of channels (*nāḍīs*) which penetrate the whole subtle body and conduct the prāṇic and spiritual energy, and it further describes special centres called *cakras* (wheels) as seats of mental and supramental faculties normally dormant in ordinary people. There are supposedly six main *cakras* placed along the main *nāḍī* called *susumṇā*, which occupies the same space in the subtle body as does the spine in the gross body. At its base is the lowest *cakra*. There sleeps *kuṇḍalinī* ('the coiled one'), man's spiritual energy. When awakened by special *āsanas*, called in this context *mudrās*, and by special *prāṇāyāma* exercises, in advanced stages combined with *maithuna* (which presumably would involve retention or reabsorption of semen), *kuṇḍalinī* rises through the *susumṇā*, activating *cakras* and their dormant psychic faculties on the way. When *kuṇḍalinī* reaches the final point at the top of the skull known as *sahasrāra padma* (thousand-petalled lotus, sometimes wrongly regarded as the seventh *cakra*), which is the gate to enlightenment, the final goal has been achieved.[42]

VIII. Yoga in the Modern World

The Beginnings

In medieval India popular involvement in the Bhakti movement and Tantrism reached its climax and Yoga in various esoteric forms played a substantial part in both of them. Haṭha Yoga developed its own occult tradition with sectarian movements derived from the activities of famous teachers such as Gorakhnath (the vernacular form of Goraksanātha) and Matsyendranath (Matsyendranātha), both of whom became mythical figures together with other so-called *siddhas* or perfect masters, eighty-four in number, rumoured to be able to demonstrate miraculous powers (*siddhis*).

The proliferation of yogic sects, some given to rather strange practices, and the spread of undisciplined left-hand Tantrism, led to the deterioration and eventual decline of the Yoga movement. Different varieties of Yoga continued, however, in some monastic centres and *āśrams* and there was never a shortage of individual truth-seekers, hermits and wanderers of the ancient type, who kept the tradition alive by passing on their knowledge and discipline to a few disciples.

The revival of public interest in Yoga in India came about in the nineteenth century mainly with the appearance of the world-famous Bengali saint Ramakrishna, with the result that Yoga aroused interest also in the West.

Ramakrishna was born in a Bengali family of Brahmin caste. He showed signs of spirituality early in his life, often achieving spontaneous ecstasy, but he also studied and liked to discuss sacred texts of Hinduism. As an adult he was appointed priest in a temple dedicated to the goddess Kālī in Dakṣiṇeśvar near Calcutta, as it then was. Here he became a devout worshipper of Kālī, who became his chosen deity (*iṣṭa devatā*). He called her the Divine Mother and was rumoured to have reached the summit of the path of Bhakti in union with her. From his studies he became acquainted with the concept of the impersonal divine and felt that he must come to terms with it by experience. At this point a wandering master of the Advaita Vedānta school, by the name of Tota Puri, approached him and introduced him to the path of Jñāna Yoga which he supposedly accomplished by reaching *nirvikalpa samādhi* in one day. Next he obtained initiation into Muslim mysticism and had visions of Mohammed followed by an experience of universal oneness. Soon he also had a vision of the Madonna with Jesus and then of Christ. His message then was that there is an essential oneness of all religious traditions.

Much of the Yoga movement is influenced by this view to the present day. This, of course, is contradicted when we compare the teachings of various religions and their sects which widely differ and frequently wage wars over them. But it may be that the yogic and mystical practices when pursued by individuals even within their denominations may bring them to the threshold of the absolute or final truth or even to its realisation, if they manage to leave behind any verbal (conceptual), metaphorical or symbolical designation of it. There is no way of knowing for sure whether Ramakrishna reached the absolutely final goal beyond his specific allegiance to his chosen deity, or just its threshold.

After his lofty experiences of the oneness of all religions Ramakrishna returned to his office as Kālī's priest and continued performing appropriate rituals in her temple.

This need not be regarded as contradicting his spiritual achievements. He would hardly have found rituals necessary for his own spiritual needs, but they were a part of his daily routine duties because he kept his position as priest instead of becoming a homeless wanderer. Besides, an accomplished or spiritually advanced person is supposed to perform every action with full awareness or in a meditative frame of mind. Ritual celebrated in this way may have profound influence on the congregation.

As Ramakrishna's fame grew, visitors of all ranks flocked to him. He was probably the first Indian master to attract also Western visitors and followers. His nearest pupil was Vivekananda (1863-1902), whose family name was Narendranath Datta; he was a graduate of Calcutta University and was well-read in Indian and Western philosophy which led him to become sceptical about religious teachings and the existence of God. He was advised by one of his College teachers to visit Ramakrishna, which proved a turning point in his life at the age of 18. The spiritual atmosphere around Ramakrishna, who immediately recognised in him a born yogi, won him over. There is a story, which may be apocryphal, that Ramakrishna touched Vivekananda with his foot whereupon Vivekananda experienced a brief ecstasy. He then visited Ramakrishna almost daily and became the foremost figure among a group of young people, also deeply impressed by Ramakrishna, who gradually implanted in their minds the idea of renouncing worldly life and becoming *saṅnyāsīs* as the best way of life aiming for the final realisation of the truth. Ramakrishna's somewhat unexpected death made them see the necessity of this step, so they took formal vows and adopted new names. It was at this time that Narendranath Datta took the name Vivekananda. The new community settled in a derelict house in Baranagar which became their monastery and was named by them Ramakrishna Math.

Later Vivekananda spent some time in solitude in the Himalayan mountains and then travelled for a few years the length and breadth of India spreading Ramakrishna's message. These activities made him widely known and he gained many followers and supporters.

The way West

The crucial event which spread Yoga worldwide was the 'Parliament of Religions' in Chicago in 1893. It was organised during the World's Columbian Exposition, a large trade fair celebrating the four-hundredth anniversary of the discovery of America by Christopher Columbus. The instigator of the Parliament of Religions was Charles Carroll Bonney, a member of the Swedenborgian church. Vivekananda was urged to attend the Parliament to represent Hinduism, with some financial assistance from Ajit Singh, the Rāja of Khetri. His speeches in the Parliament were hugely successful and resulted in lecture tours in the USA and in his giving classes and seminars in Yoga and Vedāntic philosophy, which led to the founding of Vedāntic Centres in the USA and gradually also in European countries. From the USA he twice visited England where he gained a number of pupils and he briefly stayed also in France and Germany, meeting many admirers as well as prominent scholars. He returned to India a national hero after four years of travel. In 1897 he founded the Ramakrishna Mission with a social programme and later two new monasteries, one near Almora and the other in Madras. His many lecture tours led to the foundation of numerous Vedāntic Centres all over India.

In the years 1899-1900 Vivekananda spent eighteen months on a return visit to the USA, England and Paris. He visited also Istanbul, Athens and Egypt. Back home he continued in his feverish activities which contributed to his failing health and he died on 4 July 1902. He was certainly a great Jñāna Yogi, but he had an unquestioned belief in the philosophy of Advaita Vedānta, which is in effect a conceptual anticipation of the final goal prior to realising it. Advaita Vedānta teaches, as already explained, the illusoriness of the world, the sole existence of *brahman* and also the essential unity of all beings whose common inner self is *ātman*, which is supposed to be identical with *brahman*. With his activities in the West Vivekananda certainly started the trend of world-wide popularity of Yoga, but by his style of presentation he was responsible also for the fact that it came to be and in many quarters still is regarded as a kind of 'Eastern philosophy' or Hindu religion hostile to Christianity and irreconcilable with modern science.

There was a lull after Vivekananda's untimely death, but Yoga soon started catching up. One early revivalist of its popularity was Hari Prasad Shastri (1882-1956) a Sanskrit scholar well-versed also in English literature, history and philosophy, who was steeped in Advaita Vedānta. At the instigation of his spiritual teacher, he came to London in 1929 to teach Vedāntic philosophy and meditation. In 1933 he founded Shanti Sadan, the Centre of 'Adhyatma Yoga' (Yoga of Self-Knowledge). The Centre is still active (cf. Shastri, 1950).

Another early revivalist was Paramahansa Yogananda (1893-1952), born Mukunda Lal Ghosh in Gorakhpur, Uttar Pradesh, His Guru was Swami Yukteswar Giri whom he met in 1910, at the age of 17. In a year or two Yukteswar produced in him an experience of a kind of 'cosmic consciousness' and in 1915 he gave him an initiation as a Svāmi after he gained a university degree. He was also initiated into the practice of an esoteric version of Kriya Yoga. His *guru* wanted him to take on responsibility for educating 'a much larger family' than the one he would have produced if he became a householder. He was enabled to found a school on a high school level. But in 1920, he was sent to the United States as India's delegate to the International Congress of Religious Liberals convening in Boston. Prior to that he had, according to his autobiography, a vision of a number of faces of

American people, some of whom he later met. He gave a successful lecture on board ship and his lecture in the Congress on 'The Science of Religion' was well received. He then founded the Self-Realization Fellowship (SRF) in Los Angeles to disseminate worldwide his teachings on India's ancient practices and philosophy of Yoga and its tradition of meditation and embarked on several cross-continental speaking tours. In 1935 he returned to India and it was then that his *guru* Yuktesvar gave him the title of Paramahansa, 'the supreme swan'. In 1936 he returned to America, stopping in London for sight-seeing and lectures and Yoga classes.

Paramahansa Yogananda died on 7 March 1952 in Los Angeles after finishing a talk at a banquet for the visiting Indian Ambassador to the US. His Self-Realization Fellowship and Self-Realization Fellowship Order have branches in several countries and bestow initiations and guidance in their esoteric Kriya Yoga exclusively to their members (Yogananda, 1998).

But it was mainly Haṭha Yoga which at the time fired the imagination of a great many people in the West. Perhaps the first Haṭha Yoga teacher from India to settle in the West was Yesudian, who was active in the 1930s in Hungary and from the 1940s in Switzerland. The first European Haṭha Yoga teacher was probably Boris Sacharow, who was already teaching it in the 1920s in Germany (see below). But it was probably Paul Brunton (1898-1981) who was most responsible for making Yoga and 'Eastern wisdom' popular in the 1930s and who made famous a few Indian teachers, particularly Ramaṇa Maharṣi.

Three 'Spiritual Giants' of the Twentieth Century

1. Ramaṇa (1879 - 1950)

Ramaṇa Maharṣi of Arunachala at Tiruvannamalai in South India was born Venkataraman Iyer of a Brahmin family in Tiruchizhi, Tamil Nadu, but attended an English Middle School and the American Mission High School in Madurai, where he stayed with his uncle. He also studied the lives of 63 Tamil Śaivite saints called Nayanars, famous for their realisation of the *bhakti* path, and frequently visited the impressive Meenakshi (Mīnakṣī) temple in Madurai. There was nothing exceptional about him until one day at the age of 16 he suddenly experienced a strong fear of death. He expected to die instantly and so lay down and waited to see what would happen. His senses stopped registering and his body became rigid, but his selfawareness remained undiminished. It then occurred to him that, while he was watching his body, he himself was not the body. His awareness of himself, which we refer to as 'I', was entirely separate from his body and he felt that it could not be affected by its death. The 'I am' or self-awareness was always here and now. His fear of death disappeared and he was ready to pass away, but death did not come. Gradually his senses resumed their function and his body relaxed. But his 'I am' or self-awareness was now lifted in him to the level of illumination and stayed with him uninterruptedly.

First he tried to carry on living and attending school as before, but the lessons had lost meaning for him, and he lacked any motivation for them. So after several weeks he left his uncle's home and headed for Tiruvannamalai, where there was a large temple at the foot of the sacred mountain Arunachala. He spent a few weeks in the thousand-pillared hall of the temple, then in other parts of it and eventually in an underground vault, sitting absorbed in deep meditation. He completely neglected his bodily needs and was probably unaware of the bites of insects and vermin from which his body suffered. A local Svāmi who became impressed by him brought him out of the vault and looked after him. When Ramaṇa had somewhat recovered, he moved a few times to other temples in the vicinity. Another Svāmi became so impressed by him that he attached himself to Ramaṇa as his permanent attendant. People then started taking notice of him and bringing him necessities of life. After several years, in 1898, he was traced by his family, but he did not communicate with them meaningfully, not even when his mother came and tried to persuade him to return home. A year later he moved to the foot of Arunachala where he was visited by many people who just came to have a *darśan* of the famous saint. Here he gave the first written answer to a visitor who put to him several written questions, among them how one can get to know one's true identity. Ramaṇa's written answers formed the gist of what became known as his method of self-inquiry based on the question 'Who am I?'

By then he was styled Bhagavān Śrī Ramaṇa Maharśi. In 1916 his mother and younger brother joined him and became renunciants. An *āśram* had already been built around Ramaṇa with a kitchen where his mother did the cooking. Ramaṇa gave his mother personal guidance and when she died in 1922, it was in his arms. She was buried near the foot of the mountain and Ramaṇa settled nearby in a small hut. A new *āśram* was started there around him and it gradually expanded into a large complex which is now known as 'Ramanasramam'. Ramaṇa's personality was very charismatic and many visitors felt his influence directly while he remained silent and they forgot any questions which they had intended to put to him. He did not accept disciples and never behaved as a *guru* or said anything to that effect. He had never read any Hindu scriptures and got to know some ideas contained in the Bhagavad Gītā, the Upaniṣads or Śaṅkara's works which expounded Advaita Vedānta and the *māyā* doctrine, and other works only from what visitors told him, which would hardly have been accurate. He never placed himself within any tradition or school of thought or practice. When his written answers to some questioning visitors were published by them and interpreted as, for example, Vedāntic teaching, that was an imposition. There is still disagreement and uncertainty as to how his description of Self-realisation should be understood. He expresses it first by the term *aham sphuraṇa*, 'pulsating I' or 'I-I', which is supposed to mean Self-realisation beyond thought, but it is unstable. When one persists with the method 'Who am I?', no longer by thinking it but as an attitude, the pulsating *aham sphuraṇa* subsides and the final and permanent stage of illuminating Self-realisation is attained. Nothing should be added to this attempt at explaining what Ramaṇa meant and his method should not be placed into any traditional context, not even by asking 'Isn't it a remarkable version of Jñāna Yoga?'[43]

More and more visitors flocked to the new *āśram*, just to experience Ramaṇa's presence or ask him questions. They included two former Presidents of India, Rajendra Prasad and Sarvapalli Radhakrishnan, and numerous artists, writers and academics. Inevitably, he was eventually discovered also for the West. It was Paul Brunton who played a leading role in this with his book *A Search in Secret India* (1934). His first visit to the *āśram* took place in 1931. By then Ramaṇ a was answering questions orally in Tamil which were then translated into English, the *lingua franca* used by educated Indians. He also had learned some English and could formulate short sentences. Brunton was drawn to mystical and occult pursuits from his early years, got briefly involved with the Theosophical Society and practised some kind of meditation method with encouraging results. But everything pointed to the East and in 1930 he travelled to India and met a number of yogis. He was granted an audience with South India's Śaṅkarācārya (head of one of the five Vedāntic centres founded in the wake of Śaṇkara's activities) who advised him, as did one of the yogis he was associating with, to see Ramaṇa. When Brunton faced him, all his prepared questions vanished from his mind. Subsequently there was an opportunity for questions and answers, but the outcome was always a hint that all will become clear if the method of asking 'Who am I?' is pursued till the end. After several weeks Brunton left and continued his travels and meetings with other yogis and exceptional people, but in the end he was drawn back to Arunachala, despite feeling an approaching illness. He then described in his book the many sessions of silent communication which took place between himself and Ramaṇa, eventually culminating in his temporarily experiencing the 'true Self'.

Brunton's book made him well known not only in the west, but also in India, which facilitated his subsequent longer stays in the country during which he wrote several other books. He visited Ramaṇa at least twice in subsequent years but did not achieve more durable experiences of the 'true Self'. He began to suspect that Ramaṇa's method of self-inquiry based on the question 'Who am I?' led only to calmness and a feeling of having reached the truth, but did not generate an irrefutable knowledge of truth. One had to ask further questions, such as: 'What is the meaning of the world?' 'What is the meaning of this world-experience?' and 'What is the object of all existence?' While staying in a secluded place as a guest of the Mahārāja of Mysore, he acquired a copy of the Māṇḍūkya Upaniṣad with Gauḍapāda's Kārikā which was a revelation to him and resulted in his formulation of the philosophy of 'mentalism' to be realised by Jñāna Yoga, which he translated as the 'Yoga of philosophical discernment'. It was initially a purely intellectual and rational procedure, he maintained, but became in the end 'super-mystical'. Ramaṇa's way was not really Yoga, but the path of a mystic. It was necessary to transcend it (Brunton, 1941 & 1943).

Gauḍapāda's Kārikā has been well known to Indology since about the middle of the nineteenth century and was translated into German by Deussen (1897, 573-604). Gauḍapāda lived two generations before Śaṇkara and was the teacher of Śaṅkara's teacher Govinda. Gauḍapāda's Kārikā expounds all the ingredients which form the gist of Śaṅkara's philosophical system of Advaita Vedānta — the non-reality or illusoriness (*māyā*) of the external world and the essential unity of *brahman* and *ātman*. Brunton fell into the trap of expounding at great length the nature of the final realisation of the truth ahead of reaching it. He misunderstood Ramaṇa's silence about it which, in fact, resembled the Buddha's 'noble silence' about the nature of *nirvāṇa*. But again, there is no way of telling with certainty whether Ramaṇa did reach the Absolute or was just 'a step' away from it. The Buddha who, prior to his enlightenment, grew up and was educated within the religious system of Brāhmanism abandoned all its traditional features like worship of images, ritual and prayer. Ramaṇa kept some of them — visiting the temple and showing reverence to the *liṅga* as the symbol of Śiva, although he did say that God was a 'formless being'. He also adopted the tradition of Hindu *saṅnyasis* to sit and rest on a tiger skin.

2. Aurobindo (1872-1950)

Aurobindo Acroyd Ghosh was the first modern advocate of Integral Yoga in which he tried to combine the fragmented methods of specialised Yoga practices into a holistic lifestyle with an outlook geared towards helping to spiritualise the whole world. He was born in Calcutta as the youngest of three brothers. His father was a surgeon who had studied in England and envisaged for his youngest son a career in the Indian civil service. So he sent him to England for education at the age of seven. Aurobindo eventually achieved first class in the Classical Tripos Part I in Cambridge, but did not take his degree because he did not wish to become a civil servant. On his return to India, he worked for a time for the Mahārāja of Baroda in the state administration and then as the Principal of Baroda College. But he was unhappy about the colonial status of India and became involved in a secret revolutionary movement which trained him in combat, shooting and assembling and testing home-made bombs. He accepted the position of editor of *Bande Mātaram*, a revolutionary magazine, but at the same time became interested in Yoga. He did not know much about Classical Yoga, but probably knew some of the subsequent forms of Yoga such as Haṭha Yoga which promised to enhance one's strength and vigour. He would need these qualities while engaging in revolutionary activities. In 1904 he started with *prāṇāyāma* and practised it for five hours a day. Soon he noticed that it led to heightened energy and even higher mental efficiency. Wishing to progress further, he turned to a *guru* who introduced him to meditation and he was able quite quickly to control his mind and keep it free from any intruding thoughts. As he later wrote in his autobiography, by December 1907 he had reached a state of inner stillness which remained with him ever after. His *guru* then told him that he had progressed much further in his achievements than could have been anticipated and that he himself could not teach him anything more. He advised him to listen to and follow the *guru* within himself. Aurobindo's inner experience changed his outlook so that the external world and its affairs now seemed unimportant to him. But he was still a member of the revolutionary movement and was known as such to the authorities. When in 1908 two other members of the group perpetrated a mishandled bomb attack on a magistrate, many revolutionaries were arrested as suspects, and Aurobindo was among them. Their trial lasted a year which Aurobindo spent in Alipore prison, but he in the end was acquitted.

The period in prison was a turning point for him as he spent most of the time performing Yoga exercises and meditating. His experience of the spiritual dimension deepened and developed into a stage which he later described as 'communication with the Divine Mind'. He further maintained that he was receiving from this source guidance on how to cope with his immediate situation and how to proceed in his subsequent life. His first public lecture after his release from prison took place in the Jaykrishna Public Library in Uttapara, 'the Heritage Town of West

Bengal', on 30 May 1909. He spoke about his religious experiences in prison and about Hinduism as Sanātana Dharma, but also made in that context allusions to nationalism as somehow included in Sanātana Dharma. The authorities regarded this speech as a call for a struggle for the independence of India and issued a warrant for his arrest. He then wrote a letter 'To my Countrymen' published in the *Karmayogin no. 25*, a Weekly Review, on 25 December 1909. In it he advocated the establishment of a Nationalist Council and of Nationalist Associations throughout the country which would enable planning actions with the aim of achieving the independence of India. But violence should be avoided and the law respected. He then went into hiding and the warrant was suspended. Aurobindo teased the authorities with fleeting appearances so that the warrant was re-issued on 4 April 1910, but he arrived on that date in Pondicherry, then a French colony, whereupon the warrant against him was withdrawn.

The initial concern of the French colonial administration about Aurobindo's intentions was soon dispelled as he totally withdrew from politics and settled down for four years to a contemplative life practising Yoga. Four of his former revolutionary companions joined him and a trickle of others kept arriving. A French civil servant, Paul Antoine Richard, was very impressed by Aurobindo's ideas and suggested that he publish a magazine which started appearing in 1914 under the name *Ārya: a Philosophical Review*; its publication continued until 1921. In it Aurobindo expounded his philosophical ideas and visions about evolution on a cosmic scale and laid foundations for his synthesis of different yogic techniques into what he named 'Integral Yoga'. The magazine steadily gained an international reputation and brought new followers into what was thus becoming an *āśram*.

In 1920 Aurobindo was joined by Mirra Richard. Her full original name was Blanche Rachel Mirra Alfassa and she was born in 1878 in Paris of a Turkish-Jewish father and an

Egyptian-Jewish mother a few months after her parents moved there from Egypt. She is reported to have had spiritual experiences in early life and after she had read the Bhagavad Gītā and Vivekananda's *Rāja Yoga* these experiences increased. She also studied some occult literature and was trained by an 'occult Master' in Algeria. In 1897 she had married André Henri Morisset, an artist studying under the painter Gustave Moreau. They had a son, but the marriage ended in 1908. In 1911 Mirra married Paul Richard and came with him to Pondicherry in 1914. When she met Aurobindo, she immediately felt that he was her real Master. Because of the war her husband was recalled to France in 1915 and was then posted to Japan for the rest of the war and she had to follow him. In April 1920 they returned to Pondicherry and Aurobindo acknowledged Mirra as his equal. She then took charge of the practical affairs of the *āśram.* But her husband, although an admirer of Aurobindo and his teachings, did not find the new situation congenial and left Pondicherry by the end of 1920.

After some time he started divorce proceedings which were duly finalised. With Aurobindo's approval Mirra quite quickly became involved in the spiritual practices of the community and by 1922 she was holding regular classes and meditation sessions and came to be viewed as the 'Mother' of the still only 'virtual' *āśram.* Aurobindo had total confidence in her and in November 1926 withdrew into solitude to contemplate his visions and revise his earlier writings for publication in book form. Simultaneously the Sri Aurobindo Ashram (Śrī Aurobindo Āśram) was officially founded, run by Mirra as its 'Mother'. Aurobindo's pupils could thereafter reach him solely by writing or through the Mother's mediation. Only on special occasions did he show himself to his pupils, devotees and visitors. During the second world war both Aurobindo and the Mother declared their support for the Allies. It is claimed that they worked for their victory on 'subtle levels'. When Aurobindo died on

5 December 1950 the Mother continued to build up and expand the Ashram and act as its teacher and adviser on spiritual matters. In 1968 she founded Auroville, intended to become a city for 50,000 inhabitants who would live there according to the principles of Aurobindo's philosophy, but in 2015 the population was about 2,500. The Mother headed the Ashram and supervised Auroville till her death in 1973.

The philosophy of Aurobindo can be classified as spiritual evolutionism. Evolution is not, for him, driven by the principle of the 'survival of the fittest', but there is a divine force he called the Divine Mind or Supermind behind the evolutionary process which aims for the spiritualisation of the whole universe. After the Divine Mind had produced man as the most advanced stage of the evolutionary process, evolution did not continue automatically, but required man's cooperation. Man has thus become a collaborator of the Divine Mind in this process. The way to becoming a collaborator of the Divine Mind is what Aurobindo called Integral Yoga or Purna Yoga (*pūrṇa Yoga* — 'full' Yoga). It is his answer (1) to the fragmentation of Yoga which it has undergone since its classical period and which he wanted to remedy by a new synthesis (Sorokin in: Chaudhuri & Spiegelberg, 1960, 205-212), and (2) to the requirement that the practitioner of Yoga should concentrate on his personal path without anticipating the final result. This requirement is implied in Patañjali's eightfold Yoga path, but Aurobindo rejected it and substituted for it an outlook of higher spiritual stages of achievement (Rishabhchand in: Chaudhuri & Spiegelberg, 1960, 213-222). These higher stages up to the highest level were outlined in Aurobindo's philosophical writings on the basis of his visionary experiences.

His first point has some justification and, in fact, combining two or more Yoga techniques had been done long before by some Yoga practitioners. But Aurobindo's requirement of a sort of synthesis of all yogic procedures is not realistically feasible. Besides, nowhere does he provide precise instructions for the practice of his Integral Yoga, which would presumably be a matter of his or the Mother's personal guidance. As far as the second point is concerned, Aurobindo is demanding exactly what all post-Patañjali *gurus* of specialised schools of Yoga and sectarian Yoga systems required of their followers, namely utter confidence in their teacher's realisation as being the final truth. This contradicts the spirit of Patañjali's eightfold Yoga path and is totally at variance with the clearly stated instructions for practising the eightfold path of early Buddhism. Both, the eightfold Yoga of Patañjali and the eightfold path of the Buddha are the two bases for formulating the principle of 'pure Yoga' free from speculations and premature anticipations of the final goal.

As mentioned above, Integral Yoga is supposed to be the way to becoming a collaborator of the Divine Mind. To practise for and even reach one's own individual salvation is, according to Aurobindo, a small achievement if it is enjoyed in a nirvānic isolation from the rest of creation which the liberated one has left behind in saṁsāric entanglement. The true salvation to be aimed at includes the salvation of all other beings and initiates the process of the spiritualisation of the whole earth and in the last instance of the whole universe. So Aurobindo preached universal salvation in unmistakable terms, maintaining that it was already implied in some utterances of the ancient Vedic *ṛṣis*. However, it actually sounds very much like the Buddhist Mahāyāna teaching (which started appearing some 500 years after the Buddha's death) about the inferiority of the early Buddhist achievement of individual liberation in *nirvāṇa* by *arahants.* The liberation of *arahants* is not final, they will have to pause on the threshold of *nirvāṇa* and embark on the Bodhisattva Path, vowing that they will not enter the final *nirvāṇa* until all beings are saved 'down to the last blade of grass' (Werner, 2012). It is not possible to say whether Aurobindo's idea of spiritualisation of the cosmos was a conscious reformulation of the Bodhisattva vow, but he could not have been ignorant of Mahāyāna Buddhist doctrines These went on to posit the concept of 'emptiness' as the core of all phenomena, although they did not regard it as the source out of which phenomena would have emerged. Aurobindo posits instead the Divine Supermind which is the highest level of consciousness and is in other Hindu systems referred to as *brahman*, Parameśvara (the highest Lord) or *saccidānanda*. The Supermind is seen in Aurobindo's system as the source of all that is. In its eternal dynamism it descends to lower levels of consciousness as far down as matter which is not illusory or a separate principle, but the lowest form of the true reality or Supermind. Matter is the Supermind's state of temporary repose (*nivṛtti*) which is followed by evolution upwards (*pravṛtti*) through its stages as plant and animal life up to man. From then on, as mentioned above, the Divine Supermind requires man's cooperation of which he becomes capable by adopting Integral Yoga.

When a yogi masters the integrated yogic techniques with his mind open to the Supermind, his mind transcends the acquired conceptual knowledge of the evolutionary philosophy and he develops intuition and spiritual vision to the level of cosmic consciousness which includes direct global knowledge and a sense of boundless universal self. He becomes a Superman or Gnostic Being without any sense of individuality in terms of self-centredness or self-interest. He will be one with the Supermind, yet he does not altogether cease to be an individual, retaining his body as an integrated spiritualised part of his personality. Having thus accomplished the integration and spiritualisation of the whole of his own personality, the Superman turns his attention to assisting other people towards the same or similar achievement. It transpires from Aurobindo's writings that he felt he had himself realised the status of a Superman and was radiating spiritualising influence on others and on all his surroundings.

The evolutionary dynamism of the Divine Supermind, after producing man, is in a state of *nivṛtti,* but it is prepared to descend and work through developed individuals, i.e. Supermen, as receptacles, if a particular culture needs Divine intervention for its preservation and further growth, provided that it finds in that culture a sufficient number of Supermen. The Divine Supermind can then start through them the process of spiritualisation of the rest of mankind and of the whole earth and eventually of the whole universe. But if it does not find a sufficient number of Supermen as receptacles or at least a large number of individuals who have worked intensely for their salvation and reached a certain irreversible stage of progress, the Divine Supermind cannot descend and revitalise that culture, with tragic consequences for it. The Divine Supermind then withdraws to await another opportunity for its descent. From all this it appears that Aurobindo's philosophical vision is a variety of monism inspired by the *tad ekam* of the 'Creation hymn' (RV 10.129.2; see note 4) and that it differs from Śaṅkara's Advaita Vedānta only by rejecting his notion of illusoriness (*māyā*) of the world. The world is rather in the *nivṛtti* state of the Divine mind which is the *saccidānada* or the self-delight (*līlā*) of the eternally self-existing Being. The way to experience it is through Integral Yoga (Nikam in: Chaudhuri & Spiegelberg, 1960, 143-148).

Aurobindo's is a grandiose philosophical vision. There can hardly be any doubt that he experienced in some way most of what he was describing in terms of the higher stages of consciousness, but he put on it a highly speculative interpretation, coining his own terminology which differs from the terms applied to higher levels of consciousness and existence in the Upaniṣads, Vedānta and other Hindu systems. After Aurobindo's death the Mother continued asserting that the descent of the Supermind was in progress, presumably in the belief that there were enough advanced human 'receptacles'. But not everything proceeded harmoniously. Problems arose between the local Tamil population in nearby villages and European and North Indian settlers in Auroville. Although the Mother announced that the local Tamils were the 'original Aurovillians', they in fact did not integrate with the settlers, feeling that the situation resembled colonial times. Aurovillians employed local Tamils for construction work and other menial jobs while trying to achieve their 'transformation' from ancient ways to the outlook for a future spiritual level of existence. But in fact they were using them as cheap labour and felt superior to them.

After the Mother's death tensions developed between the Ashram and Auroville which resulted in a split in 1980. The Ashram came under the administration of a newly founded Sri Aurobindo Society and the Indian government took control of Auroville. Since 1991 it has been run by the Auroville Foundation. Both institutions continue in their activities on a modest scale, while the world shows no signs of spiritualisation, but rather of deterioration in its affairs. {44}

3. Śivānanda (1887-1963)

Swami Sivananda Saraswati (Svāmī Śivānanda Sarasvatī) was born in Pattamadai near Tirunelvel in Tamil Nadu, South India, as Kuppuswamy Iyer, the youngest of three brothers, in a traditional Brahmin family. He attended medical school in Tanjore and after graduation worked for ten years in Malaysia where, after a time, he was made responsible for running a hospital and became known for providing free treatment to poor patients. He had the opportunity to acquaint himself with some other religions — Chinese forms of Buddhism, Christianity and Islam. Gradually he realised that medical treatment, although alleviating physical suffering, was insufficient, man's condition required healing on a spiritual level. One of his patients, who was a wandering mendicant, acquainted him with some Yoga procedures and with the principles of Vedāntic philosophy. The result was that he returned to India, first visiting Benares and one or two other places of pilgrimage. In 1924 he arrived in Rishikesh on the upper Ganges which had been the centre for 'holy men', *gurus* and *āśrams* since ancient times. Here he found his guru, Viśvānanda Sarasvatī, who initiated him as a *saṅnyāsī* in the Sarasvatī lineage and gave him his new name. Śivānanda then settled down in a disused hut (*kutir*) to perform intense austerities and practise meditation and some forms of Yoga. In 1927 he opened a modest dispensary where he gave medical help to wanderers, pilgrims, beggars and inhabitants of the local *āśrams.* He financed it from the lump sum which he received from Malaysia when his insurance policy, which he had taken up there, matured. The dispensary eventually grew into a full-scale hospital, supported by his followers. Some time later he became a true wanderer through the whole of India down to Rameśvaram, giving talks in temple precincts and under trees wherever people, impressed by his appearance, gathered around him.[45] On his travels he visited the Śrī Aurobindo Āoeram and had the opportunity to see also Ramaṇa Mahaṛsi in Arunachala, where he joined in the ritual dances of Ramaṇa's *bhakti* followers.

When he returned to Rishikesh, he founded, in 1932, his own *āśram* which now bears his name, Sri Shivananda Ashram (Śrī Śivānanda Āśram). It is on a bank of the river Ganges (now called Śivānanda Ghāt). Disciples flocked to him and eventually whole families were accepted and could live there, having sold their possessions and donated the proceeds to the *āśram.* Śivānanda then dedicated most of his time to writing books which became very popular in all countries with an English-speaking population and were translated into French, German and other languages. He left the running of the *āśram* to a 'committee' of senior yogis and was available for an hour a day to inhabitants and visitors for a *darśan,* giving them blessing. In 1936 he founded the Divine Life Society which soon had branches in other parts of India and in a number of other countries round the world. His writings are popular and clearly written, if sometimes simplistic and repetitious, but they were instrumental in making all varieties of Yoga, particularly Haṭha Yoga, widely known. They even penetrated behind the Iron Curtain.[46] He was never strict with his followers, but he recommended that serious aspirants should remain celibate, adopt a healthy vegetarian diet and eat moderately, abstaining from smoking and alcohol, get up every morning at 4, practise *āsanas*, twenty rounds of easy *prāṇāyāma*, and *japa* meditation. During the day they should go for a walk, read books with spiritual contents and study texts of various religions for up to an hour, setting aside two hours for silence. They should speak little and then only in a positive way and always only truth. They should reduce their needs and be charitable according to their means. They should practise *ahiṁsa*, control their anger and replace it with an attitude of love, forgiveness and compassion. They should adopt his method for protracted meditation, which is a synthesis of Karma, Bhakti, Rāja and Jñāna Yoga and finish the day with self-analysis. His advice echoes the precepts of classical Yoga, Buddhism and other systems. He particularly warned against straining oneself and being hasty and impatient. His philosophy was basically Vedāntic ('God dwells in all') and in many respects eclectic.

In 1945, Śivānanda created the Sivananda Ayurvedic Pharmacy, and organised the Allworld Religions Federation. In 1947 he established the All-world Sadhus Federation and in 1948 the Yoga-Vedanta Forest Academy. He had at least a dozen disciples who went on to found larger organisations with further branches, both in India and in the West. He was particularly keen on spreading his message in the West and even accepted as his disciple, initiating him at a distance (and possibly by telepathy?) the Russian born Boris Sacharow (1899-1959), who had studied Sanskrit and learned Yoga *āsanas* from illustrations in Indian manuscripts. He had fled bolshevik Russia in 1919, reached Berlin in 1926 and soon started giving lessons in Haṭha Yoga. He spent some time in Bulgaria propagating Yoga and on his return to Germany in 1937 founded a Yoga School in Berlin, the first ever in Europe. By eliminating religious and philosophical connections of Yoga and maintaining that *āsanas* had scientific character, his teaching activities were not stopped during the Nazi period. His school was destroyed in 1945 when Berlin was taken by the Soviet army, but Sacharow escaped to the spa Karlovy Vary (Karlsbad) in Czechoslovakia which was in the American zone. In 1947 he reopened his Yoga School in Bayreuth and Nḷrnberg. He avidly read all Śivānanda's books and wrote to him about his activities. Śivānanda was impressed, and gave him the title Yogirāj. He became known as Śivānanda's disciple 'by mail' (Strauss, 2005, 110-111). In the wake of Sacharow's activities Yoga centres spread all over Germany.

When Śivānanda visited the Śrī Aurobindo Āśram during his wandering years, he either met its Mother or at least became aware of her role in it. Was it that which gave him the idea to find a Mother for his *āśram* which he founded in Rishikesh after his return from his wanderings through India? Unusually, he summoned her from Germany. She was Charlotte Walinski-Heller, a housewife with two teenage children, who was brought up a Christian but was open-minded and sensitive to teachings that went beyond normal belief and church-going and praying in the conventional way. She was aware of the post-war spiritual trends coming from the East and knew the title of the Bhagavad Gītā, but had never read it. She was probably told some basics about 'secret doctrines' by her husband who was a theosophist and she pondered sometimes about the relation between the immortal and mortal parts of her personality. Then, on 13 February 1951, as she wrote in her book (Sarada 1954), in conversation with a female friend who was knowledgeable about 'esoteric teachings', she expressed her ardent wish to *know.* Suddenly she heard internally a voice saying "I would like to think through with you the beginning and end of all Being!" Her friend was alarmed by her unusual appearance and called her husband, who also confirmed that something unusual was happening with his wife. From then on she was receiving regular messages. Her mysterious unseen teacher asked her first to write down what views she so far held, discussed them with her and gradually introduced her to yogic and Vedāntic ideas. After five months she was able to understand to some extent the gist of it all. Her husband approved of the direction into which she was being led. On Christmas day 1951 she had a vision in which she met and spoke with Śivānanda, without his name being mentioned. A fortnight later (January 1952) came an envelope from the Yoga Vedanta Forest University in Rishikesh containing just a photograph signed on the back in his own hand: Sivananda. During subsequent months Mrs. Walinski- Heller received, as she called it, a thorough esoteric training. She 'learned to die' in several ways and then was lying as if dead for ten days, while she was drawn out of her body and moved on a different level of consciousness. Śivānanda's books were sent to her address, but she did not read them, relying solely on his direct mental training. Externally she became attractive to and was often approached by people who needed some help or advice with their life. On 4 August 1953 she was called to a man who suffered from lack of purpose and asked her to give him a new outlook. She said to him: "Wait, we'll both go to India." Her own words astonished her, but on the same day she wrote to Śivānanda to pray for her and find how she could receive money and travel documents to come to him. On 7 September 1953 a personal invitation from Śivānanda came. Her husband and eldest son encouraged her to accept the calling. People hearing about her invitation from Śivānanda provided her with personal necessities and 800 DM and the man to whom she had spoken the unexpected sentence about going to

India paid their travel expenses. They sailed from Genoa on 30 November 1953 and arrived in Bombay, as it then was, on 12 December 1953, welcomed by local followers of Śivānanda and representatives of the Divine Life Society, and by the press asking for interviews. She had many visitors in her hotel and the private home where she was accommodated from the next day and was addressed already as Mā (mother) by all, also by everybody on the train which she boarded two days later with her companion. They had to change trains twice and reached Rishikesh station in the morning of 16 December 1953 and from there came to the gate with the inscription 'Shivananda Ashram'. A young *saṅnyasi* appeared and asked; "Mrs. Walinski?" and showed her in. She lost sight of her German companion and saw him very seldom thereafter. Being taken through a hall and several rooms, she recognised the *āśram* from her vision back home. She had to wait a while in a large room where she saw a number of people sitting on the floor and typing, who seemingly did not take any notice of her. Her guide, called 'Swami Yekatesdananda', was Śivānanda's secretary and took her out of the building. Then he unlocked a bungalow called 'Ananda-Kutir' which became her temporary home. Through a window she saw the Ganges immediately below and the Himālāya mountains beyond. She was allowed to wash and change her clothes and was then taken to another building onto a long veranda full of *saṅnyasis.* At the end of the veranda sat Śivānanda. He got up, took her hand into his and said to the gathered crowd: "Look at her, she is like me, her face is my face." She said: "Siva, will you be my *guru*?" "With great pleasure," was his answer. He then took her out and down the steps to the river where he put a string of beads round her neck, watched by an ever increasing number of people. The whole procedure was filmed and a lot of snapshots were taken then and the next day of her in a new sari with Śivānanda beside her. He told her: "You look so very nice. I like to have many pictures from you."

A day or two later he came to her premises accompanied

by a group of Svāmis and sitting face to face with her with closed eyes fell into inner absorption (*Versenkung*), while she felt a kind of stream of life passing through her. Suddenly he looked at her and said: "You are Sarada!" (Śāradā, another name of the goddess Sarasvatī, is also a goddess in her own right, her name being interpreted as 'giver of essence', Harshananda, 1987, 99). Sarada became her new name. He visited her a few more times, also without anybody else present.

There were daily sessions in a big hall presided over by Śivānanda with readings (Bhagavad Gītā, Upaniṣads, Vedas and other texts) and subsequent elucidation by him or one of the resident Svāmis, loud singing in praise of deities (*kīrtana*) and heroic figures like Rāma and Sītā, and praying. Śivānanda had a good voice and told Sarada, who did not join in the singing, that she must learn to sing *kīrtan*, so she obeyed. She had to lead (*vorsingen*) a line before the congregation joined in. For those gatherings Śivānanda ordered that her seat should be placed next to his but it never was and so each time he had to order it anew. The Svāmi responsible for the arrangement thereby showed his negative attitude towards her closeness to the Master. Eventually Sarada decided to sit on the floor at the feet of her *guru*, often being touched by him. He then ordered that a carpet should be brought for her.

Throughout her stay many Indian and Western visitors came to see her, including from Germany. She received them in her bungalow, which sometimes became very crowded, and answered their questions. Occasionally Śivānanda sent for her to come to his premises and introduced her to his visitors: "This is the German. I have called her and she has come." There was only once a negative scene between them, early on at the beginning of January 1954. So that she would not miss the traditional Christmas, Śivānanda ordered a Christmas celebration in the *āśram* which was visited by many people. One of the visitors was a very revered hundred years old yogi who made an impression on her and she decided to visit him just after the New Year. He lived within walking distance, received her courteously and said straightaway: "Let me be your *guru*! You are always welcome! You are established in *ātman*! You have a mission to fulfil!" She explained she already had a *guru*, but stayed to listen further to him. On parting he said to her: "I shall always pray for you! Think of me! I shall be around you!" When she returned to the *āśram*, she saw Śivānanda standing outside his office as if waiting for her and he asked in a domineering tone: "Where are you coming from?" Taken aback, she said she had just paid a visit to a famous yogi whom even Śivānanda respected and she did not understand his concern. "Then go to him forever," said Śivānanda inflamed (*aufflammend*). "I do not need to, you are my *guru*!" said Sarada and went past him to the hall where the evening talk was soon to start. Neither of them ever mentioned the incident afterwards and she never again left the *āśram* without prior permission. But she met the old yogi by chance again, just before her return to Germany, and he repeated to her the words from their previous meeting. Curiously enough, when she had a chance to meet, in the temple on the opposite shore of the Ganges, a famous supposedly 150-years-old yogi called Nahrein who came from the mountains where he lived as a hermit and had not spoken for twenty years, he conveyed to her by sign language almost the same words: "Let me be your *guru*! You are established in *brahman*. You have a mission to fulfil!"

Śivānanda's momentary displeasure over her visit outside the *āśram* did not affect her standing with him. One day he said to her: "Sarada, always precede this name with my own," so she became Svāmī Śivānanda Śāradā. Very early on he asked her to remain in the *āśram* for good, but she could not contemplate doing so. In fact, she felt that she wished to keep a certain inner independence and proceed on the spiritual path in her own way, despite accepting Śivānanda's guidance and the mission he entrusted her with — to teach his variety of Yoga practice in the West.

There were some hostile moves against Sarada by the established Svāmis running the *āśram*'s affairs, but Śivānanda always protected her. One day in February 1954 he said to her: "I am your *guru* from life to life. We go always together..." and that was also the month when she started to go swimming every day in the Ganges. Śivānanda said it was her Haṭha Yoga. She would have preferred a bathing *ghat* on a tributary without onlookers.

Some hostility towards her also occurred when she was initiated into the Sarasvatī Saṅnyāsa Order in an elaborate ceremony with thirteen other candidates. Some of these *brahmacāris*, celibate disciples of Śivānanda, had had to wait 10 or even 15 years for initiation. Now she was being made into Swami Sivananda Sarada (Svāmī Śivānanda Śāradā) after ten weeks' discipleship. She was surprised and wondered whether the initiation was needed, but it had practical advantages. Her ochre robe was a protection outside the *āśram* and made Hindus of all persuasions treat her with reverence. By then Śivānanda had made it known that Sarada would return to Germany in April. During her stay she had experienced many events in the *āśram* — a feast given free by Śivānanda to a crowd of two hundred people in front of the Temple, a kind of staged mystery drama, even performances of Indian dancing and, of course, the showing of the films made on special occasions. Most of the time Śivānanda spent in his office dealing with abundant post, writing his books and instructing the senior yogis. But Sarada felt his presence as if he were with her all the time. When she thought of some question which she would want to ask him next day, it was answered in her own mind. When she had some wish, it was fulfilled before she could express it. One morning, on full moon day, she thought how wonderful a boat ride with Śivānanda would be. When she came into his office, he said: "Sarada, tonight you are invited onto my boat with me." It became an opportunity for a whole fleet of crowded boats, including one with a brass band, to join in. She never doubted his telepathic powers. Once he confirmed to her that he was using them with her.

Her departure day was 19 April 1954. The night before there was a gathering in which Śivānanda made clear that Sarada was returning to Germany on his behalf to fulfil her mission by founding a Śivānanda Sarada Ashram and spreading his teaching. He said to her in German: "Ich danke Dir!" Her German companion seemed envious. Śivānanda said to him: "If you do not wish to work with Sarada, go to America and teach Haṭha Yoga." Before their departure Śivānanda told her to leave her luggage behind, because she would come back, so she obeyed (but she never came back). On 2 May 1954 at 23.00 her flight left the Bombay airport (Sarada 1954). She started her Sivananda Sarada Ashram in Lindau, Bodensee, Felsburg and published several booklets the same year.[47]

Charlotte Walinski-Heller was not the only German lady who was initiated by Śivānanda into the Sarasvatī Saṅnyāsa Order, asked to precede her personal name with his and entrusted with a mission abroad. There was also Sylvia Hellman (1911–1995). She had lost her parents during the war, her first husband was executed in the Nazi concentration camp in Buchenwald and her second husband died in 1948, a year after their wedding. Depressed, she decided to leave her native country where she had suffered so much and emigrated in 1951 to Canada, where by then there were several 'Sivananda Yoga Vedanta Centres', founded by Vishnudevananda (see below). She was impressed by Śivānanda's message as presented by Vishnudevananda and decided to go to Rishikesh, where she was accepted by Śivānanda as his pupil and within a few months, on 2 February 1956, she became Swami Sivananda Radha (Svāmī Śivānanda Rādhā — Rādhā, a shepherdess, was the favourite lover of Kṛṣṇa). She returned the same year to Canada where her ochre robe attracted attention. Interviews in newspapers and invitations to lecture followed and she managed to found a 'Sivananda Ashram' in 1957, in British Columbia. When Śivānanda died she renamed it 'Yasodhara Ashram' (Yaśodharā āoeram — Yaśodharā, in Hindu mythology, is the mother of Kāmadeva, the god of love). She gave *saṅnyāsa* initiation to a number of young men, who accompanied her on her lecture tours and worked with her to establish the *āśram.* She also initiated women, including her successor, thus establishing an independent, primarily female, Western lineage in the tradition of the Saraswati Order. She opened Yoga centres in North America, Mexico and England. Informed also by transpersonal psychology, she presented Yoga as a philosophical and spiritual system, giving courses in Haṭha, Kuṇḍalinī and Dream Yoga.

The most important of Śivānanda's disciples who moved to the West at his instigation in 1957 was Vishnudevananda (Viṣṇudevānanda, 1927-1993). He founded a number of 'Sivananda Yoga Vedanta Centres', with headquarters in Canada. The most important of Śivānanda's disciples in India was Satyānanda, the founder of the Bihar School of Yoga. Out of this school emerged a remarkable *yoginī* who was known as Mā Yogaśaktī, a one time visitor to my Yoga Club in Brno (1966). She travelled the world giving talks and seminars (cf. note 46) until she was injured in an aeroplane crash whereupon she withdrew from the public eye.

As the disciples of the great masters started spreading Yoga practice and teachings into Western countries and relatively easily found listeners and followers who provided the means for establishing permanent centres and *āśrams,* some of which became prosperous and even rich, less prominent *gurus* started arriving whose motivation was not always purely spiritual. There is already a large easily accessible literature about the downside of the Yoga scene.[48]

On the other hand, Yoga gradually overcame the initial distrust of scientific and academic circles and its historical development and theory and practice have become subjects of research programmes and are taught at university level.{49}

Revival of Buddhist Practice

As with Yoga, the revival started with the 'Parliament of Religions' in Chicago in 1893. Buddhism was represented by Anagarika Dharmapala (1864-1933; family name: Don David Hewavitharane), whose address to the assembly was as successful as that of Vivekananda. He was born in Colombo, Ceylon, as it then was, and received English education in several Christian colleges, but his mother sent him subsequently to the Vidyodaya Pirivena in Maligakanda (now Vidyodaya University), a centre for educating Buddhist laymen and future monks where he acquired knowledge of Buddha's teachings and learned Singhalese and Pāli. He then felt drawn to working for Buddhist renewal. First he joined forces with the Theosophical Society, but later distanced himself from it, because of Theosophy's claim that all religions are in essence one. For him the teachings of the Buddha represented the only true world view. Early in the 1880s he took the eight precepts for life, thus becoming an *anagarika* (homeless wanderer) and changed his name to Dharmapāla. Inspired by Sir Edwin Arnold, the author of *The Light of Asia*, he visited Bodh Gayā, the site of the Buddha's enlightenment, then in Hindu hands, and initiated a struggle for Buddhist participation in the administration of the site (achieved only in 1949). On his further travels through India he put on the map Kushinagar (Kuoeśnagara), the site of the Buddha's *parinibbāna.* His appearance at the Parliament of Religions resulted in lecture tours and founding of Buddhist Centres and *vihāras* which contributed greatly to the spreading of knowledge of the Buddha's path in the West, alongside Yoga. Shortly before his death Dharmapāla was ordained a Buddhist monk of the Theravāda tradition.

This revival of Buddhism was helped by well written scholarly and popular books on Buddhism which started appearing from the middle of the nineteenth century. Soon the first Europeans ordained as Buddhist monks in Asia came back to the West as teachers of the doctrine and of meditation. Some still do so. One of the first was a Londoner, Allan Bennet (1872-1923), who was ordained in Burma (now Myanmar) in 1902 and returned to England in 1908 as Bhikkhu Ānanda Metteyya for a mission lasting about six months. He gave talks in the Buddhist Society in London and in public and some private tuition. He returned to England permanently in 1914 because of ill health, but even so he gave some lectures (later published) during the last years of his life.

Allan Bennet's example of going East for ordination impressed a German violin virtuoso, Anton W. F. Gueth (1878-1957), who was won for Buddhism in his young years by reading the works of Arthur Schopenhauer; while on a tour in Ceylon he decided to follow Bennet to Burma. He was ordained in 1904 and received the name Nyanatiloka. He became thoroughly versed in the Pāli Canon and post-canonical Pāli literature and was a skilful translator and author of a number of books in German and English which are still kept in print and studied. He ordained and taught quite a number of Westerners and established the Island Hermitage on Polgasduwa, a small island on the lake Ratgama near Dodanduwa, where he trained them. His activities were interrupted by the two world wars when he travelled from country to country and was a few times interned as a German enemy, but eventually he returned to his mission when Ceylon became independent as Sri Lanka and granted him citizenship. Nyanatiloka was very learned and his main aim, besides publishing, seems to have been to establish monastic communities in different countries, especially in Germany and England, as bases for full commitment to spiritual practice. There is no evidence that he would have taught meditation to lay Buddhists. This changed with the subsequent generation of Western monks. Nyanatiloka's disciple, Nyanaponika (1901-1994), was prominent among them (Hecker, 1995).

Born as Siegmund Feniger of a Jewish merchant family in Hanau (Hessen), Germany, he became a Buddhist as a result of reading books while running a bookshop and later working in a publishing enterprise. He met contemporary scholars and writers on Buddhism and was successively active in Buddhist societies and circles in Königsberg, Berlin and Vienna. In 1936 he left for Ceylon and was ordained on the Island Hermitage by Nyanatiloka in 1937. He was interned as a 'foreign enemy' during the war, but obtained citizenship in Sri Lanka in 1950 and settled in the Forest Hermitage in the former royal park of Udawatakelle above Kandy which is now almost like jungle. He travelled to Burma a few times to attend Buddhist councils and used the opportunity for a period of Satipaṭṭhāna meditation under the guidance of the Ven. Mahāsi Sayadaw (in 1952). He then utilised his experiences in writing a handbook of meditation in German which he afterwards reworked into a carefully worded book in English (Nyanaponika, 1962). He based it on the original discourse of the Buddha about the foundations of mindfulness (Satipaṭṭhāna Sutta, MN, 10 & DN 22), as explained above in the section on 'The Buddhist Yoga Path' (cf. also note 8). He described in it also the 'Burmese' variety of mindfulness of breathing (*anāpānasati*) devised by Mahāsi Sayadaw. The book has been very influential in Western countries, coinciding with the prolific foundations of Buddhist societies and groups, some of which organise regular group meditation sessions and temporary meditation retreats. {50} Intensive meditation courses are available for Western followers in special centres in Burma (Myanmar) and Sri Lanka. Unlike in Yoga *āśrams* led by *gurus*, the meditation masters in Buddhist centres act as advisors or guides, traditionally referred to as *kalyāna mitta* (literally 'beautiful friend') and do not, strictly speaking, accept disciples (Hecker, 1997, 60-92).

Even before the Dalai Lama and a host of highly qualified teachers of Tibetan Buddhism went into exile in 1959 following the Chinese clamp-down on their country, an organisation with a strong Tibetan background was founded in India by Lama Anagarika Govinda (1898-1985) which would have transmitted much of Tibetan style Buddhism to the West even if the exodus of the Dalai Lama and others had never occurred.

Govinda was born as Ernst Lothar Hoffmann in Waldheim, Saxony, of a German father and a Bolivian mother. As a teenager he had already read books on philosophy, mysticism and comparative religion, and became a convinced Buddhist at the age of twenty and a member of the Association for Buddhist Living (*Bund für Buddhistisches Leben*). He went to live on Capri in a colony of artists, being also a gifted poet and painter, at the same time learning Pāli in the university of Naples. In 1928 he went to Ceylon to study Pāli Buddhism, staying nine months in the Island Hermitage with Nyanatiloka, who gave him the name Govinda. In 1929 he took the vow of an *anagarika* in Burma. After giving up his home in Naples, he lived upland in Ceylon and published his translation of *Abhidhammattha-Saṅgaha* in German. Attending the 'All-India Buddhist Conference' in Darjeeling in 1931, he met the renowned *tulku* Tomo Geshe Rimpoche of the Gelugpa order and became his disciple, obtaining his Tibetan name Lama Anangavajra Khamsum Wangchuk, but remaining known as Lama Anagarika Govinda to the outside world. On his travels in Tibet he was also initiated into several other schools of the Tibetan Buddhist tradition, notably of the Nyingma and Kargyutpa lineages. At the instigation of his teacher he founded in 1933 in Darjeeling the 'Vajrayāna Buddhist Saṅgha' with initially fourteen members under the name ārya Maitreya Maṇḍala (AMM) with a focus on the future

Buddha Maitreya (Metteyya). Tomo Geshe's intention was that AMM would spread in the West.

In 1934 Govinda lectured in Rabindranath Tagore's Viśva-Bharati University in Śāntiniketan. From 1936 he taught in the University of Patna and gave guest lectures elsewhere. Exhibitions of his paintings were held in Calcutta and other towns. In 1938 he obtained British citizenship, but even so he was interned during the war in Dehra Dun, where he became friends with Nyanaponika. In 1947 he married Ratti Petit (1906-1988), a painter who had been his pupil in Śāntiniketan. She became known under her artistic name as Li Gotami. In 1948-1949 they travelled to Tsaparang in West Tibet and copied important frescoes, which have since been destroyed.

On 30 November 1952 Govinda fulfilled Tomo Geshe's wish and founded the Western branch of AMM in Sanchi and simultaneously in Berlin, where it was set up by Hans-Ulrich Rieker who had been accepted into AMM as Dapa Kassapa in January that year. Govinda lived in Kasar Devi Ashram near Almora from where he undertook several lecturing tours to most European countries and to the USA, where he settled in 1978 for health reasons. On 12-19 August 1977 he gave a seminar for AMM members in *Der Haus der Stille* in Roseburg. By then the order had several branches and local groups in Germany and spread to Holland, Austria and Hungary. Govinda visited Germany for the last time in 1977 and India in 1980 (Hecker, 1996, 84-115).

The Vajrayāna character of the Order is not exclusive, but is derived from the synthesis of the three *yānas* which is expressed in the study programme as well as in practice which does not exclude ritual. The course of study for candidates of the order covers early Buddhism, including the basics of Abhidhamma, Madhyamaka and the Yogacāra schools of Mahāyāna and the tenets of the main schools of Vajrayāna. Ordination (*dīkṣā*) into the Order involves the ceremonial taking of the Bodhisattva vow. The practice includes Pūjā in front of a specially designed altar. The Pūjā contains recitations of Pāli texts and formulas and Sanskrit *mantras* and is accompanied by *mudrās*. It represents a symbolical enactment of the path to enlightenment and has its meaning only if it is performed with meditative concentration, thereby becoming meditation made visible. In meditation sessions proper any technique is acceptable, *anāpānasati* being probably the most favoured one. Another technique is viewing a *kasiṇa*, the simplest being a circle drawn on a wall, or a traditional disk formed from clay. It is a suitable starting technique for eventual *yab yum* visualisation which is clearly a full Tantric 'right-hand' (*dakṣinācāra*) practice (Werner, 1986b).[51]

After the exodus of the Dalai Lama and many other dignitaries of Tibetan Buddhism and large numbers of Tibetan people, centres of Tibetan Buddhism of different lineages have been gradually set up in most Western countries and have found followers from among local populations. Tibetan Buddhism is prevalently Vajrayāna which means that it shares in doctrines and practices of Tantrism. It is therefore not surprising that in some Tibetan centres even the controversial elements of Tantric practice are taught. One of them was the Manjushri Institute founded in 1976 in Conishead Priory, Cumbria, where, according to personal information from one disciple it included the practice of '5 Ms' of the 'left-hand' (*vāmācāra*) variety. Reports of promiscuity outside the ritual context have also been circulated. At one point there was a controversy between the Institute and the Dalai Lama, who publicly disclosed that his life was under threat. In 1991, the Manjushri Institute was dissolved and a new organisation was set up as the Manjushri Mahayana Buddhist Centre.

The most successful Tibetan Centre has been the Kagyu Samye Ling Monastery at Eskdalemuir, near Langholm, Scotland. Originally a hunting lodge used for a time by a

Buddhist community looked after by the Theravāda monk Anandabodhi, it became a Tibetan Buddhist centre in 1965 when two Tibetan refugee lamas, Trungpa Rinpoche and Akong Rinpoche, were invited to take it over. They gave it the name Samye Ling and Trungpa became its head. Born in Tibet in 1940 Trungpa was recognized as the re-incarnation (*tulku*) of the abbot of Surmang monastery. In 1959 he fled to India and was a spiritual adviser in the Young Lamas Home School in Dalhousie until 1963. He acquired fame through the book *Born in Tibet* (1966), produced by him with a ghost-writer, and received a grant from the Spalding Foundation to study in Oxford. This was not a success, but he was often invited to speak in Buddhist circles and attracted a considerable number of resident disciples to Samye Ling. After a time it transpired that he was a heavy smoker and drinker and was having sex with his disciples, and also that a boy brought with him from India was the son he had sired on a nun even before he renounced his monastic vows. He was then banished to a nearby cottage and his son was cared for by a follower of his who lived near Eskdalemuir.

In 1970 Trungpa had a car accident which partly crippled him and when he recovered, he disrobed to become a lay teacher. Having married a 16-year-old student, Diana Mukpo, he left for America.[52] Akong took over Samye Ling with his brother Lama Yeshe Losal Rinpoche. Samye Ling has recovered and flourishes as the oldest Tibetan centre in Europe. It has branches across the country and conducts residential courses on the doctrines and practice of Tibetan Buddhism and art. It receives frequent visits from teaching lamas of high rank.

Yoga and Hatha Yoga today

As was hinted at above, when Yoga is mentioned nowadays, it more often than not refers to some system of bodily postures, i.e. to Haṭha Yoga, although books on it usually also contain summaries of '*rāja yoga*' by which is meant Patañjali's *aṣṭāṅga yoga.* After the pioneering work of Boris Sacharow and simultaneously with his later activities it was Selvarajan Yesudian (1916-1998) who greatly contributed to popularising Haṭha Yoga adapted for a wider public. He arrived in Hungary in 1937 and started successfully teaching Yoga. In 1941 he founded in Budapest the second European Yoga School and published several books in Hungarian, with the help of Elisabeth Haich. In 1948 he and Haich fled from communism and settled in Switzerland. His book on Haṭha Yoga also appeared in English (Yesudian & Haich, 1953). His approach was equally circumspect and gentle as was Śivānanda's technique which was emulated also by Boris Sacharow.

This was not always the case with some other disciples of Śivānanda. Thus Vishnudevananda even propagated in his main book (1960) difficult and strenuous *āsanas* not suitable for moderate practice, only cautioning that they should be done under the guidance of a teacher and not beyond one's capacity. But the most influential teacher of Haṭha Yoga, both in India and in the West, was B. K. s. Iyengar (1918-2014). His *guru* was Sri Tirumalai Krishnamacharya in Mysore, whose method was rather forceful and inconsistent so that Iyengar was partly self-taught. He struggled with the most difficult *āsanas* even under pain, until he mastered them as shown in his main book (1965) which is more systematic than the one by Vishnudevananda, but includes even more strenuous positions.

Iyengar, who married and raised a family, started his teaching career in Pune and gradually attracted more and more disciples, some of whom were distinguished personalities, among them the violin virtuoso Yehudi Menuhin, who brought him fame. His Western lecture demonstration tours then followed and 'Iyengar Yoga Centers' were founded in several countries. Many Western Yoga teachers and practitioners maintain that they follow

'Iyengar Yoga', but they are, in fact, rather selective in devising their daily routine. Even so cases of injury by straining muscles or tendons occur.

One remarkable account of Haṭha Yoga is by a Westerner, Theos Bernard, who was trained by an obviously competent teacher in India, probably Śrīmat Kuvalayānanda as he refers to him a few times in his book (Bernard, 1950, 14, 24, 98). The book contains 36 photographs of himself in perfect positions which cannot be bettered, with some detailed descriptions besides quotations from *Haṭha Yoga Pradīpikā* and other texts. Using cautiously and selectively his descriptions of *āsanas* and other exercises in combination with the pictures would serve as a good textbook of Haṭha Yoga. However, in his other books and in lectures the author indulged in eclectic philosophising with a touch of theosophy and visionary Tantrism. He also made exaggerated claims about his spiritual achievements in early life, prior to visiting India (Hackett, 2012). But this need not detract from making use of his valuable book.

Britain did not remain aloof from the wave of visiting *gurus.* Different Yoga centres and organisations were being founded and closed, which threatened to lead to chaos in the absence of any competent supervision. In 1965 an enthusiast by the name of Wilfred Clark (1898-1981) founded The British Wheel of Yoga and built it up into an efficient co-ordinating body of Yoga teachers and practitioners with regional branches. It still organises courses for Yoga teachers, which issue widely recognised diplomas, and an annual congress with a rich programme of demonstrations and lectures. It has a permanent central administrative office with adequate staff (www.bwy.org.uk).

Yoga's Entanglements

Throughout this historical survey of the development of Yoga in India it has become obvious that Yoga and its goal have always been presented — with two exceptions, already hinted at earlier — in the framework of a religious doctrine, a philosophical world view or a combination of the two, even though the greater stress was usually put on its practice. The early Upaniṣads, as we have already described, posited the impersonal divine principle *brahman* as the source and inner core of the whole of reality. The world according to this teaching is a temporary emanation from *brahman* just as sparks emanate from fire. That includes individual beings whose inmost self or *ātman*, which is the same in all of them, although they are unaware of it within their surface consciousness, is identical with *brahman*. Under the influence of this Upaniṣadic philosophy the final goal of Yoga practice guaranteeing liberation from rebirth came to be understood as the yogi's unification with *brahman/ātman*. This is sheer philosophy of monism which dominates most of Hindu thinking. Its starting point can be seen in 'that One' (*tad ekaṁ* of RV 10,129,2; see note 4) and its culmination is represented by Śaṅkara's 'non-dualistic' system of thought called Advaita Vedānta which maintains that *brahman* is the sole existence and everything else is an illusion (*māyā*).

In the context of the religious sects of Hinduism, at the top of reality is God the Lord.

Depending on the particular sect it may be Viṣṇu or Śiva, Kṛṣṇa or Rāma or even the elephantheaded Gaṇeśa. In each case God is seen as not only the Lord of the universe to be ritually worshipped, but simultaneously also as the timeless and unmanifest source of reality from which the manifested universe emerged and into which it will be reabsorbed at the end of the great world period. In other words he stands for the Upaniṣadic *brahman*. But an individual Hindu may worship any chosen deity (*iṣṭa devatā*) of his as the Lord and the goal of his Yoga practice. The philosophical monism is virtually omnipresent in Hinduism in various formulations. It has been expressed in very simple terms in the popular saying 'God, who sustains the world, dwells in the heart of every being'. Most if not all Indian yogic *gurus* have allegiance to a main God and Śiva, the Yogapati, is the most widely adopted. But when these *gurus* come West, they play down the religious connections of Yoga. This tendency started already with Vivekananda who stressed the 'scientific' nature of Yoga especially in his American lectures. Boris Sacharow was successful in presenting Yoga that way under the Nazi regime in Germany and I myself succeeded in getting Haṭha Yoga accepted by presenting it in my courses in communist Czechoslovakia as a physical discipline beneficial to health and alleviating stress. This approach, curiously enough, seems now to be the prevailing trend in most Yoga organisations in the West and it is also influencing the attitude to Yoga back in India. It is sometimes supplemented by statements that Yoga is benefiting mankind and the environment and only in passing by references to the spiritual uplift which Yoga practice can produce. But there must be individuals who have not lost sight of the final goal of Yoga as individual liberation from the temporality and uncertainty of life in the world into a transcendental dimension of fulfilment, even though it remains unimaginable and the traditional designations (*nirvāṇa, kaivalya, sat-cit-ānanda, mokṣa* or *vimutti*) say very little about its character.

It is highly unlikely that competent guidance in Yoga or in meditation could be found without any links to traditional Hindu or even Buddhist accretions which would be only a hindrance. Besides, there is the problem of trust in view of many instances of devious activities. One extraordinary example is Omkarananda (R.N. Jayanarayana Kannan, 1929-2000) who joined Śivānanda's *āśram* as a *brahmacāri* in 1946 and was initiated into the Sarasvatī Saṇnyāsa Order in 1947. He was intellectually alert and Śivānanda entrusted him with editing his books and booklets. He studied Western philosophy and literature at the local college and read important Vedāntic texts. After Śivānanda's death he was too junior to play a significant part in the *āśram*, so he left for Switzerland and founded the independent 'Divine Light

Zentrum' in Winterthur. In 1973 he even built a Vedic temple with an officiating Brahmin for ritual worship. Both the 'Zentrum' and the temple were disliked by the local government and population and ensuing disputes escalated allegedly into deployment of explosives by the Zentrum's inmates. Omkarananda was held responsible and was given a prison sentence. Released after 14 years, he left for Austria where he resided in a secret locality until his death. His followers have been protesting his innocence ever since. They purchased land above Rishikesh and established 'The Omkarananda Ashram International' which competes for influence on the Yoga scene locally with other Rishikesh *āśrams* and also globally (cf. Strauss, 2005, 102-107). It is rather risky to place one's total trust in a *guru.*

A Modern Messiah?

One person, a persistent travelling speaker throughout his adult life, who appeared to come closest to the image of an advocate of spiritual awakening unaffiliated to any ideology, was Jiddu Krishnamurti (1895-1986). He aimed through his speeches and writings to liberate mankind from the tyranny of mind and body. He was often asked to explain the role of sex and he usually started with reformulating the question: "Why has sex such an extraordinary importance in our life?" but answered in a broader context: "When you give tremendous importance to something which is only one part of life, you are destroying yourself.... Life is whole, not just one part. The way to reality, to that unknown immensity, is .... through the door of self-knowing." On the surface his explanations convinced thousands of people that he was truly awakened, but events in his personal life told a different story when they came to light.

Krishnamurti's father, Jiddu Narayaniah, was a Telugu Brahmin and a Theosophist employed at the headquarters of the Theosophical Society at Adyar. The teachings of the Theosophical Society stemmed allegedly from 'Masters', called also 'Mahatmas', who were living in the Himalaya, perhaps in a transcendent dimension, forming the world's Spiritual Hierarchy. They were first described by H. P. Blavatsky (1831-1891), the cofounder of the Theosophical Society. At the time the head of the Theosophical Society was Annie Besant (1847-1933), a one time social reformer, campaigner for women's rights and member of the Fabian Society. She was won for Theosophy in 1890 when she met H. P. Blavatsky. Another prominent member of the Theosophical Society was C. W. Leadbeater (1854-1934), originally an Anglican priest who converted to the Liberal Catholic Church. After he immersed himself in the study of theosophy, he claimed that he became clairvoyant and was directly guided by 'Masters', particularly Master Kuthumi. Among them was also the World Teacher or Maitreya who was supposedly the inspiration behind Zoroaster, the historical Buddha Śakyamuni and Christ. Leadbeater declared that Maitreya's next spokesman was already present in the world and he eventually 'discovered' him in Krishnamurti in 1909. Annie Besant unreservedly believed in Leadbeater's visions and that he was guided by the 'Masters'.

Krishnamurti was removed from his parents, with his younger brother Nitya to keep him company, to be groomed for his mission as the 'Messiah'. He was put through rigorous exercise and sports and given secondary education and lessons in Theosophy and religions, Yoga and meditation. The 'Order of the Star in the East' was founded for him in 1911 and twelve apostles were nominated. Both boys were taken to England the same year and the following year they travelled in Europe, just when their father, by then a widower, was suing successfully in Madras for their return to his custody. But Annie Besant won an appeal to the Privy Council in London. Krishnamurti was grateful to her and a strong tie developed between them. He saw in her his surrogate mother, but as she often travelled giving

Theosophical lectures, he also enjoyed being mothered by other older women such as Emily Lutyens, a member of the Theosophical Society since 1910. But when he reached his twenties, he became attracted to beautiful girls.

In 1913 Leadbeater discovered another possible candidate for the role of Messiah in Desikacharya Rajagopal (1900-93) to replace Krishnamurti who was showing signs of being a rebellious teenager, but Annie Besant did not allow the change. Even so Rajagopal, who was very intelligent, was being educated in Theosophy and was brought to Sydney when Leadbeater became a bishop of the Liberal Catholic Church there. Meanwhile (1914) Krishnamurti and Nitya were being tutored for Oxford. Krishnamurti failed all the examinations, but Nitya passed with honours in 1920. After that they relaxed in Paris, where they met Mme de Manziarly and her four daughters, and Krishnamurti had a romance with the youngest one, Marcelle. But marriage was out of the question because of his 'mission'. When Rajagopal was brought to London in 1920, Krishnamurti was at first apprehensive of him as a possible rival, but soon found that Rajagopal was friendly and supported his future role as Messiah. In 1921 Krishnamurti fell in love with 17-year-old Helen Knothe, an American, whom he met in Amsterdam and whose parents were supporters of Theosophy. Even so, Krishnamurti showed in 1922 that he was ready for his first lecture tour round the world in the spirit of his mission. He was accompanied by Nitya. When they finished the tour in Sydney, Krishnamurti was attracted to a beautiful English girl, Ruth Roberts, and rumours started. But Leadbeater intervened with a message for him from Master Kuthumi, who reportedly advised him to find his true self. Krishnamurti decided to take a break for the purpose. The brothers then travelled across the Pacific to California, instead of via India because of its heat, as Nitya was ailing. They arrived in the Ojai Valley where a house was acquired for them which they called Arya Vihara. It became their headquarters when

Rajagopal later joined them, taking charge of organising Krishnamurti's travelling schedules and editing his talks and books for publication.

At this time a 19-year-old American girl, Rosalind Williams, who had no connection to or interest in Theosophy, was staying in Ojai with relatives. She was asked to nurse the ailing Nitya, which she did efficiently, and soon fell in love with him. A warm relationship developed also between her and Krishnamurti, but he was still in love with Helen Knothe. In Ojai he embarked on long meditation sessions and suddenly started having strange spiritual experiences; they were accompanied by a lot of pain and during them he heard voices. When they started recurring, they came to be referred to as the 'Process' and were regarded as steps towards making Krishnamurti a channel for the Bodhisattva Maitreya. Rosalind nursed him as well through his seizures during which he often put his head on her lap and sometimes cupped her breasts. She was sceptical about the 'spirituality' of his symptoms and even suspected epilepsy, but no doctor was ever consulted. In June 1923 Nitya's health improved and the brothers went for a holiday to Austria where Krishnamurti again met Helen Knothe. Rajagopal joined them from London and witnessed the recurrence of Krishnamurti's painful ecstasies which convinced him of his vocation. It was Helen who this time consoled Krishnamurti during his seizures (he ended his tie to her a few years later to preserve his independence as a world teacher). Rajagopal then went with the brothers to Ojai and became an efficient organiser of Krishnamurti's further activities. Rosalind now looked after the three of them. But during the 'Process' which again took hold of Krishnamurti, he avoided Rosalind and called for the absent Helen, possibly out of regard for Nitya's love for Rosalind. As Nitya did not now need nursing, Rosalind was sent in 1924 to Leadbeater in Sydney to be briefed in Theosophy, while Krishnamurti, accompanied by Nitya, embarked on a world tour. In India Nitya's health suffered and he also felt distressed when his brother showed signs of doubt about his mission as the world's Messiah. When they reached Sydney in April 1925, Rosalind prevailed on Leadbeater that she must return with them to Ojai to nurse Nitya, who then recovered under her care.

When Annie Besant asked Krishnamurti to come with her to Adyar for Theosophy's fiftieth anniversary in the autumn, he insisted that Rosalind should go as well, as he felt reassured by the 'Masters' that Nitya would live. But a telegram about Nitya's death (at the age of 27) reached them on board ship from Naples to India. As a result Krishnamurti's belief in Theosophy and the 'Masters' and his role of 'Messiah' was utterly shattered, yet he continued his 'Mission' for another four years. In Adyar Krishnamurti showed tenderness to Rosalind but was often with Helen, while Rosalind turned for company to Rajagopal, who was asked by Annie Besant to organise the affairs of the Order of the Star. Rajagopal was full of admiration for Rosalind and started courting her. She, feeling lonely after Nitya's death, became engaged to him in 1926. But the engagement was cancelled when it transpired that by marrying a foreigner she would lose her American citizenship. Krishnamurti felt encouraged by this but his attentions to Rosalind led to rumours, and Annie Besant asked her to spend time living with her in London. When she went to Ommen in Holland to attend the annual gathering of the Order of the Star, she did not take Rosalind with her so as to keep her away from Krishnamurti. In her loneliness Rosalind telephoned Rajagopal, who arrived next day with flowers in hand and asked her to marry him. When Annie Besant returned, she approved and set the date for 11 October 1927 in St Mary's Liberal Catholic Church (preceded on 3 October 1927 by a civil ceremony at the Registrar's office). Annie Besant decided to play the role of giving the bride away. Krishnamurti did not attend either of the wedding ceremonies and stayed away from the reception.

Thereafter Rosalind accompanied her husband on some of his own and Krishnamurti's lecture tours, but she was often left alone in Ojai. Meanwhile Krishnamurti's misgivings about the role of Messiah imposed on him by Theosophy matured into his decision in 1929 to dissolve the Order of the Star and become an independent speaker. He proclaimed that the truth was a 'pathless land' which could not be organised and could not be 'brought down'; just as the mountain top could not be brought to the valley, it had to be climbed individually with alertness. He rejected institutionalized religion and spirituality and all philosophy and all systematised paths to liberation as deceptive products of thought. Still, one can find in his talks and books traces of Hindu-Buddhist spiritual outlook. His stress on being constantly aware of what is — 'choiceless awareness' — appears to be a variation of the Buddhist technique of mindfulness.

After Krishnamurti's proclamation, which shattered the Theosophical Society and gave a tremendous shock to Annie Besant, he continued circling the globe almost every year giving talks in his new style; they were always fully attended and efficiently organised by Rajagopal, who now founded Krishnamurti Writings Inc. (KWInc) with headquarters in Ojai to facilitate the publication of Krishnamurti's talks and books and to cover Krishnamurti's expenses from the proceeds and incoming donations. But Rajagopal never resigned from the Theosophical Society. After their daughter Radha was born in 1931, he told his wife that now there was no need for them to continue their sexual contacts, a decision which was favoured in some orthodox Brahmin clans following *Moksadharma*'s advice to abstain from intercourse after begetting offspring. He then concentrated fully on the work he was doing in the interests of Krishnamurti's mission. For an American woman like Rosalind this was not easy to accept. She now felt rejected by her husband and was frequently alone with her daughter. When Krishnamurti saw the baby, he was charmed and treated her as his surrogate daughter, practically replacing her father. His daily presence in Rosalind's flat, while spending nights in his nearby cottage, was then taken for granted and Rosalind's relation to him deepened.

In 1932 after giving a talk to a gathering held in the Ojai camp, Krishnamurti felt very elated by its success and at night left his cottage, entered Rosalind's bedroom and joined her in her bed. These visits continued daily while he was in Ojai between his lecturing tours, on which he maintained the image of a near saint independent of all ties. In 1935 Rosalind was with child and to Krishnamurti's relief decided on an abortion. Her symptoms afterwards were ascribed to mild appendicitis. A year later she became pregnant again, but suffered a miscarriage. At the age of six Radha noticed 'Krinsh', as she called him, creeping up the outside stairs into her mother's bedroom, but at the time did not take in what it meant. In 1939 Rosalind was again pregnant and considered keeping the baby but conceded to subtle pressure from Krishnamurti and had an abortion.

Krishnamurti went on his first post-war tour in 1947 and in Bombay became close to Nandini Mehta, the wife of a rich businessman, and her sister Pupul who looked after him when he was again suffering from his painful 'Process'. When he returned to Ojai in 1949, he resumed his intimacy with Rosalind, but more than once called her Nandini, denying afterwards any disloyalty. But a few months later an article on him in *Time* magazine mentioned Nandini, who was denying sexual relations to her husband. She sued for legal separation after being beaten by him but lost the case, her social standing and the custody of her three children. Rajagopal did not suspect Krishnamurti of impropriety in that case though his wife knew that Krishnamurti was not always truthful and entered into emotional involvements with other women.

In 1951 things came to a head, after friends in London told Rosalind various rumours about Krishnamurti's affairs in India. She then went to Paris where she was to meet with her husband. When Rajagopal joined her from Ojai, she voiced her suspicions and then suddenly blurted out the whole story of her relationship with Krishnamurti. It was a shock for Rajagopal, especially the abortions, but he did not blame her, his anger was directed onto Krishnamurti and he threatened to pull out of his administrative function. Yet when Krishnamurti arrived from India, he managed to calm him. Rajagopal also realised that his resignation would expose everything and harm Rosalind. Rosalind later told Krishnamurti about her confession to her husband, his acquiescence in her behaviour and his upset over Krishnamurti's deviousness and she asked him to talk things over with Rajagopal. Krishnamurti promised to do so but never did and when in India he resumed his contacts with Nandini and Pupul. The discrepancies and recurring double dealings of Krishnamurti were being patched up or glossed over by Rajagopal, but Rosalind was gradually drawing away from Krishnamurti mentally, although still complying with his carnal demands.

When all three were in Stockholm in 1955, Rosalind told her husband that she wanted to be free from Krishnamurti who agreed not to return to Ojai with them. After a period of rest he started giving talks again and was acquiring new supporters. Rajagopal still saw to the publication of Krishnamurti's talks and writings, but stopped organising his tours. Later, after recovering from an illness, he fell in love with Annalisa Beghe who was helping Rosalind in the school she ran for local children. A quiet divorce was arranged, enabling Rajagopal to marry Annalisa. The strained relationship between Krishnamurti, Rajagopal and Rosalind deteriorated and led finally to complete rupture. In 1968 Krishnamurti accused Rajagopal in the Attorney-General's office in Los Angeles of misspending KWInc funds and demanded to be put in charge of KWInc. The same year the Krishnamurti Foundation in London was formed to succeed KWInc and Brockwood Park estate was bought by his new supporters at the end of 1968. It became his new base and a school. He then continued his self-defined 'mission' with undiminished support from followers and public, despite publicity about the litigation that had already taken place.

When Rosalind realised in 1971 the inevitability of a lawsuit, and in the knowledge that she would be involved, she told everything about her life to her daughter Radha, who was now married with children. An attempt by Radha to mediate only made Krishnamurti angry. Altogether three lawsuits were started by the new Krishnamurti Foundation and again withdrawn. The final settlement was reached out of court shortly after Krishnamurti's death in 1986. Rajagopal was fully exonerated.

Krishnamurti's double life, in which the ecstatic experiences which fuelled his public speeches alternated with romantic involvements, was not generally known and the rumours circulating about him did not eclipse his reputation as a spiritual superman or world teacher (Lutyens, 1990; Sloss, 1991; Vernon, 2001). Despite everything his legacy still lives.

Brockwood Park functions as the Krishnamurti International Educational Centre, his schools and centres exist in the Americas and India, there is also a Krishnamurti Centre in Sydney, and groups of his followers are scattered in many countries. [53]

IX. Pure Yoga

Pure Yoga as practice without affiliation

The two exceptions in presentations of Yoga free from entanglements mentioned a few times earlier are of course the 'two eightfold paths', that of the Buddha and that of the *Yoga Sūtra* of Patañjali. Each one of them defined or described the pure Yoga practice in their respective historical and linguistic context and, importantly, without any religious setting or systematic philosophical background and free from speculations and premature anticipations of the nature of the final goal. If the final goal should be circumscribed at all without introducing misleading concepts, it can be done in negative terms such as freedom from conditionality, cessation of suffering or liberation from the round of rebirths, and in positive terms such as final or absolute truth, final knowledge or enlightenment. All of these and similar descriptions imply the rejection of the gross materialistic stance and the acceptance of the existence of some kind of transcendental reality beyond the material world, inaccessible to senses and scientific research. The description 'liberation from the round of rebirths' expresses the two assumptions without which serious practice of Yoga makes no sense, except for the sake of health, physical and mental fitness and an overall feeling of well-being. The first assumption involves the acceptance of the rebirth doctrine as at least the most likely state of affairs on the basis of logical probability. The second assumption is that, given the fact of the self-perpetuating round of rebirths, an individual decision can be taken to turn away from it and reach a state of being beyond it. It is therefore worthwhile to compare and analyse the two methodical procedures which promise to enable such a result and to work out from them a realistic technique which could be applied in modern conditions of life.

It should be possible to choose and follow one or the other of the two paths even today. There are *āśrams*, some perhaps also in a forest setting, and there are Buddhist monasteries. But the experiences in them, as we have seen, are not altogether encouraging. Also, too many historical accretions are attached to them which are obstacles for pure practice. So a reformulation in plain language of what is differently expressed in the two eightfold systems for the sake of individual practice in our time is worthwhile.

The way of the full-time 'pure yogi'

Could 'pure Yoga' be practised individually in living conditions prevailing in Western countries?

Maybe there are some solitary monks in Sri Lanka's protected territory living on forest fruits, roots and mushrooms, who have reached full detachment from the body so that they remain unperturbed even by discomfort caused by illness. We shall never know. But most *araññavāsas* collect the basic necessities left for them on an agreed place on the border of the protected area. So an individual practice of pure Yoga without some assistance by supporters is not entirely feasible even in the East, let alone in the West. A determined individual in a Western country could never embark on the path of pure Yoga without reliable backing by one or more committed supporters.

It would be ideal if he could live in a sheltered spot in a wooded area in the countryside. He would need a modest well insulated hut, so that he possibly could do without heating even in winter. The place should not be far from human habitation, preferably near a village, in which he would need to have one or two supporters who would provide him with a modest meal once a day and occasionally with medicine, which he perhaps could decide to do without, if he had reached sufficient detachment from his body and bodily pain by the technique of mindfulness. This situation would allow him to apply, besides regular periods of meditative absorptions, all the other intermittent procedures described earlier in this book. He would daily, weather permitting, spend some time practising walking meditation in the wood. If a hut could not be provided for him, he could live in a small room or an insulated corner in the loft of a supporter's home in the village. This would still allow him to practise walking meditation in the countryside. He would accept very few visitors, but would act as advisor to his supporters if approached for the purpose.

If such a determined individual lived in a town, he would need, similarly as in a village, a modest shelter, either a small room or an insulated corner in the loft of a building, and be supplied with necessities. He would go daily for a walk, usually at night in order to be less conspicuous when practising walking meditation, because it influences the style of walking. And again, he would accept, apart from his supporters, very few visitors. {54}

Pure Yoga as part-time practice

The first seven chapters of this book are a result of scholarly research undertaken for the purpose of providing the reader with initial definitions of Yoga, its relation to other spiritual trends, its philosophical background and the phases of its historical development. The preceding parts of this last chapter present in a selective way modern examples of yogic establishments and activities, both positive and negative, in India and the West, before turning to the *raison d'être* of this book, the 'pure Yoga', to attempt to outline what its full-time practice in Western conditions of life would look like. This last part of the final chapter goes beyond mere scholarship in the sense that it attempts to investigate how the principles of pure Yoga could be applied by practitioners living the so-called 'normal' life — having to earn a living, possibly maintaining a family and enjoying some recreation such as sport and various forms of art.

First it has again to be pointed out that a practitioner of pure Yoga, whether full-time or part-time, would not hold a religious belief of any kind or adhere to any fully formulated philosophical world view, except the philosophical background of Yoga, i.e. accepting the likelihood of the validity of the teaching on the sequence of rebirths governed by karmic laws and the possibility of liberation from the necessity of being repeatedly reborn, through consistent practice of pure Yoga. He might also accept that there are other dimensions of existence, some higher and some lower than the material world, into which beings may be reborn according to their karmic dispositions.

He would be at this point well versed in literature dealing with Yoga and its practice and would be able to decide on the technique and speed of his practice for himself. That would involve setting aside a certain time each day for a meditational session, dedicated most probably to mindfulness of breathing which is very easy in the sense that breathing as an object of meditation is always with us. Another, equally valuable technique, is '*kasiṇa* viewing'. The simplest way would be to draw a circle on the wall (cf. note 50). The more traditional object for this meditation would be a disk made from clay and placed in front of himself. There are several other methods, for example if one meditates in a hut, one can concentrate on a hole made in the wall while all the windows are shut, or place a square piece of cardboard with a hole in the middle in front of oneself and a lit candle or a weak electric bulb behind it.

As a part of the contemplation of the body a 'part-time' pure yogi would further endeavour to maintain round the clock mindfulness of his positions and movements, check them as to their purpose and usefulness and decide accordingly which position to assume and what kind of purposeful movement he would choose and when — such as various fitness exercises, jogging and walking meditation. He would not proceed with contemplation of external and internal parts of the body unless he would decide to lead a fully celibate life.[55] He could practise the contemplation of the body as composed of the four traditional impersonal elements (air, water, earth, fire) or, in the modern understanding, of atoms, particles and empty space. He would further contemplate his pleasant, unpleasant or neutral feelings and his emotional reactions and impulses to act and speak immediately. He would check them as to their purpose and usefulness and try to act on their basis only when he had beforehand consciously decided to do so.[56] This would apply also to habitual impulses to repeat superfluous words such as 'you know'. He would try to keep his mind under control by noticing the contents which spontaneously enter into it and dismiss or deal with them consciously, not allowing the mind to slip into daydreaming.

This is a whole package of requirements, a tall order, especially for a beginner. It may result sooner or later in fatigue. When one feels really tired so that further struggle would be useless, one can, so to speak, set aside the package and rest for a while and then go about one's everyday business in the usual way. As to the periods of sitting meditation, they may be at first quite brief before one gets tired, but by slowly adding minutes, one may soon arrive at half an hour which can suffice for a long time when one is leading a busy life. But during a leisurely holiday or on a retreat, one should meditate for extended periods of time and try to maintain round the clock mindfulness. After a time of part-time practice of all-round mindfulness as described earlier, an attitude of watchful observation may spontaneously emerge even amidst normal activities and one can practise mindfulness alongside the current activity without its being thereby visibly affected or anybody else present noticing.

One would naturally be inclined to occupy oneself outside strict practice with activities which would be related to Yoga or have an element of spirituality in them. Attending to bodily fitness, one would be likely to take up Haṭha Yoga in a mild way, following Yesudian's or Śivānanda's scheme and avoiding the strenuous and demanding positions (*āsanas*) bordering on contortions which were propagated by Iyengar. The correct way of practising Haṭha Yoga is with full awareness, observing the sensations in the muscles, tendons and joints, never straining them to the point at which the tension in them would start turning into pain, even if mild. In this way the daily practice of Haṭha Yoga would be simultaneously mindful contemplation of the body. Each daily sequence of *āsanas* finishes with a few minutes of relaxation in the reclining position during which one should try to empty one's mind as if one wished to fall asleep, which might happen, but when one feels that it is about to happen, one should take a conscious decision to return to normal activity by slowly getting up. If one achieves a successful relaxation, while remaining awake, one should maintain the position from two to ten minutes. It is not advisable to practise *prāṇāyāma.* Its initial procedure — breathing through alternate nostrils and withholding breath between its phases — does not in itself bring any benefits, while its further procedures which form the complicated post- Patañjali esoteric system, focussed on the subtle body, its ducts (*nādis*), spiritual centres (*cakras*) and *kuṇḍalinī,* as described in the previous chapter, would only hamper progress in Pure Yoga. As a part of mild Haṭha Yoga practice one should include instead the technique of 'full breathing' for one or two minutes after the relaxation. There are other useful procedures, mainly of Chinese origin, such as Tai Chi Chuan and Chi Qong (Chi Kung) which can be adopted.

In the periods outside strict practice one may be inclined to study other forms of spiritual endeavour, among them the Bodhisattva Path, only briefly referred to above (cf. note 36). Although it is not described in the early Buddhist sources, it is implied in them, since the Buddha was of course treading it prior to his enlightenment. Stories about his past lives as Bodhisattva, called Jātakas, although apocryphal, are a popular illustration of the Bodhisattva path. Even the Mahāyāna type meditation on emptiness may be attempted intermittently. More problematic is experimenting with Vajrayāna type meditation whose techniques are known practically only from Tibetan sources. They involve visualisation of twin effigies (*yab yum*) as described earlier (and in note 39). This is a part of the full Tantric 'right-hand' practice (*dakṣinācāra*), but it could be used also to explore whether the participants could experience any indication of the integration of male-female polarity which in the Tantric view is essential for spiritual progress. But unless one becomes proficient in the meditational technique of '*kasiṇa* viewing', the *yab yum* visualisation is hardly feasible. There is no question of experimenting with 'left-hand' practice (*vāmācāra*), but as already once mentioned above, there is no reason why married couples or partners fully committed to each other could not experiment with meditating in motionless sexual embrace. Casual relationships of course rule out even the 'part-time' Pure Yoga practice.

It goes without saying that appreciation of various forms of art would be the most valuable pursuit outside strict practice, as a source of aesthetic satisfaction. But of all the arts, listening with full concentration to classical music comes nearest to meditation. Some composers' works are as if suffused in spirituality, for example works by Scriabin. Beethoven's Ninth Symphony was during the first and second movements, in effect, an unsuccessful attempt to penetrate to the mystery of existence. Realising this,

Beethoven relaxed during the third movement and finished with the choral finale as a grandiose thisworldly culmination embracing the whole of mankind, a vision which can never be realised. But he appears to have reached the peak of his individual search for spiritual fulfilment in the Last Quartets.

There is hardly any more valuable way of life, apart from embarking on the full-time Pure Yoga path, than life with a commitment to its part-time practice on whatever level it is feasible for one. It will prepare one in the best possible way for the transition from this life into the mysterious beyond, whether it is the great void of nothingness, a kind of 'eternal peace', if in the unlikely event the prevailing belief among scientists is correct, or whether it will be another dimension of being, with possibly a sequence of further lives before one reaches the final state of liberation.

Notes :

{1} For details on Indian conceptions of the final realisation in different sects or schools of thought see Werner, 1977a, 18-19; 53-55; 59-61 & 71-92.

{2} Even the greatest personalities among physicists, starting with Einstein, had to admit that they were facing a mysterious transcendent dimension of reality which caused them to wonder (Dürr 2010). One atomic physicist took sabbatical leave from his research to explore the mystery beyond the reach of his science and delved into the study of Eastern religious and philosophical traditions. As a result he came to interesting conclusions which even changed his life (Capra, 1975 & 2002; cf. Zukav, 1980). Another one coined the term 'veiled reality' for the elusive dimension of existence suggested by quantum laws but ignored by most physicists, concluding that, as science is unable to formulate anything definite about the nature of existence, it has no right to deny the possibility of its ultimate transcendent nature (d'Espagnat, 2006).

{3} See Werner, 1985. For a comprehensive anthology on rebirth in East and West see Head & Cranston, 1977. The belief in the succession of lives (the theory of rebirth, reincarnation or metempsychosis) was widely held in antiquity and later on in diverse traditions (except in the three Abrahamic religions — Judaism, Christianity, Islam — and Bahá'í). It was without doubt held in India already in Vedic times. Hints pointing to it are scattered in various hymns, but it was clearly expressed in one hymn addressed to Savitar, the personification of the sun as the bestower of life, in the following verse:
RV 4,54,2

> *devebhyo hi prathamaṁ yajñiyebhyo 'mṛtatvaṁ suvasi bhāgam uttamam/*
> *ād id dāmānaṁ savitar vy ūrṇuṣe 'nūcīnā jīvitā mānuṣebhyaḥ //2//*
> You have first bestowed on gods, worthy of offerings, immortality as their supreme lot; then as a gift, o Vivifier, you endowed humans with lives following one after the other.

This verse was correctly translated by Ralph T. H. Griffith, *The Hymns of the Ṛgveda I,* (E. J. Lazarus and Co., Benares, 1889):

For thou at first producest for the holy Gods the noblest of all portions, immortality; Thereafter as a gift to men, O Savitar, thou openest existence, life succeeding life.

It is a mystery why most authors writing about the doctrine of rebirth or reincarnation in successive lives as evidenced in Indian scriptures misunderstood, misinterpreted, overlooked or ignored this verse and maintained that the earliest evidence of reincarnation in India can be found only in early Upaniṣads. Some of them even tried to ascribe the emergence of this belief to the influence of non-Āryan communities. This erroneous view is still perpetuated in some popular and even academic publications by authors ignorant of or poorly versed in early Indian scriptural sources. Even A. A. Macdonell (1898, 166), otherwise thoroughly knowledgeable about Vedic beliefs, wrote: "There is no indication in the Vedas of the later doctrine of transmigration..." and only knew about a hint in the ŚB 10, 4, 3, 10 about repeated death (*punarmṛtyu*). One would expect that he must have known Griffith's translation, but maybe he didn't. A. B. Keith (*The Religion and Philosophy of the Vedas and the Upanisads I-II,* 1925, 415) opined "The Rigveda and the Vedic literature of the period of the Saṁhitās and the Brāhmaṇas presents us with no clear proof of the belief in the transmigration of the dead.." He never refers to or cites RV 4.54.2.

Another hymn suggests the possibility of multiple destinations for the departed one after the cremation of his body and implies the karmic law of retribution. Cosmic constituents or forces which formed the complex structure of his individual personality are released on the death of the body, scatter and join their respective cosmic domiciles while he himself reaches, according to law, heaven or returns to earth in a new life: RV 10.16.3:

> *sūryaṁ cākṣur gachatu vātam ātmā dyāṁ ca gacha pṛthivīṁ ca dharmaṇā/*
> *apo vā gacha yadi tatra te hitam oṣadhīs. u prati tiṣṭhā śarīraiḥ //3//*
> Let vision go to the sun, breath [or spirit] to wind; you go to heaven or earth according to law, go to waters if you are so destined; [or] settle bodily in plants.

Further evidence of only temporary duration of new forms of life of the deceased one after cremation is provided by the ardent prayers of Vedic sages yearning for liberation from this transitory form of life and asking to be granted the same boon which was the lot of gods, namely immortality (*amṛta, amṛtatva*): "Lead us to immortality!" (*uto asmān amṛtatve dadhātana,* RV 5.55.4); "May I be released from death, not reft of immortality!" (*mṛtyor mukṣīya māmṛtāt,* RV 7.59.12); "Place me in that deathless, undecaying world ... make me immortal ..." (... *amṛte loke* ... *mām amṛtaṁ* ... *pari srava,* etc., RV 9.113.7-11).

As a result of good deeds one could reach heaven or return to one's original home (*punar astam*) and be reconstituted as a personality *tanū*): RV 10.14.8:

> *saṁgachasva pitṛbhiḥ saṁyameneṣṛāpūrten parame vyoman/ hitvāyāvadyam punar astam ehi saṁ gachasva tanvāsuvarcāḥ//*
> Meet ancestors and Yama along with your meritorious deeds in the highest heaven, having abandoned evil, go back to your eternal home and assume life as a brilliant personality. RV 10.15.14:
>
> *ye agnidagdhā ye anagnidagdhā madhye divaḥ svadhayā mādayante / tebhiḥ svarāḷ asunītim etāṁ yathāvaśaṁ tanvaṁ kalpayasva //14//*
> Those who have been cremated, as well as those who haven't, enjoy in the middle of heaven their draught. Being yourself, partake with them in the spirit world, reconstitute your personality as wished.

The expression *tanū* is usually translated as 'body' and so both the above verses are usually translated to indicate rebirth in another body: Griffith 10.14.8: "bright with glory wear another body"; Geldner: "vereinige dich mit einem (neuen) Leib in blühender Kraft!" and: "Nimm nach Wunsch einen (neuen) Leib an!" - Griffith 10. 15. 14: "grant them ... their own body..." - But since *tanū* figures both on the terrestrial level and the celestial level as well as the transcendent level (*punar astam*), I prefer to regard it as designating 'personality', a structure which changes the inner configuration of its character in conformity with the individual's actions (according to the laws of *karma*).

That heaven did not secure everlasting life and that one was subjected to repeated death (*punarmṛtyu*) even after being reborn in heaven is further attested by Śatapatha Brāhmaṇa (10.4.3.10; cf. 1.5.3.4; 10.3.3.8). Hence those pleas for immortality already in the Ṛg Veda quoted previously. The Ṛg Veda further proclaims that those of evil conduct "have engendered this abysmal station" (Griffith's translation): (RV 4.5.5)

> *idam padam ajanatā gabhīram*

Sāyana, the commentator to the Ṛg Veda (14th century), says that it means 'hell' (*narakasthāna*). Interestingly, the Vedic wording implies that the evildoers actually produce the abysmal place or hell by their evil actions, which is a philosophical issue worth a separate investigation.

Another hymn associates a similar fate with the lack of wisdom: "down sink the unwise": (RV 9.64.21)

majjanty avicetasaḥ

Sāyana supplements *majjanti* with *narake*, 'into hell'.

Or, according to RV 10.16.1-4, one may be sent to 'fathers' (*pitṛbhyaḥ*), go by law to heaven or earth (*dyāṁ ca gacha pṛthivīṁ ca dharmaṇā*), be embodied in plants (*oṣadhīṣu prati tiṣṭā śarīraiḥ*) or be carried to the place of 'do-gooders' (*vahainaṁ sukṛtām u lokam*).

The efficacy of the karmic aspect of the cosmic law, although implied in the above quotes, is not yet expressly described by the Vedas in terms of an impersonal force; their symbolism requires a personalised agency: it is the sun (*Suri*, *Sūrya*), the deified eye of the transcendental aspect of nature, that marks the moral quality of human actions, and various gods oversee their resulting consequences:
RV 6.51.2-3:

ṛju marteṣu vṛjinā ca paṣyann abhi caṣṭe sūryo arya evān //
stuṣa u vo maha ṛtasya gopān aditim mitraṁ varuṇaṁ sujātān aryamaṇam bhagam ...
Seeing honesty and falsehood of mortals, Sūrya notes the deeds of noble ones. I applaud you, guardians of the great Law: Aditi, Mitra, Varuṇa, the well-born ones, Aryaman, Bhaga ...

In the Upaniṣads the rebirth doctrine with karmic retribution is clearly spelled out and this is generally known and appreciated, although the earlier evidence is much less known and sometimes disputed despite the support for it by S. Radhakrishnan (1953. 113-117). He, however, viewed the "belief in rebirth" as "a natural development from the view of the Vedas and Brāhmaṇas" and says that it "receives articulate expression in the Upaniṣads" (p. 115). But what in fact developed was the language, the way of expressing the view; the view itself was undoubtedly fully understood already in Vedic times, possibly only in the higher echelons of the population, and among the homeless wanderers. That it was an elitist view among the Brahmins not shared with common folks transpires from a public debate at the court of king Janaka in which Yājīavalkya proves to be the wisest. When asked what becomes of a person after death, he takes the questioner aside not to discuss the topic in public: BU 3.2.13:

> *tau hotkramya mantrayāṁ cakrāte tau ha yad ūcatuḥ karma haiva tad ūcatuḥ atha yat praśaśaṁsatuḥ karma haiva tat praśaśaṁsatuḥ puṇyo vai puṇyena karmaṇā bhavati pāpaḥ pāpeneti*
> Having stepped aside, they deliberated. What did the two talk? Action verily they talked. What did they then praise? Action verily they praised. One becomes pure by pure action, wicked by wicked [action].

The very process of dying of a person is described in detail as losing all the sensory perceptions, thinking (*na manute*) and knowing (*na vijānāti*), but consciousness (or perhaps 'mentality') persists and goes on, no longer regarded as a real person as it is referred to by a neuter pronoun *sa*, 'that' which gets enveloped in formerly acquired knowledge, past deeds and accumulated experiences. It is then only an inactive, potential person ready for the next incarnation: BU 4.4.2:

> *sa vijñāno bhavati sa vijñānam evānvavakrāmati taṁ vidyā karmaṇī samanvārabhete pūrva prajñā ca*
> That becomes [just] consciousness, that consciousness passes on, knowledge, actions and previous experience envelop it.

This passage has been inaccurately translated, both by R. I. Hume and S. Radhakrishnan, and lately by V. J. Roebuck (2000. 84). She translated *karmaṇī* in the singular as 'action', and although in the footnote 167 she changes it to 'his actions', she comments on them as being "(particularly ritual ones), *karman*". This is unsubstantiated and out of character as far as this passage goes as well as a subsequent one which has the potent phrase: BU 4.4.5:

> *yathā kārī yathā cārī tathā bhavati*
> As he is doing, as he is behaving, so he becomes.

Not only good deeds, but also knowledge gained by discarding ignorance has an important impact on the position into which one is reborn: BU 4.4.3:

> *evam evāyam ātmā idaṁ śarīraṁ nihatya avidyāṁ gamiyitvā anyan navataraṁ kalyāṇataraṁ rūpaṇ kurute pitṛyaṁ vā gāndharvaṁ vā daivaṁ vā prajñāpatyaṁ vā brāhmaṁ vā anyeṣāṃ vā bhūtānām*

> Verily this self, having disposed of this body [and] caused ignorance to go, makes for itself a newer and more beautiful shape as that of a [departed] father, a *gandharva*, a god, a Progenitor, a Brahma or of other beings.

What is particularly interesting in this passage is that this earliest Upaniṣad already regards the positions of higher deities like Prajāpati and Brahma as available to be reborn into by anyone who manages to raise himself to their level, a view current later in Buddhism and also in Hinduism (in the epics and *purāṇas*).

As to the evidence for recurring cycles of world creation, there are clear indications of it already in the Ṛg Veda. One of its multivalent myths depicts world creation as a combat between the god Indra and the dragon Vṛtra (also referred to as the serpent Ahi), who is holding in captivity the cosmic waters, symbolising fecundity (RV 2.14.2). Indra pierces the dragon with his thunderbolt (*vajra*) and releases the life-enhancing waters (RV 1.57.6; 1.80.5; 1.103.2, etc.). The spontaneous process of creation then begins. In many hymns it is said that Indra kills the dragon, but in some the dragon is defeated but not slain, which suggests that the combat will have to be repeated: RV 3.34.3:

indro vṛtram avṛṇoc chardhanītiḥ pra māyinām aninād varpanītiḥ
As troop leader Indra surrounded the dragon (and) ran down the crafty deceiver. RV 5.30.6:

ahim ohānam apa āśayānam pra māyābhir māyinaṁ sakṣad indraḥ
Indra overcame with his wonderful powers the sly serpent. RV 10.104.9 :

indra ... vṛtra tūrye cakartha ...
Indra ... having vanquished the dragon ...

The frequent references to the combat in many hymns suggest that the combat is a recurring event which implies serial creation and repeated dissolution of the universe. On a lower level the combat is interpreted as a poetical description of the drama of the coming of the monsoon rains which is a yearly event renewing the fecundity of nature (cf. Macdonell, 1898. 59). The dark clouds represent the dragon or his castle or cave where the dragon keeps the captive waters. The lightning which heralds the oncoming downpour is Indra's thunderbolt (*vajra*) with which the dragon is pierced and eventually (temporarily) killed whereupon Indra restores the sun on the cloudless sky. The recurring nature of the fashioning of the world by the Ordainer is suggested also by the words *yathā pūrvam* (as before) in the hymn quoted below (RV 10.190.3. note 4).

The periodic emergence and reabsorption of the world is perhaps for the first time spelled out clearly in MaiU 6.17:

brahma vā idam agra āsīt, eko 'nantaḥ ... anūhya eṣa paramātmā, 'parimito, 'jo, 'atarkyo; 'cintya eṣa evaiṣa kṛstna-kṣaya eko jāgartīti, etasmād ākāoeād eṣa khalv idaṁ cetāmātram bodhayati; anenaiva cedam dhyāyate asmin ca pratyastam yāti
Originally this [world] was Brahma, the infinite one ... inscrutable [is] this supreme self. Unlimited, unborn, inconceivable, after the dissolution [of the world] he alone, unthinkable, stays awake [and] from that space he truly awakens this world's consciousness; only by him is this [world] conceived and into him it returns.

In the later texts of Hinduism — epics and *purāṇas* — the descriptions of the teaching of the cyclic creation and destruction or emergence and re-absorption of the universe, and also the evolutionary stages of world history during each period of creation, are greatly elaborated, often under the heading of Brahma's day and Brahma's night. The teaching of the cyclic sequence of universes is in one form or another accepted by all Indian religious sects and schools of Indian philosophy. It is also an integral part of the Buddhist view of the world in which, despite its somewhat mythological description, no god has any part in this process; the sequence of manifested universes and periods of rest between manifestation and dissolution is viewed as an impersonal flow of reality (Werner, 1977a, 32-46).

The teaching that the world exists in cycles of emergence and destruction was known also in ancient Greece as a part of the philosophy of stoicism which began to be taught by Zeno in the fifth century BCE. It is not possible to decide whether it was developed independently by him within the school, resulted from Indian influence or had an unrecorded pre-history in Greek thought. If the latter were the case, one could speculate about its origin in Indo-European antiquity.

Remarkably, modern cosmological theories about the origin and evolution of the universe have come round to accepting the possibility or even likelihood of an unending succession of aeons each starting with a 'space-time singularity' which explodes in a 'Big Bang' and initiates the evolution of the universe into galaxies over long periods of time in ever expanding space. But it cannot be sustained for ever and a 'gravitational collapse' results in a 'Big Crunch' or a new 'space-time singularity' which produces the big bang of the new universe, and so on. Early in the last century most astrophysicists believed that the universe had no beginning and was in a steady state. It was in 1917 that it was suggested and in 1929 confirmed by observation that the universe was in fact expanding, which led to the theory that it started by an initial explosion. In 1922 some theoretical considerations and mathematical calculations suggested the final collapse of our universe in a big crunch. Some confirmation came during the years 1964-90 from the observation of the 'cosmic microwave background' which is the most remote phenomenon observed and was produced very soon (in a matter of seconds) after the big bang (Penrose, 2011).

{4} The Vedic notions of *tapas, ṛta* and *satya* are the most important concepts ever produced by the Indian mind. They play a prominent part in the religious and philosophical thought of India over the centuries till the present day (*ṛta* in its new Hindu name as *sanātana dharma,* everlasting law or order).

In the Vedic tradition the notion of *ṛta,* the universal or cosmic law or order, is the first principle of phenomenal reality, but not its source. The primeval 'entity' or force behind everything is *tapas.* The corresponding verbal root for the word is *tap* (3rd person singular *tapati* or *tapyati,* also *tāpayati, -te*), meaning to 'blaze' or 'burn', also to 'shine', to 'heat' and to 'kindle'. The basic meaning of *tapas* is therefore usually given as 'heat', but that is already a watered down meaning (cf. Lat. *tepidus,* 'warm' and English 'tepid', which illustrates the 'demotion' of the meaning of the expression in the course of linguistic shifts which occurred progressively from the time of the presumed Indo-European parent language to languages of antiquity and to modern national languages). But in many Vedic hymns the word *tapas* has a stronger and deeper meaning in the context of human endeavour, for example as 'fervour' (RV 10,83,3), 'ardent wish' (RV 10.183.1) or 'religious or spiritual zeal' (RV 10.154.2 & 4 & 5). The most profound meaning of the word is revealed when it is used in the descriptions of the process of creation. In that context *tapas* appears to be the preexistent or primeval, latent or transcendent force which produces, in its creative fervour, phenomenal reality, the world.

In the latent state of *tapas* there are inherent in it the other two quantities: law (*ṛta*) and truth (*satya*). By its nature *tapas* is dynamic even in its latent state and this dynamism projects it into the dimension of phenomenality into which it also emanates the two quantities, law and being (what truly is, *sat-ya*, reality, truth) thus bringing about the phenomenal level of their existing. On this level *ṛta* becomes the effective universal law governing the whole of phenomenal reality. The primeval chaos is shaped into sequential time which will control living beings. The process of creation then continues with the assistance of the 'ordainer' (*dhātar*, comparable to the Greek *demiurge*) who fashions, as before (*yathā pūrvam*, RV 10.190.3), the earth and the visible universe, the heavens and the interim region. The hymn is somewhat enigmatic in its symbols, which probably had strong evocative power. The phrase 'as before' hints that the ordainer was busy even before the present creation of the world which points to the sequence of universes.

RV 10.190:

ṛtaṁ ca satyaṁ cābhīddhāt tapaso 'dhy ajāyata /
tato rātry ajāyata tataḥ samudro arṇavaḥ //1//
samudrad arṇavād adhi saṁvatsaro ajāyata /
ahorātrāṇi vidadhad viśvasya miṣato vaśī //2//
sūryācandramasau dhātā yathā pūrvam akalpayat /
divaṁ ca pṛthivīṁ cāntarikṣam atho svaḥ//3//

1. Cosmic order and reality was born from the utmost creative fervour. Thereupon was born night and then the billowing ocean.

2. From the billowing ocean was then born the year which ordained days and nights controlling all who blink the eyes.

3. Then, as before, the 'ordainer' fashioned the sun and moon, heaven and earth and the intermediary region. What splendour!

The noumenal nature of *tapas* comes across even more clearly in the most philosophical of Ṛgvedic hymns, usually referred to, not quite accurately, as the 'Creation Hymn'. which is worth quoting in full (cf. Werner, 1990a):

RV 10.129:

nāsad āsīn no sad āsīt tadānīṁ nāsīd rajo no vyomā paro yat /
kim āvarīvaḥ kuha kasya śarmann ambhaḥ kim āsīd gahanaṁ gabhīram //1//
na mṛtyur āsīd amṛtaṁ na tarhi na rātryā ahna āsīt praketaḥ /
ānīd avātaṁ svadhayā tad ekaṁ tasmād dhānyan na paraḥ kiṁ canāsa //2//
tama āsīt tamasā gūḷham agre 'praketaṁ salilaṁ sarvam ā idam /
tuchyenābhv apihitaṁ yad āsīt tapasas tan mahinājāyataikam //3//
kāmas tad agre sam avartatādhi manaso retaḥ pratahamaṁ yad āsīt/
sato bandhum asati nir avindan hṛdi pratīṣyā kavayo manīṣā //4//
tiraośīno vitato raoemir eṣām adhaḥ svid āsīd upari svid āsīt /
retodhā āsan mahimāna āsan svadhā avastāt prayatiḥ parastāt //5//
ko adhā veda ka iha pra vocat kuta ājātā kuta iyaṁvisṛṣṭiḥ/
arvāg devā asya visarjanenāthā ko veda yata ābabhūva //6//
iyaṁ visṛṣṭir yata ābabhūva yadi vā dadhe yadi vā na /
yo asyādhyakṣaḥ parame vyoman so aṅga veda yadi vā na veda //7//

A very readable metric translation of this hymn was made by Macdonell (1922) (reprinted by Radhakrishnan & Moor, 1957. 23-24). Another one is by Panikkar (1977. 58). Both were consulted in attempting the following literal rendering:

1. Neither non-being nor being then existed. There was no space nor yet heaven beyond it.

   What was concealed? Wherein? In whose protection? Was there water, deep, unfathomable?

2. Death then did not exist, not even deathlessness. Of night and day there was no sign.

   By its own force that One breathed windless. Nothing else than that existed.

3. Darkness there was by darkness at first hidden; all this was undifferentiated water.

That which was hidden by formless emptiness, that mighty One was born from primeval creative ardour (*tapas*).

4. Desire enveloped it in the beginning, which was mind's first seed.

The sages, searching in their hearts with wisdom, found the affinity of being in nonbeing.

5. Their line was extended crosswise. What was below, what was above?

Bearers of seeds were there, and mighty energy; below was self-assertion, above was thrust.

6. Who truly knows? Who can here tell from where this great emanation was born?

The gods came after this emanation. Who knows how it came to be?

7. How this emanation came to be, whether he produced it or not,

he who surveys it in the highest heaven, he only knows — or he does not know. In this hymn the pre-creational or pre-manifest latency, whose essence is the force of *tapas* and which is intent on manifestation, received a conceptual designation 'that One' (*tad ekaṃ*). It is comparable to the *to hén* of Plotinus and to the 'singularity' of modern astrophysicists before the Big Bang. Like the 'singularity', 'that One' or *tapas* was by itself in a state of unsustainable inner dynamic tension (it 'breathed windless') and so it burst into phenomenality. As is more explicitly, although in symbolical form, expressed in the hymn RV 10.190 cited earlier, creation of time and space followed, with the subsequent formation of the multiple universe. Astrophysics describes cosmic processes in mathematical formulae. This is a mental procedure within man's consciousness or mind which was, according to the theory of evolution, developed much later in the history of the cosmos after life in material form began. The Vedic texts, however, which were formulated by sages with inner, intelligent insight, recognised a mental concomitant as participating in all these processes right from the beginning or all along. Hence the desire enveloping the manifested 'mighty One' as mind's first seed. One has to assume that *tapas*, being the creative ardour, has a mental dimension even in its latency.

It would appear that the poet responsible for this hymn tried to present the process of creation or manifestation in impersonal terms as if he were translating mythological creation stories from older layers of the Vedic lore composed in symbolical language and poetic imagery, before conceptual means of expression started developing. Of the several Vedic creation myths the oldest one is centred around Aditi, the 'perfect' goddess of Infinity, mother of gods and kings and the divine mother of all that has been born and still is to be born. (The Aditi myth is fully analysed in Werner, 1990a; see also below, note 5.) It is almost certain that the author of the Creation Hymn was acquainted with the Aditi myth, but obviously carefully avoided involving in the creation process the figure of a personal deity, because he asserts a post-creational appearance of gods, probably including also the one who surveys the world from the highest heaven. Instead he chose the neutral term 'that One'. Yet throughout the hymn he is pussyfooting around the notion of some kind of a transcendent personality which would account for the mental character of the primordial *tapas* and for the post-manifest mind and the desire, its seed. This is implied already in the first stanza by the question 'In whose protection?' The expression *śarman* (house, dwelling, shelter, protection) has the overtone of a close personal sheltering. Then there is the possibility that the surveyor in the highest heaven might have been around in the transcendent and caused the manifestation and would therefore know how it came to be. The author is honest enough to admit that he is not certain about it either way. The problem whether the pre-manifest latency is an entity with the characteristics of personality or is completely impersonal would appear to be an insoluble mystery in all philosophical and religious systems. The problem is bypassed by monotheistic theologies which assert the pre-creational existence of God the Creator, a notion taken on faith. In purāṇic Hinduism Brahma the Creator, although responsible for the manifested universe, is not the creator in the proper sense of the word, but akin to the post-manifest 'ordainer' of RV 10.190.3 who figures in many other hymns under the name of Prajāpati (the Lord Progenitor). As stated before, he is akin to the *demiurge* of ancient Greek cosmogony.

In his capacity as ordainer, Prajāpati is described in the Brāhmaṇ as, the post-Vedic 'priestly' books, as the sole divine figure in empty space. He is thus the mythological equivalent of the 'mighty One' of RV 10.190, the first manifestation of the latent singularity or 'that One' brought about by the primeval *tapas*, before the process of manifestation proceeded to multiplicity. But to initiate the process of manifestation Prajāpati needed to stir himself up and that could be achieved only through *tapas*, the creative ardour. So this is the reason why *tapas* must have two levels of existing, the latent or noumenal and the manifest or phenomenal. And indeed, Prajāpati does stir himself up, which is expressed by the combination of *tapas* the noun with its verbal form *tapyati*. He is then able to carry out the diversification of phenomenal reality. This means that *tapas* with its dual form of existing is an active link between the manifest and the unmanifest, the creation and its hidden source: AB 5.32:

> *prajāpatir akāmayata: prajāyeya bhūyān syām iti sa tapo 'tapyata / sa tapas taptvā imān lokān asṛjata //*
> Prajāpati desired: let me procreate, become multiple; he kindled his zeal, having kindled his zeal, he emitted these worlds.

The active link between the primeval, pre-manifest *tapas* and the post-manifest *tapas* or creative zeal of the Progenitor became important also outside the context of philosophical and mythological cosmogony in the form of the mental endeavours of the inhabitants of this created or emanated world. In face of the repetitive nature of life with its sequence of deaths and births permeated by suffering some people found their existence so burdensome that they wanted to escape from it into the unmanifest sphere beyond time and space. There they expected to find unworldly peace in oblivion or otherworldly bliss of transcendent nature (*satcit-ānanda*) or, without speculative anticipation of the nature of their goal, simply liberation (*mokṣa*) from limited forms of repetitive existences trapped in time and space. They hoped to achieve it by developing the force of *tapas,* the post-manifest zeal, like the Progenitor did, but use it in 'reverse order'. It thus became a vehicle of reabsorption of the emitted existence of striving individuals back into transcendence. They were trying to abandon multiplicity in preference to the primeval oneness. Thus the activating of the force of *tapas* ('kindling the inner flame of zeal') was the way both to create multiplicity as well as to abolish it.

This development is reflected also in the Upaniṣads. They describe the renunciant wanderers, usually referred to as ascetics (*śramaṇas*), as 'kindling their zeal' or 'zealous endeavour', i.e. generating *tapas,* in order to overcome attachment to the world, seen as evil, and to progress on the path to liberation. The terminology of the Upaniṣads became more philosophical; the primeval unity was now conceived as being 'buried' deep down within each individual as his inner self (*ātman*). The ascetic could produce *tapas* out of himself and free himself through it from evil (*tapasā pahata pāpmā*). Then, through meditation (*cintayā*), he would develop knowledge (*vidyā*) and become liberated and united with (his inner) self (*muktas tv ātmann eva sāyujyam upaiti*) (MaiU 4,4).

The zealous endeavour of wanderers trying to eliminate all of their attachments to ordinary life often involved severe asceticism, so that *tapas* came to be identified with the practice of austerities and that is how the word is often translated.

As to *ṛta*, the notion designating the universal law inherent in the noumenal *tapas* from which it passed into the phenomenal dimension of reality occurs in many Vedic hymns in different contexts and has multifarious meanings. Usually it refers to the world, with all its dimensions, visible and transcendental, and the living beings within them. It has the character of universal validity. Among the many meanings of *ṛta* can be named, besides order and law, also rule, orderliness, regularity, reliability, balance, justice etc. It applies to all processes in all dimensions of phenomenal reality, visible and invisible, not in the sense that everything happens in conformity with it, but that any irregularity that may occur is subject, in the long run, to its balancing power. Even gods are subordinate to it.

The notion of *satya* is derived from *sat*, meaning 'being', and it also has multifarious meanings. It can be interpreted as 'that which is', alias 'reality'. But when it is pointing to noumenal reality, it stands for 'truth' in the absolute sense, 'absolute truth', often further classified as 'the highest truth' or 'the final truth'. In the context of phenomenal dimension, namely ordinary reality, it is used in assertions that something is true: 'This is truth'.[5] The principle of multi-level interpretation of the Vedas has been known in India since very early times (Werner, 1981b, 292-295). It was first expressly recorded and used by Yāska (*Nirukta* 7.1-2; cca 5th century BCE) and appreciated in modern time by Eliade (1959, 19ff. and 1979, 207). Three levels of interpretation can be adduced from Yāska's account:

(1) *ādhyātmika* or the level relating to *ātman*, the essence or inner core of man, of all beings and of reality as a whole. This meaning of the expression *ātman*, known since the early Upaniṣads, was current in Yāska's time, but in Vedic texts its meaning is 'breath'. The underlying core or innermost basis

of reality is referred to in the RV as *aja*, the 'Unborn'. All beings depend on it and it underlies the concept *tad ekam*, 'that One', whose nature is inner dynamism even in its transcendent state (it 'breathed windless', see above, RV 10.129.2). That One got going the 'primeval germ' which already harboured all gods and was resting on the 'navel' (in the centre) of the Unborn and was received by waters (which are always a symbol of phenomenal reality prior to its bursting into existence). The priests reciting the hymns during their sacrificial rituals will never discover a creator of all this since they are after worldly rewards, not truly searching for truth. So again, as in the creation hymn (RV10.129), the following hymn suggests that there was no creator of the world, or if there was one, he cannot be known. The hymn is dedicated to Vioevakarman, the 'all-doer', but this is no contradiction, because Vioevakarman is just one of the gods, who were originally harboured in the primeval germ before they emerged from it into space. Vioevakarman then had the function equivalent to the Greek demiurge and fashioned the universe when it emerged from the waters. RV 10.82.5-7:

paro divā para enā pṛthivyā paro devebhir asurair yad asti /
kaṁ svid garbham prathamaṁ dadhra āpo yatra devāḥ samapaśyanta viśve //5//
taṁ id garbham prathamaṁ dadhra āpo yatra devāḥ samagachanta viśve /
ajasya nābhāv adhy ekam arpitaṁ yasmin viśvāni bhuvanāni tasthuḥ/ /6//
na taṁ vidātha ya imā jajanānyad yuṣmākam antaram babhūva /
nīhāreṇ a prāvṛtā jalpyā cāsutṛpa ukthaśāsaoe caranti //7//

5. That which is prior to heaven, prior to earth, prior to gods and demons, is verily the primeval germ; the waters received it with all gods seen together.
6. The waters received the primeval germ with all gods assembled in it; it first rested on the Unborn's navel, the One upon which all beings depend.
7. You do not know him who may have produced these [beings], something else came between you.

Rapt in confusion, muttering and satisfied with their life, the reciters of praises carry on.

In a rare moment of utmost curiosity the poet asks why has this phenomenal world with its different dimensions of existence been brought about at all and demands an answer, but no answer is forthcoming; the rest of the stanza resorts to mythological imagery of the manifested world:

RV 1.164.6-7:

acikitvāñ cikituṣaś cid atra kavīn pṛchāmi vidmane na vidvān /
vi yas tastambha ṣaḷ imā rajānsy ajasya rūpe kim api svid ekam //6//
iha bravītu ya īm aṅga vedāsya vāmasya nihitam padaṁ veḥ /
śḥrṣṇah. kṣīraṁ duhrate gāvo asya vavriṁ vasānā udakam padāpuḥ //
7//

6. Myself lacking understanding, unknowing, I ask wise seers for knowledge.

Why has the One established these six regions as the external appearance of the Unborn?

7. Let him who knows proclaim it here. The glorious bird is firmly placed, cows draw milk from his head and water lingers in its shelter.

The translation of the second sentence in the last stanza is tentative. The text is obscure, but it points to a region of the external world and thereby abandons the *adhyātmika* level. (Sāyana interprets the bird as the sun and cows as clouds which absorb milk/water and temporarily hold it.)

The notions of 'the One', the 'Unborn' and 'primeval germ' could emerge only when the language of the hymns developed a relatively advanced conceptual idiom exhibiting the ability of abstraction. But most Vedic hymns are composed in a language which employs symbols, metaphors and mythological imagery. Yet there are even in them passages pertaining to the *ādhyātmika* level, particularly in cosmogonical myths featuring the goddess Aditi, as was already explained. Her name means 'infinity' and 'boundlessness' and rules out any appearance by her in any shape so that there are no descriptions of her features, except that she is luminous (*jyotiṣmatī*, RV 1.136.3). She is, in fact, the oldest symbolical representation of the primeval source of reality (and thus equivalent to the philosophically understood *tapas* of RV 10.129) prior to her incarnation in the phenomenal world among other gods. She is behind everything and is even identified with all that ever was or will be born, thus anticipating Vedāntic pantheism:

RV 1.89.10:

aditir dyaur aditir antarikṣam aditir mātā sa pitā sa putraḥ /
viśve devā pañca janā aditir jātam aditir janitvam //
Aditi is the infinite heaven, Aditi is the space between [heaven and earth; or the intermediary sphere between the spiritual and the material], Aditi is mother and father and son [as well as] all gods and the five classes of humans, Aditi is all that has been born, Aditi is all that will be born.

In many hymns Aditi is specifically mentioned as mother of gods (*mātā devānām*, RV 1.113.19) and particularly of a group of the most prominent gods, such as Indra, Vāyu, Bṛhaspati, Mitra, Agni, Pūṣan, Bhaga (RV 1,14,3), Varuṇa (RV 1.25.13), Aryaman (RV 8.47.9), Savitar (RV 8.18.3-5) and Dakṣa (RV 10.72.4), who bear the collective name Ādityas.

(2) *ādhibhautika* or the level relating to everything that has 'being' — elements, natural phenomena such as thunder, lightning, heavens (supported from the transcendence by one 'foot' of the Unborn), rivers, oceans etc. This level, as we saw above, emerged from the transcendental level represented in one myth by Aditi, in another by 'that One' and elsewhere by Aja, the Unborn. The poet here addresses the gods asking them to hear his words of praise which continue in subsequent stanzas and in a further hymn. He expects some boon in return. In the same tone the following stanzas continue also onto the next (theological) level.

RV 10.65.13:

pāvīravī tanyatur ekapād ajo divo dhartā sindhur āpaḥ samudriyaḥ / viśve devāsaḥ śṛnavan vacānsi me sarasvatī saha dhībhiḥ puram dhyā / /13//

Thunder, the daughter of lightning, the Unborn which supports heavens with one foot, Sindhu, waters and oceans, all gods, hear and mark my words, with SarasvatÓ, giving abundantly.

RV 10.66.11:

samudraḥ sindhū rajo antarikṣam aja ekapāt tanayitnur arṇavaḥ / ahir budhnyaḥ śṛnavad vacānsi me viśve devāsa uta sūrayo mama //11//
The ocean, Sindhu, the interim region, the one-footed Unborn, reverberating thunder, the Dragon of the Deep, listen to my words, all gods and my patrons.

(3) *ādhidaivika* or the level relating to gods, i.e. the theological-liturgical context in which the Vedas have been used for the purpose of worship, sacrificial rites and traditional religious observances. Individual gods, groups of gods and 'all gods' are invoked in numerous hymns and asked for various boons. Among them is again the personified one-footed god Aja Ekapād, the individualised emanation of the Unborn. One can speculate that his 'one-footedness' means that he is diminished, because phenomenal reality is the incomplete manifestation of absolute reality.

RV 6.50.14:

uta no' hir budhnyaḥ śṛṇotv aja ekapāt pṛthivi samudraḥ / viśve devāḥṛtāvṛdho huvānā stutā mantrāḥ kaviśastā avantu //14//
Also the Dragon of the Deep should hear us, the One-footed Unborn,, the Earth, the Ocean, all gods, upholders of law, as praying poets offer you hymns of praise.

RV 7.35.13:

śam no aja ekapād devo astu śam no 'hir budhnyaḥ śam samudraḥ / śam no apām napāt perur astu śam naḥ pṛśenir bhavatu devagopā //13//

May the One-footed Unborn God grant us blessing, so, too, the Dragon of the Deep and the ocean, and the effervescent Son of Waters, may the god-protected (heavenly) Cow grant us blessing.

Finally we have here on the *ādhidaivika* level the most interesting proclamation about the goddess Aditi, mother of gods, representing on the *ādhyātmika* level the primeval source of phenomenal reality, that she was born into the world of her son Dakṣa which makes her the sister of Ādityas. This reappearance of the personified transcendent primeval creative force as a goddess on the phenomenal level of reality may be regarded as an anticipation or origin of the later Hindu doctrine of divine incarnations:

RV 10.72.4-5:

bhūr jajña uttānapado bhuva āśā ajāyanta /
aditer dakṣo ajāyata dakṣād v aditiḥ pari //4//
aditir hy ajaniṣṭ a dakṣa yā duhitā tava /
tām devā anv ajāyanta bhadrā amṛtabandhavaḥ //5//
4. The world was born from the World mother [Aditi], the space was born from the earth. Dakṣa was born from Aditi, Aditi in turn from Dakṣa.
5. For Aditi was born, Dakṣa, as your daughter. Subsequently other gods were born, the shining ones, bound for immortality.

{6} The first finds which led to the discovery of this highly developed pre-Vedic civilisation were made at the present-day Harappa on the river Ravi, a tributary of the river Chenab which joins the river Sutlej before they together reach the upper Indus. According to the rules accepted among archaeologists this civilisation should properly be called Harappan. But the main bulk of excavations of remnants of this civilisation was carried out at Mohenjo-daro on the lower Indus by Sir John Marshall in the 1920s and was reported on by him first in the *Illustrated London News* on 20th September 1924 (Taddei, 1970). His monumental account of the whole undertaking followed several years later (Marshall, 1931). Because Mohenjo-daro is more impressive than Harappa and many archaeological finds kept being dug out along the river

Indus, the original name Sir John Marshall used in the title of his work, Indus Civilisation, was subsequently, and often still is, used by some authors and so is the other designation, namely Mohenjo-daro civilisation.

It took more than a decade before the first very readable and still important comprehensive presentation followed (Piggot, 1950). It was succeeded by a scholarly survey, which, one would think, could hardly have had popular appeal (Wheeler, 1953), yet it was reprinted several times; its 3rd edition was published as a supplementary volume to the *Cambridge History of India* (1968, repr. 1972). (The author later wrote an interesting postscript to his researches in India in a little book which is a good read, see Wheeler, 1976.)

Another decade and a half was needed to produce a scholarly work which would take into account all further discoveries up to the date it was written. It was the achievement of a husband and wife team who themselves, besides utilising the work of others, did important archaeological field work (Allchin, 1968). They are only rather overcautious in dating the civilisation. This is even more the case in the work whose author relied too much on the then not very accurate samples of carbon dating (Fairservis, 1971). But this latter book has its merits. At that time the well publicised Harappan civilisation needed to be put into a wider prehistoric, historical and geographical context. It was necessary to frame it with accounts of local earliest human settlements, a kind of prelude to civilisation, and with the still quite primitive village communities in neighbouring regions. It was further opportune to deal, after the peak of the Harappan civilisation, with the process of its slow deterioration before it was partly overwhelmed by incoming āryans. Then there was the problem of what survived from the Harappan civilisation after its downfall and possible integration into the Vedic and post- Vedic culture. The most important result of this integration of Harappan civilisational achievements resulted in the urbanisation of the post-Vedic āryan culture. This is what the book by Fairservis describes with the added bonus of being very readable. Many other expert research articles and monographs followed, supplemented by further comprehensive surveys (for example Wright, 2010, to name but one). The chronology was corrected to take account of longer phases of the development and decline of the Harappan culture: Early Harappan 3300–2600, Mature Harappan 2600–1900 and Late Harappan 1900–1300, the latter coinciding and mingling with early āryan culture (Shaffer, 1992).

As to the attempts to decipher the Harappan script on the seals, there is a comprehensive account of them by Parpola (1994, latest edition 2009). Subsequently he developed a theory according to which the language of the inscriptions on the seals is of Dravidian type (Parpola, 2010). This theory is almost universally disputed.

Another attempt has been made by a solitary private researcher on the fringe of academic credibility, Egbert Richter (2001). He believes that he can read some inscriptions and identify them with corresponding lines in several Ṛgvedic hymns. He further believes that the statuette of a man in a ceremonial garment represents a priest-king whose name was Ushanas. He added this name to his own name to form a pseudonym (personal communication, 2014). His views have not found support in academic circles as his methodical approach does not meet the strict criteria of research.

{7} RV 7.21.5:

na yātava indra jūjuvur no na vandanā śaviṣṭha vedyābhiḥ /
sa śardhad aryo viṣuṇasya jantor mā śiśnadevā api gur ṛtaṁnaḥ//
We are not impelled, Indra, by spirits, nor by mighty demons unwittingly. Let our noble race prevail and let not those whose god is phallus get hold of our holy rituals.

RV 10.99.3:

sa vājaṁ yātāpaduṣpadā yan svarṣātā pari ṣadat saniṣyan /
anarvā yac chatadurasya vedo ghnañ chioenadevān abhi varpasā bhūt//
He goes surefooted to battle to victoriously achieve heaven; invincible, he cleverly destroyed the hundred gates of the haunt of those whose god is phallus, slaying them.

{8} DN II. 291:

idha ... bhikkhu araññagato vā rukkhamūlagato vā suññāgāragato vā nisīdati pallaṅkaṁ ābhujitvā ujuṁ kāyaṁ paṇidhāya parimukhaṁ satiṁ upaṭṭhapetvā so sato va assasati sato passasati
here ... a monk, having gone into a forest or to the roots of a tree or into an empty room, and having set his mindfulness alert, sits down cross-legged, while keeping his body erect. Thus he mindfully inhales and mindfully exhales.

{9} The most important of the medieval sources are: Gorakṣanātha's *Gorakṣa Saṁhitā* (possibly from the 12th century), Svātmārāma Yogindra's *HaṭhaYogapradīpikā* (14th century) and Gheraṇḍ anātha's *Gheraṇḍa Saṁhitā* (17th century).

{10} In some works it is wrongly asserted that the invading Āryans were nomads, but they were already settled and advanced in agriculture some 3,000 years earlier in their original home in Southern Russia. When the growth of population caused them to migrate, taking their cattle with them, they proceeded slowly to the East, temporarily settling down for longer periods to grow food. The most important long stops were in Central Asia and in Īrān, followed by the crossing of the Hindukush mountains to India (Werner, 1987).

{11} Cf. Werner (1989b), particularly 22-24.

{12} A *muni* is described in vivid terms in a late hymn of the Ṛg Veda as the phenomenon of the 'long-haired one' (*keoein*). The hymn comes from the time when the true Vedic seerhood may virtually have vanished and was probably composed by an unknown intrigued outsider who was broad-minded enough to give this undistorted account of a conspicuous phenomenon existing outside his own tradition:

RV 10.136:

Keśy agniṁ keśī viṣaṁ keśī bibharti rodasī /
keśī viśvaṁ svar dṛśe keśīdaṁ jyotir ucyate //1//
munayo vātaraśanāḥpiśaṅgā vasate malā /
vātasyānu dhrājiṁ yanti yad devāso avikṣata //2//
unmaditā mauneyena vātān ā tasthimā yayam /
śarīred asmākaṁ yūyam martāso abhi paśyatha //3//
antarikṣeṇa patati viśvā rūpāvacākaśat /
munir devasya-devasya saukṛtyāya sakhā hitaḥ //4//
vātasyāśvo vāyoḥ sakātho deveṣito muniḥ /
ubhau samudrāv ā kṣeti yas. ca pūrva utāparaḥ //5//
apsarasāṅ gandharvāṅ ām mṛgāṇāṁ caraṇe caran /
keśī ketasya vidvān sakhā svādur madintamaḥ //6//
vāyur asmā upāmanthat pinaṣṭi smā kunannamā /
keśī viṣasya pātreṇ a yad rudreṇ āpibat saha //7//

1. The long-haired one carries within himself fire and poison and both heaven and earth. To look at him is like seeing heavenly brightness in its fullness. He is said to be light itself.

2. The sages, girdled with the wind, are clad in dust of yellow hue. They follow the path of the wind when the gods have penetrated them.

3. 'Uplifted by our sagehood we have ascended upon the winds. You mortals see just our bodies. '

4. The sage flies through the inner region, illuminating all forms below. Given to holy work he is the companion of every god.

5. Being the wind's horse, Vāyu's companion and god-inspired, the sage is at home in both oceans, the eastern and the western.

6. Wandering in the track of celestial beings and sylvan beasts, the long-haired one, knowing their aspiration, is a sweet and most uplifting friend.

7. For him Vayu churned, even pounded that which is hard to bend, as the long-haired one drank poison from the cup, together with Rudra.

This hymn is full of mythological imagery and poetic

metaphors and therefore requires interpretation verse by verse:

1. 'Carrying within oneself fire and poison, heaven and earth' expresses the wide scope of human experience, ranging from enthusiasm and creativity to depression and agony which the sage has mastered, reconciling within himself these contrary forces and thus becoming a visible embodiment of accomplished spirituality (*svar*) and radiating light.

2. The phrase 'girdled with the wind' obviously means that the long-haired sage went about without clothes, only the yellow dust of the Indian soil covering his skin (which may be the origin of the usual colour of the traditional robes of Indian mendicants and Buddhist monks which was later adopted). Being penetrated by gods would mean that the long-haired sages were raised beyond the earthly dimension, perhaps living permanently in a kind of meditative state of mind.

3. While the first two verses were descriptive, the third one is a quotation in which one of the sages confirms that, as spiritual personalities, they have reached a different level of existence from that of other people who, as ordinary mortals, cannot see them as they really are, but see only their bodies. This is a hint that they themselves are no mere mortals but have reached the plane of immortality, an achievement desired and often prayed for by traditional Vedic worshippers as has been shown above.

4. This verse asserts that the sage moves in the inner dimension of reality (*antarikṣan*) where he perceives and understands 'all forms', i.e. the archetypes of everything that exists. He is dedicated only to worth while effort and can communicate with any god.

5. The imagery of this verse suggests that the sage is in tune with life at large, both as far as the biological vitality,

the lower aspect of life, is concerned (being Vāta's 'horse') and (as Vāyu's companion) also with respect to the subtle aspect of the cosmic force of life. It follows from the previous verse that he has reached this situation by his dedication to some form of spiritual discipline, the only worthwhile task for men. No intervention of divine grace, help or assistance is mentioned, yet he is penetrated by the divine or is god-inspired and at home in both oceans, the eastern and the western, the east being a symbol for the world of light, spirit and wisdom, while the west symbolises the world of darkness, matter and ignorance. The sage's mastery of both worlds virtually anticipates the later notion of Mahāyāna *bodhisattvas* equally at home in both *nirvāṇa* and *saṁsara.*

6. The spiritual achievements of the long-haired sage enable him to follow the tracks of all beings, even the superhuman and subhuman ones, to know their hearts and, by fully understanding them, to become their real friend and help by uplifting them. This is yet another anticipation of a Buddhist notion, namely that of a 'beautiful' or spiritual friend (*kalyāna mitra*), an expression occasionally used for a personal teacher also in the Theravāda tradition (*kalyāna mitta*), but mainly in the Mahāyāna Buddhist context where it contrasts with the Hindu image of a stern *guru.* The ability to read other beings' hearts is among the Yogic powers (*siddhis*) later listed by Patañjali as well as being a quality said to have been possessed by the Buddha in unequalled measure and used by him particularly when instructing and helping his pupils and listeners on the path of their moral and spiritual progres.

7. This last verse of the hymn presents some real difficulties to interpreters, as the history of its misrepresentation testifies. Help is available if one draws on the materials contained in the *purāṇas.* The image of churning and pounding connects this verse with the purāṇic myth of churning the cosmic ocean to obtain the drink of immortality. The purāṇic myths, although usually recorded

relatively late, undoubtedly have a long history and the contents of some of them may have stemmed from very ancient times indeed and therefore the allusion to one of them in the RV need not be surprising. If one again takes Vāyu as standing for universal life, one may understand the first part of the verse as stating that having reached harmony with the universal life, the sage also reached immortality, the highest goal of spiritual life. The second part of the stanza then indicates that he did so while still active in ('drinking from') the stream of mortal (poisonous) life in the material world through having a material body (represented probably by the image of the cup). One can paraphrase the situation in Buddhist terminology: having realised *nirvāṇa,* he remains active in *saṁsāra* untouched by its defilements.

In the purāṇic legend poison is released as a by-product during the process of churning the cosmic ocean to obtain the drink of immortality before it is won, and it thus symbolizes the unavoidable phenomenon of death within the manifested universe. Only when death is overcome by one's spiritual power is true immortality obtained. The gods do not manage to do so in the legend. Only Śiva is capable of drinking the poison without being harmed and he is, significantly enough, the popular Hindu symbol of spiritual progress through Yoga. As the Vedic Rudra was the same as, or developed into, Śiva, the image of drinking poison in his company suggests the spiritual achievement gained by Yoga, and as Rudra/Śiva saved by his deed the gods and other beings from the deadly poison, the image also suggests the idea of the assistance which the long-haired sage gives or is capable of offering to others. But he does not do so as a saviour, for he is not and has not become a god or divine incarnation; he is still a human being who has reached accomplishment and thereby the realm of immortality, but who can only assist the world rather than save it, an idea which again points in the direction of the Mahāyāna Buddhist teachings as expressed in the Bodhisattva doctrine.

Thus what clearly emerges from this unique hymn is a picture of the noble figure of a spiritual hero, an ideal which has been the focal point of spiritual aspirations in India throughout millennia and which has retained its appeal up to the present day. (For a full analysis of the *keśin* hymn see Werner, 1989a.)

{13} For comprehensive information on Vrātyas refer to Hauer, 1927, a thorough and most important research work on the subject. Some supplementing material was later included in Hauer, 1958. An informative book in English, heavily dependent on Hauer, to be used critically, is Choudhary, 1964. For *puṁścalī* see Hauer 1927, 246ff. and Hauer 1958, 36.

The tradition of the teams of three continued in post-Vedic centuries until their tracks eventually disappeared, but there are reasons to believe that they reappeared under the name of Bāuls - wandering religious poet-singers who form a loose sect within the *bhakti* movement. Some Bāul songs and poems were collected in the 19th century and inspired the poetry of Rabindranath Tagore. Their beginnings are usually regarded as stemming from the activities of Caitanya (1486-1533), an ecstatic devotee of Kṛṣṇa, but there are indications that they should be seen as being of a more ancient origin. Those who roam in groups of three, one of them being a female dancer, bear a striking resemblance to the ancient Vrātya teams of three. In modern times all Bāuls resisted for a long time commercial offers to perform in concert halls, but eventually some of them succumbed in the second half of the last century.

{14} ChU 7.6.1:

dhyānaṁvā cittād bhūyaḥ dhyāyatīva pṛthivī dhyāyatīvāntarikṣan dhyāyatīva dyauḥ dhyāyatḥvāpoḥ dhyāyatḥva parvatāḥ dhyāyatḥva devamanuṣyāḥ tasmā ya iha manuṣyāṇām mahattvam prāpnuvanti dhyānāpādāṁśā ivaiva te bhavanti atha ye 'lpāḥ kalahinaḥ pioeunā upavādinas te atha ye prabhavaḥ dhyānāpādāṁśā ivaiva te bhavanti dhyānam upāsveti /

> Contemplation is verily superior to mentation; the earth in a certain manner contemplates, space in a certain manner contemplates, heaven in a certain manner contemplates, waters in a certain manner contemplate, mountains contemplate in a certain manner, gods and humans contemplate in a certain manner. Therefore whoever of men achieve here greatness, they become partakers of the state of meditation. But those who are small are contentious, backbiting [and] accusing. Those who are distinguished become partakers of the state of meditation. Be devoted to meditation.

{15} The sources for the Vedic conception of the human personality are funeral hymns which describe the process of dying. From them it is obvious that the Vedic view of the human personality was one of a composite structure whose constituents were dynamic cosmic forces called deities (*devatās*). That means that they were not understood as blind mechanical or physical forces, but as possessing inherent intelligence of different grades which led them to combine into functional units with inner hierarchical structures on both cosmic and individual levels. Thus cosmos emerged out of primeval chaos and individual beings out of the interplay of these cosmic forces, with the 'unborn' (*aja*) underlying all as catalyst. When a man dies, the *devatās* constituting his personality return to their cosmic abodes. His sight goes to the sun which represents the element of light and his breath, i.e. his individual life force, merges with the wind, i.e. cosmic life force (*sūryaṁ cakṣur gachatu vātam ātmā*, RV 10.16.3).

References to further constituents of man's personality have to be assembled from other hymns and texts. In RV 10.9013-14 we find the mind (*manas*) whose cosmic counterpart is the moon, which stands for the element of mentality. The mouth, i.e. speech or the capacity to communicate and understand meanings, corresponds to the cosmic element of fire represented by Agni, the divine flame, symbolising the light of consciousness. Indra, the ruler of lightning, brings the flash of insight enabling higher understanding and knowledge. Hearing (*śrotra*) has its cosmic abode in space. A passage in AB 2,1,6,13 mentions another constituent dispersed on death, namely *asu*, the animating principle, which figures as such in many hymns (RV 1.113.16; 10.15.1; AV 6.104.1; 8.1.3; 8.1.21; 8.2.1). It corresponds to the interim region (*antarikṣan*) which is on the one hand the space between heavenly worlds and earthly abodes and on the other is the inner space of man's mind (cf. RV 10.136.4). A hymn in AV 11.8 elaborates further on the constituents of the personality, listing among them various physiological processes and psychological capacities, all held together in the core of man:

> AV 11.8.32 *tasmādai vidvān puruṣam idam brahmeti manyate/*
> *sarvā hy asmin devatā gāvo goṣṭa ivāste //32//*
> Therefore he, who knows this person, thinks: he is *brahman*,
> for all these deities are [in him] like cattle in [their] pen.

The 'pen' is what makes loose cattle into a herd. This stanza suggests that by being composed of divine powers (*devatās*), man is divine, also by having *brahman* as his core. What AV already names *brahman*, RV terms *aja*, the unborn, as mentioned earlier; the unborn supports the earth and heaven (*ajo na kṣaṁ dadhāra pṛthivīṁ tastambha dyām* ..., RV 1.67.6 = in Griffith's translation 1.67.3). 'Earth and heaven' stands for the universe as a whole, and within it the One established six regions or levels of existence as the external emanation of the Unborn (RV 1.164.6. see above, note 5). Besides mental or subtle constituents of the personality there is of course the gross structural unit called body (*śarīra*, RV 10.136.3) which gets burned on the funeral pyre. The subtle structural unit which holds together the mental constituents and is, like the whole universe, sustained by *aja*, is, on the phenomenal level, represented by *tanū*, the subtle structural unit harbouring the individualised cosmic forces or 'deities' (similarly as the 'pen' creates a herd out of loose cattle in the above AV quote). Even when enveloped in the gross body, *tanū* is the person as an individual and its inner composition or configuration of the constituent deities makes for a person's character by which one is known to others and which has the power to reflect itself also in the outward bodily likeness, i.e. in one's face. Gods and other beings in higher regions who have no gross body, nevertheless have *tanū*, a visible shape (sometimes somewhat misleadingly rendered 'subtle body'), for *tanū*, when the deities disperse after bodily death, remains very briefly an empty structure before the deities return to fill it in a new configuration and the person reappears again fully reconstituted on some level of existence, perhaps even with a new material body. Thus the Vedic notion of the complex personality structure in three layers implies that the Vedic man had an elaborate and quite profound psychological understanding of the subject. The fact that it has been preserved for us only in a non-systematic way in the hymns must not prevent us from acknowledging its profundity and value (more in Werner, 1978b & 1988 & 1996).

{16} Some more details are given in Werner (1986a, 1-7). The passages of the TU discussed in the text have never been analysed and interpreted in this way before. Hauer (1958, 96) mentions TU only as evidence that Yoga was known in the Brāhmanic circles at the time, but was systematically pursued outside them. Before him Paul Deussen (1938. 230. 3rd ed. 1938) did not attach importance to the word Yoga in the passage and translated it as 'Hingebung' (devotion). It was made even more obscure in the recent English translation of Deussen's book where the word Yoga is rendered 'resignation or devotion'. In English Hume (1931. 285) and Radhakrishnan (1953. 545) translate Yoga as 'contemplation'. Neither of them attempted any explanation why the term should have been employed in the TU. Eliade (1969. 117) only lists the passage as the first occurrence of the term "in its technical sense" without any explanation of its significance in the TU.

{17} The Brāhmanic scheme of four stages of life (*āśramas*) was developed for the members of the three higher castes at about the time of the earliest Upaniṣads: a youngster became first a pupil (*brahmacārī*) for a period of up to 12 years, during which he learned his father's trade; then as an adult he married, became a householder (*gṛhastha*) and started a family; when he had an adult son following in his footsteps and saw the births of his grandchildren, he left home and became a forest-dwelling hermit (*vānaprastha*). Towards the end of his life he should have left even his hermitage and become a wanderer (*saṅnyāsi*). The scheme was an ideal programme and was never universally followed. It was developed by the Brāhmanic establishment probably at the time when the movement of *śramaṇas* became attractive to many young people of rich families who, satiated by easy pleasures and at the same time disillusioned with ritualistic religion, were joining famous teachers in forest hermitages or were becoming wanderers, as did Maskari Gośāla, who became the founder of the Ājīvika school, Vardhamana Jñātriputra, who became Jina Mahāvīra, or Siddhatha Gotama, who became the Buddha. As a result the Brahmins recognised the value and need of searching for final truth with full commitment, but insisted that one should first fulfill one's duty to one's family and society by securing the family line and with it also the continuation of the ritual offerings for the benefit of departed ancestors and their well-being in the afterlife.

{18} For the criteria of perfect enlightenment as described by the Buddha in some of his discourses, see Werner, 1981a.

{19} Virtually every book on basic Buddhism describes the four noble truths and the eightfold path and attempts their interpretation. Many books on wider topics with passages on Buddhism in them do the same (cf. Werner, 1977a, repr. 1980, 1998 and 2016, 120-130. This book can be used to obtain a survey of the teachings of Buddhism by piecing together passages dealing with it with the help of the index). A good anthology of texts from the Pāli Canon arranged so as to illustrate the four truths and particularly the path is by Nyanatiloka: *The Word of the Buddha*, Buddhist Publication Society, Kandy 1959 (13th ed.; 1st in 1907; 1st in German 1906). Two specialised books on Buddhist meditation are highly instructive: Vajiraīāṇa, Paravehera Mahāthera, *Buddhist Meditation in Theory and Practice*, Gunasena, Colombo 1962.

Nyāṇaponika Thera, *Satipaṭṭhāna. The Heart of Buddhist Meditation*, Rider, London 1962, and many subsequent reprints and editions. Nyāṇaponika favours the later Theravāda commentarial division in the practical progress of meditation efforts into two varieties of methodical approach. One is geared to developing absorptions (*jhānas*) and is called 'tranquillity meditation' (*samattha-bhāvanā*) which by itself supposedly does not lead to final liberation. The other one can be applied after developing *jhānas* or even right from the start and is called insight meditation (*vipassanā-bhāvanā*). It can supposedly bypass full absorptions by developing insight into the three characteristics of existence, impermanence (*anicca*), suffering (*dukkha*) and non-self (*anatta* — which Nyanaponika translates, I think inaccurately, as impersonality) and can result in final liberation. However, this division has no basis in the actual wording of either of the two Suttas which deal with the practice of meditation, Satipaṭṭhāna Sutta (MN 10) and Mahā Satipaṭṭhāna Sutta (DN 22). In them there is described the whole comprehensive method of practice on the basis of 'foundations of mindfulness' (*satipaṭṭhāna*) which should result in liberation. The *vipassanā* method as a 'shortcut' bypassing *jhānas* was developed in Burma, possibly in the 19th century and became widely used in meditation centres there and on Sri Lanka.

{20} The Buddha's account of his enlightenment:

MN I.26. PTS p. 167:

asaṅkhiliṭṭaṁ anuttaraṁ Yogakkhemaṁ nibbānaṁ ajjhagamaṁ / ñāṇañ ca pana me dassanaṁ udapādi / akuppā me vimutti ayam antimā jāti natthi dāni punabhavo ti//
Unblemished, incomparable, bond-free *nibbāna* has been reached; wisdom and vision arose in me: unshakable is my liberation, this is the last birth, there is now no further repeat of becoming.

{21} For quick information on Jainism the reader may consult a chapter in a book on the history of religions or an encyclopedic work. For deeper study see Dundas, 1992 or Schubring, 2000.

{22} OEU I. 1-3:

brahmavādino vadanti: kiṁ kāraṇam brahma, kutaḥ sma jātā, jīvāma kena, kva ca sampratiṣṭhāḥ, adhiṣṭ hitāh kena sukhetareṣu vartāmahe brahmavido vyavasthām. kālaḥ svabhāvo niyatir yadṛcchā bhūtāni yoniḥ puruṣa iti cintyā samYoga eṣam na tvātmabhāvād ātmāpy anīśaḥ sukhaduḥ khahetoḥ.
te dhyānayogānugatā apaśyan devātmaśaktiṁ svaguṇair nigūḍhām; yaḥ kāraṇāni nikhilāni tāni kālātmayuktāny adhitiṣṭhati ekaḥ.
Those who discuss *brahman* say: What is the origin? Brahma? From where comes birth, through what do we live, on what established, through what determined do we abide in bliss or opposite, you knowers of Brahma? Time, spontaneity, necessity, fortuity, elements, procreation force, primeval person are unthinkable as are all of them together because of self; even self is helpless with respect to the cause of bliss and hardship.
Those who took up the technique of yogic absorption saw the power of the self of God vested in his own qualities, who alone superintends all these causes lumped together, starting with time and finishing with the self (cf. RV 10.90, *puruṣa Sūkta,* and ŚU III, 11-19).

ŚU I. 6-7: *sarvājīve sarvasamsthe bṛhante asmin hamso bhrāmyate brahma cakre pṛthag* ātmānam preritāram ca matvā juṣṭ as tatas tenāmṛtatvam eti

utgītam etad paramaṁ tu brahma tasmims trayam supratiṣṭhākṣaram ca atrāntaram brahma-vido'viditvā līnā brahmaṇi tat-parāyoni-muktāḥ

In this vastness of all life and all things the swan [individual soul] roams about in the wheel of Brahma [= the round of rebirths], believing itself to be different from the Turner [of the wheel, i.e. Brahma]; yet, welcomed by him, he reaches immortality. Songs praise this as the highest *brahman* and in it is grounded the imperishable triad; having found out what is in it, those who know [and are] merged in *brahman* [and] thus [gone] beyond, [are] liberated from the womb [i.e. rebirth].

ŚU I, 8-9: *samyuktam etat kṣaram akṣaram ca vyaktāvyaktam bharate viśvam īśaḥ; anñśas* cātmā badhyate bhoktṛ bhāvāt jñātvā devam mucyate sarva pāoeaiḥ

jñājñau dvāv ajāv īśanīśāv ajā hy ekā bhoktṛ-bhogyārtha yuktā anantaś cātmā viśvarūpo hy akartā trayam yadā vindate brahman etad

The powerful one sustains all this within, the perishable and the imperishable, the manifest and the unmanifest, yet, when [it becomes] an enjoyer and thereby bound, the self is powerless; but when God is known, one is released from all fetters. There are two [who are] unborn, connected together, one knowing and one unknowing, one powerful and one powerless; one is the enjoyer [and the other] one is here for the sake of being enjoyed; and then there is the infinite Self, all-embracing, inactive. When this triad is known, [one becomes] *brahman.*

ŚU I. 12:

> *etad jñeyam nityam evātmasamstham nātaḥ param veditavyam hi kiñcit bhoktā bhogyam preritāram ca matvā sarvam proktam trividham brahman etad*
> That [triad] should be known as innate, truly established in [one's own inner] self; nothing higher remains to be known; when the enjoyer, the object of enjoyment and the impeller are understood, all has been explained; that is the threefold *brahman.*

{23} A survey of the problems around the authorship of the *Yoga Sūtra* is in Eliade 1969, note I.2 (not 1.3 as given in

Connolly 2007, 245. note 28) and in White 2014. 226-234; cf. Maas 2006.

{24} I have slightly modified Hauer's terminology in summarising his views, because I differ from him in the interpretation of the meaning of some of the terms he used.

{25} "Over the past forty years in particular, critical scholarship on Yoga has become a growth industry in the American and European academies" (White 2014. 9).

{26} My translation of this chapter and all other chapters is rather tentative, but tries to penetrate to the spirit of the text of the Ys. It differs from practically all other extant translations, because it does not draw hints from commentaries. It cannot be a smooth explanatory text since it would then be another commentary, but it gives a good idea of the unsystematic nature of the YS which can be used to support the theory, mentioned earlier, that the chapters dealing with practice (2. 3. 4 and 5) are based on notes taken by pupils when listening to their teachers, sometimes supplemented from memory outside the teaching sessions. For that reason they cannot be entirely reliable in all details.

A tentative translation of the chapter on cessation (*nirodha*, I.1-22):

I.1 *atha yoga-anuśāsana*

Now [follows] the instruction on Yoga. I.2 *yogaś citta vṛtti nirodhah.*

Yoga is elimination [or cessation] of the fluctuations of the mind.

I.3 *tadā draṣṭuḥ* svarūpe 'vasthānam

Then the perceiver's state [is as] in his own nature.

I.4 *vṛtti sā-rūpyam itaratra*

Otherwise the fluctuations shape him.

I.5 *vṛttayaḥ pañcatayaḥ kliṣṭa-akliṣṭāḥ*

The fluctuations [i.e. activities of the mind, either] harmful [or] benign, are fivefold:

I.6 *pramāṇa-viparyaya-vikalpa-nidrā-smṛtayaḥ*

Cognition, error, mentation, [deep, i.e. dreamless] sleep, memory.

I.7 *pratyakṣa-anumāna-āgamāḥ pramāṇāni*

Cognitions [come from] observation, inference and testimony.

I.8 *viparyayo mithyā-jñānam atadrūpa-pratiṣṭham*

Error is incorrect knowledge, not based on actuality.

I.9 *śabda-jñāna-anupātī vastu-śūnyo vikalpaḥ*

Mentation is based on verbal knowledge and lacks substance.

I.10 *a-bhāva-pratyaya-ālambanā vṛttir nidrā*

Deep sleep is sustained by the absence of perception.

I.11 *anubhūta-viṣaya-asampramoṣaḥ smṛtiḥ*

Memory does not allow experienced phenomena to vanish.

I.12 *abhyāsa-vairāgyābhyām tan nirodhaḥ*

The cessation [of the fluctuations of the mind is achieved] by practice and dispassion.

I.13 *tatra sthitau yatno 'bhyāsaḥ*

Practice [requires] continuous effort.

I.14 *sa tu dīrgha-kāla-nairantarya-satkāra-āsevito dṛḍha bhūmi*

If maintained for a long time uninterruptedly, correctly and assiduously, it [becomes] a firm foundation.

I.15 *dṛṣṭa-anuśravika-viṣaya-vitṛṣṇasya vaśīkāra-samjñā vairāgyam*

Dispassion is conscious subjugation of the thirst for objects of experience whether seen or heard.

I.16 *tatparam puruṣa-khyāter guṇa-vaitṛṣṇyam*

That, ultimately, is no more thirsting for attributes [of nature], [it is] assertion [of oneself] as [pure] person.

I.17 *vitarka-vicāra-ānanda-asmitā-rupa-anugamāt saṁprajñātaḥ*

[While there is still] discernment it is accompanied by deliberation and reflection associated with bliss and a form of I-ness.

I.18 *virāma-pratyaya-ābhyāsa-pūrvaḥ saṁskāra-śeṣo 'nyaḥ*

By sustained practice is achieved discontinuance of these processes, but they leave behind residual impressions.

I.19 *bhava-pratyayo videha-prakṛti-layānam*

These impulses continue [into the next existence], after the body is gone, merged with nature.

I.20 *śraddhā-vīrya- smṛti-samādhi-prajñā-pūrvaka itareṣām*

For others, [who cultivate] faith, heroic energy, mindfulness, contemplation and wisdom,

I.21 *tīvra-samvegānām āsannaḥ*

[and] ardently desire emancipation,* it is near,

I.22 *mṛdu-madhya-adhimātratvāt tato 'pi viśeṣaḥ*

depending on [their] mild, average or exceeding [effort].

*[In translating *samvega* as 'emancipation', I follow Hauer, 1958, 465, note 8: 'samvega ist ein seltenes Wort, das ich sonst nirgends in der eigentlichen Yogaliteratur angetroffen habe. Seine Bedeutung war offenbar auch den Kommentatoren nicht mehr klar. Vācaspatimiśra setzt es einfach mit *vairāgya* gleich, was sicher nur eine Vermutung ist. Die richtige Deutung geht aus Hemacandras Yogaoeāstra II,15 hervor. Dort ist es mit *mokṣābhilāsa* 'Verlangen nach Befreiung' erklärt.]

{27} A tentative translation of the *īśvara praṇidhāna* chapter (I,23-33):

I.23 *īśvara praṇidhānád vā*

Or [realisation can be achieved] by devotion to the Lord.

I.24 *kleśa-karma-vipāka-āśayair puruṣa viśeṣa īśvaraḥ*

The Lord is a special kind of person unaffected by karmic actions, their fruitions and residues.

I.25 *tatra niratiśayam sarvajña-bījam*

That is the cause of his perpetual omniscience.

I.26 *purveṣām api guruḥ, kālena anavacchedāt*

Unrestricted by time, he was the very teacher of the earlier [yogis].

I.27 *tasya vācakaḥ praṇava*

His significant sound is murmuring *om.*

I.28 *taj-japas tad-artha-bhāvanam*

Whispering it realises the goal

I.29 *tataḥ pratyakcetanā-adhigamo 'py antarāya-abhāvaś ca*

through implanting it into consciousness, and as a result obstacles disappear.

I.30 *vyādhi-styāna-saṃśaya-pramāda-ālasya-avirati-bhrānti-darśana-alabdhabhūmikatvaanavasthitatvāni citta-vikṣepās, te 'ntarāyāḥ*

Disease, languor, doubt, carelessness, idleness, indulgence, misconception, inability to progress by stages, inconstancy, mental distractions — these are obstacles.

I.31 *duḥkha-daurmanasya-aṅgamejayatva-śvāsa-praśvāsā vikṣepa-sahabhuvaḥ*

Distractions are accompanied by sorrow, despondency, trembling of limbs and irregular breathing.

I.32 *tat-pratiṣedha-artham ekatattva-abhyāsaḥ*

This can be warded off by purposeful practice of one single procedure:

I.33 *maitrī-karuṇā-muditā-upekṣāṇām sukha-duḥkha-puṇya-apuṇya-viṣayāṇām bhāvanātaścitta-prasādanam*

The mind becomes tranquil by radiating friendliness, compassion, sympathetic joy and equanimity towards all, whether good or evil.

{28} A tentative translation of the *samādhi* text (I.34-51)

I.34 *pracchardana-vidhāraṇābhyām vā prāṇasya*

Or (one can proceed) by retaining breath before its expulsion

I.35 *viṣayavatī vā pravṛttir utpannā manasaḥ* sthiti nibandhanī

or one gains stability of mind by focussing on arising mental phenomena

I.36 *viśokā vā jyotiṣmatī*

or on those which, being luminous, bring about cessation of sorrow,

I.37 *vītarāga-viṣayam vā cittam*

or on those which leave the mind desireless

I.38 *svapna-nidrā-jñāna-ālambanam vā*

or on those based on insights from deep sleep

I.39 *yathā-abhimata-dhyānād vā*

or on those brought about through meditative absorption.

I.40 *parama-aṇu-parama-mahatva-anto 'sya vaśīkāraḥ*

Thus mastery on all levels [is won].

I.41 *kṣīṇa-vṛtter abhijātasya iva maṇer grahītṛ-grahaṇa-grāhyeṣu tatatha-tadañjanatā samāpattiḥ*

Thus, without mind's fluctuations, being like a transparent jewel, the perceiver, unaffected by perceiving and by what is perceived, is in unified contemplation.

I.42 *śabdārtha-jñāna-vikalpaiḥ samkīṇā savitarkā samāpatti*

As long as there is verbal knowledge and conceptualisation, it is unified contemplation mingled with deliberation.

I.43 *smṛti-pariśuddhau svarūpa-śūnyā iva arthamātra-nirbhāsā nirvitarkā*

When [it has] wiped off all memories [and become] empty in itself, it shines without any deliberation.

I.44 *etayā eva savicārā nirvicārā ca sūkṣma-viṣayā vyākhyātā*

Similarly is explained the subtle experience with reflection and without reflection.

I.45 *sūkṣma-viṣayatvam ca aliṅga-paryavasānām*

This subtle region is an abode without marks.

I.46 *tā eva sabījaḥ samādhiḥ*

This is verily completion [still] with seedṣ

I.47 *nirvicāra-vaiśāradye 'dhyātma prasādaḥ*

From perfection of non-reflection comes the transparency of the inner self

I.48 *ṛtambharā tatra prajñā*

and in it is truth bearing wisdom

I.49 *śruta-anumāna-prajñābhyām anyaviṣayā viśeṣa-arthatvāt*

which has quite different results than wisdom based on scriptures or inference.

I.50 *taj-jaḥ saṁskāro 'nya-saṁskāra-pratibandhī*

[Subtle] mental formations born from [the truth bearing wisdom] prevent grosser formations from developing.

I.51 *tasya api nirodhe satva-nirodhān nirbījaḥ samādhiḥ*

When even [the subtle mental formations] are stilled, everything being stilled, there is just the seedless completion.

{29} A tentative translation of the *kriyā* text (II,1-27)

II.1 *tapas-svādhyāya-īśvarapraṇidhānānikriyā yogaḥ*

Active Yoga involves austerity, own study [and] respect for the Lord.

II.2 *samādhi-bhāvanā-arthaḥ kleśa-tanūkaraṇa-arthaoe ca*

Its purpose is to diminish afflictions and develop concentration.

II.3 *avidyā-asmitā-rāga-dveṣa-abhiniveśāḥ kleoeāḥ*

Adherence to ignorance, egoity, passion [and] hatred — these are afflictions.

II.4 *avidyā kṣetram uttareṣām prasupta-tanu-vicchinna-udārāṇām*

—Ignorance is the field of further dormant and weak [afflictions] to be intercepted before they get aroused.

II.5 *anitya-aśuci-duḥkha-anātmasu nitya-śuci-sukha-ātma-khyātir avidyā*

Ignorance is viewing of impermanence, impurity, suffering and non-self as permanence, purity, pleasure and self.

II.6 *dṛg-darśana-śaktyor ekātmatā iva asmitā*

The viewing ability may present the I-am-ness as if it were unique selfhood.

II.7 *sukha-anuśayī rāgaḥ*

Consequence of pleasure is lust.

II.8 *duḥkha-anuśayī dveṣaḥ*

Consequence of suffering is hatred.

II.9 *sva-rasa-vāhī viduṣo 'pi tathā rūḍdho 'bhiniveśaḥ*

Even the knowing one is burdened with the instinct of self-preservation.

II.10 *te pratiprasava-heyāḥ sūkśmāḥ*

These subtle [tendencies] are to be overcome by reversal.

II.11 *dhyāna-heyās tad vṛttayaḥ*

All mental activities are overcome by meditative absorption.

II.12 *kleśa-mūlaḥ karma-āśayo dṛṣṭa-adṛṣṭa-janma-vedanīyaḥ*

Rooted afflictions and accumulation of *karma,* whether seen or unseen, will be felt when born.

II.13 *sati mūle tad-vipāko jāty-āyur-bhogāḥ*

If there is a cause, its effects are experienced after birth during one's lifespan.

II.14 *te hlāda-paritāpa-phalāḥ punya-apunya-hetutvāt*

The consequences of delight or anguish are caused by pure or impure actions.

II.15 *pariṇāma-tāpa-samskāra-duḥkhair guṇa-vṛtti-virodhāc ca duḥkham eva sarvam vivekinaḥ*

The latent tendencies of sorrow may exhaust painful afflictions [so that] the opposite [i.e. relief] [results]; conflicts within forces [of nature] may fluctuate, but to the discriminating one all is truly suffering.

II.16 *heyam duḥkham anāgatam*

Future suffering can be avoided.

II.17 *draṣṭṛ-dṛśyayoḥ samyogo heya hetuḥ*

The association of perceiver and the perceived is the cause [of suffering] to be avoided.

II.18 *prakāśa-kriyā-sthiti-śīlam bhūta-indriya-ātmakam bhoga-apavarga-artham dṛśyam*

The perceived, with its character of brightness, activity and continued existence, and consisting of elements, senses and selfhood may aim either for experiencing [the world] or for emancipation.

II.19 *viśeṣa-aviśeṣa-liṇgamātra-aliṇgāni guṇa-parvāṇi*

The manifestations of forces [of nature] are with or without distinction [and] with or without marks.

II.20 *draṣṭā dṛśi-mātraḥ śudho 'pi pratyaya-anupaśyaḥ*

The perceiver is nothing but perceiving; [he is] pure, but even so he conceives ideas.

II.21 *tad-artha eva dṛśyasya ātmā*

The purpose is truly (to see) the essence of what is perceived.

In some manuscripts there is an extra aphorism:

III.22 *etena śabdâdyantardhânam uktaṁ*

Thereby, it is said, sounds and other capabilities disappear (cf. Hartranft online 2003).

The result is that the numbering of subsequent verses would be changed and chapter III would have 56 aphorisms instead of the usual 55.

II.22 *kṛtārtham prati naṣṭam apy annaṣṭam tad-anya-sādhāraṇatvāt*

When the goal is reached, its opposite [phenomenality] is discarded, but it is not discarded by others who are still filled [by it].

II.23 *sva-svāmi-śaktyoḥ sva-rūpa-upalabdhi-hetuḥ samyogaḥ*

By reason of one's drive one gets hold of a form [i.e a body], thus getting yoked [in a new incarnation].

II.24 *tasya hetur avidyā*

The cause [of it is] ignorance.

II.25 *tad-abhavāt samyoga-abhāvo hānam tad dṛśeḥ kaivalyam*

In the absence [of ignorance] there is no getting yoked, there is escaping, that is the perceiver's emancipation.

II.26 *viveka khyātir aviplavā hāna-upāyaḥ*

Continuous discriminative viewing is the means of escaping.

II.27 *tasya saptadhā prānta-bhūmi-prajñā*

That is the last stage of the sevenfold wisdom.

{30} A tentative translation of the *aṣṭāṇga yoga* chapter (II.28-55 & III.1-55 & IV.1)

II.28 *yogāṅgānuṣṭhanāt aśuddhi-kṣaye jñāna-dīptir ā viveka-khyāteḥ*

By practising the limbs of Yoga impurities decrease and the light of knowledge increases by upholding discrimination.

II.29 *yama-niyama-āsana-prāṇāyāma-pratyāhāra-dhāraṇā-dhyāna-samādhayo 'ṣṭav aṅgāni*

The eight limbs [are]: restrictions, obligations, posture, breath control, withdrawal [of attention from sensory perception], holding [meditation object], [meditative] absorption, completion.

II.30 *ahiṁsā-satya-asteya-brahmacarya-aparigraha yamāḥ*

The obligations are nonviolence, truthfulness, non-stealing, 'divine faring' [chastity], non-acquisitiveness.

II.31 *ete jāti-deśa-kāla-samaya-anavanachinnāḥ sārvab-haumā mahā vratam*

Practised irrespective of status by birth, place, time or circumstance and at all levels, these [precepts] represent a Great Vow.

II.32 *śauca-saṅtoṣa-tapas-svādhyāya-īśvarapraṇidhānāni niyamāḥ*

Observances are: purity, contentment, austerity, self-development, respect for the Lord.

II.33 *vitarka-bādhane pratipakṣa-bhāvanam*

Hindering thoughts should be countered by generating their opposite.

II.34 *vitarkāhimsādayaḥ kṛta-kāritānumoditā lobha-krodha-moha-pūrvakā mṛdumadhyādhimātrā duḥkhājñānānanta-phalā iti pratipakṣa-bhāvanam*

Thoughts of harming etc. or condoning it when done by others [result from] mild, moderate or intense greed, anger and delusion; their result is endless fruition of suffering; they should be countered by generating their opposite.

II.35 *ahimsā -pratiṣṭāyām tat-samnidhau vaira-tyāgaḥ*

With nonviolence established, the presence of enmity will be forsaken.

II.36 *satya-pratiṣṭāyām kriyāphalāśrayatvam*

With truthfulness established, acting and its fruits [in future lives] will proceed accordingly.

II.37 *asteya-pratiṣṭāyām sarva ratna-upasthānam*

With non-stealing established, there is scope for [wearing] all jewellery.

II.38 *brahmacarya-pratiṣṭāyām vīrya-lābhaḥ*

Through abstaining from sex vigour is acquired.

II.39 *aparigraha-sthairye janma-kathantā sambodhaḥ*

Steadfastness in non-grasping results in understanding the 'why' of birth [i.e. how *karma* works].

II.40 *śaucāt svāṅga-jugupsā parair asamsargaḥ*

From [mental] purity comes detachment from own limbs and avoidance of grasping [those] of others.

II.41 *sattva-śuddhi-saumanasyaikāgratendriya-jayātma-darśana-yogyatvāni ca*

The purification of mind makes for its happiness and for capabilities of one-pointed mastery of senses, one is [then] seeing just oneself.

II.42 *samtoṣād anuttamaḥ sukha-lābhaḥ*

From contentedness [comes] the attainment of incomparable happiness.

II.43 *kāyendriya-siddhir aśuddhi-kṣayāt tapasaḥ*

Perfection of body and senses and elimination of impurities [result] from ascetic practice.

II.44 *svādhyāyād iṣṭa devatā-samprayogaḥ*

From the study of [i.e. recitation of and meditation on] sacred texts [one establishes] communion with one's chosen deity.

II.45 *samādhi-siddhir īśvarapraṇidhānāt*

The perfection of concentration [results] from devotion to the Lord.

II.46 *sthira sukham āsanam*

The position [should be] firm and comfortable.

II.47 *prayatna-śaithilyānantya samāpattibhyām*

Effort brings an infinite reward in unified contemplation.

II.48 *tato dvandvānabhighātaḥ*

Then [one is] beyond opposites.

II.49 *tasmin sati śvāsa-praśvāsayor gati-vichedaḥ prāṇāyāmaḥ*

This being so, while breathing in and out, the achievement of suspension of [this] flow is the control of breath.

II.50 *bāhyābhyantara-stambha-vṛttir deśa-kāla-samkhyābhiḥ paridṛṣṭo dīrgha-sūkṣmaḥ*

Its outgoing, ingoing and stationary phases [are to be] observed as to the place [at the nostrils, in the throat and in the movement of the abdomen] and [their] duration [and] subtleness [and they are to be] counted.

II.51 *bāhyābhyantara-viṣayākśepī caturthaḥ*

The fourth stage is beyond the domain of outgoing and ingoing breath [which may mean that it ceases completely].

II.52 *tataḥ kśīyate prakāśāvaraṇam*

Thus the veil obscuring clarity is removed.

II.53 *dhāraṇāsu ca yogyatā manasaḥ*

The mind then is capable of holding [the meditation object or procedure].

II.54 *sva-viṣayāsamprayoge cittasya svarūpānukāra ivendriyāṇām pratyāhāraḥ*

Disassociation of one's mind from objects [of experience] and the same with respect to one's body and the senses [is] withdrawal.

II.55 *tataḥ paramā vaśyatā indriyāṇām*

Then there is the ultimate mastery of the senses.

III.1 *deśa-bandhaś cittasya dhāraṇā*

The bonding of the mind to [or focussing it on] one point is holding.

III,2 *tatra pratyayaikatā-natā dhyānam*

Then, bent on oneness, it [becomes] absorption.

III.3 *tad evārtha-mātra-nirbhāsam svarūpa-śūnyam iva samādhi*

Its true and only purpose is revealing the emptiness of one's own form [which is] indeed completion.

III.4 *trayam ekatra samyamaḥ*

These three [*pratyāhāra, dhyāna* and *samādhi*] as a unit [represent] global mastery.

III. 5 *taj-jayāt prajñālokaḥ*

From that achievement [is derived] the lustre of wisdom.

III.6 *tasya bhūmiṣu viniyogaḥ*

It is arrived at in progressive stages.

III.7 *trayam antar-aṅgam pūrvebhyaḥ*

The earlier three [*pratyāhāra, dhyāna* and *samādhi*] are inner limbs.

III.8 *tad api bahir-aṅgam nirbījasya*

But even they are external limbs beside the seedless.

III.9 *vyutthāna-nirodha-saṁskārayor abhibhava-prādur-bhāvau nirodha-kṣaṇa-cittānvayo nirodha-parināmaḥ*

When the stilling of latent impressions gets under way and the mind, linked to it, appears momentarily subjugated, [it is] a development [towards] cessation.

III.10 *tasya praśānta-vāhitā saṁskārāt*

Its tranquillised flow is due to latent impressions [which are on the way to stilling].

III.11 *sarvāthataikāgratayoḥ kṣayodayau cittasya samādhi-pariṇāmaḥ*

The sole purpose of the mind reaching the dominion of one-pointedness is maturing for completion.

III.12 *tataḥ punaḥ śāntoditau tulya-pratyayau cittasyaikāgratā-pariṇāmaḥ*

There again, the lofty tranquillity and similar achievements result in the perfection of mind's one-pointedness.

III.13 *etena bhūtendriyeṣu dharma-lakṣaṇāvasthā pariṇāmā vyākhyātāḥ*

By all these elements is explained the transformation of characteristics and conditions of what has been established.

III.14 *tatra śāntoditāvyapadeśya-dharma-anupātī dharmī*

So the arisen calm is indefinable as is the bearer of the consequent state.

III.15 *kramānyatvam pariṇāmānyatve hetuḥ*

The succession of variations is the cause of further transformations.

III.16 *pariṇāma-traya-samyamād atīta-anāgata-jñānam*

Through development and holding together the three [achievements — *pratyāhāra, dhyāna* and *samādhi* — comes] knowledge of the past and future.

III.17 *śabdārtha-pratyayānām itaretarādhyāsāt saṅkaras tat pravibhāga-samyamāt sarvabhūta-* ruta-jñānam

Owing to superimposition of word, meaning and idea — one on the other — confusion arises; their disciplined discernment [results] in understanding the utterances of all beings.

III.18 *samskāra-sākṣātkaraṇāt pūrva-jāti-jñānam*

By [being able] to view directly latent impressions knowledge of previous births [is acquired]

III.19 *pratyayasya-para-citta-jñānam*

[and by direct] perception the knowledge of the minds of others,

III.20 *na ca tat sālambhanam tasyāviṣayī-bhūtatvāt* [but] not their causes [which are] out of reach.

III.21 *kāyarūpa samyamāt tad-grāhya-śakti-stambhe cakṣuḥ-prakāśāsamyoge 'ntardhānam*

By controlling the bodily form, having seized it with the power of suspension, the eye loses vision and [there is] disappearance [one becomes invisible].

III.22 *sopakramam nirupakramam ca karma tat samyamād aparānta jñānam ariṣṭebhyo vā*

Karmic results may be immediate or delayed, concentration on omens brings knowledge of the end [the time of one's death].

III.23 *maitryādiṣu balāni*

By [radiating] friendliness etc. [compassion, sympathetic joy and equanimity towards all as in I,33] powers [are developed].

III.24 *baleṣu hasti-balādini*

By [focusing] on the strength of the elephant, powers etc. [are developed].

III.25 *pravṛttyāloka-nyāsāt sūkṣma-vyavahita-viprakṛṣṭa-jñānam*

By concentrating on one's capacity of vision, [one gains] knowledge of subtle, concealed and distant objects.

III.26 *bhuvana-jñānam sūrye samyamāt*

By concentrating on the sun, [one gains] knowledge of the universe,

III.27 *candre tārā vyūha-jñānam*

on the moon, knowledge of stellar constellations,

III.28 *dhruve tad-gati-jñānam*

on the polar star, knowledge of stellar movements,

III.29 *nābhi cakre kāya-vyūha-jñānam*

on the navel, the energy centre, knowledge of bodily structure,

III.30 *kaṇṭ ha-kupe kṣut-pipāsā-nivṛttiḥ*

on the pit of the throat, one overcomes hunger and thirst,

III.31 *kūrma-nāḍyam sthairam*

on tortoise duct, [one gains] steadfastness,

III.32 *mūrdha-jyotiṣi siddha-darśanam*

on the [mystic] light on top of the head, [one can] see the Perfect Ones.

III.33 *prātibhād vā sarvam*

Or all that [may be won] by sudden illumination.

III.34 *hṛdaye citta-samvit*

By [focusing] on the heart, [one gains] comprehensive understanding of one's mind.

III.35 *sattva-puruṣayor atyantāsaṇkīrṇ ayoḥ pratyayāviśeṣo bhogaḥ parathānya-svārthasamyamāt puruṣa-jñānam*

[Everyday] experience does not distinguish between the notion of nature and between the person [as such] which are absolutely distinct; by concentrating on the difference between the one and the other, [one gains] knowledge of oneself as [pure] person.

III.36 *tataḥ prātibha śrāvaṇa-vedanādarśāsvāda-varttā jayante.*

As a result of this illumination the senses of hearing, feeling, seeing, tasting [and] smelling are enhanced.

III.37 *te samādhāvupasargā vyutthāne siddhayaḥ*

The emergence of supernormal powers may become an impediment of completion.

III.38 *bandha-kāraṇa śaithilyāt pracara-samvedanāc ca cittasya paraśarīrāveoeaḥ*

By loosening the mind's binding to sense organs and by sensation of going, taking possession of another's body [is possible].

III.39 *udāna-jayāj jala-paṅka-kaṇṭakādiṣv asaṅga' utkrāntiś ca*

By mastering the vital air rising upwards one can walk over water, mud, thorns etc. without touching them.

III.40 *samāna-jayāt prajvalanam*

By generating vital air [circulating through the solar plexus] one becomes radiant.

III.41 *śrotrākāśayoḥ sambandha-samyamād divyam śrotram*

By concentrating on the connection between hearing and space, [one gains] divine [distant] hearing.

III.42 *kāyākāśayoḥ sambandha-samyamāl laghu-tūla-samāpatteoe cākāoea-gamanam*

By concentrating on the relation of body to space and the relation of lightness to cotton, one can travel through space.

III.43 *bahir akalpitā vṛttir mahāvidehā tataḥ prakāśāvaraṇa-kṣayaḥ*

When the [mind's] activities are no longer generated from outside, then this great disembodiment [dissociation from materiality] lifts the veil from illumination.

III.44 *sthūla-svarūpa-sūkṣmānvayārtthavattvasamyamād bhūta-jayaḥ*

By concentrating on one's gross form and linking it to pervasive subtlety one masters the elements.

III.45 *tato 'ṇima-ādi-prādurbhāvaḥ kāya-sampat tad-dharmānabhighātaś ca*

From that comes the power to appear as small as an atom etc. as the body is now perfect and no longer subject to laws [of nature].

III.46 *rūpa-lāvaṇya-bala-vajra-saṃhananatvāni kāya-sampat*

The perfection of the body [includes] beauty of form, grace, strength and diamond-like durability.

III.47 *grahaṇa-svarūpāsmitānvayārthavattvasaṃyamād indriya-jayaḥ*

By concentration on the purpose for grasping one's form and the pervasiveness of the function of I-am-ness, [one] masters one's sensory apparatus.

III.48 *tato manojavitvam vikaraṇa-bhāvaḥ pradhāna-jayaś ca*

Thence the quickness of the mind transcends sense organs and [direct] understanding triumphs.

III.49 *sattva-puruṣānyatā-khyāti-mātrasya sarva-bhāvādhiṣṭ hātṛtvam sarva-jñātṛtvam ca*

Having established the total otherness between nature and the [pure] person, [one wins] supremacy over all conditions of being and total omniscience.

III.50 *tad vairāgyād api doṣabīja-kṣaye kaivalyam*

Owing to non-attachment even to that, the flawed seeds are destroyed and emancipation [follows].

III.51 *sthāny-upanimantraṇe saṅga-smayākaraṇam punar aniṣṭa-prasaṅgāt*

Even when higher abodes beckon, [one should] abstain from desire for their wonders, otherwise [what is] undesirable will follow.

III.52 *kṣaṇa-tat-kramayoḥ samyamād vivekajam jñānam*

Concentrating on the sequence of moments [leads] to knowledge born from discrimination.

III.53 *jāti-lakṣaṇa-deśair anyatānavachedāt tulyayos tataḥ pratipattiḥ*

Thence [comes] the understanding of the difference between [phenomena] with equal characteristics and origin as not being the same.

III.54 *tārakam sarva-viṣayam sarvathā-viṣayam akramam ca vivekajam jñānam*

Knowledge born from discrimination enables transcending all objects of experience and their total disorderliness.

III.55 *sattva-puruṣayoḥ śuddhi-sāmye kaivalyam*

When the true essence of persons equals purity, there is [total] emancipation.

IV.1 *janma-auṣadhi-mantra-tapaḥ-samādhijāḥ siddhayaḥ*

Magic powers [may be] inborn [in some people], [may be developed by drinking potions from certain] plants, [may be won through recitation of] formulas, by ascetic practice or be generated [when] completion [is achieved].

This last aphorism, traditionally placed at the beginning of the next (last) chapter of the YS, on 'Manifestations of the Mind' (*nirmāṇacitta*), certainly does not fit into that position and is misleading. It caused problems to commentators' interpretation of that chapter. It may be a later interpolation (cf. Hauer 1958, 469, note 1) or it may be an afterthought referring to the above aphorisms dealing with powers and wishing to explain in detail the instances of how powers are generated.

{31} A tentative translation of the Manifestations of the Mind (*nirmāṇacitta* - IV.2-34)

IV.2 *jāty-antara-pariṇāmaḥ prakṛty-āpūrāt*

The transmigration into another birth [takes place] through the abundance of nature [the original substance].

IV,3 *nimittam aprayojakam prakṛtīnām varaṇa-bhedas tu tataḥ kṣetrikavat*

The cause of it is not by nature aimless but an act of choosing, like a farmer dividing [a stream of water to drive it through channels for irrigation].

IV.4 *nirmāṇa-cittāni asmitā-mātrāt*

Out of the matrix of I-am-ness emerge [individual] minds.

IV.5 *pravṛtti-bhede prayojakam citam ekam anekeṣām*

Thus out of such active division the one [cosmic] mind generates many [individual minds].

IV.6 *tatra dhyānajam anāśayam*

But as a result of deep absorption there is no residue [in the individual mind, i.e. it becomes no-mind].

IV.7 *karmāśuklākṛṣṇam yoginas trividham itareṣām*

The actions of [accomplished] yogis are not white and not black [or: neither good nor bad, meaning: without generating future effects]; of others they are threefold [good, bad and neutral].

IV.8 *tatas tad-vipākānuguṇ ānām eva abhivyaktir vāsanānām*

Therefore their [future] effects are of corresponding quality, being manifestations of latent imprints.

IV,9 *jāti-deśa-kāla-vyavahitānām apy ānantataryam smṛti-saṁskārayor eka-rūpatvāt*

Although separated in succession by birth, place and time, the latent impressions connect cause and result, being in essence like memory [doing the same within one life]

IV,10 *tāsām anāditvam cāśiṣo nityatvāt*

and they [the latent impressions] are without beginning because of the perpetuity of the urge to exist.

IV.11 *hetu-phalāśrayālambanaiḥ saṅgṛhītatvāt eṣam abhave tadabhāvaḥ*

Because of the interdependence of cause and effect and their contiguity, when one ceases to be, so does the other.

IV.12 *atītānāgatam svarūpato 'sty adhva-bhedād dharmāṇām*

The past and the future have each its own specific character by splitting the time-flow of phenomena.

IV.13 *te vyakta-sūkṣma guṇa-ātmānaḥ*

They are evident, though intangible, subordinate parts of the life process

IV.14 *pariṇāmaikatvād vastu-tattvam*

By the transformation of oneness [into manifoldness], objects [become] reality [as phenomena].

IV.15 *vastu-sāmye citta-bhedāt tayor vibhaktaḥ panthāḥ*

The same object [is perceived] by different minds in a different way.

IV.16 *na ca ekacitta-tantram vastu tad apramāṇakām tadā kim*

But the object is not dependent on one mind, what would it be when unobserved?

IV.17 *tad-uparāgāpekṣitvāc cittasya vastu jñātājñātam*

Depending on whether an object colours [=affects] the mind, it becomes known or [remains] unknown.

IV.18 *sadā jñātāś citta-vṛttayas tat-prabhoḥ puruṣasya apariṇāmitvāt*

Fluctuations of the mind are always known to the [transcendent] person, yet his splendour [remains] unchanged.

IV.19 *na tat svābhāsam dṛśyatvāt*

[The mind] as an object of seeing is not self-illuminating.

IV.20 *eka-samaye cobhayānavadhāraṇam*

They both [the mind and an object of seeing] cannot be held [in attention] at the same time.

IV.21 *cittāntara-dṛśye buddhi-buddher atiprasaṅgaḥ smṛti-saṇkaraśca*

If the mind could be [directly] seen by another [mind], [there would be] endless succession of these mental entities and confusion of memory [would follow].

IV.22 *citer apratisaṅkramāyās tad-ākārāpattau sva-buddhi-samvedanam*

When the pure awareness (*citi*) [of the person], being basically unchanging, does take notice of a phenomenon, it is its mental act of perceiving.

IV.23 *draśṭṛdṛśyoparaktam cittam sarvārtham*

The mind, reflecting perceiver as well as the perceived, [serves] fully the purpose [of release].

IV.24 *tad asaṅkhyeya-vāsanābhiś citram api parārtham samhatya-kāritvāt*

Even though penetrated by uncounted variegated impressions, [the mind] is working together with the other [i.e. with the free perceiver (*draśṭṛ*) for its own release].

IV.25 *viśeṣa-darśiṇātma-bhāva-bhāvanā-vinivṛtti*

When the perceiver realises the distinction between essence (*ātma*) and existence, cessation follows.

IV.26 *tadā viveka-nimmam kaivalya-prāgbhāram cittam*

Then the previously burdened mind, now bent on discrimination, [reaches] autonomy.

IV.27 *tac-chidreṣu pratyayāntarāṇi samskārebhyaḥ*

Lapse in upholding it [allows into the mind] other [mental contents] from latent formationṣ

IV.28 *hānam eṣam kleoeavad uktam*

These are to be got rid of as the [earlier] discussed afflictions.

IV.29 *prasaṅkhyāne 'py akusīdasya sarvathā viveka-khyāter dharma-meghaḥ samādhi*

Reaching the highest states of mind without ever indulging in them because of preserving discrimination makes for direct cognitive union with the totality of truth.

IV.30 *tataḥ kleśa-karma-nivṛttiḥ*

The result is cessation of karmic afflictions.

IV.31 *tadā sarvāraṇa malāpetasya jñānasyānantyāj jñeyam alpam*

Once all obstructing impurities have been removed, knowledge becomes boundless with little left yet to be known.

IV.32 *tataḥ kṛtārthānām pariṇāma-krama-samāptir guṇānām*

Thereby the purposes of the forces of nature have been accomplished and the sequence of their transformations ceases.

IV.33 *kṣaṇapratiyogī pariṇāmāparānta-nirgrāhyaḥ kramaḥ*

The succession of instances of perceivable, dependent existence [comes] to an end.

IV.34 *puruṣārtha-śunyānām guṇānām pratiprasavaḥ kaivalyam svarūpa-pratiṣṭ hā vā citiśaktir iti*

The return of the forces of nature to their original state — having no longer any purpose for the [pure] person — is emancipation or the capacity of [the individual's awareness] to abide in its own nature.

{32} BhG IV, 6-9:

ajo 'pi sann avyayātmā bhūtānām īśvaro 'pi san //

prakṛtim svām adhiṣṭhāya sambhavāmyātma māyayā //6//

yadā yadā hi dharmasya glānir bhavati Bhārata //

abhyutthānam adharmasya tad ātmānaṁ sṛjāmyaham //7//

paritrāṇāya sādhūnāṁ vināśāya ca duṣkṛtām //

dharma saṁsthāpanārthāya saṁbhavāmi yuge yuge //8//

janma karma ca me divyam evam yo vetti tattvataḥ //

tyaktvā deham punarjanma nai 'ti mām eti so 'rjuna //9//

6. Even though being the unborn, imperishable self and the Lord of [all] beings, I enter existence, owing to my nature, through my creative power.

7. Whenever the decrease of righteousness occurs, o Bhārata, and the increase of unrighteousness, then I myself enter existence.

8. For the protection of the good, for the destruction of

the evil-doers, for the sake of re-establishing law I enter existence age after age.

9. Who knows thus my divine births and actions as they truly are, having discarded his body, he does not go on to rebirth, he goes to me, o Arjuna.

BhG III. 3:

loke 'smin dvividhā niṣṭhā purā proktā mayā 'nagha //

jñāna yogena sāṅkhyānāṅ karma yogena yoginām //3//

3. In this world two kinds of application have been hitherto proclaimed by me, o blameless one:

through pursuit of knowledge by the ponderous ones and through performing actions by the endeavouring ones

BhG XIII. 24:

dhyānenātmani paśyanti kecid ātmānam ātmānā //

anye sāṅkhyena yogena karma yogena cāpare //24//

24. Through deep absorption some selves see the Self by way of their self, others by the pursuit of knowledge and yet others through the path of action.

There are numerous translations of the BhG, some of them with the Sanskrit text, vocabulary and word for word rendering. For serious study it is advisable to use at least two translations. For systematic research the handbook by Minor (1982) is essential.

{33} For information on Yogavāsiṣṭha see Atreya, 1966. Also useful is the chapter 'The Philosophy of the *yoga-vāsiṣṭha*' (Dasgupta 1952. 228-272). For a sample of the text propagating the unreality of the world see Shastri, 1980. The whole translation of the *Yogavāsiṣṭha Rāmāyāṇa* by B. Lal Mitra was published in four volumes in Calcutta, 1891-99, repr. Haratiya Publishing House, Varanasi, 1976. A chapter on Yoga (*Yoga Kāṇḍa*) from a later popular work, *Vāsiṣṭha Saṁhitā,* was published, with Sanskrit text and English translation, by the Kaivalyadhama Institute in Lonavla, 1969.

{34} BhG: IV. 33:

śreyān dravyamayād yajñāj jñāna yajñaḥ paran tapa //

sarvaṅ karmā 'khilam pārtha jñāne parisamāpyate //33//

33. Better than offering possessions as sacrifice is offering knowledge, o foe-tamer; all works without exception, o Pārtha, reach completion in knowledge.

BhG: IV. 36-37:

api ced asi pāpebhyaḥ sarvebhyaḥ pāpakṛtamaḥ //

sarvañ jñāna plavenaiva vṛjinam santariṣyasi //36//

yathaidhāmsi samiddho 'gnir bhasmasāt kurute 'rjuna //

jñānāgniḥ sarva karmāṇi bhasmasāt kurute tathā //37//

36. Even if you were of all villains, the worst miscreants, just by the boat of knowledge you will cross over (the sea of) wickedness.

37. Just as fuel set on fire produces ashes, o Arjuna, so the fire of wisdom reduces all works to ashes.

{35} For more details on Advaita Vedānta and Jñāna Yoga see Werner, 1977a, 36-38, 66-70, 83-85, 143-145. See also: Sharma, 2004, and Deutsch, 1969. I am not dealing with the school of 'qualified non-dualism' (Vioeiṣṭa Advaita) of Rāmānuja (12th cent. CE), who provided a philosophical basis for the Bhakti movement.

{36} For a brief outline of the Bodhisattva doctrine see Werner, 1977a, 86-89. For a fuller treatment see Har Dayal, 1970 and Werner, 2012.

{37} BhG V. 2:

saṅnyāsaḥ karmayogaś ca niḥśreyasa karāvubhau /

tayos tu karmasaṅnyāsāt karmayogo viśiṣyate //2//

2. Renunciation and Yoga of action are both conducive to salvation; of those Yoga of action is better than renouncing action.

BhG III. 4-5:

na karmaṇām anārambhān naiṣkarmyam puruoeo 'śnute /

na ca saṅnyasamād eva sidhim samadhigacchati //4//

na hi kaścit kṣaṇam api jātu tiṣṭhatyakarmakṛt /

kāryate hyavaśaḥ karma sarvaḥ prakṛtijair gunaiḥ //5//

4. Not by not undertaking actions does a person gain relief from (bonds of past) actions, nor does he through renunciation arrive at perfection.

5. Not for a moment can he remain a non-performer of action, for he is made to do impulsively all actions through tendencies born from nature.

BhG III. 19:

tasmād asaktaḥ satataṅ kāryaṅ karma samācara /

asakto hyācaraṅ karma param āpnoti pūruṣaḥ //19//

19. Therefore, unattached, constantly perform acts which are to be done; performing actions while unattached, a person gains the highest.

BhG II. 12-13:

na tvevāhañ jātu nāsan na tvan nemejanādhipāḥ//

na caiva na bhaviṣyāmaḥ sarve vayam ataḥ param //12//

dehino 'smin yathā dehe kaumāram yauvanañ jarā //

tathā dehāntara prāptir dhīras tatra na muhyati //13//

12. Never ever was I non-existent, neither you, nor these kings; nor ever will we all henceforward truly not exist.

13. As to the owner of this body, as he passes from boyhood to youth and old age, just so he acquires another body; the wise do not get confused thereby.

BhG II. 31:

svadharmam api cāvekṣya na vikampitum arhasi //

dharmyād dhi yuddhāc chreyo 'nyat kṣatriyasya na vidyate / /31//

31. Having taken into consideration your own duty, you have no right to be tremulous; there is nothing better for a warrior than fighting out of duty.

BhG III. 30:

mayi sarvāṇi karmāṇi saṅnyasyādhyātma cetanā //

nirāśīr nirmamo bhūtvā yudhyasva vigata jvaraḥ //20//

30. Surrendering all actions onto me, being Self-conscious, having become desireless, non-possessive and free from grief, fight!

{38} BhG VIII. 16:

ā brahma bhūvanāl lokāḥ punar āvartino 'rjuna //

mām upetya tu kaunteya punar janma na vidyate //16//

16. From Brahma realms down to these worlds there is repeated recurring, o Arjuna; but after coming to me, o son of Kuntī, there is no more rebirth.

BhG XIV. 27:

brahmano hi pratiṣṭhāham amṛtasyāvyayasya ca //

śāśvatasya ca dharmasya sukhasyaikāntikasya ca //27//

27. For I am the foundation of *brahman*, the immortal

and imperishable, of the eternal ordinance and of absolute beatitude.

BhG, XVIII. 55:

bhaktyā mām abhijānāti yāvan yaś cāsmi tattvataḥ//

tato mām tattvato jñātvā vioeate tadantaram//55//

55. Through devotion (the devotee) comes to know me as I truly am and having known me in my true state, he enters into me.

{39} In Tantric practice ritual union of the yogi and yoginī in motionless embrace with penetration (*maithuna*) cannot be regarded as a sexual act in the current meaning of the term, if pursued in a genuine frame of mind. Nevertheless, according to some sources it does result in the issue of semen, but it requires retention and reabsorption of it by the yogi and of her issue by the yoginī. Special preparatory training is needed to achieve this before one reaches the stage of Anuttara Yoga. This training may be started even earlier, as soon as one decides to study and take initial steps in Tantra Yoga. To my knowledge such a training is or at least was in the past provided for selected aspirants in the Yoga Institute in Santa Cruz, Bombay (Mumbáí), as reported to me personally by a participant, a German, at the time a student of medicine.

As regards the visualisation of a plain effigy of a yogi and yoginí in embrace which may not be easily available, experienced meditators may be able to assemble one in their imagination on the basis of a photograph. For example, the Tibetan *yab yum* effigy with no obvious affiliation (pictured) consists of entirely naked figures without adornments. The male figure with a Buddha hairstyle holds his hands in meditation *mudrā* behind the yoginí's buttocks while she, embracing him round his neck, holds a *vajra* in one hand and a small bowl in the other.

As to the obscure and dubious practices in Tantric Yoga, one of the main controversial ones is the *pañcamakāra sādhanā*, 'spiritual practice with performing five Ms'. It is a ritual procedure using ingredients and performing acts normally viewed as incompatible with a spiritual path, each beginning with the letter 'm'. They are five, hence the '5 Ms'. They are *madya* which is an intoxicating drink, usually wine; *matsya*, meaning fish; *māṁsa*, i.e. meat; *mudrā*, whose basic meaning is 'seal' or 'sign', refers in a religious context to ritual gestures by hands with specific positions of the fingers, but Tantric texts give it the meaning of 'parched kidney beans', supposedly an aphrodisiac; the last is *maithuna*, copulation, which has differing rules in different Tantras. In the process of a complicated ritual the first four Ms are being gradually consumed as a preparation for the last M, because they are regarded as enhancing potency and therefore make for a successful *maithuna*. Some Tantras maintain that a correct *maithuna* requires utmost self-discipline which is more effective than traditional renunciation and asceticism on the path to liberation. Whether it is so or not, it is easy to imagine that 5 Ms sessions may easily turn into orgies. (Chattopadhyaya, 1978, 10-29; Briggs, 1998, throughout.)

{40} The pioneer of Tantric studies was Sir John Woodroffe (1865–1936), who wrote, to begin with, under the pseudonym Arthur Avalon. His voluminous works are now more or less outdated, although some parts of them may still be useful as a starting point. Academic research works are not easy reading and have to be studied with caution, because they often disagree with each other on important points. Most of available Tantric literature on a popular level is far from reliable. Some popular works, however, draw conclusions for the modern application of Tantric practice which might merit close scrutiny. But the subject has not been researched enough to allow a considered assessment of the field. Besides, many manuscripts still wait for critical editions and translation.

{41} Haṭha Yoga is the most popular part of the Yoga tradition in modern times around the world, but the term under which it is often, misleadingly, written about is simply yoga or Yoga. Methods of purification of the body are in some contexts very elaborate and at least in one context become virtually an advanced path on a cosmic scale (Flood, 2000).

{42} The literature on Kuṇḍalinī Yoga is unreliable and contains many speculative elements, even though it purports to present the topic from the point of view of scientific knowledge (Rele, 1927). There are also deliberate mystifications in some works on the topic, as in the case of Theos Bernard. Besides, as the tradition insists that the practice can be successful only under the guidance of an accomplished *guru* whose disciples are bound by secrecy, no authentic accounts can be extant.

{43} In 1975 I wrote: "He (Ramaṇa) did not bring any new teaching or philosophy and he might be described as fitting within the tradition of Advaita Vedānta. Neither is his method new. His instructions ... can be classified as following the path of Jñāna Yoga. But they are formulated so as to be easily understood today. They offer a method of self-inquiry that is basically analytical and proceeds, first discursively and then meditationally, to eliminate the meditator's identification with insubstantial constituents of his personality — which are his body, his feelings and his thoughts — in order to enable him to penetrate to the experience of his hidden essence or 'real self'." (Werner, 1977a, 159-160) Forty years later I see that this description was inadequate.

{44} Aurobindo's works are numerous, but there is a lot of repetition in them; those few listed in the Bibliography would suffice for thorough study. For Auroville see Namakkal, 2012.

{45} One little incident, conveyed personally to me by a Czech astronomer, Professor Karel Hujer of Chattanooga University, USA, is perhaps worth recording. He was travelling through India in the 1930s and was struck by the spiritual atmosphere around a figure sitting half naked under a tree. Being interested in Indian religions, he approached him and finding that he spoke almost perfect English, had a long conversation with him which he found quite impressive. It was Śivānanda, some of whose books Prof. Hujer already knew.[{46}]

To this I can testify on the basis of my own activities. When I was deprived in 1951 in communist Czechoslovakia of my appointment as university lecturer in Indology, because I refused to become a member of the communist party, I was forced to work in manual jobs, which included for a time coal-mining, and I decided that Yoga exercises could improve my physical ability to cope. Illustrations in line drawings of Yoga *āsanas* from Indian manuscripts (Schmidt, 1921) were not much help, but by that time there was a clandestine network circulating forbidden literature in typescript copies to which I also contributed with translations of religious texts from Pāli and Sanskrit. Through this means I obtained a typescript copy of Śivānanda's book on Haṭha Yoga (1965) with precise drawings copied by someone from the original photographs in the book. I was then able to start learning the Yoga positions together with a flexible teenager who was helping me, while I was teaching him to proceed slowly with mindfulness. I managed to master some 25 *āsanas* and practised them daily alone and weekly together with a dozen or so others. When I discovered that *āsanas* were included in obligatory morning exercises (called in Russian *fyzminutky*) in the offices of the Soviet Academy of Sciences in Moscow (introduced there by one Russian academic who had learned some *āsanas* during a year in India), I persuaded the Czech authorities to allow me to give public lectures on Yoga with demonstrations of *āsanas*.

Eventually a trade union club in Brno (where I was living) employed me to take Yoga classes in the club. They were open to the public for a fee. I was even allowed to found within it the Yoga Club (1964), the first one in communist Czechoslovakia. Its membership was open to the public, but its bulk was recruited from the 'graduates' of my Yoga classes. Besides delivering monthly lectures I held clandestine meetings of smaller groups with talks and discussions about spiritual aspects of Yoga. The reputation of the Yoga Club spread by word of mouth even into yogic circles in neighbouring countries. In 1966 it was visited by Mā Yogaśaktī who had heard of it while lecturing in Vienna. On the basis of my teaching experience I then wrote a textbook of Haṭha Yoga which was published with many delays after the censors removed passages which in their eyes contained hints about a spiritual dimension behind the physical Yoga exercises. I filled the blank pages with more photographs and more detailed instructions on how to practise. The book quickly sold 95,000 copies in two editions but the third one was stopped when I emigrated to England after the Soviet invasion of Czechoslovakia (21.8.1968). After the collapse of communism, the book was republished without change (the publisher's illustrated extracts from the book can be seen online at: http://www.cadpress. sk/hathajoga.htm). It is regarded as the best Czech textbook of Haṭha Yoga for moderate practice, avoiding the excesses of forceful techniques propagated by some Indian *gurus*, such as B.K.S. Iyengar. The Yoga Club survived my emigration in the wake of the 1968 Soviet invasion and carried on its activities into the new era after the collapse of communist rule in 1989. I gave my first lecture for it on my visit in 1990. By then Yoga and its organisations had spread all over the country, eventually forming a centralised Union of Yoga. I gave my last seminar on the basis of my textbook for 141 Yoga teachers organised by the South Moravian Union of Yoga on 20 November 2010 in Brno.

The book served me well also as the basis for my lectures in the diploma courses for aspiring Yoga teachers organised by the British Wheel of Yoga.

{47} Her *āśram* did not survive. I visited her in 1967 and 1968 in her home, when she was just Frau Walinski-Heller, and got from her a personal account of what had happened. Her *āśram* on Bodensee was in an area in Bavaria which was notorious for religious bigotry and it was resented by the Christian population. Soon the parish priests of catholic as well as various protestant denominations condemned her for spreading a pagan religion and even accused her of being in collusion with the devil. Stones were frequently thrown through the windows of her *āśram* and other damage was inflicted on the building until her friends and initial disciples became frightened and stayed away. She gave up further attempts at running a Yoga centre on her own and negotiated with Boris Sacharow to join him in his Yoga School in Nürnberg, but they had not yet reached an agreement when he tragically died in a horrific car accident. She told me that she had a strong telepathic message from him calling for help. He had been hanging upside down from a tree for a considerable time before he was found and it was already too late to administer medical treatment to rescue him. After the closure of her *āśram* Frau Walinski-Heller continued to receive visitors in her home, giving advice and tuition in Yoga, and in the process she realised that she had a healing effect on some of them. Her husband, who did not join the Nazi party after Hitler assumed power and as a result lost his position as director of police in Gdansk, received compensation and a generous pension from the Federal Republic, enabling them to move into a luxurious home. At that time she started thinking of opening a clinic if she could find a qualified therapist as partner. When I visited her in 1967, I was, by that time, employed by the Psychiatric Institute in Kroměříž, Czechoslovakia, on a research project for 'Yoga therapy', and she asked me to head her prospective clinic while retaining my position in the Psychiatric Institute in Kroměříž, where cases she could not cope with would be sent for treatment. My director agreed with the plan, encouraged by the 'Prague Spring' heralding Dubček's 'communism with a human face' in January 1968. All came to nothing when the Warsaw Pact forces invaded Czechoslovakia on 21 August the same year. I then followed up an invitation to lecture in the London Buddhist Society's Summer School, and on the way visited Frau Walinski-Heller for the second time. She still cherished her plan for a clinic with my participation after I would finish my lecturing assignment in London and perhaps return to Nürnberg. However, when I wrote to her from England that I had accepted a permanent appointment in Indian Studies at the University of Durham, she felt disappointed if not somewhat hurt by my decision and lost interest in keeping in touch with me.

Besides the account of the failure of her Bodensee *āśram,* she had given me during the few days of my first visit in 1967 a summary of her sojourn in Śivānanda's *āśram* which was less enthusiastic than the account of her stay which she gave in her book. Her oral account was more critical in some respects and contained quite a few details which were left out in the book. She was very disappointed, for example, that no one came to meet her at the Rishikesh railway station so that she and her companion had to hire a horse-drawn cart. When they reached the gate of the *āśram,* it took some while for the Svāmi to appear and show them in. But Śivānanda did welcome her with great courtesy and joy, and when he took her down to the river, many photographs were taken. She gave me one in which she is standing on the left wearing a sārī-like wrap down to her ankles and Śivananda is on the right with his staff, facing her and smiling at her. He signed the photograph as a dedication with the name he later gave to her, Sarada. On the back of the photograph is the date, 16 December, 1953. Her description of her reception sounded to me more like a ceremonial installation of her as 'mother' of the *āśram* which does not come over as such in the book. When Śivānanda explained to her that she had been his companion for several lives, he also said that he had been a philosopher in ancient Greece in pre-Socratic time in a past life when she was his pupil. In a commotion, when there was public anger against sophists, they were stoned to death. She then escaped from him into a life in medieval Europe and then into modern Europe and he had been looking for her since then in order to win her back. She also described to me in more detail the visit she made without prior permission to the old yogi in Rishikesh. In addtion to what she recorded in the book, she told me that the yogi said to her that there was no real spirituality around Śivananda because he was too involved in superficial writing and in expanding his world-wide network of Divine Life Society's branches. She should not expect spiritual progress with him. He reportedly said: "If you are really interested in following a spiritual path and in making progress on it, stay with me and I guarantee that you will be enlightened within a year." She said that she had been very impressed by what he told her during their further conversation. He made no attempt to persuade her, but spoke in a sober and straightforward manner, leaving her to think about what he had said. She said to him that she could not make such a momentous decision. She felt loyalty towards Śivānanda and could not contemplate suddenly resigning her function as Mother of the *āśram.*

When she saw Śivananda waiting for her, he looked "like a god of revenge" and she was flabbergasted by his outburst and could not understand it. After that she sometimes felt that she was closely watched by the senior Svāmis and felt at times like a caged bird. She had a strong impression that her presence was particularly resented by the Svāmi who was a kind of minister of finances, who looked at her as a rather expensive non-paying guest of the *āśram.*

When Śivānanda accepted that she would not stay for good, he announced in the *āśram* that she had a special mission in Germany which, he maintained, was in fact his original plan, and he duly announced the time of her departure. After her return home she learned how the journey was paid for. The Federal Republic of Germany was established on 23 May 1949 and soon the government was seeking links with other countries. After the war India was very popular, not least because of *gurus* from India giving talks and offering classes of Yoga all over the West. There was then in India a German consul, and a diplomat or perhaps even a Minister came there on a goodwill mission, bringing with him not only an entourage that was in part technical and commercial, but also a donation from the Republic of some expensive electrical equipment to illuminate the outline of a temple. As a matter of course, the Minister came to visit also the famous yogi Śivānanda in Rishikesh, who told him about the problem of financing the return journey of his two German guests. The Minister arranged the passage.

{48} Two different cases of less than genuine *gurus* may be mentioned as examples. For the first one's early attempt to establish himself in Europe I obtained a witness's account from the husband of Mrs Walinsky-Heller. He went to see Mahesh Yogi when he came in the early 1950s to Hamburg in Germany. He styled himself Maharishi Mahesh Yogi. The hall for his lecture was full of expectant listeners, but he arrived one hour late, by which time about half of the audience had left. Without any apology he started his talk by saying something like "You may have heard from other *gurus* that the Yoga practice is arduous and that it takes a long time to reach the goal. It can be likened to travel in medieval time by a stage coach. But if you follow me, it will be like taking a jet and off you fly to enlightenment." The audience started laughing and my witness left the hall. This early visit of Mahesh Yogi in Europe is not mentioned in any publication about him and the start of his foreign travels is usually given as 1959. He no doubt learned from his initial experience and was subsequently more cautious so that he gradually established himself. He was not a *saṁnyāsi* or a wanderer, but took a vow of *brahmacarya* (celibate discipleship) under his *guru*. He taught a traditional *mantra* meditation which he renamed Transcendental Meditation (TM) and which caught on with the public and became even a subject of research by one or two psychologists. His fame took off when in 1968 the Beatles enrolled in his well-attended course on TM in his comfortable *āśram* in Rishikesh, although they started leaving one after the other before the course finished, one reason being that he reportedly made sexual advances towards a film actress and a few other women, with some successfully. However, his movement spread, with centres being established round the world. Claims were made that TM produced 'yogic flying' and that when done in coordination in his centres, it influenced world politics. Mahesh lived all his life in luxury and eventually settled in Holland, where he died in 2008.

The other example is the notorious 'sex *guru*' Rajneesh, known also as Osho, who gave up a university teaching post as boring and opened his *āśram* in Pune in 1974 in which he conducted naked meditation classes and introduced promiscuous therapeutic sessionds. Violent incidents were not unusual in the *āśram*. Because of tensions with the Indian government, he relocated his *āśram* to the state of Oregon in the USA. Here he became obsessed with Rolls- Royce cars, having bought 93 of them, and drove daily in one around the *āśram*, thus giving *daroean* to his followers. The leadership of the *āśram* became corrupt and there were criminal machinations geared to taking over the local municipality. Rajneesh was forced to leave the USA in 1985. Many countries around the world refused him entry and he returned to his *āśram* in Pune in January 1987. Still popular with many, mainly Western, followers, he resumed teaching sessionsds. But ailing health resulted in his death in 1990 at the age of 58. His teaching as outlined in many books was highly eclectic, often imitating the Zen style, with touches of megalomania and self-aggrandisement.

{49} As Spalding lecturer in Indian philosophy and religion in the School of Oriental Studies of the University of Durham, I introduced soon after my appointment in 1969 courses in Yoga, parallel to my academic courses in Sanskrit, Indian civilisation, religions and philosophy. My courses in Yoga were eventually adopted by the Extramural Department of the University and ran for five years in several localities in Northeast England. My postgraduate tuition in Yoga studies was in due course noticed and appreciated in a convocation speech given by the Vice-Chancellor of the university who, commenting on the themes of higher degree theses, mostly of a scientific character, was struck by the title of the thesis of one of my students and said: "Rather towards the other end of the spectrum we have one on 'Studies in Classical Yoga' - not perhaps a subject for which the popular word 'relevance' springs to mind. But it seems to me absolutely right when an activity has rather suddenly awakened the interest of many thousands of people in this country, a university should study and try to expound its real intellectual and historic roots. " *University of Durham Gazette*, vol. XXII (New Series), no. 31, January 1977, p. 8. Since then substantial progress has been made. One example will suffice. When, in my retirement, I was appointed Honorary Professorial Research Associate in the Department of the Study of Religions in the School of Oriental and African Studies in the University of London in 1993, my endeavours to get Yoga studies on the syllabus eventually resulted in an invitation to give a keynote lecture during the first session of the new MA degree course in 'Traditions of Yoga and Meditation' on 4 October 2012. The course started with about thirty students and courses dealing with Yoga have become a staple feature of the department's syllabus, with many students enrolling each year.

{50} Nyanaponika himself, after the period of intense meditation in Burma, settled in the Forest Hermitage as a scholar and editor for the Buddhist Publication Society (BPS) in Kandy. Later in his life he admitted to me that he could just as well have reached the same stage of his spiritual development if he had not become a monk and had settled in Switzerland in conditions more favourable for his work. I had been in correspondence with him since the early 1960s, met him for the first time in Vienna in 1968 and spent a week with him in the Forest Hermitage in 1975. This was not a retreat for me, but a comfortable stay in luxury with a daily abundant meal before midday (fruits, vegetables, usually also fish or meat or both) brought by an errand boy going to and fro between BPS and the Forest Hermitage a few times every day. (Monks in Sri Lanka do not beg for food on an alms round as do monks in Burma and Thailand.) One day the meal was extremely lavish. Nyanaponika explained to me that 30 families secured the privilege of gaining merit by sending him the daily meal in turn. This one was from the household of General Bandaranaike (uncle of the then prime minister). He had to send the best his kitchen could provide, otherwise his reputation would suffer, because everybody in town would know what was sent from his house to the famous scholar monk. The abundant leftovers were taken to Kandy to be distributed to people in need.

Once I followed a narrow footpath through the jungle and came across a cave inhabited by a monk. The cave had been in use for generations. The interior had been enlarged and the entrance was fitted with a door with a *kasiṇa* (a circle for visual meditation) carved above it.

The monk was sitting on a stone seat and addressed me in good English. Unlike Nyanaponika he had ideal conditions for prolonged meditation, but obviously was not practising fully in the way the Buddha described as leading quickly to *nibbāna.* When the monk could not get on with strict meditation, he preoccupied himself with astrophysical theories. By his side were notebooks filled with summaries from books his lay supporters had borrowed for him from libraries. He knew both Einstein's theories of relativity, the big bang theory and even the theory of the 'pulsating universe' from some source, long before Penrose (2011) had a change of heart and abandoned the theory of the 'steady state' universe for the likelihood of a sequence of universes. I was quite impressed by him, but when I mentioned him to Nyanaponika, he was rather dismissive of his pursuits, possibly because he preferred spending his time outside strict meditation in Buddhist scholarship and propagation of Buddhism rather than studying scientific theories about the universe.

{51} Govinda, a scholar, poet, painter and experienced practitioner of meditation as well as of rituals, appeared to be a truly integrated personality. Having watched him performing the Pūjā, I could agree with his description that it was visible meditation which should not be omitted or discarded in high stages of spiritual achievement as being superfluous, as is done in other systems. The movement of his hands and his recitation had also an aesthetic quality. His paintings of meditative absorptions (*jhānas*, in: Govinda, 1962) have a similar effect.

{52} I heard Trungpa lecturing to a packed hall in Cambridge in 1968 when I was supervisor of Sanskrit for Churchill College. A friend of mine, who was a Fellow of Christ College, was so impressed that he gave up his post, followed Trungpa north and bought a disused farmhouse near Samye Ling in Eskdalemuir (which he restored). It was he who eventually looked after Trungpa's son, whom I encountered when visiting him. During the first year of my appointment in the University of Durham, when I heard about Trungpa's car accident nearby, I went to see him in the Newcastle-upon-Tyne General Hospital (1969). He was unable to talk to me, as a bottle of whisky had been smuggled in to him, but his secretary suggested another day and promised to keep him sober for the occasion. True enough, Trungpa was then able and willing to grant me a private hearing during which he showed undoubted knowledge of traditional Tibetan Buddhist lore. When answering my questions on the phenomenon of the *tulku* and how it was to be understood that, for example, he himself was a part incarnation of Chenrezig (the Bodhisattva Avalokiteoevara), he explained that a *tulku* was a reincarnating person in his own right, but a "ray" issued by the Bodhisattva was reincarnating with him. That association had a beginning in the past and would last as long as did his mission in helping others to liberation. "What would happen if a *tulku* strayed from the right path?", was my last question. This may have prompted a moment of truth. After a pause came the reply: "The ray may be withdrawn." As he was saying it, his face looked rather sad and on impulse I took a picture of him at that very moment (I had secured permission to take a photograph of him beforehand). It is, for me, a reminder of my esoteric lesson in Tibetan buddhology. I wonder whether the expression "stray dog of the *tulku* tradition" was later adopted by him in reminiscence of our conversation? (My account of him and our meeting titled 'On Chogyam Trungpa', in: *Tibet Alive. The Journal of the Tibet Society Relief Fund of the UK 43/4, 19,* contains a black and white copy of my picture of him whose original is in colour, but my article was heavily censored without my permission.)

In the USA Trungpa founded the Naropa University in Boulder, Colorado, the first Buddhist academic institution, and other organisations. He acquired a large following by his charismatic lectures, but his habit of carrying supplies of beer everywhere earned him the nickname "beercan guru". He referred to himself, as mentioned above, as a "stray dog of the *tulku* tradition". He eventually died of cardiac arrest and respiratory failure in 1987 in an intensive care unit in Halifax, Nova Scotia, leaving a widow and five sons.

His legacy is extraordinary. When his 'dharma heir', Tendzin (Thomas F. Rich), who was appointed the 'Vajra Regent' of the 'Vajradhatu International Buddhist Church' in 1976, stood accused of passing the AIDS virus through sexual intercourse to his male and female disciples for several years (before he himself died of it in 1990), he claimed that he had had the assurance from Trungpa, given to him in 1985, that he "could change the *karma*", because he had "some extraordinary means of protection" (*New York Times*, February 21, 1989). Institutions and centres founded by Trungpa and others in his "lineage", even in Europe, still flourish under the aegis of his son Rangdröl Mukpo. The belief in Trungpa's spiritual status seems to remain undiminished among his followers.

{53} I read Krishnamurti's published talks and books when I was running the Yoga Club in Brno in the 1960s and I recognized in his style the influence of the Buddha's 'right mindfulness', the seventh step of his eightfold path. Krishnamurti's talks seemed to me repetitive and basically just variations of the same inquiry carefully thought through but never with any answers which were left to the listener to 'see', not to formulate in words. His talks were clearly products of thought, yet he condemned thought as a limiting and misleading process. To prove this to myself, I experimentally adopted Krishnamurti's style for my monthly talks to the members of the Yoga Club who had been attending my Haṭha Yoga classes. The effect was that they became deferential and started treating me as their *guru*; when I addressed someone on his or her own, they showed signs of shyness, almost like stage fright. I soon dropped the experiment, yet some of its effect lingered on in my listeners. (I was careful not to land in a similar position after my emigration to England when I was taking Yoga classes and lecturing on Yoga topics for the extramural departments of Durham and Leicester Universities and Stockton's YMCA.) When I was invited to lecture in different towns in

Czechoslovakia during the brief period of the 'Prague Spring', a group of listeners to my talk in Moravská Ostrava took me late at night to the home of a small disabled man who was married with children, was nicknamed 'little Krishnamurti' and was rumoured to be enlightened. His flat was crowded with his disciples, a small sample of his following, I was told. There must have been, and perhaps still are, imitators of Krishnamurti in other parts of the world.

After emigrating to England in 1968 and taking up my appointment in Durham University the following year, I visited the new Krishnamurti Foundation office in London. There I was asked if I could arrange an invitation for Krishnamurti to give lectures at my university, but I never considered it feasible. I was given two books for review and I also happened to watch the BBC television interview with Krishnamurti on 21 March 1969 in which he was asked whether, after having been talking for nearly fifty years, he thought he saw some change in the people or in the world as a result. His answer was: "I doubt it." Inspired by this question I wrote a review article, 'Half a Century of Krishnamurti' (Werner, 1969). After pointing out that his demand for continued 'choiceless awareness' was basically the Buddha's way of right mindfulness, I continued: "What is missing in his attitude, however, is the allembracing understanding and compassion of a Buddha who would not dismiss even little worries of ordinary people (who are not yet ripe for the arduous path of mindfulness), but would advise them even on their everyday affairs to make their lives brighter and to bring them, eventually, also to the path. Krishnamurti, on the other hand, speaks only to a certain part of the intellectually advanced elite. He does not possess the capability of talking the language of different people on different levels, he speaks only his own language. Perhaps this is the reason why he has to doubt that any change was brought about by his lectures. Contrary to this we know that the Buddha's teachings have changed many a wild Asian folk into a peaceful nation..."

I first listened to a talk by Krishnamurti on 7 September 1969. It was attended by about 800 people and delivered for the first time in a large tent erected in the grounds of Brockwood Park. His talk was emphatic and increasingly passionate as if he were working himself up into an ecstasy. When he finished and left the tent through a gap behind the stage, I followed him. He turned round and I congratulated him on an effective lecture. He took my hand and during our conversation held it in his. I started feeling a subtle vibration passing through my hand and arm and slowly suffusing my whole body. It was a very pleasant feeling which lasted several hours. I had been driven to Brockwood by John Walters whom I was visiting in his home in Farnham. (He was the author of the book *Mind Unshaken. A Modern Approach to Buddhism* which I had translated into Czech in the early 1960s for clandestine circulation in typescript copies; he wrote it when he found one night in Thailand that he in fact had become a Buddhist.) He waited discreetly for me further off and when I joined him for our packed lunch, I told him about the contents of my conversation with Krishnamurti and the feeling which he had passed from his hand into my body and which had not yet diminished. John stopped eating and looked at me in amazement. When he had recovered, he said: "I have travelled the whole of Asia visiting places of pilgrimage and meeting yogis and Buddhist monks, but I have never had any experience of that kind. When I found myself to have become a Buddhist after a night of meditation, it was more like 'the penny dropped', a kind of conceptually grasping the truth of the Dhamma."

I went to several more of Krishnamurti's annual talks in the tent at Brockwood which was packed each time by more than 1,000 listeners. I encouraged my students in Durham to accompany me. Some did and we subsequently held discussions in my class. None of them was won to become a follower of Krishnamurti. Now that independent accounts of his life and activities are available, it is obvious that he was a product of invention and delusion. To begin with he was a victim of the Theosophical grandees (Leadbeater and Annie Besant) who wished to produce a contemporary Messiah akin to Jesus. According to the Theosophical doctrine, Jesus and the future saviours were supposed to be spokesmen or 'vehicles' of the Bodhisattva Maitreya, the future Buddha. Being educated for the role of the future Messiah in fact deformed Krishnamurti's adolescence and on the threshold of adulthood the need to appear to live up to the image created a conflict in him with his strong need of erotic fulfilment. For several years he was still under the influence of Leadbeater, who acted with the authority of the supposed 'Masters', but he simply could not resist feminine charms. This forced him into role playing, maintaining the image of the future Messiah. The instances of the so-called 'Process' under which he suffered physically and mentally may have been symptoms of this inner conflict. He can hardly be blamed for continuing his tours between his seizures and acting as an ostensibly inspired teacher while he was not yet quite sure where the truth lay. But once he stopped believing in the existence of the 'Masters' and shook off the charade of a Messiah with twelve apostles, the responsibility for his future actions became solely his. He continued the deception and chose a life of carefree luxury while all the complicated arrangements for his public appearances and private life were shouldered by others to whom he showed little gratitude. While denying that he accepted disciples, he cleverly manipulated his adherents into total dependence on him. Many followed him wherever he went to deliver talks. He was an embodiment of a latter-day mobile Indian *guru* in all but name.

{54} I knew a man in Prague in the 1960s who seemed to me to be an approximation to a determined individual living in a town who may have embarked on the path of pure Yoga. I obtained his address from the clandestine circuit which circulated forbidden literature on spiritual topics and to which I was contributing with translations of Buddhist texts and booklets (as mentioned earlier). With the address came also a message that he would accept my visit should I decide to seek him out. I found him in a secluded corner in the loft of an old block of flats not far from the centre of Prague, but with a park nearby. The only furnishing he had in his 'abode' was a chair for visitors and a straw mattress on which he was lying. He seemed to me to be in his upper sixties. He spoke correct language like someone who had received a good education on at least grammar school level or had done a lot of reading or both. He knew works by H. P. Blavatsky and had been a member of the Theosophical Society, but left when Annie Besant and C. W. Leadbeater announced the coming of a new Messiah in the person of J. Krishnamurti and named twelve apostles for him. He did not mention Krishnamurti's activities after his parting with Theosophy and his new 'mission' as an itinerant 'world teacher', which in itself suggested that he did not have any regard for him. Silence was sufficient for the purpose, as he never spoke in a negative way about anybody. But when he mentioned some names of past and contemporary personalities such as St Teresa of Avila, Ramana Maharshi, Śivānanda, Karel Weinfurter, a pre-war prolific Czech writer on occult, mystical and Indian religious topics, and Leopold Procházka, the author of five Czech books on Buddhism published in the 1930s, it was a sign of approval. He knew everything about my writings, public lectures and Yoga classes. I visited him several times, in fact each time I came to Prague to lecture or meet with Yoga practitioners. He obviously approved of my approach of combining scholarship with personal involvement in the practice of Yoga. We had extensive conversations on spiritual topics with some indirectly implied hints about my search for the meaning of life. But he asked me not to disclose the contents of our conversations in my writings. His way of life of course inspired my description of 'a determined individual', whether living in town or countryside, 'who may have embarked on the path of pure Yoga'. I do not know what became of him and I could not pay him a last visit, because of my hasty departure from Czechoslovakia after the Soviet invasion. I had to avoid Prague where there were clashes between the invading army and protesters, with some loss of life.

{55} Contemplation of external and internal parts of the body is a very effective means to free oneself from being attracted to the physical beauty of the opposite sex and from the sexual drive altogether to which I can personally testify. During the second world war when I was thirteen I lost my Roman Catholic faith and indeed faith in any religion, but it intrigued me why people could have firm faith in diverse religions whose teachings contradicted each other. So after a time I started reading historical books about religions in addition to my other interests (films, poetry, novels, some art books) and found them absorbing. At seventeen I discovered the five books by Leopold Procházka on Buddhism. I read all five of them and the Buddha's explanations of life and existence immediately struck me as realistic. I practically adopted Buddhism wholesale, including the belief in the rebirth doctrine and the undesirability of carrying on with ordinary life. I did have some fleeting encounters with girls of my age, but now I started experiencing the sexual drive as an unwelcome disturbance. Procházka's book on Buddhist meditation also contained descriptions on the contemplation of bodily parts and the discourse on the foundation of mindfulness, which had great power despite being a translation into Czech of the German translation of the English translation from the Pāli original. I immediately started, besides regular meditation, the contemplation of bodily parts, applying it alternately to myself and externally to others, as the instruction goes. Soon, when meeting a girl, I saw within her body all her entrails — the bladder half full with urine, the colon with faeces etc. It was easy for me and it gave me a sense of freedom. Otherwise my life was 'normal' within the wartime conditions in an occupied country with fighting far away. The easy way I was able to assume the contemplation of bodily parts made me think that I must have been in the past life a Buddhist monk, perhaps on Ceylon, practising it, but gave it up for some reason and eventually disrobed, possibly lured by the way of life in Europe. In youthful enthusiasm I now started preparing myself for monkhood as soon as it would become possible to travel to Ceylon.

However, even though I was successful in this unusual exercise, I occasionally wondered whether I was on the right track. When after the war I enrolled in the university and mingled in its premises with female students, it seemed to me unfair to them and inappropriate to view them in that way, so I set the practice aside and soon regained normal perception. Then came an early academic appointment and a kind of pride in it and deep involvement in scholarship which pushed spiritual pursuits into the background, although I did not entirely stop my meditational sessions. Meanwhile I even married and had two children. But the rude awakening after I lost my university post three years after the communist putsch (February 1948) brought home to me again the Buddha's dictum about the transitoriness of life's achievements and its overall unsatisfactoriness. I started dedicating more time to meditation and resumed my round the clock practice of mindfulness when on a retreat. Then after a few years the results of my contemplation during my teens came suddenly back to me and, without actively practising the viewing of the bodily parts, I became celibate. My wife respected it. But two years later it came to an abrupt end. I was on a ten day retreat in a forest hut and was so successful with the results of my round the clock mindfulness that I even thought of attempting to leave the country illegally in order to join the Saṅgha in Sri Lanka. This would be dangerous, but I thought that if caught, I could just as well meditate in prison and could even face death if the worst should happen. However, early in the morning on the last day of my retreat when I came out of the hut, I experienced an unusual symbolical hint combined with a kind of vision not easy to describe. It was a figure formed by clouds and resembling vaguely Bodhisattva statues. It appeared as walking towards me but never reaching me. The hint may have been that it was not my path to attempt total renunciation, but to take an alternative route.

Later in the day I was sitting in the open trying to meditate, not very successfully because of the strange hint early in the morning, when I saw some figures in the distance which had never happened before. It was a solitary place reached by a journey by train and bus and after a long walk. Soon I recognized my wife with both children. She told me that she had woken in the morning with the thought that I was dead. This was the time in the morning when I was no longer contemplating leaving for Sri Lanka to become a monk, but did not yet gear myself to embark on the Bodhisattva path so that I was somehow suspended outside empirical time. This severed the usual telepathic link between my wife's and my mind and produced in her a feeling that I was dead.

After returning home I slowly resumed normal life, including our marital relations.

{56} Checking reactions and impulses to act or speak as to their purpose and usefulness at a given moment and act or speak only after making a conscious decision to do so — this was a practice I was already quite proficient in, when I found myself under interrogation by the communist secret police. As a lecturer in the university, I had postal contacts with a few Weste1itutions and continued in them even after my dismissal. I also had published a few scholarly and popular articles in English, German and Ceylonese journals, mostly on Buddhist topics. The suspicion was that they were a cover for sending messages abroad about the dire situation in the country, which was being drained of resources by the Soviets for supporting North Korea in its war against the South. It was a time of show-trials in the 1950s in which several death sentences were passed, even against some leading communists accused of treason (e.g. the foreign minister V. Clementis). If oral or written evidence was not available, the sentence could be passed only if the accused confessed. This was often achieved by severe beating or torture. There was no evidence against me and my answers to leading questions probably sounded veracious to the interrogator. The possibility of beating was mentioned but not carried out. Instead a psychological method was chosen of a quick succession of questions, not related to each other, to which I had to answer without the slightest hesitation. Six or seven interrogators intermittently shot questions at me for up to two hours during which individual interrogators left the room in turn to relax with a cigarette. I gathered that the aim was to provoke me into saying a negative word about the socialist order or perhaps even only to show hate by the expression of my face or eyes; they would then work on it and make a case. The interrogation went on twice a week for three months. On all these occasions I was able to decide in a split second what to answer and to remain relaxed. Towards the end I even noticed a kind of respect in the interrogators' attitude to me. During the last session their chief remained alone with me and tried to start a friendly conversation which was not a success as we had hardly any common interests.

My ability to watch calmly my reactions and the contents of my mind also served me in good stead in the coal mines, to which I was assigned after the interrogations for a year, for 're-education', although I had to sign a contract stating that I had decided to volunteer to help build socialism in my country. I worked in a team looking after the ventilation of the mine 900 metres underground. The shafts we dug or maintained were sometimes so small that one could only crawl in them or even move only centimetre by centimetre lying on one's back. It was very claustrophobic and one could easily panic. My mates were willing to exempt me from accompanying them through such shafts and were surprised that I went along with them. I cannot imagine being able to cope now with a similar situation, especially after years of comfortable life in England.

Bibliography

Allchin, Bridget and Raymond (1968), *The Birth of Indian Civilisation. India and Pakistan before 500 B.C.*, Penguin Books Ltd., Harmondsworth.

Alter, Joseph S. (2004), *Yoga in Modern India: the Body Between Science and Philosophy,*

Princeton University Press, Princeton, NJ.

Anand, Mulk Raj (1991), *Kama Yoga: Some Notes on the Philosophical Basis of "Erotic" Art of India 1905-2004,* Aspect, New Delhi.

Anantharaman, T. R (1996), *Ancient Yoga and Modern Science, Science, Philosophy and Culture,* Delhi.

Atreya, Bhikhan Lal (1966), *The Yogavāsisṭha and its Philosophy,* 3rd rev. ed., Darshana Printers, Moradabad, Benares.

Aurobindo, Sri (1955), *The Life Divine,* Sri Aurobindo Ashram, Pondicherry.

Aurobindo, Sri (1953), *Sri Aurobindo on Himself and on the Mother,* Sri Aurobindo Ashram, Pondicherry.

Aurobindo, Sri (1988), *The Synthesis of Yoga,* The Sri Aurobindo Library, New York.

Banerji, Sures Chandra (1995), *Studies in Origin and Development of Yoga: from Vedic Times, in India and Abroad,* Punthi Pustak, Calcutta.

Bernard, Theos (1950), *Haṭha Yoga. The Report of a Personal Experience*, Rider & Company, London.

Bharati, Agehananda (1965), *The Tantric Tradition*, Rider & Company, London.

Bhatkal, G. R. (1960), *Shri Aurobindo. His Life and Teachings*, Popular Prakashan, Bombay.

Bhatt, G.P. (2004), *The Forceful Yoga. Being the Translation of HaṭhaYoga-Pradīpikā, Gheraṇḍa-Saṁhitā and Śiva-Sam. hitā*, Banarsidass, Delhi.

Billion, Anna (1979), *Kundalini, Secret of the Ancient Yogis*, Parker Pub. Co., West Nyack, N.Y.

Bolle, Kees W. (1971), *The Persistence of Religion. An Essay on Tantrism and Sri Aurobindo's Philosophy*, Brill, Leiden.

Briggs, George Weston (1998), *Gorakhnāth and the Kānphata Yogīs*, Banarsidass, Delhi (First Calcutta, 1938).

Bronkhorst, Johannes, *The Two Sources of Indian Asceticism*, Banarsidass, Delhi, 1999.

Brunton, Paul (1934), *A Search in Secret India*, Rider, London.

Brunton, Paul (1941), *The Hidden Teaching beyond Yoga*, Rider, London.

Brunton, Paul (1943), *The Wisdom of the Overself*, Rider, London.

Bryant, Edwin (2009), *The Yoga Sūtras of Patañjali.* A New Edition, Translation, and Commentary with Insights from the Traditional Comentators, North Point Press, New York.

Burley, Mikel (2007), *Classical Samkhya and Yoga: an Indian Metaphysics of Experience*, Routledge, London.

Capra, Fritjof (1975), *The Tao of Physics. An Exploration of the Parallels Between Modern Physics and Eastern Mysticism*, Shambhala, Boulder.

Capra, Fritjof (2002), *The Hidden Connections*, HarperCollins, London.

Chakravarti, Chintaharan (1972), *Tantras. Studies on their Religion and Literature*, Punthi Pustak, Calcutta.

Chattopadhyaya, Sudhakar (1978), *Reflections on the Tantras*, Banarsidass, Delhi.

Chaudhuri, Haridas & Spiegelberg (1960): *Integral Philosophy of Aurobindo. A Commemorative Symposium*, Allen & Unwin, London.

Choudhary, Radhakrishna (1964), *Vrātyas in Ancient India*, The Chowkhamba Sanskrit Series Office, Varanasi.

Clements, Richa Pauranik (2005), 'Being a Witness: Cross-examining the Notion of Self in Śaṅkara's *Upadeśasāhasrī*, Īśvarakṛṣna's *Sāṅkhyakārikā*, and Patañjali's *Yogasūtra*' (Jacobsen, 2005 , 75-97).

Coney, Judith (1998), *Sahaja Yoga*, Curzon, Richmond.

Connolly, Peter (2007) *A Student's Guide to the History and Philosophy of Yoga*, Equinox, London & Oakville, CT (2nd ed. 2014).

Connolly, Peter (ed., 1986), *Perspectives on Indian Religion. Papers in Honour of Karel*

Werner, (Bibliotheca Indo-Budhica No. 30), Sri Satguru Publications, Delhi.

Coward, Harold G. (2002), *Yoga and Psychology: Language, Memory, and Mysticism*, State University of New York Press, Albany, New York.

Cozort, Daniel (1986), *Highest Yoga Tantra: an Introduction to the Esoteric Buddhism of Tibet*, Snow Lion, Ithaca, N.Y.

Dam, Jyotishman (1998), *Shiva Yoga. Indiens groșer Yigi Gorakshanatha*, Eugen Diederich Verlag, München.

Dasgupta, Sashi Bhushan (1974), *An Introduction to Tantric Buddhism,* Shambhala, Berkeley.

Dasgupta, Sashibhushan (1969), *Obscure Religious Cults,* Mukhopadhyay, Calcutta.

Dasgupta, Surendranath (1952), *A History of Indian Philosophy II,* Cambridge University Press, Cambridge.

Desikachar, T. K. V. (1980), *Religiousness in Yoga: Lectures on Theory and Practice,* University Press of America, Washington, D.C.

D'Espagnat, Bernard, (2006), *On Physics and Philosophy.* Princeton University Press, Princeton.

Douglas, Nik (1971), *Tantra Yoga. With Original Photographs by the Author,* Munshiram Manoharlal, New Delhi.

Deussen, Paul (1920), *Die Philosophie der Upanishad's,* Leipzig, Brockhaus (4th ed.).

Deussen, Paul (1897), *Sechzig Upanisad's des Veda,* Brockhaus, Leipzig. (3rd ed. 1938)

Deussen, Paul (1980), *Sixty Upanisads of the Veda,* translated from German by V.M. Bedekar & G.B. Palsule, Delhi.

Deussen, Paul (1906), *Vier philosophische Texte des Mahabharatam.* In Gemeinschaft mit Otto Strauss aus dem Sanskrit übersetzt, F. A. Brockhaus, Leipzig,

Deutsch, Eliot (1969), *Advaita Vedānta: A Philosophical Reconstruction,* University of Hawaii Press, Honolulu.

Dewana, Mohan Singh Uberoi (1965), *Dhyana Yoga,* Dhyana Yoga Mandira, Chandigarh.

Dikshit, Rao Bahadur K. N. (1939), *Prehistoric Civilisation of the Indus Valley,* University of Madras, Madras.

Douglas, Nik (1971), *Tantra Yoga,* Munshiram Manoharlal, Delhi.

Dundas, Paul (1992), *The Jains*, Routledge, London,.

Dvivedi, M.N. (tr.1983), *The Yoga Sutras of Patanjali*, Sanskrit Text, Transliteration and English Translation, with an intr., append. & notes on each sutra based on several authentic commentaries, Satguru Publications, Delhi.

Dürr, Hans-Peter (ed. 2010), *Physik und Transzendenz. Die grossen Physiker unseres Jahrhunderts über ihre Begegnungen mit dem Wunderbaren* (Niels Bohr, Max Born, Albert Einstein, Werner Heisenberg, Wolfgang Pauli, Max Planck, C.F. von Weizsäcker u.a.), Drieriger Verlag, Bad Essen.

Edgerton, Franklin: (1952), *The Bhagavad Gītā. Translated and Interpreted I-II.*, Harvard UP, Cambridge, Massachusetts.

Ehrich, R. W. (ed.) (1992), *Chronologies in Old World Archaeology*, 2nd ed., University of Chicago Press, Chicago.

Eliade, Mircea (1969), *Yoga, Immortality and Freedom*, Routledge & Kegan Paul, London, 2nd edition (1st ed. London, 1958, French ed. Paris, 1954).

Eliade, Mircea (1959), *Cosmos and History*, Princeton University Press, N.J.

Eliade, Mircea (1979), *History of Religiou Ideas I*, Collins, London.

Fairservis, Walter A., Jr. (1971), *The Roots of Ancient India. The Archaeology of Early Indian Civilisation*, London.

Feuerstein, Georg (1975), *Textbook of Yoga*, Rider & Company, London.

Feuerstein, Georg (1990), *Encyclopedic Dictionary of Yoga*, Paragon House, New York.

Feuerstein, Georg (1980), *The Philosophy of Classical Yoga*, Manchester University Press, Manchester.

Feuerstein, Georg (2002), *The Yoga Tradition: its History, Literature, Philosophy and Practice*, Bhavana Books, Delhi (1st Hohm Press, Prescott, Arizona, 1998).

Feuerstein, Georg & Miller, Jeanine (1971), *A Reappraisal of Yoga. Essays in Indian Philosophy*, Rider & Company, London.

Flood, Gavin (2000), 'The Purification of the Body', in: White, David Gordon, 2000, 509-520.

Frost, Gavin & Yvonne (1994), *Tantric Yoga : The Royal Path To Raising Kundalini Power*, Motilal Banarsidass Publishers, Delhi.

Gonda, Jan (1963), *The vision of the Vedic poets*, Mouton & Co., The Hague.

Govinda, Lama Anagarika (1977), *Creative Meditation and Multidimensional Consciousness*, Unwin Paperbacks, London.

Govinda, Lama Anagarika (1959), *Foundations of Tibetan Mysticism*, Rider & Company, London.

Govinda, Lama Anagarika (1962), *Mandala. Meditationsgedichte und Betrachtungen*, Origo Verlag, Zürich.

Govinda, Lama Anagarika (1966), *The Way of the White Clouds*, Rider & Company, London.

Grassmann, Hermann (1873), *WĪrterbuch zum Rig-Veda*, F. A. Brockhaus, Leipzig.

Gyatso, Geshe Kelsang (1996), *Guide to Dakini Land: the Highest Yoga Tantra Practice of Buddha Vajrayogini*, Tharpa, Ulverston.

Hackett, Paul G. (2012), 'Theos Bernard and the Early Days of Tantric Yoga in America', in: White, 2012, 353-364.

Har Dayal, Lala (1970), *The Bodhisattva Doctrine in Buddhist Sanskrit Literature*, Banarsidass, Delhi (1st London 1932).

Harshananda, Swami (1987), *Hindu Gods and Goddesses*, Shri Ramakrishna Ashram, Mysore.

Hartranft, Chip (2003), *The Yoga-Sūtra of Patañjali. Sanskrit-English Translation & Glossary*, http://www.lightweaver.com/ys/ys_linkṣhtml.

Hauer, J.W. (1922), *Die Anfänge der Yoga-Praxis im alten Indien*, Kohlhammer, Stuttgart.

Hauer, J.W. (1958), *Der Yoga. Ein indischer Weg zum Selbst*, Kohlhammer, Stuttgart.

Hauer, J.W. (1927), *Der Vrātya I. Die Vrātya als nichtbrahmanische Kultgenossenschaften arischer Herkunft*, Kohlhammer, Stuttgart.

Head, Joseph & Cranston, s. L. (1977), *Reincarnation. The Phoenix Fire Mystery. An East-* West Dialogue on Death and Rebirth from the Worlds of Religion, Science,

Psychology, Philosophy, Art, and Literature, and from Great Thinkers of the Past and *Present*, Julien Press/Crown Publishers, New York.

Hecker, Hellmuth (1995), *Der erste deutsche Bhikkhu. Das bewegte Leben des Ehrwürdigen*

Nyānatiloka (1878-1957) und seine Schüler, Universität Konstanz, Konstanz.

Hecker, Hellmuth (1996), *Lebensbilder deutscher Buddhisten. Ein bio-bibliographisches*

Handbuch Band I: Die Gründer, Universität Konstanz, Konstanz.

Hecker, Hellmuth (1997), *Lebensbilder deutscher Buddhidten. Ein bio-bibliographisches*

Handbuch Band II: Die Nachfolger, Universität Konstanz, Konstanz.

Hopkins, Jeffrey (1987), *Emptiness Yoga: the Middle Way Consequence School*, Snow Lion Publications, Ithaca, N.Y.

Hroznl̲, Bedìich (1941), *Älteste Geschichte Vorderasiens und Indiens*, Melantrich, Praha.

Hume, Robert Ernest, (1931), *The Thirteen Principal Upanisads*, Oxford University Press, Oxford, 2nd revised edition (1st ed. 1921).

Iyengar, B.K.s. (1965), *Light on Yoga*, Allen & Unwin, London.

Jacobsen, Knut A. (ed) (2005), *Theory and Practice of Yoga : Essays in Honour of Gerald*

James Larson, (Numen Book Series, Volume110), Koninklijke Brill NV, Leiden.

Joshi, Kireet (1989), *Sri Aurobindo and Integral Yoga, Dharam Hinduja International Centre of Indic Research*, New Delhi.

Kaul, H. Kumar (1989), *Yoga in Hindu scriptures*, Surjeet, Delhi.

Key Chapple, Christopher (2012), 'The Sevenfold Yoga of the *Yogavāsiṣṝ ha*', in: White, 2012.

Killingley, Dermot, 'Yoga-Sutra IV, 2-3 and Vivekananda's interpretation of evolution, *Journal of Indian Philosophy 17* (1989), 91-119.

Lamb, Ramdas (2005), 'Rāja Yoga, Asceticism, and the Rāmānanda Saṁpradāy', (Jacobsen, 2005, 317-331).

Larson, Gerald James (2012), 'Pātañjala Yoga in Practice', in: Gordon 2012, 73-96.

Leggett, Trevor (1990), *The Complete Commentary by Śaṅkara on the Yoga Sūtras.* A Full Translation of the Newly Discovered Text, Kegan Paul International, London & New York.

Lutyens, Mary (1990), *The Life and Death of Krishnamurti, John Murray, London.*

Maas, Philipp A. (2006), *Samādhipāda: das erste Kapitel des PātañjalaYogaśāstra zum ersten Mal kritisch editiert*, Shaker, Aachen.

Macdonell, Arthur A. (1922), *Hymns From The Rigveda : Selected And Metrically Translated*, The Heritage of India Series, Calcutta, London.

Macdonell, Arthur A. (1898): Vedic Mythology, De Gruyter & Co., Strassburg, (repr. Banarsidass, Delhi, 1974).

Mackay, Ernest John Henry (1938), *Further excavations at Mohenjo-Daro, being an official* account of archaeological excavations at Mohenjo-Daro carried out by Government of *India between the years 1927 and 1931*, vol. I & II, Munshiram Manoharlal Publishers, Delhi (new ed. 1998).

Mainkar, Trimbak Govind (1977), *The Vāsiṣṭha Rāmāyanṇa: a Study*, Meharchand Lachhmandas, New Delhi.

Mallinson, James (2012), 'The Original *Gorakṣaoeataka*' in: White 2012, 257-272.

Marshall, Sir John (1931), *Mohenjo-daro and the Indus Civilisation* I-III, Arthur Probsthain, London.

Matchett, Freda (1993), 'The Pervasiveness of *Bhakti* in the Bhāgavata Purāṇa', in: Werner, 1993, 95-115.

de Michelis, Elizabeth (2005), *A History of Modern Yoga: Patañjali and Western Esotericism*, Continuum, London & New York.

Minor, Robert Neil (1982), *Bhagavad-Gītā. An Exegetical Commentary*, Heritage, Delhi.

Munsterberg, Hugo (1970), *Art of India and Southeast Asia*, Harry N. Abrams, Inc., New York.

Münsterberg, Hugo (no date), *Der indische Raum*, Naturalis Verlag.

Namakkal, Jessica (2012), 'European Dreams, Tamil Land: Auroville and the Paradox of a Postcolonial Utopia', *Journal for the Study of Radicalism 6/1* (Spring 2012), 59-88, Michigan State University Press.

Newberry. John (1985), *Indus Seal and Moldings* from Mohenjo-daro, Victoria, British Columbia, Canada (published by the author). Nyanaponika Thera (1962), *Satipaṭṭhāna.* The Heart of Buddhist Meditation. A Handbook of *Mental Training Based on the Buddha's Way of Mindfulness,* Rider, London.

Nyanasatta Thera, *Foundations of Buddhism*

Panikkar, Raimundo (1977), *The Vedic Experience, Mantramañjarī. An Anthology of the Vedas for Modern Man and Contemporary Celebration,* Darton, Longman & Todd, London.

Pant, Apa (1970), *Surya Namaskars: an Ancient Indian Exercise,* Orient Longman, Bombay.

Parpola, Asko (1994), *Deciphering the Indus Script,* Cambridge U.P, Cambridge (latest edition 2009).

Parpola, Asko (2010), 'A Dravidian Solution to the Indus Script Problem', Kalaignar M. Karunanidhi Classical Tamil Research Endowment Lecture, World Classical Tamil

Conference 25-6-2010, Coimbatore, Central Institute for Classical Tamil, Chennai, India.

Penrose, Roger (2011): *Cycles of Time. An Extraordinary New View of the Universe,* Vintage Books, London.

Pensa, Corado (1969), 'On the Purification Concept in Indian Tradition, with Special Regard to Yoga', *East and West 19,* 194-228.

Pfleuger, Lloyd W., 'Person, Purity and Power in the *Yogasūtra*' in: Jacobsen, 2005 , 29-59).

Piggot, Stuart (1950), *Prehistoric India to 1,000 B.C.*, Penguin Books Ltd., Harmondsworth.

Radha, Swami Sivananda (1978), *Kundalini. Yoga for the West*, Timeless Books, Spokane, USA.

Radhakrishnan, S. (1953), *The Principal Upaniṣads*, Allen & Unwin Ltd., London.

Radhakrishnan, S. & Moore, C.A. (1957): *Source Book in Indian Philosophy*, Princeton University Press, Princeton.

Radhakrishnan, S (1960), *The Bhagavad Gītā. With an Introductory Essay, Sanskrit text, English Translation and Notes*, Allen & Unwin, London (1st ed. 1948).

Rele, Vasant. G. (1927), *The Mysterious Kundalini. The Physical Basis of the "Kundalini"*

(Hatha) Yoga in Terms of Western Anatomy and Physiology, Taraporevala Sons & Co. Privat Ltd., Bombay.

Richter-Ushanas, Egbert (2001), *The Indus Script and the R.g-veda*, Motilal Banarsidass, Delhi (first 1997).

Rishabhchand (1959), *The Integral Yoga of Sri Aurobindo*, Sri Aurobindo Ashram, Pondicherry.

Roebuck, V. J. (2000), *The Upaniṣads*, Penguin, London.

Sacharow, Boris (1983), *Yoga aus dem Urquell*, Drei-Eichen-Verlag, München (3rd ed.)

Samuel, Geoffrey (2008), *The Origins of Yoga and Yantra: Indic Religions to the Thirteenth*

Century, Cambridge University Press, Cambridge.

Sankaracāryā (1990), *The complete commentary by Śankara on the Yoga Sūtras*: a full translation of the newly discovered text, Kegan Paul, London.

Sarada, Swami Sivananda (1954) (Charlotte Walinski-Heller), *Der Ruf. Eine moderne* Pilgerfahrt nach Indien auf persönliche Einladung zu dem heiligen, weisen und *grossen Yogi Sri Swami Sivananda Saraswati Rishikesh-Himalaja,* Sivananda-Sarada Ashram, Lindau/Bodensee.

Sastri, Asoke Chatterjee (1989), *Upanioead Yoga and PātañjalaYoga - a Comparative Approach,* University of Calcutta, Calcutta.

Satprem (1968), *Sri Aurobindo or The Adventure of Consciousness,* Sri Aurobindo Ashram, Pondicherry.

Schmidt, Richard (1921), *Fakire und Fakirtum im alten und modernen Indien. Yoga-Lehre und Yoga-Praxis nach den indischen Originalquellen,* zweite Auflage, Verlag von Hermann Barsdorf, Berlin.

Shaffer, Jim G. (1992), 'The Indus Valley, Baluchistan and Helmand Traditions: Neolithic Through Bronze Age', in: Ehrich, R. W. (ed.) (1992), *Chronologies in Old World Archaeology,* 2nd ed., University of Chicago Press, Chicago.

Sharma, Arvind (2004), *Advaita Vedānta. An Introduction,* Banarsidass, Delhi.

Shastri, Hari Prasad (1950), *Meditation, Its Theory and Practice,* Shanti Sadan, London.

Shastri, Hari Prasad (1980), *The world within the mind: Yoga-Vasishtha: extracts from the* discourses of the sage Vasishtha to his pupil, Prince Rama, and the story of Queen

Chudala, translated from the Sanskrit of Valmiki, Shanti Sadan, London.

Shrivastava, G.M.L. (1990), *Aurobindo and Patanjali: a Critical and Analytical Study,* Criterion Publications, New Delhi.

Schubring, Walther (2000), *The Doctrine of the Jainas: Described after the Old Sources,* Banarsidass, Delhi.

Singleton, Mark (2010), *Yoga Body. The Origins of Modern Posture Practice,* Oxford University Press, New York.

Singleton, Mark & Byrne, Jean (ed.) (2008), *Yoga in the modern world: Contemporary Perspectives,* Routledge, London & New York.

Singleton, Mark & Goldberg, Ellen (ed.) (2014), *Gurus of Modern Yoga,* Oxford University Press, Oxford.

Singleton, M. (2012), *Yoga in Practice,* Princeton University Press, Princeton, N. J.

Sivananda, Swami (1980), *Autobiography,* The Divine Life Society, Shivanandanagar.

Sivananda, Swami (1965), *Yoga Practice for Developing and Increasing Physical, Mental and Spiritual Powers,* Taraporevala, Bombay.

Sivananda, Swami (1986), *Japa Yoga: a comprehensive treatise on mantra-sastra,* Divine Life Society, Shivanandanagar.

Sivananda, Swami (1994), *Sex, Love, and Marriage from a Yogic Viewpoint: from the Mating Dance to the Cosmic Dance,* UBS Publishers' Distributors. New Delhi.

Sloss, Radha Rajagopal (1991), *Lives in the Shadow with J Krishnamurti,* Bloomsbury, London.

Strauss, Sarah (2005), *Positioning Yoga. Balancing Acts Across Cultures,* Berg, Oxford & New York.

Svātmārāma (1970), *Haṭhapradīpikā,* ed. Sw. Digambarji & R. G. Kokaje, Kaivalyadhama, S. M. Y. M. Samiti, Lonavla.

Taddei, Maurizio (1970), *India,* Nagel Publishers, Geneva - Paris - Munich.

Tripathi, Preeti (2010), *Indian Religions: Tradition, History and Culture,* Axis Publications, New Delhi.

Venkatesananda, Swami (2005), *The Supreme Yoga Vāsiṣṭha,* Banarsidass, Delhi. (4th repr. 2010)

Vernon, Roland (2001), *Star in the East. Krishnamurti: The Invention of a Messiah,* Palgrave, St. Martin's Press, New York.

Vivekananda, Svami (1896), *Raja-Yoga or Conquering the Internal Nature,* Longmans, Green and Co., London.

Vivekananda, Svami (1974), *Bhakti-Yoga: the Yoga of Love and Devotion,*

Vishnudevananda, Swami (1960), *A Complete Illustrated Book of Yoga,* The Julian Press, New York.

Wayman, Alex (1973), *The Buddhist Tantras. Light on Indo-Tibetan Esotericism,* Routledge & Kegan Paul, London.

Werner, Karel (1969), 'Half a Century of Krishnamurti', *World Buddhism XVIII/2,* 51-52.

Werner, Karel (1975), 'Religious Practice and Yoga in the Time of the Vedas, Upaniṣads and Early Buddhism', *Annals of the Bhandarkar Oriental Research Institute LVI,* Poona, 179-194.

Werner, Karel (1977a), *Yoga and Indian Philosophy,* Motilal Banarsidass, New Delhi (repr. 1980, 1998 and 2017)

Werner, Karel (1977b), 'On Interpreting the Vedas', *Religion 7/2,* London, 189-200.

Werner, Karel (1978a), 'A Note on *karma* and Rebirth in the Vedas', *Hinduism 83,* London, 1-4.

Werner, Karel (1978b), 'The Vedic Concept of Human Personality and its Destiny', *Journal of Indian Philosophy* 5, The Hague, 275-289.

Werner, Karel (1981a), '*Bodhi* and *arahattaphala.* From Early Buddhism to Early Mahāyāna',

The Journal of the International Association of Buddhist Studies 4, 1981, 70-84.

Reprinted in: *The Bodhisattva Ideal: Essays on the Emergence of Mahāyāna*, ed. Bhikkhu Nyanatusita himi, Kandy, Buddhist Publication Society, 2013, 51-67.

Werner, Karel (1981b), 'The Teachings of the Veda and the *ādhyātmika* Method of Interpretation', *Golden Jubilee Volume, Vaidika Saṁśodhana Maṇḍala* (Vedic Research Institute), Poona,, 288-295.

Werner, Karel (1985), *The Doctrine of Rebirth in Eastern and Western Thought* (Bodhi Leaves No 100), Buddhist Publication Society, Kandy.

Werner, Karel (1986a), 'Yoga and the Old Upaniṣads', *Perspectives on Indian Religion: Papers in Honour of Karel Werner*, ed. Peter Connolly, Sri Satguru Publications, Delhi, 1-7.

Werner, Karel (1986b), 'Arya Maitreya Mandala - a Buddhist Vajrayana Sangha', *Realist 1986*, 45-47, Buddhist Realists' Centre, Penang.

Werner, Karel (1987), 'The Indo-Europeans and the Indo-āryans: The philological, archaeological and historical context', *Annals of the Bhandarkar Oriental Research Institute LXVIII* (Ramakrishna Gopal Bhandarkar 150th Birth-Anniversary Volume), Poona, 491-523.

Werner, Karel (1988), 'Indian Concepts of Human Personality in Relation to the Doctrine of the Soul', *Journal of the Royal Asiatic Society* 1988, no. 1, 73-97.

Werner, Karel (ed. 1989), *The Yogi and the Mystic. Studies in Indian and Comparative Mysticism* (Durham Indological Series No. 1), Curzon Press, London (repr. 1994).

Werner, Karel (1989a), 'The long-haired Sage of Ṛg Veda 10,136; A Shaman, a Mystic or a Yogi?' in: Werner, 1989, 33-53.

Werner, Karel (1989b), 'Mysticism and Indian Spirituality', in: Werner, (ed., 1989), 20-32.

Werner, Karel (1989c), 'From Polytheism to Monism - Multidimensional View of the Vedic Religion', *Polytheistic Systems* (Cosmos 5), ed. Glenys Davies, Edinburgh University Press, 12-27.

Werner, Karel (ed. 1990), *Symbols in Art and Religion. The Indian and the Comparative Perspectives* (Durham Indological Series No. 2), Curzon Press, London (repr. Motilal Banarsidass Publishers PVT. Ltd., Delhi, 1991).

Werner, Karel (1990a), 'Symbolism in the Vedas and its Conceptualization', in: Werner (ed. 1990), 27-45.

Werner, Karel (ed., 1993), *Love Divine. Studies in* bhakti *and Devotional Mysticism* (ed.), (Durham Indological Series No. 3), Curzon Press, London.

Werner, Karel (1996), 'Indian Conceptions of Human Personality', *Asian Philosophy 6/2,* 93- 107.

Werner, Karel (2008), 'Death, Rebirth and Personal Identity', *International Journal of Buddhist Thought and Culture 10,* Dongkuk University, Seoul, 19-39.

Werner, Karel (2012), 'The Last Blade of Grass? Universal Salvation and Buddhism',

International Journal of Buddhist Thought and Culture 18 & 19 (Dongguk University, Seoul), Part 1&2 (February 2012 & September 2012), 7-24 & 7-22.

Wheeler, Sir Mortimer (1953), *The Indus Civilisation,* Cambridge University Press, Cambridge (3rd edition 1968, repr. 1972).

Wheeler, Mortimer (1976), *My Archaeological Mission in India and Pakistan,* Thames and Hudson.

Whicher, Ian (1998), *The Integrity of the Yoga Daroeana: a Reconsideration of Classical Yoga,* SUNY Press, Albany, New York.

Whicher, Ian & Carpenter, David (eds,, 2003), *Yoga. The Indian tradition,* Routledge Curzon, London.

Wile, Douglas (1992), *Art of the bedchamber: the Chinese sexual Yoga classics including women's solo meditation texts,* State University of New York Press, Albany, N.Y.

White, David Gordon (2009), *Sinister Yogis,* University of Chicago Press, Chicago & London.

White, David Gordon (2003), *Kiss of the yogini: 'Tantric Sex' in its South Asian Contexts,* University of Chicago Press, Chicago & London.

White, David Gordon (ed.) (2000), *Tantra in Practice,* Princeton University Press, Princeton, N.J.

White, David Gordon (2012), *Yoga in Practice,* Princeton University Press, Princeton, N.J.

White, David Gordon (2014), *The Yoga Sutra of Patanjali: A Biography,* Princeton University Press, Princeton, N.J.

White, John (ed.) (1979), *Kundalini, Evolution and Enlightenment,* New York.

Wolff, Otto (1967), *Sri Aurobindo in Selbstzeugnissen und Bilddokumenten,* Rowohlt, Reinbek.

Worthington, Vivian (1982), *A History of Yoga,* Routledge & Kegan Paul, London.

Wright, Rita P. (2010), *The Ancient Indus: Urbanism, Economy, and Society,* Cambridge University Press, Cambridge.

Yesudian, Selvarajan & Haich, Elisabeth (1953), *Yoga and Health,* Unwin, London.

Yogananda, Paramahamsa (1998) *Autobiography of a Yogi*, Self-Realization Fellowship, Los Angeles (13th edition; first 1946)

Yogendra, Shri (1966), *Yoga. Physical Education*, The Yoga Institute, Santa Cruz, Bombay (12th ed., 1st ed. 1928).

Yogendra, Shri (1958), *Haṭha Yoga Simplified*, The Yoga Institute, Santa Cruz, Bombay (9th ed., 1st ed. 1931).

Zaehner, R. C. (1969), *The Bhagavad Gita with Commentary based on Original Sources*, Clarendon Press, Oxford.

Zimmer, Heinrich (1973), *Yoga und Buddhismus. Indische Sphären*, Insel Verlag, Frankfurt am Main.

Zitko, Howard John (1974), *New Age Tantra Yoga. The Cybernetics of Sex and Love*, World University Press, Tucson.

Zukav, Gary (1984), *The Dancing Wu Li Masters. An Overview of the New Physics*, Flamingo, London.

List of Abbreviations

AB - Aitareya Brāhmaṇa

AU - Aitareya Upaniṣad

AV - Atharva Veda

BCE - before common era

BhG - Bhagavad Gītā

BU - Bṛhadāraṇyaka Upaniṣad

cca - *circa*

cf. - compare

CE - common era

ChU - Chāndogya Upaniṣad

DN - DÓgha Nikāya

IU - ḍsā Upaniṣad

J - Jātaka

KathU - Kaṭha Upaniṣad

KauU - Kauoeiśtakī Upaniṣad

KenU - Kena Upaniṣad

MaiU - Maitrayānīya (Maitrī) Upaniṣad

ManU - Māṇḍūkya Upaniṣad

Mbh - Mahābhārata

Mdh - Mokṣadharma

MN - Majjhima Nikāya

MunU - Muṇḍ

aka Upaniṣad

P. - Pāli

PU - Praśṇa Upaniṣad

RV - Ṛg Veda

Ry - Rāmāyaṇa

OE - Śatapatha Brāhmaṇa

OEU - Śvetāoevatara Upaniṣad

Skt. - Sanskrit

SN - Saṁyutta Nikāya

SV - Sāma Veda

TU - Taittirīya Upaniṣad

Ud - Udāna

Vin - Vinaya Piṭaka

YS - Yoga Sūtras of Patañjali

YV - Yajur Veda

Yvas - Yogavāsiṣṭha